SHIELDS OF PRIDE

Also by Elizabeth Chadwick

THE WILD HUNT

THE RUNNING VIXEN

THE LEOPARD UNLEASHED

CHILDREN OF DESTINY

SHIELDS OF PRIDE

Elizabeth Chadwick

MICHAEL JOSEPH
LONDON

MICHAEL JOSEPH LTD

Published by the Penguin Group
27 Wrights Lane, London W8 5TZ
Viking Penguin Inc., 375 Hudson Street, New York, New York 10014, USA
Penguin Books Australia Ltd, Ringwood, Victoria, Australia
Penguin Books Canada Ltd, 10 Alcorn Avenue, Toronto, Ontario, Canada M4V 3B2
Penguin Books (NZ) Ltd, 182–190 Wairau Road, Auckland 10, New Zealand

Penguin Books Ltd, Registered Offices: Harmondsworth, Middlesex, England

First published in Great Britain 1994
Copyright © Susan E. Hicks 1994

Typeset by Datix International Limited, Bungay, Suffolk
Set in $11\frac{1}{2}$/13 pt Monophoto Bembo
Printed in England by Clays Ltd, St Ives plc

ISBN 0 7181 3764 7

ACKNOWLEDGEMENTS

On this page, I want to take the opportunity of thanking everyone who has helped me in the writing of this novel. As always, the advice, friendship and tireless endeavour of my agent Carole Blake has been a solid foundation stone, as has the quiet, strong support of my husband, Roger. It is always a pleasure to work with Maggie Pringle, my editor at Michael Joseph, and I would also like to thank my copy editor Arianne Burnette and Fanny Blake at Signet for their time and trouble. A very special thank you goes to the members of Regia Anglorum, Early Medieval re-enactment Society, who have taught me so much more than I could ever glean from research books alone. I am grateful to Janine Brown for sharing with me the arts of tablet-weaving, nailbinding, baking and dyeing. For patiently answering my questions and demonstrating the warrior skills, I am indebted to Graham Turner, Lyndon and Adrian Sanderson, Nick Hogben, Nigel Simms, Patrick and John Lowe, Simon Carter (whom I would also like to thank for the bone needles and dragon amulet), David Southgate, Gary Golding, and Karl Oldham, may their sword arms never wither and their hauberks never tarnish.

The verses on pages 246–7 are taken from *The Restoration of Cock Robin* by Norman Isles, published by Robert Hale.

CHAPTER 1

Summer 1173

SWEARING THROUGH HIS teeth, Joscelin de Gael drew rein at the head of his troop of mercenaries and scowled at the covered baggage wain that was slewed sideways across the Clerkenwell road, blocking access to all other traffic. He had been in the saddle since dawn. It was late afternoon now, and it had been raining all day. The comfort of his father's London house was still five miles away on the other side of the obstruction.

An assortment of knights and men-at-arms surrounded the wain like witnesses clustering around a fresh corpse. At their centre a man was examining a damaged wheel. He was a noble, for his cloak was trimmed with sable and the horse his squire held was clean-limbed and glossy, with a harness of Cordovan leather. A handful of women huddled together in the anonymity of full cloaks and headshawls, and watched the men from beneath the inadequate shelter of an ash tree overhanging the road.

Dismounting, Joscelin tossed his reins to his own squire and approached the crippled wain. The soldiers stiffened, hands descending to sword hilts and fingers tightening upon spear shafts. The nobleman, who had turned round at the first sound of horses on the road, narrowed his eyes as he recognized Joscelin.

Joscelin regarded him with similar disfavour. Giles de Montsorrel was a young baron, distantly related to the Earl of Leicester, thus he considered himself high nobility. He viewed Joscelin, the mere bastard of a warrior who had carved his own nobility by the sword, as dung beneath his boots. They had encountered each other occasionally on the French tourney circuits, but no amity had sprung from these meetings. Montsorrel was not a man to forgive being bowled from the saddle on the blunt end of a jousting lance.

Forced by circumstance to be civil, Montsorrel gave Joscelin the iciest of nods, his lips tight as a drawn purse, dusky colour seeping into his face.

Joscelin returned the nod in the same spirit, and turned his attention to the broken cart-wheel. Not just broken, he could see now, but hopelessly shattered where an ill-fitting iron tyre had pulled the frame out of true. 'You haven't a hope in hell of cobbling that mess back together,' he said impatiently. 'You'll have to hire a cart from the nearest village. Clerkenwell isn't far.' He walked slowly around the stricken carcass of the wain, examining it thoughtfully from all angles before halting in front of the three sturdy cobs still harnessed in line between the shafts. 'How much weight do you carry?'

'None of your business!' A gold torque at Montsorrel's throat jumped with the rapid throb of his pulse. He shook rain from his fair hair and glared.

'Oh, but it is,' Joscelin contradicted. 'I cannot bring my own wain through while yours is obstructing the road. If it's not too heavy, I'd be more than willing to help you drag it to one side.'

Montsorrel's entire face was scarlet by now. 'You think I'll stand aside for hired scum like you!' he choked.

One of the women murmured swiftly to her companions and, detaching herself from the anonymity of their group, stepped forward to place herself between the two men. She faced Joscelin so that he was forced to divert his attention from Montsorrel. Her headshawl of striped green and brown wool was beaded with rain and short tendrils of damp brown hair wisped on her brow. She had soft grey-blue eyes and delicately wrought features that put him in mind of a waif. Holding his gaze with her own, she indicated the broken wain.

2

'By the time we have found a wheelwright or hired another cart, the city gates will have closed for the night.' She hesitated and bit her lip as if to prevent it from quivering. 'I notice that your own wain is twice the size of ours and but lightly laden. I am sure that if you lent it to us my husband would compensate you for any inconvenience.'

Joscelin gaped at her like a codfish, words deserting him. She returned his stare with eyes suspiciously liquid and clutched the wet headshawl beneath her chin.

'Linnet!' Montsorrel raised his fist, his anger diverting from Joscelin to the woman. 'Do you dare to interfere?'

She flinched slightly, but her voice was steady as she turned and gave him reply. 'I was thinking of your son, my lord. He must not catch a chill.'

Montsorrel cast an irritated glare in the direction of the other women. Joscelin looked too. Protruding from a bundle of cloaks and blankets, a little hand was held in the grasp of a nursemaid. He had the merest glimpse of wide, frightened eyes and a snub nose set in a wan, small face. Amid the anger at finding himself trapped because he could not for shame refuse the woman, he discovered compassion for her frightened courage, and a deeper pain, born of memories ten years buried with the son he had lost in Normandy.

Montsorrel said stiffly to Joscelin, 'All right. You're a mercenary. I'll pay you the rate to deliver the goods to my house.'

Joscelin bit back the urge to laugh and the retort that he was not so much of a mercenary that he would allow the likes of Giles de Montsorrel to buy his obedience. 'I'll not serve you,' he said derisively, 'but your lady did speak of compensation. Perhaps we can reach an agreement.'

Montsorrel clenched his fists and glared, light eyes bloodshot with temper.

'No?' Joscelin shrugged and started to turn away.

'Damn you, get on with it!' Montsorrel snarled.

Joscelin flourished a sarcastic salute and sauntered away to instruct his men to strip and reload his own sound wain.

3

Linnet de Montsorrel rejoined the women. The pit of her stomach was queasy with fear. Everything had its price, and she knew she would have to pay hers later when she and Giles were alone.

'I'm cold, Mama,' her son whimpered and, leaving his nurse, he ran to cling to her skirts.

She stooped to chafe his hands, noting that his eyes were heavy and his complexion pale with exhaustion. 'It won't be long now, sweetheart,' she comforted, and folded him beneath the protection of her cloak like a mother hen spreading her wing over a chick, availing him of her body warmth.

'Madam, I know that man,' whispered Ella, her personal maid, jutting her chin towards the mercenary whom Linnet had just shamed into helping them. 'It's Joscelin de Gael, son of William Ironheart.'

'Oh?' William Ironheart she knew by reputation. They said he was so hard he pissed nails, that he was stubborn, embittered and dangerous to cross. Linnet looked at Ella, then at de Gael. Her expression neutral, she asked, 'And how do you come to be acquainted with such a one?'

The maid blushed. 'I only know him by sight, Madam. He was at my sister's wedding in the spring as a friend of the groom. They were both garrison soldiers at Nottingham castle.'

'I see.' Linnet assessed de Gael thoughtfully. She judged him to be in his mid or late twenties, hardly a younger son with nothing but a sword to his name. 'What is he doing in the mercenary trade if he's Ironheart's son?'

'He's only Lord William's bastard. His mother was a common mercenary's daughter, or so my mother says.' Ella folded her arms, hugging her shawl against her body and hopping from foot to foot. 'Apparently when de Gael's mother died in childbed, Lord William went mad with grief and tried to kill himself, but his sword broke and he was only wounded. After that men started calling him Ironheart because his breast was stronger than the steel. My mother said Brokenheart was more appropriate.'

4

Ella's gaze returned to their reluctant rescuer who was now standing back from the wain, one hand on the sword at his hip, the other pushing his rain-wet hair off his forehead.

Linnet, all romantic notions literally knocked out of her head by six years of marriage to Giles, said nothing, her feeling one of irritation rather than pity. She knew what it was like to be usurped by another woman in your own hall, and how much that other woman's status also depended on arrogant masculine whim.

Two panting men-at-arms struggled out of the broken wain carrying a large, iron-bound strongbox between them.

'Make haste!' Giles snapped and Linnet saw him glare at de Gael, who was eyeing the money chest with undisguised curiosity.

'I see now the exact kind of weight you do carry,' the mercenary remarked, refusing to be intimidated. 'Small wonder that your wheel broke.' And in his own good time he withdrew his scrutiny and approached the women.

Linnet retreated behind downcast lids, knowing that she would suffer if de Gael chose to take his impertinence further. Giles might think twice about assaulting a man of the mercenary's undoubted ability, but no such restraint would prevent him from beating her. She heard the men puffing and swearing as their strongbox was manœuvred into de Gael's wain. Giles's voice was high-pitched with impatience and bad temper, and inwardly she quailed.

De Gael crouched on his heels and gently peeled aside a soaked fold of her cloak. 'And who have we here?' he asked.

'My son, Robert.' Her throat dry, she glanced rapidly at her husband. He was still occupied in ranting at his guards, but in a moment he would turn round.

De Gael did not miss her darting look. 'You have a high courage, my lady,' he murmured. 'I won't make it harder for you than it already is.' And, plucking the child out from beneath her cloak, he swept him up in his arms. 'Come on, my young soldier, there's a dry corner prepared especially for you in my cart.'

5

Linnet stretched her arms towards her son with an involuntary cry. Robert peered at his mother over de Gael's shoulder, his eyes wide with shock, but the move had been so sudden that he had had no time to cry, and by the time he did let out a wail of protest he was being placed on a dry blanket in the good wain, a lambskin rug tucked up to his chin.

Linnet, following hard on de Gael's heels, found herself taken by the elbow and helped up beside her son. Robert stopped crying and began to knead the lambswool like a nursing kitten. Linnet stroked his brow and looked at de Gael. 'You have my gratitude,' she said. 'Thank you.'

De Gael shrugged and affected a pragmatic tone. 'No sense in keeping him out in that downpour when he can be warm in here. I expect your husband's compensation to reflect my care of his goods.' He started to withdraw. 'There is room for your women too, my lady. I'll tell them, shall I?'

Rain thudded on the roof of the wain. She looked out through a canvas arch on a tableau of hazy green and brown. The smell of her wet garments clogged her nostrils. She watched Joscelin de Gael walk across to her maids. He moved with a wolf's ungainly elegance and she did not think that the similarity stopped there. And yet he had been considerate beyond the bounds of her knowledge of men.

Giles was still shouting. Behind her, at the other end of the wain, their soldiers were depositing her clothing coffer with much bumping and cursing. Robert's eyelids drooped and closed. Linnet leaned her head against her son's, her arm around him, and shut her own eyes.

CHAPTER 2

'J OSCELIN, YOU ROGUE!' cried Maude de Monsart with delight, and folded her nephew in an embrace he remembered from childhood. His nostrils were overpowered by a mingling of lavender, sweat and the marchpane she adored which had rotted most of her teeth to stumps. For the last five years she had been a widow and, having no children, now dwelt in the de Rocher household as a companion and housekeeper to the Lady Agnes, his father's wife. 'What brings you down to London?'

He returned her hug and smiled. 'I've come for the horse fair. I have to replace some war gear and I'm thinking about buying a palfrey.'

'I thought you'd be in France by now, doing the round of the tourneys?' She handed his wet, heavy cloak to a servant and drew him down the hall to the low dais where stood a wine flagon and some fine glazed cups. After filling one from the other, she watched him drink. Four rapid, deep swallows he took, then breathed out hard. His shoulders relaxed and his smile this time was less perfunctory.

'Not this season. I've a contract to serve Justiciar de Luci until Michaelmas at least. It may be that he will send me and the men to Normandy to join the King's troops there, but it's more than likely we'll be kept at Nottingham.' He refilled the cup and looked around the hall.

Two maidservants were lighting the candles and closing the shutters on a thickening but calm dusk. The rain had stopped an hour since and the sun had glimmered through the clouds in time to set. Another woman was stirring a pot of soup over the central hearth and the smoke rising

7

from the fire was woven with an aroma of garlic and onions.

Since his last visit a year ago there were some hangings on the wall he had not seen before and he noticed that his father had finally bought a new box chair for himself. The old one, through a combination of splinters and wood-worm, had been lethal. The cups were new also. He recognized Maude's taste in the jolly horse and rider scenes painted in thick white slip on the red background.

'It's a bad business, the King's own sons turning against him.' Maude folded her arms beneath her ample bosom and clucked her tongue. 'I'm old enough to remember how it was before Henry sat on the throne and I never want to live through the like again. What was he thinking of to have his eldest boy anointed? Bound to give him ideas beyond himself.'

'He already has ideas beyond himself, feckless whelp.' Joscelin took another long swallow of wine and felt it glide smoothly down his throat, followed by a slight sting in his nostrils. 'The lad was only crowned to keep him quiet; now he's realized that for all the frippery and promises, he's no closer to power than he was as a swaddled infant. As far as his father's concerned, he can be a king all he wants, as long as it's king of nothing, and I'm inclined to agree.' Grimacing, he twitched his shoulders. The rain had soaked through his cloak and there was an uncomfortable clamminess across the back of his neck. 'What does my father say?'

'The same as you, but he's less polite.'

Joscelin's hazel eyes brightened with amusement. 'Where is the old wolf anyway? I'd have expected him to have bellowed my backside off by now.'

'He's dining with the Justiciar.'

'Is he so?' Joscelin raised his brows and sat down in his father's new chair. Richard de Luci was the nominal ruler of England while the King was absent in Normandy. Fiercely loyal to Henry, he was a civil servant of the highest order with superb ability. Joscelin's father and

Richard de Luci were friends of long standing and frequently pleasure marched hand in glove with business.

'Apparently the Earl of Leicester and others are in London for the purpose of asking de Luci's permission to leave England with troops and money for King Henry's army,' Maude said. Beckoning a servant, she told him to bring food.

Joscelin's brows rose higher. Robert of Leicester was self-seeking and arrogant without an honest bone in his body. If he was going to war, it was to line his pockets with power at the expense of other, weaker men. King Henry was certainly not weak – but his son was. 'I saw some of that money today,' he said thoughtfully, and tilted his cup to examine the dark sediment lurking in the bottom. 'Indeed I helped bring it into the city. It was in the custody of one of Young Henry's lick-boots, and if I have not walked in here with Giles de Montsorrel's blood all over my hands, it is by God's grace and not my own.' His eyes were suddenly battle-lit.

Maude sat down beside him, leaned her elbows on the trestle and gave him her full attention as he told her about his encounter with Giles de Montsorrel, his tone growing vehement with disgust as the tale progressed. 'He looked at me as if he had a stink beneath his nose that he was too high-bred to mention. I tell you, if it were not for the women and the little boy, I'd have struck him in the teeth and withdrawn my aid. You should have seen his men struggling with his strongbox. There was more in it than a few shillings to buy himself a couple of nags at Smithfield and trinkets for his wife.'

'He's lately come into an inheritance if my memory serves me correctly.' Maude screwed up her face in concentration. 'Yes, that's right. Old Lord Raymond died of a seizure at Eastertide, although he'd been having falling fits for almost a year.'

'Yes, I'd heard.' Joscelin did not add the information that Raymond's final seizure, on Easter Sunday immediately before mass, had taken place between the thighs of a servant's daughter at the moment of supreme pleasure. The incident had been the source of much ribald comment in the alehouses and barracks of Nottingham. Giles de Montsorrel had either a family reputation to keep up or one that he would never live down. That thought reminded Joscelin of his own half-brothers, and he grimaced without even realizing that he had done so.

'Are Ragnar and Ivo here?'

The serving man mounted the dais and set before Joscelin a steaming bowl of pork and bean pottage and an oblong loaf cut with a cross.

'Indeed they are.' The softly pleated lines around Maude's mouth deepened. 'Not that we often see them, the amount of time they spend carousing in brothels and taverns. Your father says they're just sowing their wild oats and that they'll tire soon enough.'

'But you are not as convinced.'

'Would you be?' She gave him a look from the corner of her eye.

Joscelin cut a chunk from the bread and dipped it into the pottage. 'You know how matters stand between myself and my half-brothers,' he said quietly, mindful of the servant still within earshot. 'I'm the bastard, Ragnar's the heir, and he rams it down my throat at every opportunity. Some things he never tires of.' He chewed and swallowed, his expression suddenly grim. 'And Ivo's like a sheep – he follows Ragnar's lead even if it happens to be off the edge of a cliff. Thank Christ I won't be here much above a week.'

'You've only just arrived!' Maude protested.

'I've a bad memory,' he said ruefully. 'It's not until I come home that I remember the reasons why I left in the first place, and by then it's too late.'

CHAPTER 3

LINNET DE MONTSORREL stared at a cobweb veiling an oak roof beam. A spider was sucking the life from a fly, which was still twitching feebly in the dark, vampire embrace. Giles bit into the soft skin between her throat and shoulder. His fingers gouged her buttocks, drawing her up to meet the crisis of his thrusting body. Clinging sweat; raw, stabbing pain. He whined and bit down. Linnet arched in silent agony, a prisoner of his weight. His jaws relaxed and he collapsed on her. She felt his tongue slide upon her shoulder, licking the blood, his quivering flesh still rigid within her own.

She lay stiffly under him, desperate to throw him off and knowing that she could not. On the web above, the fly no longer twitched, a mercy not permitted to her. She remained Giles's victim, to be unwrapped, impaled and used at his whim.

Leaving her shoulder, he moved lower, seeking the comfort of her nipple like a monstrous child. His weight settled, crushing her into the mattress. He sucked in drowsy pleasure. Her ribs started to ache and small spots of colour fluctuated before her eyes. 'Please!' she gasped. 'Please, Giles, you're crushing me!'

He jerked awake and, raising his head, glared at her reproachfully. 'God's eyes, don't you ever do anything but complain?' He slid out of her. She averted her eyes from his red, glistening shaft and closed her aching thighs. Her shoulder stung.

'Don't just lie there, fetch me a clean tunic!' he snapped impatiently. 'I've a rendezvous at Leicester's house tonight.'

'Yes, my lord,' she said meekly, her mind seething with a resentment she was careful to conceal. Sitting up, she drew on her chemise and went silently to the clothing pole. Crumpled on the floor were his discarded shirt and tunic, the latter torn in his haste to bed her. He would expect it mended by morning.

'If you don't like it, you should hurry up and quicken with a babe,' Giles said coldly as he snatched the fresh garments from her hands. 'The only child you've borne to me in six years of marriage is that milksop weakling out there, and you know what I think about him!'

Swallowing, Linnet turned away to get his belt and meat dagger. Bearing Robert had almost killed her, for her hips had still been childishly narrow. Giles had told the midwives to save the infant – he could always take another wife and what use was a bad breeder anyway? But she had survived and one of the midwives had advised her how to avoid quickening again too soon. It involved vinegar douches and small pieces of trimmed sponge or moss soaked in the same. Of late she had stopped using them in the hope of conceiving again, but thus far there had been no interruption to her monthly bleeds.

Giles stepped into his braies and jiggled his now recumbent genitals into a comfortable position. 'You think I enjoy ploughing a corpse?' he flayed her, his blue gaze savage. 'I might as well spread the legs of an effigy for all the response I get from you!'

She risked a single, frightened glance at his lean, tense frame, then looked at the floor. How could she reply that when he touched her she did indeed wish to be dead or turned to stone? It had always been so with Giles, although there had once been another who had taught her the pleasure and sin of lust.

'Mayhap you dream elsewhere,' he said darkly as he plunged into his shirt and tunic. 'You must know that I was displeased with your boldness this afternoon.'

'I'm sorry, my lord; I was only thinking of Robert's welfare.'

'Were you indeed? I saw the way de Gael looked at you after you spoke to him. A man of his ilk needs very little encouragement.'

'I swear I gave him none, my lord.' Cold fear climbed a ladder up Linnet's spine. 'On my soul.'

Giles seized the belt out of her hands and she flinched. 'On your soul?' he enquired softly. 'Shall we not say rather "on your hide"?' He ran the leather through his fingers until they stopped against the dragon's-head buckle.

'On my hide, I swear it,' Linnet said, looking at the intricate curlicues of Norse workmanship on the cold, solid brass and knowing how much their impact hurt. 'I swear it.'

Giles drew out the moment like a needle drawing thread through flesh, letting her suffer. 'I might have trusted you once,' he said huskily, and a shadow of pain tensed his eye corners. 'Then I discovered that any bitch in heat will run to be serviced by the nearest dog!' He jerked the belt around his lean waist, latched the buckle through a notch, and knotted the loose end. 'If you give me cause to reprimand you again, you know the consequences.'

Linnet lowered her eyes and stared at the floor. She could see his legs, the right one thrusting belligerently forwards, encased in gilded soft leather. 'Yes, my lord,' she whispered, feeling cold and sick.

The feet shifted and moved towards the door. 'Hurry up and get dressed, you've a household to order,' he snapped. 'Make yourself useful for something at least!' He flung himself out of the door and she heard him descend the stairs, yelling at one of his squires to summon a boatman to row him downriver to Leicester's house.

Slimy moisture crawled down the inside of her thigh. Shuddering, she sat on the edge of the bed and, taking a narwhal comb from her coffer, began to tidy her hair. She did not want to summon her maid; she needed a moment of solitude to compose herself, to fix in position the calm façade she would present to her household. Controlling the servants meant first of all controlling herself. Returning

13

the comb to the coffer, she picked up a small clay jar of marigold salve to soothe her injuries.

It was not the first time that Giles had bitten her, nor the most painful, but as she broke the creamy beeswax seal and took a daub of ointment on her fingertip, her eyes stung with tears. Jesu, how she hated being at his mercy, trapped like a fly in a web.

Vision blurring, she sat down on the strongbox which stood against his clothing chest. The studs on the stout iron bands reinforcing the carcass dug into the backs of her thighs, which were still tender from the grip of Giles's fingers. Beneath its twin locks lay the coin from the sale of their entire wool clip, and all the rents and toll monies from their villages. The silver plate from the keep at Rushcliffe was also there. It was part of her dowry and Giles had no right to bestow it upon Robert of Leicester for some dubious scheme in Normandy. Giles needed this coin to keep the moneylenders at bay. Promises did not put bread on the board and Giles had already taxed his villeins to the limit of their means. If there were a bad harvest this year, some of his people would starve for the cause of a sixteen-year-old boy with delusions of grandeur.

Giles was supposedly accompanying Leicester across the narrow sea to offer support to King Henry's efforts to crush his rebellious sons, but Linnet had deduced that treachery was intended. Giles disliked the controls that King Henry had imposed on baronial rights and would certainly not beggar himself to go to the King's aid. To her husband the prospect of an untried adolescent on the throne held endless possibilities, especially for the men who helped to place him there. It was a gamble, it was treason, and she had never seen Giles so excited – irritable and exhilarated at the same time. And it was she who bore the brunt of his mood swings.

Rising from the coffer, Linnet impatiently wiped away her tears on the heel of her hand. They were a release, nothing more. Giles was not softened by them and she would have dismissed them from her armoury long ago had she not discovered that other men were less impervious to their effect. This very afternoon the threat of tears, the appearance of quivering, feminine vulnerability had moved the mercenary Joscelin de Gael to sell his aid despite his obvious dislike of Giles. And she had paid the price.

She set her jaw and summoned her tiring maid Ella with a stony composure that did not falter even when the woman's eyes flickered over the ugly, blood-filled bruise on her shoulder with knowing, unspoken pity.

'You'll be wanting warm water and a towel first,' Ella said practically, and went to fetch them.

Linnet lit a taper from the fat white night candle and crossed the room to the small, portable screen at the end. Behind it, exhausted by the journey, her son slept in his small truckle bed. Against the pillow, his hair stood up in waifish blond spikes. He was fine-boned and fragile, light as thistledown, and she loved him with a fierce and guilty desperation. Frail children so often died in infancy; she would find herself watching him intently, waiting for the first cough or sneeze or sign of fever to have him swaddled up and dosed with herbal possets. And if he did live to adulthood, what kind of man would he make? Never such a one as his father, she vowed, although God alone knew the ways in which he would be twisted when he left the safety of her skirts for the masculine world beyond the bower.

'Never,' she vowed, her hand cupped around the candle flame, protecting her child from the hot drip of the wax. If only it were as easy to protect him from his future.

CHAPTER 4

RICHARD DE LUCI reclined in his pelt-spread chair, his goblet resting comfortably on the neat curve of his belly, and regarded his guest out of lugubrious, bloodhound eyes. 'What do you think about this latest news from Normandy?'

William de Rocher, nicknamed Ironheart, thrust his shoulder into the angle of his box chair and sucked his teeth, such as remained to him. In contrast to de Luci's surplus display of jowl, his flesh was drawn tightly over gaunt, prominent bones. Indeed, de Luci was wont to jest that given a black robe and a scythe, William de Rocher would personify the grim reaper.

'You mean about Queen Eleanor being caught defecting to Paris to join her sons in rebellion? Nothing would surprise me about her,' he snorted, 'not even the fact that she was disguised as a man when she was captured – it wouldn't be the first time.' He cast a dark look at his own wife. Dumpy and plain, she sat like a lump of proving dough beside de Luci's elegant wife. At least Agnes knew her place, and if she ever approached the borderline of his tolerance, a bellow and a raised fist sent her scuttling back to her corner with downcast eyes and a trembling mouth. But some women, brought up without benefit of discipline, were wont to snarl and bite the hand that fed them. 'I trust she's well under lock and key now?'

'Oh indeed yes, but it doesn't make the rebellion any less dangerous.'

Ironheart looked at de Luci from beneath untidy silver brows. 'I hear that the Earl of Leicester has approached you for permission to cross to Normandy and offer his

16

support to the King?' He made patterns on the tablelinen with the haft of his eating knife. 'Rumour has it too that he has amassed no small amount of bullion to fund his expedition.'

De Luci stared at him, then laughed and shook his head. 'I swear to God, William, you know more than I do half the time!'

'I listen at the right keyholes,' Ironheart retorted with a grin. 'Besides, Leicester's not exactly been making a secret of the fact, has he?'

'You've never approved of Robert of Leicester, have you?'

The grin faded. 'His father was as solid as granite; you could trust him with your life, but I wouldn't trust his heir further than I could hurl a lance. And before you ask, I've no evidence to prove him unworthy. It's a feeling inside here, a soldier's gut.' He patted the area between heart and belt.

'Then it's not jealousy because your sons spend more time in his company than they do in yours?' asked de Luci shrewdly.

Ironheart tossed and caught the meat dagger and looked along the bright length. 'Why should I be jealous?' he scoffed. 'I am their father, he is just a turd wrapped in cloth of gold. Let them have their little flirtation. Once they've unwrapped Earl Robert's bindings, they'll back away.'

De Luci pursed his lips, not so sure. 'I'm willing to give Leicester a chance,' he said and, with a rueful smile, patted his own paunch. 'A diplomat's gut, William.'

Ironheart snorted rudely and held out his wine cup to be refilled. 'I know which I'd rather trust.'

De Luci chose to ignore the remark, and changed the direction of the conversation. Raising his own cup, he rolled a mouthful of wine around his teeth and looked speculatively at Ironheart. 'Did you know I'd commissioned Joscelin for the rest of the summer?'

'No, but I thought you might, the situation being what it is.'

'If the opportunity arises, I'd like to give him a seneschal's post in one of the royal castles. He's proved his abilities in my service time and again this last year and a half.'

William stared down at his scarred, knotted hands. 'I forget how old the boy is,' he muttered, 'and how old I am.' Then he gave a laugh which held more snarl than amusement. 'Your wine's potent tonight; I'm growing maudlin! Aye, he'll make you a good seneschal, one of the best.'

An atmosphere, rather than anything said, caused de Luci to glance at the women who had stayed out of the conversation thus far. Behind her dough-like impassivity, Agnes de Rocher's rage was seething like rising yeast. Her fists were clenched as tight as rocks on the board and there were hectic red blotches on her throat. But then he and William had been discussing Joscelin's advancement, which was, he supposed, tantamount in Agnes's presence to drawing a yard of naked steel.

'Rohese, why don't you take Agnes above and show her those bales of fabric that arrived yesterday from Italy,' he said quickly to his wife in order to rectify the lapse of his diplomat's gut.

'By your leave, my lord,' murmured Rohese de Luci, giving him a look compounded of irritation and sympathy as she signalled for the finger-bowl.

De Luci returned her look with one of apologetic gratitude and knew that he would now have to purchase the bolt of peacock-coloured silk she had been angling after.

As the women curtsied and left the hall, William's breath eased out on a long sigh of relief and his tension visibly slackened. 'When Martyn enters your household next year to be a squire, I'm going to buy her a pension in a nunnery,' he said, his eyes upon his wife's disappearing rump.

De Luci rubbed his chin. 'Does Agnes know?'

'Not yet,' Ironheart shrugged. 'I can't see that she'll object. She keeps to her rooms most of the time at Arnsby anyway. I should have put her away long since.'

18

De Luci said nothing, although he gave his friend a wry glance. If Agnes de Rocher was scarcely the ideal wife, William de Rocher was certainly less than the perfect husband. Richard had been a groomsman at their wedding almost thirty years ago and had watched them labour under the yoke, mismatched and tugging in opposite directions. And once Joscelin's mother had left her mark on their lives, any chance of marital harmony had been utterly destroyed.

William sheathed his meat knife and, picking up his goblet, took a long swallow of wine. 'To future freedom,' he toasted. 'Enough of Agnes. Let's talk of other matters.'

Ironheart's squire handed Agnes from her litter and set her down in the courtyard at the rear of the house. William dismounted. The perfume of rain-wet grass and leaves drifted from the orchards beyond the stables and warred with the smell of the saturated dung and straw underfoot. At the end of the garden the Thames glinted in the last green glow of twilight. A groom and his apprentice emerged from the depths of the stables, the latter bearing a horn candle-lantern on a pole. By its light William saw that the stalls were crowded with horseflesh, little of it his own.

Bestowing his palfrey's reins upon the lad, he stooped under the lintel and, hands on hips, regarded the additions. A handsome liver-chestnut with distinctive white markings swung its head from the manger and, munching, regarded him with a liquid, intelligent eye. He knew Whitesocks well, for he had bred him from his own stud herd and gifted him to Joscelin four years ago when he was still a leggy, untrained colt.

Agnes sniffed furiously. 'How long are these animals going to eat us out of house and home?' she demanded, goaded by resentment to a boldness that she would not usually have dared to display.

'It will only be for a couple of days. He'll be stabling them at the Crown's expense after that,' William answered in a preoccupied voice.

19

The mildness of his response encouraged Agnes to press harder. 'You know that Ragnar and Joscelin hate the sight of each other,' she carped. 'This is just asking for a confrontation.'

'And I am master in this house. There will be no trouble,' he said coldly, and stroked the satin liver-chestnut hide. 'Besides, Ragnar's not here. He's out there wasting his substance in some den of fools.'

Agnes glared at her husband's long, straight spine and swept-back mane of unkempt badger-grey hair. As a bride of sixteen she had loved him so hard that even to look at him had made her queasy with joy. And in those first months he had been kind enough for her to imagine that he at least returned a measure of her affection. She had borne him two daughters one after the other and became pregnant again within three months of Katharine's birth. Exhausted, sick and miserable, she had watched William ride away to war, and every day she had prayed for him, callusing her knees on the cold chapel floor.

Her pleas to God had been answered after a fashion, for three months later he had returned unscathed, bringing with him a contingent of Breton mercenaries to garrison their castle. He had also brought a woman, the sister of one of the mercenaries. The glow of early pregnancy had been upon her, making her shine like a candle among common rush dips. She had been dark-haired, green-eyed and regal of bearing, and she had given William his first son to replace Agnes's own stillborn baby boy. It was then, seeing the blaze of joy, triumph and naked love in William's eyes, that Agnes had begun to learn hatred.

Three sons she had given him since then, but her success was tarnished. The shadow of Morwenna and her bastard had turned all her own efforts to dross. 'There is always trouble when Joscelin shows his face,' she said bitterly.

William rounded on her with a look that threatened violence. 'Watch your tongue or you'll be wearing a scold's bridle to curb it,' he said roughly.

Compressing her lips, she turned from him and marched

angrily across the yard and up the exterior stairs to the upper floor of the house. She would not go into the hall, for that would mean acknowledging Morwenna's bastard. A maid opened the door for her, but it was Agnes who slammed it shut, the sound reverberating across the soft summer dusk.

William's eyelids tensed. 'Sulky bitch,' he muttered, knowing that he was not being fair, but not caring enough to set his attitude to rights. Never in the farthest corner of his soul would it have occurred to him to placate or apologize.

When he entered the hall, Joscelin was sprawled in his box chair before the central hearth. His squire sat in the rushes near his feet, his head bent over a dagger grip he was rebinding with new strips of hide. A different dagger twisted in William's heart as he approached the fire and his son raised his head. God's life, he was so much like his mother. The green-hazel eyes and the expression in them were all hers, and they brought back unbearable bitter-sweet memories.

Joscelin sprang to his feet and engulfed his father in a bone-crunching embrace. They were of similar height and build, for William still had a tough, muscular body on which no softness had been allowed to encroach. Only his granite features betrayed more than fifty years of harsh life.

'I swear you grow more like a plough ox every time I see you!' he gasped and, thrusting his son aside, prowled to the hearth. The flaxen-haired squire scrambled to his feet in deference, his blue eyes wary.

'Fetch wine,' William commanded, 'two cups.' He glanced at the thick cloak spread upon the chair and spilling to the floor. 'I trust you'll stay to drink a measure with your old father?'

Joscelin's colour heightened. 'Of course, sir. I was waiting for you.'

William grunted and gave him an eloquent stare, but did not further spike it with words. If Joscelin intended going out into the city at night, it was none of his business,

21

but nevertheless he was curious. Joscelin was not usually one for the vices that were to be found in the alehouses and stews on the wrong side of curfew.

The squire returned with the wine.

'Was your journey free of hazard?'

Joscelin grinned and, shaking his head, looked at the floor for a moment before raising laughter-bright eyes. 'How do you always know where to strike a nut to crack the shell and come to the meat?'

'Call it grim experience.'

For the second time that evening Joscelin related the tale of his encounter with Giles de Montsorrel. 'It stinks like a barrel of rotten fish,' he concluded. 'Why should he want to bring his worldly wealth all the way to London?'

From the upper floor came the muffled sound of women's voices and the loud thud of a coffer lid opening and slamming. William flickered an irritated glance aloft. 'He's related to Robert of Leicester, is he not? And Leicester has obtained de Luci's permission to sail for Normandy in the next week or so with men and money to succour King Henry . . . or so Leicester would have us believe. Myself, I've heard more truth in a minstrel's lay.'

Joscelin nodded thoughtfully at his father's comments. 'And Montsorrel is contributing his bit to Leicester's endeavour. From what I know of Giles, he has no passionate loyalty to the King. If he was going to take sides, I would say that he would choose Young Henry's.'

Ironheart snorted disparagingly. 'I certainly wouldn't chance my all on an untried youth of sixteen with a reputation for being as fickle as a Southwark strumpet both on the battlefield and off. Mind you, it's easier to manipulate a vain, spoiled boy than it is to obtain satisfaction from a man well versed in statecraft who's had his backside on the throne for the past twenty years.' William took a swallow of wine. 'Giles de Montsorrel is a fool.'

'A wealthy fool with the Rushcliffe inheritance new in his purse,' Joscelin said.

'Not for long,' Ironheart snorted. 'He's already

squandered a good portion of the money his wife brought to their marriage bed, not to mention what she inherited from her father.'

'Her father?'

'Robert de Courcelles – too soft for his own good, but decent enough. The family lands are mostly in Derbyshire – such as Giles hasn't sold off to finance his jousting habit.'

'I remember Robert de Courcelles,' Joscelin murmured. 'He was a friend of the sheriff and he was often in Nottingham. They used to go hunting together.' After a pause he added casually, 'Linnet de Montsorrel resembles him very much.'

The very nonchalance of Joscelin's tone caused Ironheart's ears to sharpen. 'Took your fancy this afternoon, did she?' he asked with a sly grin.

Joscelin's colour heightened. 'I felt sorry for her, and a little curious. I suppose that makes me "too soft for my own good" too.' He took a fast gulp of the wine and glared at his father.

Ironheart continued to grin, not in the least deceived. The way Joscelin had fired up was proof that the woman had got to him. 'Indeed it does,' he said. 'Giles de Montsorrel is known to be a jealous husband.'

'He has nothing to be jealous about.'

'Do not bristle at me, I but speak out for your own good.'

'There is no need.'

Ironheart eyed his son impatiently, then laughed brusquely and abandoned the subject. 'Very well, there is no need. Let us talk of other things. De Luci informs me that he is keeping you on throughout the summer.'

Joscelin relaxed, but his eyes remained wary. 'The rewards are greater on the tourney circuit, but so are the risks. Garrison duty's usually boring but, if there's food in my belly and money in my pouch, who am I to grumble?'

William winced. There was no rancour in Joscelin's tone, no intention to complain, but still he felt the burden of guilt hit him like the counterbalance on a quintain.

23

Joscelin was his first-born son, the only child Morwenna had given him, but because he was bastard-born, he was debarred from inheriting any of the de Rocher lands. Instead he had to make his own way in the world, and that meant either by the priesthood or by the sword. William had done his best, educating Joscelin for both vocations and furnishing him with the tools of his chosen trade, but it would never be enough for his bleeding conscience.

'I doubt you'll have time for boredom to be a hazard,' he said wryly as Joscelin drained his cup. 'Richard didn't say much, but I gather he's got more in mind for you than just garrison duty.'

Joscelin forced his cloak-pin through the good blue Flemish cloth. 'Such as?'

'That's for de Luci to tell you.'

Joscelin's narrow, restless brows arched and came level. 'I'd best make the most of my freedom then,' he said, and gestured round. 'As you've noticed by the emptiness of the hall, my men are already about it with gusto.'

Ironheart could sense an undercurrent of turbulence in Joscelin's manner, probably a residue of his meeting with Montsorrel that afternoon. A night in a tavern might settle it, or a woman who knew her trade, but it was a dangerous burden to bear into London after dark. 'Have a care, Josce,' he said, frowning.

'As always.' Joscelin dismissed the caution far too lightly for his father's liking and, with a casual parting salute, disappeared into the night.

William sighed heavily. Gesturing the wide-eyed squire away to his pallet, he sat down before the banked central hearth to drink the rest of his wine. His thoughts of their own wayward volition turned to Joscelin's mother. Morwenna. Even the name whispered on his tongue twisted the knife in his heart.

She had been a mercenary's daughter whose favours he had bought one spring evening during the campaign of '46. Until Morwenna he thought he had women in perspective, but she had broken all rules and moulds and, finally, his heart. Five years it had lasted, from the night she unbound her hair for him at an army campfire to the night they combed it down over the silent, cold breast of her corpse, a swaddled stillborn daughter in the crook of her arm. Nothing of her existence had remained except a bewildered little boy of four years old and an even more bewildered man of thirty-two.

Oh God, how he had hated Agnes in the months following Morwenna's death. All the tolerance in his nature, all the gentleness had died too. He should have been delighted at how swift Agnes was to quicken with child, at how easily she was delivered, but he had felt nothing but cursed. He knew that he treated his dogs better than he did his wife, but it was ingrained now. Every time he looked at her he saw Morwenna's grey, lifeless body and rejected the image with violence. They said that it was a tragic accident, the fall downstairs so late into her pregnancy. The afterbirth had come away, she had started to bleed, and two days later she and the baby had died. And he had not reached her in time even to have the grace of a last farewell.

The candle on the pricket near him sputtered petulantly and he emerged from his dismal reverie with a start. In the shadows beyond the light the servants were asleep on straw mattresses. Normally they would have drawn them nearer to the fire, but no one dared to encroach on his solitude. Ironheart heaved himself to his feet, tossed the wine dregs on to the fire where they hissed into vapour, and wearily sought his bed.

Further along the Strand, the Earl of Leicester's house stood open to the last of the gloaming. It was a new dwelling, constructed of traditional plaster and timber with a red-tiled roof. Tiles were more expensive than thatch, but a symbol of status and far less of a fire hazard. Both indoors and out, torches blazed in high wall brackets, illuminating the revellers who either sat at long trestles in the puddle-filled courtyard or crowded into the main room, jostling each other for elbow room. Herb-seasoned mutton, shiny with grease, hissed over firepits in the garth, tended by a spit boy half-drunk on cider. He wavered erratically between the carcasses, a tankard in one hand, a basting ladle in the other.

Joscelin hesitated. He could see some of the Justiciar's men at one of the trestles – soldiers of his acquaintance who would welcome him among their number. The light and laughter beckoned. So did a wench with slumberous dark eyes and the slender body of a weasel. She smiled as Joscelin hovered, and suggestively twitched her hips. Against his better judgement, lured by her invitation, he stepped across the threshold and entered the crowded room.

The tables lining the walls were packed solid with Leicester's knights and retainers. He saw a Flemish mercenary captain he knew from the tourney circuits and two renowned jousters who had been over-wintering at the Earl's board. On the dais at the far end of the room, beneath criss-crossed gilded banners, sat Leicester himself. He was a heavily fleshed man in his early thirties, handsome in an overblown, florid sort of way that would yield to grossness as age converted muscle into fat. At the moment, one arm embraced his guest, Giles de Montsorrel of the broken cart-wheel, who was well on the way to being drunk, if his exaggerated gestures and overloud voice were any indication. At his other side, hunched forwards listening to the conversation and chewing on a chicken bone, sat another relation of Leicester's, Hubert de Beaumont. The family tendency to corpulence was already ballooning his gut and setting a ruffle of fat around his throat. Joscelin knew him vaguely – a disreputable roisterer who had squandered the last three years in the dubious company of the King's disgruntled sons.

Deciding that the girl was not worth the discomfort of drinking in such a rancid den of rebels, even with a leavening of de Luci's men present, Joscelin turned to leave.

'Ho villein!' crowed a mocking voice he knew only too well, and his shoulder was thumped with bruising force. 'Come scrounging like the rest, have you?'

Joscelin turned slowly to face his half-brother.

'Elflin, fetch wine for our exalted guest!' commanded Ragnar de Rocher with a sarcastic flourish.

The dark-eyed girl giggled and disappeared. Ragnar reseated himself and made room for Joscelin on the crowded bench, but the gesture held more of challenge than generosity. At the same table among other young knights and squires sat Ivo, who was younger than Ragnar by two years and a shadowy replica of his hawk-featured red-blond brother.

'Have you come to sell your sword?' Ragnar enquired. 'Leicester's paying good rates and you look as if you need the coin.' His narrow, light brown eyes disparaged Joscelin's garments which, although of good quality wool, showed evidence of hard wear and were almost devoid of embroidery or embellishment.

'I already have a commission,' Joscelin said. 'I'm not so poor that I cannot choose a decent paymaster.'

'Oh-ho!' Ragnar's lips parted in a feral grin. 'Living on principles, are we?' He stuck his finger down his throat and made a retching sound.

Ivo gave a high-pitched nervous laugh. 'Have you ever known a mercenary with principles?' His glance sidled slyly between Ragnar and Joscelin. Anticipation gleamed through his sparse, sandy lashes.

'You wouldn't know a principle, Ivo, if one walked up to you and struck you in the face,' Joscelin said contemptuously.

The girl returned with a yellow glazed pitcher and refilled the empty cups at the trestle with rough red wine. Ragnar caught her wrist and swung her round on to his lap. She squealed but did not resist as his hard arm encircled her waist and his hand took liberties upwards.

'So you're already commissioned?' Ragnar asked.

'To the Justiciar until Michaelmas.' Joscelin took a gulp

of the wine and knew that there was going to be trouble. Anger simmered in his blood, a fraction from boiling point. It lurked too in Ragnar's narrowed eyes and the curl of Ivo's lip.

Ragnar yanked down the girl's tunic and shift to plant a kiss in the cleft of her breasts. 'You reckon you'll live that long?' he asked, the words muffled by his companion's soft flesh.

'Longer than you,' Joscelin retorted, sweeping the crowded trestles with a scornful stare. 'If you think this trek to Normandy is the easy way to glory then your brains must truly dwell up your backside.'

Ivo sniggered. Ragnar jerked his head out of the girl's bosom, his chin jutting aggressively. 'You'll take that back,' he said, his fine-grained skin white with anger.

'Why should I? It's the truth.'

Ragnar coiled himself to strike, then paused, his eyes flickering sideways to a heavily set knight easing past their trestle. 'Hubert.' He set a detaining arm on the man's sleeve. 'Have you met my brother Joscelin?'

Hubert de Beaumont was fumbling with the drawstring of his braies, making it obvious that he was on his way outside for a piss. He gave Joscelin a brusque nod of acknowledgement. 'Your face looks familiar,' he said. 'Didn't I see you in Paris at Easter?'

'Try the midsummer joust in Toulouse last year.'

Beaumont frowned. His lips moved, repeating Joscelin's words and his expression suddenly changed. 'Yes, I remember.' His tone was not altogether complimentary. He turned back to Ragnar. 'He's your brother you say?'

'Only my half-brother,' Ragnar replied, and added with malicious delight, relishing each word, 'he's my father's bastard out of a tourney whore who'd had more lances in her target than a worn-out quintain shield by the time she came to his bed.'

The serving girl screamed as she was sent flying and the brothers hit the trestle, Joscelin uppermost, fist raised. Cups flew in all directions, their contents splattering far and wide. The pitcher crashed on its side and split in two, bleeding a lake of wine across the scrubbed oak. The two brothers rocked for a moment on the board, the red Anjou soaking like a huge bloodstain into Ragnar's tunic, and then they crashed to the floor, rolling amidst the rushes.

Open-mouthed, his full bladder forgotten, Hubert de Beaumont stared. Ivo brushed wine from his tunic with the palm of one hand and shifted his position the better to watch the brawl, his usually pallid complexion pink with glee.

Ragnar came uppermost, his hand flashing to his dagger hilt. Nine inches of greased steel sparkled free. Joscelin brought up his knee and kicked hard, hurling Ragnar back towards the central firepit. Ragnar sprawled, his head almost striking a hearth brick, but he recovered swiftly, rolled to one side and regained his feet, dagger held low to gut. Joscelin wove under the slashing attack and again thrust Ragnar backwards. His own hand streaked to his poniard, closed on the leather grip, then stopped, holding hard, for Ragnar lay where he had landed, and a soldier's tough leather boot was crushed firmly down across both his dagger and wrist.

The foot belonged to a tall, powerfully built man with exquisitely barbered blond hair and shrewd grey eyes that were surrounded by fine premature weather-lines. Joscelin recognized Brien FitzRenard of Ravenstow, one of de Luci's hand-picked team of messengers and reconnaissance men.

'Enough,' said FitzRenard, and stooped to remove the offending weapon from Ragnar's fingers. He looked through the smoke haze at Joscelin, his gaze irritated, but not unfriendly. 'Best if you leave now before anything uglier develops.' His voice, like his movements, was measured without being in the least way slow.

Joscelin glanced round the room. A low hum of conversation had started again, but he was aware of being scrutinized with a mixture of hostility, contempt and downright curiosity. On the dais, Leicester's expression was one of

29

cold anger. Giles had succumbed to the wine, his head flat on the board, his mop of fair hair trailing its edges in the finger-bowl.

FitzRenard lifted his boot and permitted Ragnar to regain his feet, but displayed not the slightest inclination to return the dagger. Breathing heavily, Ragnar sat up, his expensive tunic ruined by an enormous wine stain and stubbled with bits of floor straw.

'One day, I'll kill you!' he snarled at Joscelin, his face bleached white by rage.

'Then I'll make sure to guard my back,' Joscelin retorted. 'It's the only corner from which I fear your attack.' Wiping a thin trickle of blood from the corner of his mouth, he stormed outside into the damp summer evening. His breath came unevenly and tears of fury and humiliation stung his eyes. He was aware of having failed himself, of not wanting to care, and of caring too damned much.

CHAPTER 5

THE MOUSE SAT on its haunches, industriously manipulating an ear of grain in its forepaws, its sharp teeth nibbling through the husk to reach the sweet, starchy kernel. Sunlight wove through the crack in the stable door, patterning the straw with glints of fiery yellow and threading up the daub and wattle walls to spread the hide of the dozing liver-chestnut stallion with a cloth of gold.

Joscelin watched the busy rodent with the half-open, slightly glazed eyes of the newly awakened. His head throbbed gently and his mouth was painfully dry and tasted of kennel sweepings – payment for last night's sins, of which, after the fight with Ragnar, he remembered very little. Nor did he wish to.

A brindled and white blur suddenly shot past the tip of his nose and pounced in a flurry of straw. Joscelin jerked upright, his heart thrusting vigorously against his ribs, his dagger already out of its sheath. The tabby stable cat regarded him, a mixture of wariness and disdain in its jewel-green eyes, a mouse dangling in its jaws like a chestnut moustache. Keeping him in view, the cat slunk sideways across the stable and undulated through the narrowly open door into the courtyard.

Joscelin relaxed and, with a soft groan, put his head down between his parted knees. Outside he could hear the sounds of his father's house coming to life in the bright summer morning – two maids gossiping at the trough, the cheeky wolf-whistle of a soldier and the good-natured riposte. He smelt smoke from an outdoor cooking fire and heard hens crooning and scratching in the dust. Then feet scuffled immediately outside the stable door and laid shadows across the stripes of sunlight on straw. Two people consulted in low tones, one voice adolescent, the other a mature baritone.

'. . . have to tend the horses, sir, but he's still asleep in there.'

'Not surprising the state he returned in last night,' commented the baritone. 'All right, go and break your fast. I'll see if I can rouse him up.'

'No need,' Joscelin said, pushing open the stable door to the full glory of the sunlit morning and squinting blearily at the groom and his goggle-eyed apprentice. He scraped his hand through his rumpled hair and paused to pluck out a stalk of straw. 'I would have made my way to bed in the hall, but the stables were closer and I wasn't sure my feet would hold me up for the extra distance.'

A grin split the groom's weather-brown face. 'You were a trifle unsteady, master Joscelin,' he agreed.

'I was gilded to the eyeballs,' Joscelin snorted, 'and I've a head to prove it this morning.'

The apprentice sidled away to get his food before the groom should press him to his duty now that the obstacle had removed itself.

Joscelin loosened the drawstring of his braies and relieved himself in the waste channel that ran the length of the stable block.

'Master Ragnar didn't come home at all,' the groom volunteered and, picking up the dung fork, looked round in exasperation for his lad. 'Your lord father's not best pleased.'

Joscelin finished, adjusted his garments and went to wash his hands and face in the rain butt against the gutter pipe. His cut lip stung and his ribs ached. His lord father was going to be even less pleased when he heard about the fight. Perhaps he already knew; Ivo excelled at carrying tales.

'What about Ivo?'

'Sick as a dog,' said the groom, a gleam of malicious satisfaction in his eyes.

Joscelin's lips twitched. It might be possible to avoid the reckoning until he was fit to cope with it after all.

'Joscelin!' A bruising weight struck him in the middle of the back. Wiry arms and legs wrapped themselves monkey-fashion around him and their owner swarmed aloft to his shoulders. 'Will you take me to see the dancing bear at Smithfield fair?' A freckled face topped by a mop of unruly reddish-brown curls peered down into his at an angle that made focusing a nauseous pain. Joscelin raised his arms, grabbed the agile small body and somersaulted it over his shoulder, setting it on its feet before him.

His youngest half-brother, Martyn, gazed up at him, an urchin grin polishing his face. At eight years old he was soon to fly the nest for a squirehood position in de Luci's household. He possessed his full share of the de Rocher self-assurance, although at the moment it was innocent rather than arrogant.

'Why in the world should I take you anywhere?' Joscelin demanded with amusement.

Chuckling, the groom departed in search of his wily apprentice.

'I'll be good, I promise!'

'I've heard that one before too!'

'Please,' Martyn beseeched with eyes as soulful as a hound's so that Joscelin had to bite his lip.

'Let me settle my wits and my gut first and I'll see,' he said, and started towards the house. Martyn skipped beside him like a spring lamb and chattered nine to the dozen about the dubious fairground delights offered on Smithfield's perimeter.

'And there's a real mermaid too!' he declared as they entered the hall together. 'All bare up here . . . but it costs a whole penny to see her.'

Joscelin knew the 'mermaid' well since fairgrounds and tourneys frequently travelled sword in sheath together. The nearest she had ever come to being a fish was servicing sailors in a Southampton brothel. Her long blond hair was a wig and her 'tail' was made of cunningly stitched snakeskins. He supposed that she had good breasts if that was the only opportunity you ever got to see a pair, but hardly a full penny's worth. 'Gingerbread's better value,' he advised gravely and halted, his expression becoming blank as Lady Agnes descended upon them, her face puckered with lines of temper.

'Where have you been?' she snapped at Martyn and grabbed his arm in a pincer grip. 'Go and change your tunic, hurry. We're due at the Justiciar's hall within the hour. You look like something disreputable in a mercenary baggage train!' She released him with a push.

Self-assured Martyn might be, but not stupid, and he obeyed her command at a run, grimacing over his shoulder at Joscelin as he reached the end of the hall.

Her insult had been all for Joscelin. Last night he had responded to Ragnar's baiting with violence. Now he offered the Lady Agnes a stony courtesy, his manners precise. She might claim that he had been bred in the gutter, but she was the one who stooped to it to sling mud.

He sat down at a trestle and took a small loaf from the shallow bread-basket in the centre of the table. Then he poured himself a leather mug of ale. He could have insisted on taking his place at the high table and commandeering white manchet bread and good wine, but he could not be bothered with that sort of battle this morning.

'Where's my father?' he asked, a glance round the hall showing him a suffering, bleary handful of his own men, the steward and servants, but scarcely any of the de Rocher retainers. For a moment he thought that she was not going to reply. Her small eyes narrowed and her fastidious nostrils quivered. None of your business her expression said, but the reaction to male dominance was so ingrained that she did not openly defy him. 'He's gone to fetch Ragnar back from Leicester's house,' she said frostily, and turned her back on him to chivvy the servants.

Joscelin arched his brow and began to eat. Small joy his father would have of Ragnar, he thought. At three and twenty, brimful of anger and resentment, his half-brother was too old and dangerous to be whipped to heel like a raw adolescent. He regarded the skinned knuckles of his own right hand, flexed them, and winced.

Agnes swept past the trestle with compressed lips and eyes like stones. The servants suffered. Joscelin thought about holding his ground, and decided that it would just be cutting off his nose to spite his face. Cramming a final piece of bread into his mouth with unmannerly haste, he took his cup outside to finish his ale in peace. It was a mistake. As he sauntered into the warm morning air, his father rode into the yard, Ragnar a few paces behind and both of them obviously in filthy tempers.

Ironheart dismounted, cuffed the groom's apprentice across the ear for being a fraction too slow at the bridle, and stamped towards the hall. His pace checked for an instant when he saw Joscelin and a muscle ticked in the long hollow of his cheekbone. Then he came on, his body stiff with anger.

'Leicester's house!' he snarled at Joscelin as he came level. 'You couldn't have chosen a more public place to brawl had you scoured all of London! You shame me and you shame your blood!'

Joscelin looked beyond his father's mottled fury to where Ragnar still sat on his horse. 'I had good reason,' he said quietly, his fist tightening on the mug handle.

'Leicester says you were drunk. He was only too pleased to regale me with all the details while I haled Ragnar off some strumpet he'd fallen asleep on,' Ironheart retorted, not in the least mollified. 'I'd have been better advised to take a vow of celibacy than beget the brood of half-wit sons collaring me now!'

'I wasn't drunk, just very angry,' Joscelin said.

'And spoiling for a fight before you left me last night. A dozen eyewitnesses say that you started it!'

Joscelin's chin jerked slightly as if he had taken a blow, but he said nothing, his stare wooden.

'Oh, get out of my way!' Ironheart snapped. 'Let me swallow a drink before I choke!' Thrusting past Joscelin into the house, he bellowed at his wife like a wounded bear.

Ragnar rode over to Joscelin, deliberately fretting the horse, making it prance dangerously close. 'I thought for the good of your hide you'd be long gone by now,' he sneered.

'As usual, you thought wrong,' Joscelin answered with a shrug, his dislike of Ragnar tinged with weariness.

Ragnar's complexion was pale and sweaty. An ugly bruise marred his left eye socket where Joscelin's fist had connected the night before. 'One day I'll be lord of all my father owns and you'll be nothing,' he said, each word limned with bitterness. The horse stamped and its tail swished, clipping the cup in Joscelin's hands.

Joscelin refused to be intimidated. 'You really don't know the difference, do you Ragnar, between having nothing and being nothing,' he said scornfully and poured the dregs of his cup on to the ground. The dust lumped together and glistened. 'I might sell my sword for money, but never my integrity.'

For a moment the prospect of another brawl hung imminent, but the sound of Ironheart's choler-choked voice barking through the open hall doors held the two antagonists to caution. Ragnar bestowed upon Joscelin a single, glittering look that spoke far more eloquently than words and, knuckles white upon the reins, snatched the horse round towards the waiting, apprehensive groom. In the course of its turn, his mount's glossy shoulder brushed Joscelin, forcing him to take a step backwards. A hoofprint bit open the dark stain in the dust where the drink had spilled. Joscelin stared at it, and then at his brother's back. It was long and broad, and the amount of blue velvet required to make the sumptuous overtunic must have cost Lady Agnes's domestic budget several shillings.

Ragnar did not know the privation of lying down at a roadside because there was nowhere better to sleep. He had never had to fight for each mouthful of food or gather firewood in freezing, sleety rain when he was so weary he wanted to lie down and die, but couldn't because people were depending on him. Ragnar did not know what real hunger was.

Ragnar moved restlessly around his mother's chamber, touching this and that without any real purpose. Agnes watched his progress with troubled eyes. She could still feel the dry imprint of his kiss on her cheek. He stank of wine, sweat and the cheap gillyflower scent of whores. She was disappointed, but not surprised; nor did she blame him. It was all William's fault.

'Shall I find you some salve for your eye, beloved?'

Ragnar shook his head and fiddled with a piece of tablet-woven braid lying on top of her work-basket. 'It doesn't hurt,' he muttered.

'Are you sure?'

'Yes, Mama.'

His voice was soft and flat. Agnes dried her damp palms on the full skirt of her gown. He dropped the braid and moved to the window. She admired his spare, angular grace and the gleam of his sun-bright hair. In Ragnar the Norse heritage of his forefathers was apparent in more than just his name. He was golden and fierce and she had given him life. Her daughters had possessed similar colouring but both had died in infancy.

'Joscelin should have fetched up in gaol,' she seethed. 'You might have been blinded.'

He gave a non-committal grunt and did not look round, his gaze upon the toings and froings in the courtyard. 'I need money,' he said. 'I don't want to ask Papa, and even if I did, he would not give it to me.'

'How much?'

'Enough to see me comfortable while I'm in Normandy with Leicester's troops.'

Her heart plummeted. 'You are truly going?'

He said nothing, but after a moment he turned his head and fixed her with a stare that held a world of discontent and frustration. His eyes were her own narrow light brown.

With the sun striking them obliquely, they held small flakes of suspended gold. The swollen purple bruise was an affront to his beauty.

'Have you told your father?'

'Not in so many words, but he knows.'

And would do nothing to help him, Agnes thought, because he thoroughly disapproved of Robert of Leicester. If she herself disapproved, it was because of the danger to Ragnar's safety, but she knew she could no more hold him or persuade him to do her bidding than she could handle William's savage Norway hawk. In her mind it thus made sense to ensure that Ragnar had everything he needed to survive.

'How much?' she questioned again, and from the house-wife's keys jingling at her waist she selected the one to her enamelled jewel casket. Every penny that she spent had to be accounted for to William, but she still had the pieces of jewellery that were part of her dowry and those were hers to dispose of as she wished. William never noticed whether she wore trinkets or not, and she seldom felt the need to adorn herself in finery. If they would spare Ragnar even a minute of hardship, she would not begrudge giving them up.

Ragnar left the window niche and crossed the room to stand at her shoulder as she raised the casket lid. There were rings and brooches, jewelled belt clasps and a tablet-woven girdle that her waist had outgrown in the course of a dozen pregnancies, its surface sewn with tiny freshwater pearls. Ragnar ignored all these and, leaning over, pounced upon a reliquary cross on a heavy gold chain.

'This will do,' he said and held it up to the light, his fist claiming the links. Amethyst and moonstone, agate and beryl flashed amid a fire of sun-caught gold.

Agnes inhaled to protest. The cross was one of the few pieces that she still liked to wear, and certainly the most expensive. Seeing the smile on Ragnar's lips, however, she sighed out again softly, and was rewarded by another kiss, less perfunctory this time.

38

'Thank you, Mama, I can always count on you for an ally,' he said and, ducking the cross around his neck, headed for the door.

On the threshold he encountered his Aunt Maude, a dish of marzipanned dates in her hand. He kissed her too, filched several of the sweetmeats off the tray and, whistling loudly, pounded away down the stairs.

Maude looked curiously at Agnes, who, pink-faced, was closing and locking her jewel casket.

'Ragnar's uncommonly cocky to say that William almost flayed him alive earlier,' she remarked, setting the dish on the coffer and biting avidly into one of the dates. 'Have you been helping him out again?'

Greedy interfering sow, thought Agnes. 'It's none of your business,' she said coldly. The hoop of keys jangled on her waist as she adjusted them.

'Just be careful. I don't think William would approve.'

Agnes narrowed her eyes. 'Are you going to tell him?'

Maude shrugged and licked her fingers. 'No,' she said, giving her sister-in-law a hard look. 'It's none of my business, is it?'

CHAPTER 6

LINNET WATCHED THE dancing bear shamble in slow circles to the tune its corpulent owner was playing on a bone flute. A moth-eaten bearskin was pinned on the man's shoulder by a tarnished silver brooch, and around his throat was a necklace of bear teeth interspersed with long, curved claws of a clear, tortoise-shell yellow. She had no doubt that they were the remains of the showman's former animal.

Linnet eyed the stout chain that attached the bear to a stake and hoped that it had no weak links. The beast itself looked weary to death. Its coat was scabby with mange, its small eyes listless, and the stench of its body was so great that she held her veil across her nose. Poor creature, she thought even as she did so, for she knew what it was to be trapped, forced to dance at another's will until nothing of self remained.

A glance around showed her that Giles and some other young knights of Leicester's mesnie were trying out the paces of the war-horses at a coper's booth near the fairground. Strange how there was money for what he wanted, but never sufficient for her own requests. That morning she had almost had to beg him for the coin to purchase needles and thread and some linen to make a summer tunic for Robert. It made her sick with bitterness when she thought of all that silver in their strongbox and how it was going to finance a stupid war.

Robert hid behind her skirts and peeped out at the bear, his grey eyes enormous with wonder and fear. A honeyed fig was clutched tightly in his hand and Linnet was well aware that her gown would be covered in sticky fingerprints before the morning was out.

'Joscelin, look, here's the bear, I told you!' a child's voice shrilled.

Turning her head, Linnet saw an excited little boy of about eight years old pointing towards the bear with one hand and dragging a laughing, resigned man with the other. Today Joscelin de Gael had discarded his mail for a tunic of russet wool, the sleeve ends banded with tawny braid to match the tight-sleeved undertunic and chausses. The excellence of the cloth was only emphasized by its lack of embellishment and by the slightly worn but good quality belt slanting between waist and hip, drawn down by the weight of a serviceable poniard. He and the child bore a resemblance to each other in the sculpture of brow and jaw and the proud carriage of body, giving her cause to be curious.

Fascinated by the bear, too young to see the tarnish of its moth-eaten plight, the boy stared. De Gael shook his head and smiled indulgently. Glancing sideways, his expression suddenly became one of surprised pleasure.

'Lady de Montsorrel!'

Linnet's maid moved defensively to her side and the two soldiers whom her husband had posted over her as escort and guard eyed him with sour disfavour, their hands hovering suggestively close to the weapons on their belts.

'Sir Joscelin,' she murmured and lowered her gaze, knowing that Giles would blame her for any familiarity. And yet de Gael was owed a courteous response. 'I must thank you again for yesterday.'

'I didn't have much choice, did I?' Laughter quivered in his voice, which held the hint of a Breton accent.

Linnet knew that she was blushing because her face felt as hot as a furnace. She dared not look up or reply to his admiring, slightly teasing gambit. Joscelin de Gael rode the tourney circuits; flirting with women was just another of the accoutrements of his trade. His very presence at her side was a danger to her reputation, especially after yesterday.

41

He suddenly crouched on his heels, hands dangling in the space between his bent knees. 'And you look much brighter young man,' he said to Robert. 'Do you like the bear?'

Robert clutched her hand for reassurance and pressed himself against her.

De Gael wrinkled his nose. 'I confess I don't, but I've been dragged to see it none the less.' He spoke softly to the little boy, but his words were directed at Linnet.

She nodded towards the older child. 'Is this your son?'

'My half-brother Martyn. The kind of existence I lead is no recommendation for marriage and children.' A shadow briefly crossed his face and when his smile resumed it was cynical. 'The fortune-teller yonder informs me that I am going to wed a beautiful heiress and die in idle comfort, but she was just lying to get at my purse. If I married an heiress, beautiful or not, I'd spend all my time defending my new-found fortune by writ and by sword.'

'Instead you defend other men's fortunes,' Linnet said, warming to his rueful candour despite herself.

'Oh yes, strongboxes full of them, for whatever purpose.' He slanted her a look from cat-hazel eyes and Linnet physically recoiled from his knowing insinuation.

'Come, sweetheart,' she said to Robert, 'it is time to go.' Grasping his sticky, small hand, she inclined her head in a per-functory, formal farewell to the mercenary. He unfolded from his crouch and returned her salute, his gravity marred by the sparkle of humour deepening the creases at his eye corners.

Linnet hurried away from the danger of his proximity. She heard de Gael's small brother asking if he could have some gingerbread and the mercenary's good-natured response. Risking a glance over her shoulder she discovered that de Gael was staring after her in speculation, and her throat closed with fear.

'What did he want with you?'

Linnet came to an abrupt halt, her path blocked by her husband. He sat astride a fancy tan war-horse whose paces he was trying. The beast had a rolling, wicked eye and

Giles was barely in control, his knuckles white on the reins which were drawn to their tightest limit.

'Nothing,' she croaked, and had to swallow before she could speak again. 'He was just passing the time of day.'

'Then why are you blushing? What did he say to you?'

'Nothing, I swear it; he was talking to Robert.'

'To a whey-faced brat?' The horse plunged and she had to step aside quickly to avoid being barged by its powerful shoulder. 'You expect me to believe that?'

'He has his own younger brother with him. Please, my lord, everyone is watching us. You will make a scandal out of nothing.'

Scowling, Giles cast his glance around. Hubert de Beaumont and Ragnar de Rocher were watching the scene without even trying to conceal their enjoyment. Richard de Luci, who had come to inspect the war-horses himself was looking politely elsewhere, but a heavy frown weighted the lines of his bloodhound features. William Ironheart, who was in the Justiciar's company, was staring at both of them with rude intensity, his hands clamped around his sword belt. 'I hope for your sake that it is a nothing,' Giles threatened, but lowered his voice. 'Is it any wonder that I am loth to bring you anywhere when you shame me like this? You are no better than a whore!'

Linnet quivered at the final word as if he had struck her with the coiled whip in his fist. Hating him, sick with fear, she stood submissively before him, knowing that she had no defence. Robert, frightened by the atmosphere, by the sidlings of the huge horse and the thunderous expression on his father's face, began to grizzle into her skirts.

'Go home and wait for me,' Giles commanded, tight-lipped.

Linnet bowed her head and wondered if the convent of St Mary in Southwark would open its doors to a runaway wife. Or perhaps she could join the camp followers clustering around the mercenaries assembling for embarkation to Normandy. Surely that kind of life could be no worse than the one she led now.

Giles wrenched the tan horse around and pranced him back to his audience. She could tell from the looks on their faces and Giles's strutting manner that her humiliation sat well with them. Summoning the tatters of her dignity, she lifted Robert in her arms and went towards her waiting horse litter on the side of the field.

Joscelin indulged Martyn with a square of gilded ginger-bread from the booth adjacent to Melusine the Mermaid and, with that bribe, removed the child from the dubious attractions of the fairground to the more sober business of the selection and purchase of an all-purpose riding mount from the dozens offered for sale.

Taught first by his father and then by his uncle, Conan, upon the battlefields of Brittany, Normandy, Anjou and Aquitaine, Joscelin was an excellent judge of horseflesh. Sometimes a good mount was all that had stood between himself and death in the thick of the fray. He examined with a critical eye the various animals paraded before him, discarding several high-mettled glossy beasts with the most perfunctory of glances despite the horse coper's assurances of their breeding and quality.

Martyn was very taken with a dainty white mare, but Joscelin shook his head. 'She'd do well enough on good roads in summertime but she hasn't got the heart-room for hard work and her legs are too spindly. Also she'd never ford a stream without balking. See how nervous she is?'

Martyn pursed his lips. 'She's still very pretty.'

Joscelin chuckled. 'So are many women, but that's no recommendation to buy.'

'Lady de Montsorrel's pretty.'

Joscelin busied himself examining the teeth of a stocky bay cob. 'So she is,' he agreed, half his mind on the horse, the other half dwelling upon the memory of Linnet de Montsorrel's soft grey eyes and elfin features. His usual preference was for large-boned, buxom women; they adapted best to the vagaries of mercenary baggage trains, but occasionally he found himself yearning for daintier

44

fare. Breaca had been bird-boned and slender, quick of movement and raven-black of hair and eye. He still thought of her sometimes on freezing winter nights when his own body heat was not enough to keep him warm. And of Juhel too. Of him he thought constantly.

Abruptly he commanded the horse coper to trot the cob up and down so that he could study its gait with a critical eye.

Martyn nibbled on the gingerbread and stared around the enormous field, bursting at the seams with colour and life. The market was held every sixth day of the week and Martyn loved to come here if his family were in London. The atmosphere exhilarated his senses. Everyone was here: rich, poor, lord, merchant, soldier and farmer, all of them drawn by the common interest of livestock. Here you could buy anything from a plough horse to a palfrey, from a child's first pony to a fully trained war-horse costing in excess of seventy marks. You could wager on the races between swift, thin-legged coursers and see hot-blooded Arab and Barb bloodstock from the deserts of Outremer. And if you became tired of looking at the horses, there were cattle and sheep, pigs and fowl of every variety. There were farm implements to be purchased and craftsmen to watch at their work. And, best of all, there was the fairground.

'A knight's riding over from the destriers,' he told Joscelin. 'I think he wants you.'

The horse coper ceased showing the cob's paces and hastened to lead the animal to one side, his expression suddenly anxious. Joscelin swung round and saw Giles de Montsorrel riding towards him. He sat upon a sweating tan destrier that sidled and pranced, almost out of control. Giles was riding him on a pack saddle and his stirrup straps were far too short, designed for a much smaller man. Giles himself was wattle-red with a face sour enough to curdle a dish of new milk.

'If I see you near my wife again, I'll garter my hose with strips of your flayed hide!' he snarled.

Joscelin stared up into the red-rimmed blue eyes. 'We but exchanged courtesies. Should I have turned the other way and slighted her?'

'You're a common mercenary. I know only too well what was in your mind.'

'Not having a mind of your own above the belt that you so freely use,' Joscelin retorted, his first astonishment rapidly turning to anger.

'Joscelin . . .' Martyn whispered in a frightened voice.

Giles clapped his ornate prick spurs into the destrier's flanks and it plunged towards boy and man, forehooves performing a deadly dance. Martyn shrieked as he was flung from a powerful forequarter. He hit the ground hard, the gingerbread flying from his fingers. Giles leaned over the saddle to strike at Joscelin with his whip. The blow slashed across Joscelin's face, narrowly missing his eye and raising an immediate welt. The stallion's sweat-darkened flank sent him staggering. Giles pursued, whip raised in his right fist, his left clenched white upon the reins.

Martyn scrambled to his feet and dashed for safety. Joscelin, about to be ridden down by a metal-shod fury, grabbed the horse coper's three-legged stool and swung it full at the oncoming destrier's head. The stool shattered across rolling eye and forelock and the horse went mad. Giles, fighting to keep his seat, snatched at the right rein and hauled hard, but it was far too late for that kind of control. Half-blinded, wild with terror and rage, the tan stallion reared, came down on all fours and bucked. Then, before the horrified gaze of a gathering crowd, it lay down and deliberately rolled upon its rider.

Giles screamed and screamed again. There was a sickening sound of snapping bones, and still he screamed. Joscelin discarded the remains of the stool and ran to lay hold of the stallion's head stall. Others hurried forward to restrain the horse and prevent it from rolling again while the coper and another merchant dragged Giles clear. Someone else brought a rope to bind the destrier.

Panting, Joscelin dropped to his knees beside Giles and

discovered that he was still alive, but for how long was a moot point. Blood bubbled out of his mouth with each released breath, a sign that one or more of his broken ribs had punctured a lung.

'Let me pass!' cried a woman's voice, imperative with fear. 'In God's name, let me pass. I am his wife!'

Linnet de Montsorrel fought her way determinedly through the crowd, many of whom had diverted from the fairground to view this far more interesting spectacle. Reaching the centre of the circle, she knelt beside her husband. 'Giles . . .' she touched his hair with her fingertips, a look of disbelief on her face. Then she raised her eyes to Joscelin.

He shook his head. 'His ribs have broken inwards and torn his lungs. Someone has gone for a priest. I am sorry, my lady.'

She shuddered. 'I saw you arguing.'

'There was nothing else I could have done but to strike the horse. He was going to ride me and Martyn down.' He looked rapidly around the crowd and breathed a sigh of relief when he saw Martyn standing with his father. The child was pale, more eyes than face, and his tunic was stained and torn, but he appeared otherwise unscathed as he sheltered within the protection of Ironheart's steadying arm. Ironheart himself was frowning, not so much with anger, but more as if he had just been presented with an interesting idea.

'I wished myself free of him yesterday,' Linnet whispered. 'But not now, not like this.'

The expression on her face filled Joscelin with an uncomfortable mixture of pity and guilt. 'It was his own fault and a little of my own,' he said, laying his hand over hers. 'Never think it was yours.'

She shook her head and removed herself from his touch. 'But it is,' she replied. 'You do not understand.'

The crowd, encouraged by the Justiciar's men, started to disperse, and a moment later Richard de Luci himself stooped over Giles. He grimaced at the physical signs of

47

internal damage. 'I saw that horse earlier and thought he was a rogue,' he commented grimly. His brief glance at Joscelin was piercing, but he said nothing aloud about the human conflict that had played its part in the tragedy.

De Luci stood aside to permit a tonsured cleric to take his place. 'My personal chaplain, Father Adam,' he said by way of introduction as he assisted Linnet to her feet, a courteous elbow beneath her own. 'I will ensure that your husband has the comfort of God in his extremity and that you are seen safely home.'

'Thank you, my lord, I am grateful,' Linnet murmured, the response automatic, her expression blank with shock. Two dusty brown patches smeared her gown where she had been kneeling.

De Luci patted her hand and, turning from her, began making arrangements to bear Giles home, arrangements which involved delegating Joscelin to provide escort.

'My lord?' Joscelin looked at de Luci askance, and touched the angry red weal traversing the left side of his face. The chaplain was shriving Giles lest he should die on the journey home. Linnet de Montsorrel had taken her son from her maid and was hugging him tightly in her arms, her face ashen.

'Are you sure you want me for this duty?'

Again de Luci gave him that piercing look. 'You may not think it now, but I judge you the best man I have. I could send Brien; he's a superb diplomat, but I really need him elsewhere.' He gnawed on his knuckle, briefly pondering. 'I'll send someone over to relieve you before compline. With Montsorrel stricken like this, it will be prudent, I think, to have royal troops keep a friendly eye on his household.'

'Yes, my lord,' Joscelin said heavily, and resigned himself to de Luci's command.

CHAPTER 7

IN THE BEDCHAMBER above the hall, Linnet listened to her husband's breathing; the sound was akin to a dull-bladed saw dragging through wood. Mad, she thought, I will go mad, and turned away to pace the floor before she was tempted to seize a pillow and press it over Giles's face. She clenched her fists and halted as she reached the wall of whitewashed dung and plaster. Outside a storm wind rattled the shutters trying to gain entry, while within herself a storm fought to escape. 'Jesu,' she whispered, closing her eyes.

Giles groaned her name and she returned quickly to his bedside. He tossed his head, moaning softly in the grip of a dream induced by the poppy-in-wine she had given him. She laid a calming hand across his forehead, but his eyes jerked wide open and fixed on her, the pupils black pin-points in the fogged blue iris.

'The strongbox!' he bubbled, and seized her wrist in a grip that was still viciously strong.

'Lie still, my lord,' she soothed. 'You must conserve your strength.'

His grip tightened painfully. 'The strongbox . . .' he repeated through blood-stained teeth. 'Give it . . . to Leicester.' He fell back against the pillows, breath rasping, and his grip slackened. She snatched back her wrist and rubbed it, her own breathing loud with distress. If she permitted Leicester to take their coin, she would beggar her son's inheritance for another man's glory. She could not do it, and yet, if Young Henry's rebellion were successful, she would face terrible repercussions for denying his cause valuable funds.

49

'How does he fare, Madam?'

With a stifled cry she spun round to face Hubert de Beaumont. Her knees almost buckled with terror. Beaumont was squat, but powerful. His ugly tenacity had always reminded her of a bull-baiting dog, and he was certainly known to be as vicious. 'My husband needs rest,' she managed to swallow, and leaned against the wall for support.

Beaumont considered her narrowly and clicked his tongue against his palate. 'A bad business. The horse coper's in the stocks and he'll be lucky to escape the gibbet, selling a killer like that. He must have known the brute had that trick.' Advancing to the bed, he leaned over the dying man.

Linnet struggled to regain command of her gelatinous body. An acrid mingling of sweat and hearth smoke clung to Beaumont's garments and his hair curled across a broad bald patch on the back of his skull like two demonic horns.

'I beg you not to disturb him,' she whispered.

Beaumont straightened, and turned to look at her, his round cheeks dimpled by a smile. His eyes were as cold as stones. 'As soon as I have possession of the silver that your husband promised to Lord Leicester for his Normandy expedition, I'll leave you both in peace.' Without lowering his gaze, he removed a parchment from his scrip. 'Here's my writ of authorization from the Earl himself.'

The seal of the house of Beaumont dangled on its ribbons, heavy with the weight of authority and obligation – far too heavy for her to accept into her own hands. 'My husband said nothing to me of such a promise. I'm afraid I cannot give you what you ask.' She raised her chin and returned his stare steadily.

Hubert's brows drew together across the wide bridge of his nose. 'Why should Giles have told you?' he said scornfully. 'This is men's business. You would do well to do as you are told.'

Linnet clasped her hands. Her eyes widened with innocent distress. 'You are right, this is men's business and I am unable to deal with it. Perhaps when Giles has improved . . .'

'Improved, my arse, he's as good as a corpse now!' Beaumont snorted, losing his thin veneer of civility. 'Lord Leicester wants that silver now.' His glance flickered to the money chest beside the bed.

Linnet bit her lip. 'My lord Leicester will have to wait on the Justiciar's will,' she said and, going to the chest, sat down upon it deliberately.

Giles made a horrible strangling sound as he strove to sit up. Beaumont's eyes bulged and reddened. In two strides he had reached the strongbox and hurled her off it. 'Give me the key!' he snarled.

'I don't know where it is,' she said tearfully from the rushes and, regaining her feet, rubbed her bruised side.

Beaumont turned to the bed. 'Key?' he demanded of the choking Giles, who garbled his wife's name and pointed an accusing finger.

Linnet flinched before Beaumont's wrath and slowly backed away from him until her spine struck the wall and she could retreat no further.

Beaumont's arm flashed out and he seized her round the neck. 'Where is it, you bitch?' He shook her, his thumb pressing on her windpipe.

Breath crowing in her throat, Linnet struggled, but his grip was too strong.

Ella, who had gone downstairs earlier to fetch her mistress a milk and nutmeg posset, halted in the doorway, taking in the scene with horror. With a gasp she turned and ran back down the stairs, the posset spilling down her skirts in white rills.

'Tell me!' Hubert roared, his unclipped nails gouging Linnet's skin. She kicked in panic at his shins and did not answer, but he became aware of a tough leather cord beneath his squeezing fingers and saw how it disappeared beneath undergown and tunic, concealing whatever was strung upon it. Panting with exertion and triumph, he set his fist around the cord and twisted.

★

51

Joscelin heard Westminster's bells strike the hour of compline as he unburdened his bladder in the latrine pit at the foot of the garth. Unseasonal wind and rain buffeted and spattered him. There was still an hour until dusk, but the sky over the cathedral was darkly overcast, closing hard on a thin, silver rim of light over the Tyburn.

Readjusting his clothing, Joscelin started back towards the house. The garden was neglected, but showed signs of having been hastily tidied. There were no neatly planned and well-tended herb beds as there were at his father's house, just straggles of half-wild sage and lurching green clumps of rosemary. He supposed that, although Giles probably used this place for bachelor pursuits when he was in the city, it very seldom became a domestic household.

He glanced up at the shuttered window above the hall where Giles was slowly bleeding his life away. The horse was already killing wild before he had struck out with the stool, he told himself, but the gnawing feeling of guilt refused to go away.

Giles's heir was a frail small boy of five whose lands would have to be administered by a representative of the crown for the next ten years at least. Either that or the crown would sell the estates by right of marriage to the highest bidder and entrust whoever he might be with the child's well-being. From what he had seen, Giles de Montsorrel had been no kind of husband or father, but his successor would not necessarily be any more competent.

His ruminations were curtailed by Malcolm, a young, red-haired Galwegian soldier in his troop, who was sauntering on his own way to the latrine pit.

'Lady Montsorrel's got a visitor, sir,' he saluted in a broad Scots accent. 'A paunchy wastrel from Leicester's household. Said he was a friend of the Montsorrels', but I didna like his manner, so I took his sword before I let him go on up.'

'What was his name?'

'Beaumont, sir, Hubert de Beaumont.'

Joscelin nodded. 'Paunchy wastrel about sums him up. You did right to confiscate his sword.' He slapped the young soldier's brawny arm and walked on to the house. He was on the verge of re-entering the hall, about to wash his hands and face at the laver, when Linnet de Montsorrel's distraught maid seized his sleeve, gibbered something about her mistress being murdered by the visitor and pointed frantically at the stairs to the upper floor. Joscelin heeled about and, drawing his sword as he ran, took the stairs two at a time, clashed aside the embroidered curtain and hurtled into the bedchamber.

On the bed Giles de Montsorrel gurgled in a spreading stain of blood, fingers outstretched towards his scabbarded sword which was propped against the wall only just out of his reach. Joscelin leaped across the bed to the choking woman on the floor and the man poised over her. Grabbing a handful of Beaumont's oiled hair, Joscelin wrenched him off his victim and threw the knight down on the floor, a sword point levelled at his windpipe.

'Christ's blood, what goes forth here!'

Linnet de Montsorrel clutched her bruised throat and drew great gulps of air, her breathing no less desperate than her husband's.

His complexion a deep, wattle-crimson, Beaumont glared up the sword's blood-gutter at Joscelin. 'It's a private matter,' he snarled. 'None of your interfering business!'

Joscelin was heartily sick of being told what was and was not his business. 'Almost a private murder,' he retorted, following Beaumont with the steel and his eyes. 'Don't move.'

'No, let him go,' Linnet choked. Her gown had risen to her thighs in their struggle and she pulled it decently back down.

Not believing his ears, Joscelin stared at her. Beaumont used the instant's loss of concentration to lunge sideways, past the bed, and out of the door. Swearing, Joscelin turned to run after him.

'Please, I beg you, let him be!' Linnet implored.

53

'But he would have killed you, my lady!' Joscelin said incredulously but, after a hesitation, he sheathed his sword and helped her to her feet.

'I thank you for your concern but, as he said, it was a private matter.'

Joscelin raised his brows. Red fingerprints blotched the white skin of her throat and there was an ugly graze where Beaumont had tried to tear off the leather cord she was now clutching. Joscelin suspected that the key to the Montsorrel strongbox nestled upon her bosom beneath the various layers of clothing. 'I don't think so,' he said.

Avoiding his needle-sharp stare, she brushed past him and knelt at the bedside to take her husband's hand. Her hoarse entreaties to the Virgin were drowned out by Giles's rasping struggle for air. He stiffened, exhaled on a choking bubble of blood and did not draw another breath. His body sank against the mattress and the spreading stain of blood became a lake.

Linnet bowed her head. Against the shutters the rain spattered in lieu of the tears she would never cry. She was free, unanchored, and driving towards the point where she would smash on the rock wall of her own guilt.

De Gael came quietly to her side. Leaning over, he gently closed Giles's staring eyes, and murmured the appropriate words of Church ritual before instructing the maid to fetch Father Adam from his meal in the hall.

'You know Latin?' she asked, trying to fill the dangerous spaces in her mind.

'I was educated for more than just selling my sword,' he said curtly, and she sensed his unease. He desired to pursue Hubert de Beaumont and could not comprehend her reluctance. She could feel his thoughts pulling at him like a bloodhound pulling on a leash. Rising abruptly, she went to the shutters and flung them open to let the fresh air dispel the reek of blood and death. In the distance over the steeples of the abbey and palace at Westminster the lightning flashed, but here there was only the heartbeat patter of the rain, veiling in grey the overgrown garden. Involuntarily her hand crept up to clutch the leather thong around her neck.

'I assume he wanted the contents of the strongbox?' de Gael said.

Linnet was irritated by his persistence. She snatched her hand from the cord. 'Assume what you wish,' she said coldly, then added, 'he was Giles's friend, not mine.'

He grunted. 'Hubert de Beaumont is no one's friend.'

There was a short silence. Linnet looked over her shoulder and saw that he had stopped at the screen behind which Robert slept on his small truckle bed. Drawing it slightly to one side, he looked down on her sleeping, vulnerable son, Giles's heir, and as valuable as the iron-bound box standing sentinel beside his dead father. The man smiled, but on his face there was fleetingly a look of such haunting sorrow that Linnet resisted her first instinct, which was to run across the room, tear the screen from his hand, and stand protectively over her child like a she-wolf.

He became aware of her scrutiny and gently pulled the screen back into position. When he faced her, his expression was neutral. 'I can see you object to my questions,' he said, 'but you will let me post a guard at the door and send word to the Justiciar.'

His tone was courteous enough, but it held authority and expectation of obedience. Nor was it her wish to challenge him, for she was beginning to feel shaky and cold.

He took her cloak from the back of a chair and draped it around her shoulders. 'You need someone to stay with you, another woman of your own rank to help where your maid cannot. Do you know anyone?'

Linnet shook her head. 'My husband did not permit me to meet with other men's wives and sisters except on the most formal occasions when he had no choice.' She grimaced. 'I suppose the Countess of Leicester is my kinswoman after a fashion, but I would rather not turn to her for succour.'

'No,' he agreed wryly, his tone revealing that his opinion

of Petronilla of Leicester differed little from her own. 'I have an aunt here in the town, not half a mile away. She's a widow herself and I can vouch for the excellence of her character.'

'To be my gaoler?'

His brows drew level across the bony bridge of his nose. 'I don't blame you for being suspicious, but it was truly an offer of comfort,' he said with dignity.

The outer door swung open and the hissing sound of the rain followed Father Adam into the room. Linnet touched her bruised throat and thought rapidly. She was as good as a prisoner already if a guard was to be set on the door. Another woman's company would make her fears less overwhelming because there would not be so much time for her to brood alone and magnify them out of proportion. Besides, she believed de Gael when he said that the offer was made out of a genuine concern for her welfare. He had been almost offended when she had called his aunt a gaoler.

Father Adam was brushing rain from his robes and tut-tutting over the corpse. Giles demanded her attention. There were rituals to observe for the sake of his soul and his body to prepare for its final resting.

'I apologize,' she murmured to Joscelin. 'Your aunt will be most welcome if she will come.'

The guarded expression did not leave his eyes, but his mouth relaxed. He bowed to her, crossed his breast to the priest, and left. She heard his footsteps clattering down the stairs, as Giles's had done only yesterday.

The memory was close enough to touch, but it seemed to belong to someone else.

CHAPTER 8

I T WAS MID-MORNING when Joscelin had the dream. He was riding through a forest of mature hazel and birch trees, dusty sunlight diffusing through the foliage, turning the world a luminous green-gold. He could hear birdsong, the drone of bees, and the chock of a woodsman's axe muted by distance.

Beside him, on a white-faced roan mare, a woman rode. Breaca he thought at first, but when she turned to speak to him, her eyes were not dark brown, but a misty blue-grey, experienced of the world in a way that was totally different to Breaca's.

Behind them his troop escorted a coffin on which there was neither lid nor pall. Open to the air, Giles de Montsorrel stared up at the green lacework of branches with dry, dead eyes. At first Joscelin thought that the corpse was wearing a hauberk, but then he realized, his scalp crawling, that Giles was in fact clothed in a mesh of silver pennies. The coins flashed and slithered and Joscelin felt a scream gathering in his throat as the corpse started slowly to sit up. The linen jaw bandage slipped from its anchoring and Giles's mouth laughed open. Blood-stained teeth and sewn-down tongue; the stench of rot. 'As I am, so shall ye be.'

The woman spoke to Joscelin in a softly anxious voice. Struck dumb with horror, he was unable to respond. The birds ceased to sing and the flash of sun on steel in the trees ahead caught the corner of his eye, and he realized that he had ridden into an ambush. Even while the thought staggered through his brain, the attack was launched. His shield was on its long strap behind his back, his sword still in its scabbard, and he had only half-rectified the deficiency when the bright blade of a hand-axe took him square in the chest.

Agony such as he had never experienced ripped through him with the knowledge that here was death. He screamed his denial, and woke shivering and drenched in cold sweat. Disorientated, he stared at the smoke-blackened rafters and the leather curtain screening the pallet on which he lay from the main room. The clatter and bustle of a busy domestic household rang hollowly in his ears, drowning out the echo of his last cry.

He jerked upright and, groaning, put his head in his hands. The dream had been so real that he could almost have touched it, and the fading images still held their colours and emotions.

'Jesu!' he muttered shakenly. His breathing was short and harsh with the residue of terror. A blinding pain thumped behind his eyes, impairing his vision with small dancing circles of light.

The leather curtain parted and Stephen entered the tiny alcove bearing a horn cup of watered wine. 'Justiciar de Luci is waiting to see you,' he announced as he presented the drink.

Joscelin took a tentative swallow and his stomach churned. He swore beneath his breath.

'Is something wrong, my lord?'

Slowly Joscelin reached for his undergown and tunic. They were rumpled, still damp from last night's rain. His whole body ached with bruises from his fight with Ragnar, and the whip welt on his face hurt. 'I slept badly and I can do without my father and the Justiciar this morning,' he said and hissed through his teeth with pain as he raised his arm to push it into his shirt. Stephen made haste to help him, easing the shirt down and holding the looser outer garment in such a way that his master did not have to stretch to don it. Even so, by the time he had latched his belt, Joscelin was pale and sweating. He pressed his hands over his eyes for a moment.

'Go and find a maid, lad, and ask her for a willow bark potion before my skull splits in two,' he requested, swallowing hard.

The youth left at a run. Joscelin's own gait was a slow shamble as he followed him out into the hall. A lyme hound scented the fear still lingering on his body and growled softly. He ignored the dog even as he ignored the gossiping serving women who pretended to be busy while he passed and then returned to their chatter. Two priests and a clerk sat at a trestle dining on fat bacon and wastel bread and a scribe had set up his lectern on the dais and was writing steadily.

Joscelin walked very gingerly down the hall to the hearth, trying not to jolt his precarious stomach and even more precarious skull. Richard de Luci and his father were deep in conversation, but when they saw him approaching they broke off and looked quickly at each other like a pair of conspirators.

'You desired to speak to me, my lord?' Joscelin's lips fumbled over the words. The circles of light before his eyes had expanded and were now seriously impeding his vision. He hoped that de Luci was not going to procrastinate.

De Luci's garments were immaculate, not so much as a speck of fluff daring to mar the perfection of his dark blue tunic. Crisp gold embroidery decorated the collar, sleeves and hem, and his well-fed face wore the smooth gleam of recent barbering. Concern settled on his features as he looked Joscelin up and down.

'It has been a rough night,' said the Justiciar.

Joscelin winced a reply and rubbed his aching forehead. He had not finished reporting to de Luci until after midnight and by the time he had come off duty and arrived at his father's house, the matins bells had been sounding from the abbey on errant drifts of breeze.

'Leicester's claiming the blood-right to be the warden of Montsorrel's heir,' de Luci said. 'He served me notice at first light and I told him that the Crown's right was

59

greater and that either myself or the King, depending on circumstance, would appoint the right man to the post in our own good time.'

Joscelin struggled to concentrate. His wits had not gone wool-gathering – they were the wool itself: grey, fuzzy, and tangled. De Luci was looking at him expectantly. What was he supposed to deduce or say? 'What about the silver?' he managed to unravel off his tongue.

'Ah yes, the silver.' Smile creases deepened the folds of de Luci's heavy jowls. 'Lord Leicester was not slow to raise the subject either, nor the fact that when his representative went to the Montsorrel house last night to make enquiries, he was summarily seen off the premises by one of my men – "A drunken, brawling, trouble-causing oaf", so you were described to me.'

Joscelin avoided de Luci's sparkling gaze and wished himself a hundred leagues away and dreamlessly asleep. 'Hubert de Beaumont's manner did not lead me to believe his errand was legitimate. The only reason I did not arrest him was that Lady de Montsorrel pleaded for leniency.'

'Oh, I applaud your diligence,' said the Justiciar. 'That coin no more belongs to Leicester than does the boy's wardship, and I have no intention of letting it go to Normandy.'

'Just how much is there?' Ironheart enquired curiously. 'Have you had a chance to find out?'

'Oh yes, Linnet de Montsorrel was very cooperative. Including the plate, I would say about seventy marks.'

William whistled through his chipped teeth. 'That's enough to field a troop like Joscelin's for an entire season.'

'I confess I did not realize the extent of the sum myself until I opened the chest,' de Luci rubbed his hand back and forth across his barbered chin. Then he stopped and raised his forefinger, a chunky seal ring gleaming. 'Joscelin, I want you and your men to escort the widow and her household home to Rushcliffe. You are to remain there as acting castellan until you receive further orders. The strong-box will travel with you since it is the boy's inheritance and you'll need monies to run the keep. You can cast accounts, can't you?' It was a rhetorical question, for de Luci was fully aware of Joscelin's abilities. 'I am told that the coffin will be ready the day after tomorrow.'

There was a pregnant silence. Joscelin knew that the Justiciar was waiting for him to reply decisively and with gratitude, but in his mind's eye he was seeing the open coffin of his dream and feeling very sick indeed.

De Luci looked at him and frowned. 'Of course, if the commission is not to your taste, I can always find someone else.'

Joscelin battled to focus. 'No, my lord, I'll be pleased to fulfil any commission that you lay to me,' he said sluggishly. 'Have I your leave to go and make preparations?'

De Luci stared at him in open amazement. 'What in God's name is wrong with you? Anyone would have thought I'd kicked you in the teeth, not offered your career a substantial hoist.'

'It's not that, my lord. Truly, I'm grateful . . .' Joscelin swallowed jerkily.

Ironheart said quickly, 'Let the boy go, Richard, before he's sick all over Agnes's new-strewn rushes. You'll be able to get more sense out of him later, I promise.'

The Justiciar lifted his brows, knowing that William did not give a damn for the rushes or the extra work it would cause Agnes to replace them. His concern was all for Joscelin. 'Very well,' he said, and dismissed Joscelin with a curt nod.

Hardly bothering to salute, the young man staggered from the room.

'Would you care to explain?' de Luci turned frostily to Ironheart. 'If he's going to let me down, then I'll allot the task elsewhere.'

'He won't fail you,' Ironheart said impatiently. 'What you saw now was an affliction he gets sometimes – like Becket used to after a crisis. A sickness comes upon him and a headache worse than anything you'd get out of a flagon of bad wine. All he needs to do is sleep it off. His mother was the same.'

De Luci grunted, reassured, but not entirely convinced. 'All the same, he seemed disturbed at the command.'

Ironheart took his time answering, but when he did it was in his usual blunt fashion. 'That's because he's attracted to the widow and knows that if he abandoned his honour and the trust you have in him, he could have her out from beneath your nose, and her fortune too.'

'He told you this?' De Luci stared at his friend.

William laughed sourly. 'Christ, my sons never tell me anything! No, I have eyes in my head. Joscelin's not like Ragnar to rut indiscriminately all over the town. He's more selective and he'll do without rather than take anything just for the sake of sheathing his sword. Your young widow appeals to him and she's only just beyond his reach. If he could steal out on a limb, he might just touch her.'

De Luci thoughtfully stroked his smooth, razored chin. Clever and shrewd was William de Rocher, and a realist too. He also loved his bastard son with a painful intensity that he was careful never to parade. De Luci full knew his friend's vulnerability, and also his ambition. He was aiming high for Joscelin, but not hopelessly so, given de Luci's own opinion of the young man.

'This needs thinking about more deeply than I have time for just now, William,' he said to give himself a breathing space, then tucked a secretive smile into the folds of his face. 'You wouldn't have given me the benefit of your wisdom a moment ago if you thought it would cause me to dismiss Joscelin.'

Ironheart returned the smile and did not attempt to press the matter further. 'I think we know each other well enough by now,' he said.

CHAPTER 9

STRIPPED TO THE WAIST, wearing only his braies and short leggings, Ragnar worked at putting an edge on his sword-blade. With powerful sweeping motions of his long arms he smoothed the oiled Lombardy steel over the huge grindstone, evening out the nicks and brightening the grey with a border of shining, bluish silver like the underbelly of a fish. Honing a blade was something Ragnar did well if he was in the mood to be patient, and not even the Earl of Leicester's own personal armourer could have bettered his work today.

He blotted his sweating brow on his forearm and paused for breath. The courtyard was heaving with activity, for the Earl was preparing to leave London for Southampton the next morning. The girl Elflin smiled intimately at him across the yard, her arms piled high with linens for the Countess Petronilla. Ragnar looked in the opposite direction, his gaze upon a wain that had become stuck in the muddy wheel-ruts by the gateway. Pleasure he had had from the wench in the stables not an hour since but, as far as he was concerned, the silver penny he had given her was a release from obligation.

The sun disappeared into shadow and, glancing upwards and sideways, he discovered Hubert de Beaumont standing over him, thumbs thrust through his wide buckskin sword-belt. 'May I?' he asked and, without waiting for Ragnar's consent, took the bare sword from his knee and hefted it, testing the balance and then the edge. 'Excellent,' he commented, then grinned. 'You could make your fortune as a swordsmith.'

Ragnar snorted. 'Do I look like a tradesman?'

Beaumont eyed him up and down. 'I suppose not. You're too disreputable by far without half your clothes and sporting that purple eye.' He returned the sword.

Ragnar applied more oil to the blade. He wondered why Beaumont had sought him out. The knight was a seasoned member of Leicester's mesnie and not given to applying the lard of friendship to newcomers unless he had wheels to grease.

'Your brother's fast on his feet for one so tall,' Beaumont remarked.

Ragnar scowled and touched his puffy, tender eye. 'I'd have got the better of him if Brien of Ravenstow hadn't poked his nose where it didn't belong.'

'I was thinking of my own tangle with him last night.'

Ragnar laid the sword edge to the grindstone and rasped it across. His lower lip pushed his upper into a smile. He might hate Joscelin with every inch of his being, but there was a certain perverse delight in seeing the de Rocher blood triumph in a fight. 'Why are you interested in my bastard brother?'

Beaumont was silent for a while, watching the hypnotic rhythm of Ragnar's arm. Then he said, 'Lord Leicester wants the Montsorrel silver for our cause and your brother is its guardian.'

'I see.'

'Is he open to bribery?'

The sword shrieked on the grindstone as Ragnar choked on his mirth. 'Good Christ, no!' he spluttered. 'Why do you think he's in such high favour with the Justiciar? Whatever you offered him would not be enough to make him bend his precious honour. He knows that you are Leicester's man through and through.' He wiped his eyes and sheathed the sword in its scabbard. 'The only way you'll get that silver out of Joscelin is over his dead body.'

Beaumont wrapped his fist around his own weapon hilt. 'I'm prepared to do that,' he said, 'but I'm curious about him. He is my adversary, and I need to know more.'

Ragnar looked at him darkly. 'You are taking a risk by asking me.'

'I don't think so. I saw all I needed of your "brotherly love" for each other two nights ago. Look, come to the Peacock and we'll talk over a jug of wine.' Beaumont jingled the leather purse lying against his dagger grip.

'Is that by way of a bribe to me?' Ragnar pushed his damp red-gold hair off his forehead.

'You appear to have finished your work for the moment, and you look thirsty.'

Suddenly Ragnar smiled, the somewhat narrow line of his lips redeemed by a display of fine, white teeth that no chirurgeon's pincers had ever been remotely near. 'The Peacock, you said. Lead on, I am indeed a very thirsty man.'

'Joscelin's always been my father's favourite,' Ragnar said, and drew the shape of a dragon in a puddle of spilled wine on the trestle. His other hand propped up his head, which felt both light and heavy at the same time. The task of sharpening his sword in the hot yard had made him very thirsty and he had gulped the first two cups of Anjou without moderation. The third had followed a little slower, matching pace with Beaumont, and he was now more than half-way down his fourth. 'I know that if the Arnsby lands were not mine by right of blood, he would give them to Joscelin – his first-born son.' Unconscious frown lines appeared vertically between his light brown eyes.

'But you said the other night his mother was a whore.'

'She was. My father picked her up among the loose women of the army camp during some battle campaign. Supposedly she had noble blood, but I don't believe that. No decent woman follows the troops for a livelihood.'

Ragnar lifted his cup and drank again, rapidly. 'After she died in childbed my father built a chapel to her memory and endowed a chantry of nuns to sing her praises for ever. God's death, do you know how much it sticks in my craw to see him riding off to visit the place every month like a damned pilgrim? She wasn't a saint, she was a witch!'

Beaumont made sympathetic sounds and refilled Ragnar's cup before tipping the final half-measure into his own. Then he took a contemplative swallow and set his enquiries back on their original course. 'So how did your brother come to be a mercenary? Surely your father could have found him an heiress with lands?'

'Originally Joscelin was going to be a priest. He boarded with the monks at Lenton for three years, until one of them tried to make him into his bum boy and Joscelin knocked his teeth down his throat. Papa decided then that his true vocation lay with the sword. Besides, the church would not have him back.'

'And then?' Beaumont prompted, as Ragnar returned to dabbling his finger in the spilled pool of wine.

'There's little else to tell,' Ragnar said moodily. 'When Joscelin was fifteen, he quarrelled with our father – Joscelin and I had been arguing and Joscelin threw his weight around so much that he almost killed me – I was only ten or eleven years old at the time. Papa thrashed him, and Joscelin packed his saddle roll and ran away to France, to the battlefields and tourney circuits. Papa said he would not last a month, but we didn't see him again for seven years. When he came home, it was at the head of his own troop of mercenaries. He was treated like the prodigal son, put on a pedestal and held up to me as a shining example.' Ragnar stared at his hand, the fingertips wine-laced and trembling. 'For seven years I had dared to dream that he was dead, out of my life for ever, amen.'

Beaumont folded his arms across his broad belly. 'So what happened to him in those missing seven years?'

'I don't know. He never spoke about it, but to survive those first few months he must have gone to his uncle Conan, his mother's brother. He's a whoremonger and a mercenary. Where else would Joscelin have learned to brawl like a common cut-purse?' Ragnar raised drink-fogged brown eyes to Beaumont. 'How are you intending to kill Joscelin?'

66

Beaumont pursed his lips. 'I can see a way to obtain the Montsorrel silver without directly confronting your brother, a way that will be a far greater blow to his pride.'

'Are you afraid to face him?' Ragnar's voice was contemptuous.

The older knight reddened. 'I fear no one,' he growled. 'Fortunate for you that you're drunk or I'd break your arm for that remark. If you want to be rid of your brother, best do it yourself. My first concern is recovering Lord Leicester's money.' Rising from the bench, he tossed a coin on the trestle to pay for the wine.

'Where are you going?' Remaining seated because he suddenly did not trust the steadiness of his legs, Ragnar blinked up at him.

'To hire a boat to take me upriver. I fancy a little sightseeing.' Beaumont smiled at Ragnar. 'I'd take you with me, but you'd probably puke all that wine over the side.'

Ragnar listened to him clatter from the alehouse. For a moment he stared bleakly at the recently lime-washed walls, already grey around the sconces with candle soot. The serving wench approached to take the money and the empty flagon. Ragnar fumbled in his purse for a coin and commanded another jug. There was no point in only being half-drunk.

Beaumont's sightseeing consisted of paying a River Thames boatman three silver pennies to row him upriver from Leicester's house until they were opposite the far more modest building that constituted the Montsorrel dwelling. From his bench on the prow of the boat Beaumont studied the small shingle beach and wooden steps leading up to the unkempt garth. He heard a rooster crowing and saw hens pecking among the high grass and brambles. The buildings were of the old Saxon type – dung and plaster with thatched roofs. Only the main house was covered with the more expensive red tile. In the heat of the day the white window shutters facing the river had been flung wide.

'Want me to beach her, m'lud?' enquired the boatman who was struggling to hold his craft steady on the tide.

Beaumont shook his head. 'No. I've seen enough. Row me over to the Southwark side. I've business there now.'

The boatman arched his brow but did as he was requested without demur. You got all sorts hiring Thames boats, especially these days when so many nobles were in the city seeking permission to join the war in Normandy. The Southwark side had been very popular recently. You could purchase anything you wanted there, from a good time to one that in future you would rather forget. Souls were easily bought and sold in the dark alleyways of the Southwark stews. The boatman eyed the fancy sword and long dagger on the knight's tooled belt, the well-fed gut hanging over it. 'Is it a bath-house you're wanting, m'lud? I can suggest several good ones. Nice clean country girls, no hags.'

Beaumont smiled. 'Later perhaps. First I want you to row me to the landing nearest the Maypole. You know it?'

'Yes, m'lud.' The boatman tipped a forefinger against the broad felt brim of his hat. He knew the Maypole all right. It was a dingy back alley tavern that housed the worst den of thieves and cut-throats this side of Normandy. 'You won't be wanting me to wait for you.'

Beaumont produced another silver penny from his purse and held it up between forefinger and thumb, glimmering like a silver fish scale. 'I've got business there,' he said. 'I won't be long, and it's full daylight. This will be yours if you're there when I return.'

The boatman eyed the money and wondered if the Norman knew what the odds were against returning alive from the Maypole. 'I'll wait an hour, no longer,' he said grudgingly and began working his boat out into the heaving grey sheet of water.

CHAPTER 10

CHEAPSIDE, LONDON'S MAIN market-place, simmered with activity in the afternoon heat. From the fly-plagued butcher's shambles at the far west side through the prestigious stalls of the goldsmiths, the drapers and the spice-sellers in the centre, to the poultry, grain and fish markets leading down to Oystergate on the east side, hundreds of shopkeepers stood by their booths and stalls, enticing the townspeople to buy their wares. And buy some of them certainly did, with much alacrity and very little discrimination.

Clutching a packet of sugared plums, a cage containing two black coneys, a skein of scarlet wool and a box of green peppercorns, Joscelin was still marvelling at the speed with which his aunt Maude had whisked him away from his essential duties to escort herself and Linnet around the stalls of the Cheap.

'That poor girl, cooped up in that house with naught to do but worry and pray!' she had clucked at him as though it were his fault – which he supposed in the most indirect of terms it was. 'She needs a respite. I know that I most certainly do!'

Joscelin had opened his mouth to protest, but that was as far as he got, as Maude overrode him, a look in her eyes which said *I knew you when you were a squawling brat in tail clouts, so don't presume to know better*. 'There are things she needs to buy before she leaves – women's things, needles and thread and the like. A man wouldn't understand – not until his backside wore through his braies. And you need a freshening too. Have you still got that megrim? Did you drink the betony posset I sent down to you?'

It was impossible to swim against a flood-tide and he had capitulated, if not gracefully, then at least with a reasonable degree of resignation. For his pains he was now a sweltering pack-beast for Maude's various impulse purchases, although he had managed to persuade her out of buying an extremely smelly goatskin from a tanner's stall on the corner of the Jewry. His head had started to throb with a gentle, exquisite insistence. So had his feet. The women had reached the Soper's lane haberdashery booths in their quest for a bargain and were talking animatedly to a seller of threads.

Yawning widely, Joscelin leaned against a colonnade pole and watched them haggle. His aunt, as to be expected, was as vociferous as a plump barnyard hen and the merchant parried her assaults with cheerful vigour. Linnet de Montsorrel, however, was a surprise. Instead of leaving Maude to do all the bargaining this time, she made offers herself and held firmly to them. When the merchant refused, Linnet's grey eyes grew large and tragic and her lower lip drooped. When he conceded defeat, she transfixed him with a shy, radiant smile. The gentle mixture of pathos and coaxing achieved far more success than Maude's blustering threats to take her custom elsewhere.

Linnet de Montsorrel looked soft and vulnerable, Joscelin thought, but there was a tough core, a will to survive. And there in the crowded market-place he began to understand why she was attractive to him. Breaca had been like that – quietly unremarkable until something kindled the flame and her spirit shone through.

Robert detached himself from Ella and came to Joscelin to look at the coneys. The usual colour was a greyish brown, but these were dark, almost black, and lustrous as sables.

'Are you going to eat them?' he asked Joscelin solemnly.

'They're not mine, they belong to Lady Maude,' Joscelin replied, crouching down to be on a level with the child. 'I know for a fact that she dislikes the flavour of coney, so I expect she has another purpose in mind.'

Robert touched the soft fur through the wickerwork bars. 'I don't like coney to eat either. Papa showed me how to kill one once, but I was sick and he beat me.'

Joscelin said nothing, but his mouth corners tightened. No one could live through November without seeing at least one pig slaughtered for salting down during the winter months, but the age of three or four was overly young to be taught to kill for food, especially using a coney. To a child's eye, the rodents were pretty and soft, something to cuddle. And Robert would not have the strength to make a clean kill.

'Papa's dead now,' Robert added. 'That means he's gone away and he won't come back.'

There was a hint of a question in the statement, a desire for reassurance that constricted Joscelin's throat. 'No, he won't come back,' he said gently and decided to have a word with Linnet and Maude and make sure that the boy was not present when Giles's body was displayed in its open coffin tonight before being packed in salt and sewn up in a deerhide.

After the thread-seller had been bartered down to his lowest price, Linnet and Maude assaulted another stall-holder to purchase needles, some of bone and some of brass for different uses, and then moved on to a draper's booth to buy necessary supplies of linen and trimmings. Maude's ankles started to swell and Robert, who had been very good all afternoon, began to grizzle with fatigue. Joscelin lifted him on to his shoulders and gave the maid the various packages to carry as they repaired to the livery stables in West Cheap to recover their horses.

Linnet returned to Joscelin the purse of silver he had given her at the outset. 'You will need to make a record for the Justiciar of how much I have spent,' she said. 'I obtained the best bargain that I could.'

'So I noticed.'

Linnet turned a delicate shade of pink and lowered her eyes.

Joscelin handed her the purse. 'Keep the coin. I've already

71

set it down in the accounts for your personal use – "two marks to the Lady Montsorrel for the purchase of household items". I don't think you've spent any more than ten shillings altogether.'

Her colour deepened. 'You are generous, Sir Joscelin.'

He gave her a sharp look, unsure whether to take her remark at its innocent face value or read sarcasm into it. Not only were her lids downcast, but she had turned her head a little to one side, ensuring that their eyes would not meet. He saw not so much anger as embarrassment, and was intrigued. But the opportunity to question her was not forthcoming, for they arrived at the livery stables and his attention was taken up in helping his charges into their litter and mounting his horse. And when they arrived at the house on the Strand, the thought was blanked from his mind by the frantic chaos that greeted his eyes.

Smoke and flames were rising in thick gouts from the kitchen building and a chain of men were passing leather buckets furiously from the water trough in the yard to the source of the fire, while others used long, hooked poles to drag the burning thatch off the roof. Joscelin's troops were battling to prevent the fire from spreading to the stables. In the garth, the grooms were trying to gentle the frightened horses, which had been removed to safety.

'Dear God!' gasped Maude as the litter was set on the ground, a half-eaten sugar-plum suspended on its way to her mouth.

Joscelin flung himself down from his mount and ran across the yard to the bucket chain. 'Milo, what in God's name is happening?' he demanded of his senior adjutant who was toiling hard with the other men.

'Kitchen fire, sir!' panted Milo and stepped out of line for a moment. He was long of body with an ungainly heron-like stride. His linen robe was saturated from the water buckets he had been helping to carry, and his chausses clung to his legs. 'Started not long after nones – a stray spark in the tinder for the bread oven, or so the cook thinks. He was called away to look at the wares of an

72

oystermonger, and when he returned to the kitchens they were well ablaze.' He rubbed his long jaw, leaving behind a black smear. 'A good thing the main house is roofed with tile the way the wind's blowing, else we'd all be sleeping in the almshouse tonight.'

It was a common enough way for a fire to start, but Joscelin felt his scalp prickling. He looked along the row of men on the bucket chain and his unease deepened. 'You took Gilbert off guarding the strongbox?'

'Yes, sir.' Milo said, confident of his decision. 'I gave Walter the task instead. He'd have been no use on the buckets with that bad shoulder of his.'

'Leave that, come with me,' Joscelin said brusquely and stalked towards the main building.

'What's wrong, sir?'

'Nothing, I hope.' Joscelin mounted the external stairs to the upper chamber. The door at the top was closed, a good sign, but matters deteriorated the moment Joscelin set his hand to the latch. Although it yielded to his pressure, the door would not move, as if there was something behind it, blocking entry.

'Walter, open up!' shouted Milo, beginning to look alarmed. He thudded the door with his fist, receiving only the vibration of the blow in response. Together with Joscelin, he threw his weight at the door. It gave way the tiniest crack, not even enough to see through with one eye.

'I'll get an axe,' Milo said and pelted away down the stairs. Joscelin threw his weight against the door again, venting his frustration and anger, then took a grip on himself, breathing hard. Milo returned at the run, brandishing a Danish war axe that belonged to one of the men. Joscelin grabbed the weapon out of his hands, swung it, and sank the curved blade into the door close to the hinges. Splinters leaped out of the wood like white javelins. Joscelin wrenched the axe-head free and launched it again with all the strength in his upper arms. A split opened in the oak and he worked on this. A couple more strokes north and south, and wood parted from metal. Milo thrust at the door with his shoulder and it fell inwards, slamming down like a drawbridge upon the corpse that had been lying behind it.

'Christ on the Cross!' Milo leaped over the door and, with Joscelin, heaved it off the body. It was obvious that Walter was dead. There was a huge wound in his throat, although it had not killed him immediately. The whitewashed wall was sprayed with blood and there was a glistening trail of it on the rushes across which he had crawled to reach the door to try and fetch help. The room reeked like a slaughterhouse.

Making a rapid mental inventory of the room, Joscelin saw without surprise that the strongbox no longer stood in its place beside the great bed. Other items had been taken too – Giles's hauberk no longer gleamed on its pole, and the fine Flemish hangings had been stripped from the walls.

'Whoever it was can't have gone far,' he said, rapidly assessing the span of time that had passed between now and the fire starting, and setting it against the sheer weight and bulk of the goods that had been taken.

'No one has gone out of the front entrance on to the street, I'd swear my life on it!' Milo's voice was hoarse with shock, but he was a mercenary, a man who lived by the sword, and his thinking processes remained sharp. 'The only way to get such weight out in a hurry is by the river!'

'Go and get some men, take them off the bucket chain if you have to, and meet me at the wharf,' Joscelin ordered. 'And post another man here, a servant will do, but tell him on no account to allow the women into the room and especially not the child.'

'Yes, sir.'

Joscelin ran down the stairs, sprinted across the neglected garden and down through the small orchard to the wharf bordering the rear of the property. A set of slippery, weed-covered steps descended to the gravel shoreline where several small rowing boats in varying stages of decrepitude were beached.

74

The tide was out and on the expanse of shingle, two men, their tunics drawn high through their belts, were striving to push a beached Thames shallow boat into deeper water. A third man sat aft of the boat upon the missing strongbox, exhorting them to greater effort. Before him were heaped several waxed linen sacks, probably containing the other missing items which were easily worth their weight in silver. The rower's exhortations rapidly changed to a cry of warning as Joscelin's approach was noticed. The men on the beach looked over their shoulders and then began to push harder than ever, trying to free the boat.

Joscelin half-ran, half-slithered down the weed-green stairs, only saved from falling by the firm grip of his cropped leather boot soles. He thrust with his toes on the final step, sprinted across the short expanse of shingle, and launched himself upon the robber to his left. So hard and swift was the impact that the man had no chance of remaining upright, and toppled into the river, bringing Joscelin down with him. The water was shockingly cold and very rapidly saturated their garments, increasing the weight to a level that seriously hampered their every move. They threshed and floundered. Joscelin, having landed uppermost, used the advantage to drive his opponent's head under the water. He lost his grip and the thief broke the surface, choking, but by then help had arrived from Joscelin's troops and the man was seized and dragged ashore.

The second thief had succeeded in pushing the boat free, but had lost his footing as he tried to scramble into it and had been caught by Milo and another panting soldier. The rower worked frantically to cull his craft into deep water, away from the danger on the bank.

Stripping off his sodden tunic and shirt, Joscelin plunged into the river and swam towards his quarry — it was quicker than trying to run, for he was armpit deep by the time he laid his hands to the prow and hauled himself on board. The small vessel rocked alarmingly from side to side as the robber rose to a crouching stand and raised a dripping oar to strike at Joscelin. Joscelin rolled and the oar missed his skull but landed a bruising blow on his shoulder blade. His attacker struck at him again and the boat see-sawed as if in a gale, water sloshing over the prow and stern to form a deep puddle in the caulked bottom.

Joscelin lashed out with his feet and the oarsman staggered backwards and fell heavily against the side. Immediately Joscelin was upon him, using the oar between them to bear down and crush the man's thorax. Panic-stricken, the thief kicked frantically. Joscelin grunted in pain as his body absorbed the blows, but he did not yield his inexorable pressure. The resistance slackened; the thief choked. Joscelin held him within a hair's breadth of death. One more push and the windpipe would collapse. His victim's body went limp as it slipped from consciousness.

'Enough,' Joscelin said with a grimace of distaste. There had been too much death and destruction already. It would be too easy to add to it while the barriers were down. Unbuckling the belt around the man's waist, he rolled him on to his stomach and lashed his hands firmly behind his back, wrapping the tongue of the belt around twice and jerking the latch viciously on to the last hole of the leather. The thief groaned and started to recover his senses. His head moved feebly as he tried to avoid the water that had pooled in the bottom of the boat.

'Don't give me any trouble,' Joscelin said, lifting the man's head by the hair and shoving Giles's hauberk beneath it to prevent him from drowning. 'I'm quite likely to throw you to the fish, and in that padded jerkin you'd sink like a chest full of silver, wouldn't you?' Patting the strongbox, he seated himself upon it, retrieved the oars and fitted them into the rowlocks, and turned the boat for shore.

It was late, well past compline before Joscelin was sufficiently free of his responsibilities to think about sitting down with the women to take a cup of wine and a cold venison pasty – one of a batch fetched by Stephen from a cookshop on King Street, the Montsorrel kitchens being little more than smouldering ruins.

A new door had been improvised out of planks from one of the rowing boats down on the shoreline and the floor had been laid with new rushes borrowed from a neighbour. All traces of blood had been either removed or covered up. Out of sight but not out of mind, Joscelin thought as he sat down on a stool and leaned his back against the wall. The stolen hanging had been replaced and it cushioned his spine from the scrubbed, damp patch on the plaster. Once he had eaten and reassured the women, he had to go and spend at least the small hours in vigil over Walter's body. His men were the outer ring of his family, and to lose one hurt. Some deaths hurt more badly than others. Walter had been a staunch companion, one of the first to join his banner the year that Juhel died.

In the privacy of the women's domain, Linnet de Montsorrel had removed her wimple. A thick braid of honey-brown hair fell over her shoulder and touched her girdle of plaited leather. The colour of her hair surprised him, for he had expected it to be darker, matching her brows. The tendrils he had glimpsed on their first encounter had been deep brown like his own because they were damp.

'I have three men below in the hall, guarding the strongbox,' he said. 'And more within immediate reach should the necessity arise, although I do not believe we'll be troubled again in London. Leicester and his retinue are leaving at first light, so I gather.'

'Have you spoken to Richard de Luci yet?' asked Maude.

Joscelin dusted crumbs from his spare tunic. It was more threadbare than the one he had ruined in the river, and only just respectable. It was better for a mercenary to invest his coin in the best weapons and horses he could afford rather than robing himself in finery. 'No, he wasn't at home. It can wait until morning now. His prisoners are

77

securely confined, although I doubt he'll get much out of them before they swing.' He fell silent for a moment and stared into his half-empty cup. When he spoke again, it was to Linnet, not his anxiously hovering aunt.

'Perhaps you will tell me now about Hubert de Beaumont, about this private quarrel of yours. I think that perhaps it is not so private after all.'

Linnet put her hand upon the necklet of blue and yellow bruises at her throat. A red burn mark showed livid where Beaumont had tried to tear off the leather cord upon which the strongbox key had hung. Joscelin was its custodian now. 'If you had made an issue of it, there would have been a scandal and I would have been branded a harlot at the very least. Hubert de Beaumont has a murky reputation and there have been several incidents involving other men's wives. You ride the tourney circuit, you know the type.'

Joscelin inwardly flinched as her barb hit home. Being a tourney champion himself and an itinerant mercenary, he was by association linked to such men. Nor could he claim to be a lily-white innocent himself.

'He wanted the silver. It was Giles's wish too, but I denied them both. I had to decide how to act in my own interests and my son's, since the strongbox belongs to him now. Even now I'm not sure that I have done the right thing. There is no surety that King Henry will emerge from this rebellion the victor. To lean too far in either direction seems dangerous to me.'

Joscelin had been taking a drink of wine and he almost choked at hearing her deliver these less than honourable sentiments in a thoughtful, pragmatic voice. 'Playing a double game is even more dangerous,' he croaked.

She lowered her head and watched her hands smoothing the soft blue wool of her gown over her knees. All he could see was the curve of her cheek and the golden highlights polishing her heavy braid. Then, after a moment, she drew a deep breath, as if of courage, and lifted her gaze to his. 'And sometimes safer I do believe. No, please, hear

78

me out.' She lifted her hand quickly to stay his protest. 'I have a suggestion to put to you about tomorrow's journey.'

Joscelin looked at the hand she had stretched out to him. It was well-formed and generous, with short, clipped nails; a quick and capable hand, the fingers not tapering, but of a similar breadth from base to tip. 'Yes?' he said cautiously.

'The strongbox is obviously a target. Leicester knows that if he takes his claim to court, he is likely to lose. He also knows that we are leaving for Rushcliffe tomorrow and that we will have to travel through lands where his influence is almost as powerful as the Justiciar's.'

'Y . . . es,' Joscelin said again, beginning to frown.

'What I suggest is that to protect my son's inheritance, we take...' She stopped speaking abruptly, her gaze darting to the makeshift door as it was heavily thumped by the fist of the guard outside.

'Come,' Joscelin commanded.

Malcolm the Galwegian poked his head around the door, his flaming hair concealed within a boiled leather cap helm. 'The Justiciar and your lord father have just arrived, sir, and want to see ye doonstairs,' he announced, his Scots accent so broad that Linnet and Maude both stared at him blankly. Joscelin, more accustomed than the women to the Galwegian manner of speech, rose to his feet with a heavy sigh. 'All right, I'll be there directly,' he said, and turned to Linnet. 'I shall be interested to hear what you have to say when I get back,' adding ruefully as he reached the door, 'if I can stay awake that long.'

Joscelin walked into the main hall downstairs, and found his father and the Justiciar waiting for him. Ironheart's expression was smug and Joscelin was immediately put on his guard. It was a relief to have the culprits under lock and key awaiting interrogation, but set against it, a man had died, and the kitchens and stables were naught but heaps of smoking cinders.

Joscelin made a concise report that bordered on the curt because he was tired and because the sharper he became, the more his father's lips curved. De Luci, too, seemed to find it necessary to smile as he seated himself on a padded bench along the wall of the room. Beside him was a wicker cage lined with straw, and inside it, curled at the back, two small black rabbits slept nose to tail.

'Food for your journey?' de Luci asked, peering inside.

'They are a gift from my aunt to Robert Montsorrel,' Joscelin answered stiffly.

Ironheart snorted with contempt. 'Maude's got more wool in her head than a downland sheep.'

'And more sense than most,' Joscelin snapped, and then, aware that both men were staring at him, shrugged. 'I lost a good man today, and got thoroughly belaboured by an oar when I went after the strongbox on the boat. Between one and the other, I'm not fit company.'

De Luci sobered. 'It is always a grief to lose a companion. In token of respect, I will pay for masses to be said for him once you are gone. We won't keep you much longer, but I have a proposal to set before you, one that is very much to your advantage, and it has a direct bearing on the task I have set you.' His bloodshot brown eyes flickered briefly to Ironheart and back to Joscelin.

It was a night for proposals, Joscelin thought. He saw that his father was openly grinning now, his body almost pulsating with delight.

De Luci steepled his fingers beneath his blurring, pugnacious jaw. 'Originally I wanted you to escort Linnet de Montsorrel and her son back to Rushcliffe and take up the reins of government, while I found a suitable warden for the boy. Well, I am pleased to tell you that I have found one already.'

Joscelin eyed de Luci. How could that be of advantage to him unless de Luci was offering him a higher post, which he very much doubted. The qualifications were means, breeding and influence, and he possessed none of these. 'My lord?' he questioned, because it was required of him to play the game out.

'I came here tonight to offer you the wardship of

Robert de Montsorrel by right of marriage to the widow.'

The words entered Joscelin's consciousness in jumbled disorder and slowly rearranged themselves, but still they made little sense to his reeling mind. His eyes widened and his lips moved, silently repeating the final part of the sentence.

De Luci smiled in self-satisfied glee. He loved to toss surprises like snakes and then watch his victims juggle frantically. It was one of his few vices, but mischievous rather than malicious. 'There will be a relief to pay to the crown for the right to take the lady to wife, but you'll still have enough to live on while you set the lands to rights.' He chuckled into his jowls. 'Don't look so stunned. If I did not believe you were capable of putting on baronial robes, I'd not have offered you the Rushcliffe estates. Of course they'll only be yours until the lad comes of age, but there is still his mother's dower property, and that's worth a decent sum in itself. What do you say?'

Joscelin swallowed. His mind was so full of conflicting thoughts and emotions that nothing coherent could be sifted out and presented to the Justiciar. 'I do not know what to say, my lord.'

De Luci laughed. 'I have thought for some time that you should settle down and breed some sons to follow you in service to the Crown.'

Joscelin's fists tightened at his sides. You did not need to settle down to breed sons. You could see them born on a freezing midwinter road between Paris and Nantes, with the nearest shelter a derelict charcoal burner's hut, and no midwives to hand but yourself and a hard-bitten troop of mercenaries. From rich beyond compare, adorned in fierce and tender love, to the bitter rags of inconsolable grief it was a short, black plunge. But how should de Luci know?

'Women should be kept busy,' Ironheart agreed vigorously and exposed his chipped teeth and cavities in a wide grin. 'The bed, the distaff and the cradle; that's the way to run your household.'

Joscelin had seen what the bed, distaff and cradle had done for his father's wife and wondered if Ironheart really believed what he was advocating, or spouted it blindly out of the comfort of habit. 'I would rather not season my dinner with wormwood,' he said tartly, and turned to de Luci. 'My lord, I will be pleased to accept what you offer me, providing the lady is willing.'

'She has no choice in the matter,' Ironheart growled.

'Then I am giving her one.' Joscelin looked defiantly at his father until Ironheart dropped his gaze and spat copious disapproval into the rushes.

'Very well,' said de Luci gravely, 'only if the lady is willing.' His lips twitched and it took a determined effort to straighten them. His own wife had had no say in the matter of their marriage, but he remembered wanting her to agree to the match of her own volition. First and foremost it was pride. He did not believe that there was the slightest possibility of Joscelin giving up an opportunity like this for the sake of a woman's word. De Luci wagged a finger at Ironheart. 'It damages a man's esteem, William, to think that he has to force his bride to marry him.'

'It never damaged mine,' Ironheart snapped. 'Good Christ, if anything, Agnes was forced on me, the sulky bitch.'

'And if you had had to force my mother?' Joscelin asked.

A shadow crossed William's face. 'Then perhaps she would still be alive,' he said bitterly. 'I warned her to be careful on those stairs in that trailing gown, but she went her own way as usual and I was idiot enough not to confine her to the bower until she was safely delivered.'

An uncomfortable silence seized the room. Joscelin knew that he had stepped upon forbidden territory, but sometimes it was the only way of fighting back. It was very seldom that the subject of his mother was raised in conversation. For all that Ironheart believed in plain speaking and honesty, she was one subject that he kept locked away in his own personal, dark hell. He blamed himself for her death, and his guilt was a wound so deep that it still bled with rage and bewilderment.

Joscelin drew breath to speak so that the stifling silence should be broken, but a draught from the door curtain made him stop and glance quickly over his shoulder and then widen his eyes in dismay.

Linnet de Montsorrel stood on the threshold and, from the look on her face, it was obvious that she had heard every word of their discussion and was fully prepared to be as unwilling as a heifer smelling a slaughter shed.

Ironheart, a superb general, came off the defensive and straight into the attack. 'Is it your habit to eavesdrop?' he demanded scathingly, and glared her up and down, making it obvious what he thought of her uncovered hair and the lack of overtunic to her white wool gown.

Joscelin watched her face blanch of colour, but she stood her ground bravely. 'No, my lord,' she answered with dignity, a slight tremble in her voice. 'I came down to fetch the coneys. My son has had a nightmare about them being killed and I want him to see that they are safe. I heard you talking and, since it concerned me most intimately, I had no qualms about listening.'

William spluttered.

Linnet faced Joscelin. 'You want me to consent to be your wife?'

'I ask of you that honour, my lady,' he answered, his colour high, and thought how trite it sounded. Straight out of a minstrel's ballad, and the scorn in her eyes was a fitting payment.

'Honour,' she said wearily. 'What an overused word that is.'

Ironheart, still speechless, clenched one fist upon his belt buckle as if he were contemplating unlatching it to use upon her. De Luci's well-fed face wore an expression of utter shock, as if a butterfly had just bitten him.

'My son has need of me.' Quickly taking the coney cage from beside the Justiciar, she raked the men one and all with a look of utter contempt, and walked out.

'By Christ she needs her hide lifting with a whip, the wanton!' William ground out, his fists clenching and unclenching on his belt, the great vein in his throat a pulsing worm.

'I don't want a wife like Agnes who cowers every time you raise your voice,' Joscelin answered, his gaze upon the swaying door curtain.

'That is precisely the kind of wife you do want!' Ironheart choked out. Striding across the room to the nearest flagon, he sloshed a measure of mulberry wine into a cup and, raising it on high, toasted his son. 'To the lady's willingness!' he mocked, his eyes bright with cruelty and, taking a deep gulp, he wiped his mouth on the back of his hand and his braided tunic cuff.

'William, enough!' de Luci sharply admonished.

'I will gain her willingness.' Joscelin's eyes glittered on his father's in challenge and the hammer-stroke of every heartbeat was clearly visible in his throat. 'And I won't have to beat her to do it.'

Ironheart returned the look just as fiercely. 'Nay, I know you. You will flay your own hide and offer it to her for a saddle blanket.'

'Perhaps I'll offer her yours instead,' Joscelin snarled. 'You don't know me at all!' And stormed out of the room before he committed patricide.

Reassured that no one had butchered his coneys, Robert had fallen asleep, one small hand lightly touching the cage. A lump grew in Linnet's throat and her eyes stung with tears. Slowly she rose from his bedside and went to the laver. Tilting the brass reservoir, she poured water into the pink and cream marble basin beneath, and splashed her hot face. De Gael's words had been courtly, but she knew them for dross. He was as calculating and ambitious as any other landless wolf. A keep, a comfortingly heavy strong-box, someone to mend his clothes, see to his food and pleasure his bed. Servants, herself included, to call him 'my lord' and fetch and carry at his whim. And she was supposed to be honoured. Arrogant bastard, as if she had a choice. Say no, and the soft words would disappear and the bludgeons emerge. A wave of dizziness assaulted her and she held her wrists in the cold water and tried to breath more slowly.

'Whatever's the matter?' Maude advanced on Linnet from the other end of the room where a maid had been preparing her for bed. She wore a chemise and bedrobe and her grey hair lay in a frizzy plait on her bosom.

Linnet laughed bitterly. 'Giles is barely in his coffin and already I've been given a new "protector".' Her mouth twisted on the final word.

Maude regarded her blankly. 'You mean de Luci has appointed a permanent ward to look after Robert's inheritance? What about Joscelin? Is he still taking you north tomorrow?'

Linnet looked through waterlogged lashes into the older woman's bemused, homely face. 'Joscelin,' she said stiffly, 'has been given full custody of everything by right of marriage. My son, myself and our lands. All he requires is my consent, and even that can be obtained by a handful of silver to the right priest.'

Maude's small eyes popped with astonishment. 'Richard de Luci has offered you in marriage to Joscelin?'

'Yes.'

'Well, well, well.' Maude folded her arms upon her plenteous bosom and assimilated the fact with pursed lips. 'What did Joscelin say?'

'That wedding me was an honour, that he desired my willingness, but I could see that his desire was not for me to be happy, but for him to take what he wants without a bleat from his conscience. He was paying lip service to honour, and I told him so.'

'You said that to Joscelin?' Maude looked horrified.

'I said it to all three of them,' Linnet answered defiantly and dried her hands on the rectangle of bleached linen hanging at the side of the laver. 'Giles believed in honour too.' She yanked her gown and chemise to one side and showed Maude the livid mark of a bite on her shoulder, the yellow smudges encircling her throat, the friction graze of the leather key cord. 'Here's the proof.'

Maude unfolded her arms and quickly put them around Linnet. 'Not all men are so tainted, my dear,' she said in a voice tender with compassion. 'My husband never took his fist to me nor did he reproach me even once because I was barren. We were very fond of each other. I still miss him terribly.' Her eyes brimmed.

Linnet refused to be diverted from her course by the older woman's tears. 'And your nephew, how does he treat women?'

'Joscelin would not abuse you, I know he would not.'

'With his father for an example?'

Maude squeezed Linnet's shoulder against the fatty pad of her own. 'Once you know William, he's more bark than bite. I'm not saying that he's an easy man; sometimes he can be downright obnoxious, but his bad temper is a shield to stop anyone from wounding him. Besides, Joscelin has always had the strength of will to go his own way. That's one of the reasons he and William sometimes quarrel fit to fly the doors off their hinges.' She hesitated, then said on a different, less conciliatory note, 'Do you object to Joscelin because he is base-born?'

'Giles had the blood of the Dukes of Normandy in his veins and the habits of a pig. I don't give a cursed bean for the circumstances of your nephew's birth.'

'Aunt Maude, I'd be grateful for a moment alone with Lady Linnet,' said Joscelin from the doorway.

Linnet pulled away from Maude. 'I have nothing to say to you,' she answered coldly. She could see the checked temper and tension in the way he was standing and had no intention of being its victim.

Maude stepped protectively in front of the younger woman. 'I think tomorrow would be better for us all,' she suggested.

'No.' The word was uttered with a quiet determination, informing her that while she might badger him and win on trivial issues such as shopping trips, she would have no success on a matter as important as this. He seated himself on the coffer where he had earlier sat to eat his pasty, and settled his back against the wall, indicating that he was prepared for a long wait if necessary.

Maude held her ground for a moment longer, then capitulated with a deep shrug and an apologetic glance for Linnet. She retired to the far end of the room and would have left the partitioning curtain open, but Joscelin signalled her to draw it across. After a brief, silent battle of wills, she yielded with an exasperated twitch of her hand.

Nausea threatening, hands icy, Linnet faced Joscelin.

'If not me,' he said, 'it will be someone else and soon. You cannot remain a widow, you must know that.'

His tone was reasonable, but she was not deceived. He was as tense as herself, and struggling to contain his anger. She had seen the signs often enough in Giles.

'My husband has yet to be decently buried and you speak to me of marriage? Mother of God, you even pursue me here to press your claim? You must be eager indeed!'

'I would have discussed it in the hall, but you showed no inclination to stay.'

'With the three of you staring at me like hucksters deliberating over a choice piece of ware?'

'I suppose it must have appeared like that to you,' he admitted candidly, 'but the Justiciar has not made me this offer out of pure generosity for services rendered in the past. He sees me as a choice piece of ware too.'

'So he uses me and my son to buy your loyalty.'

'Hell's death, woman, will you use your brain instead of your tongue!' Joscelin snapped, then slumped on the coffer and rubbed his eyes. 'I'm sorry,' he said heavily. 'I'm tired and sore and my temper's not of the best. I don't mean to frighten you. Look, de Luci has offered me something that will never come within my grasp again. Most mercenaries die in the ditch. Those who don't might rise as high as the post of seneschal in a modest keep if they are fortunate. It's a glittering prize and I would be mad not to desire it with all my being.'

Linnet had flinched when he snarled at her, but his

apology gave her the courage to fight back. 'Rushcliffe is my son's by feudal right. You make it sound like a choice morsel that has landed on your trencher to be devoured.'

Joscelin first pursed and then relaxed his lips in what was almost, but not quite, a smile. 'It is true,' he said, 'that being the warden of a small child who is heir to wide estates is a lucrative post. I pay de Luci for the privilege and then make good my loss and hopefully a profit out of the estate's revenues. It would be dishonest of me to claim otherwise; but unless I'm a competent steward, those profits are going to be negligible, and in the end they will dry up.'

His words held the ring of common sense, but Linnet was not yet prepared to be mollified. And she certainly had no intention of trusting him. 'Giles was not averse to selling his own child's inheritance to the French,' she said, the hostility still in her voice. 'Why should you as a stepfather be any more tender?'

'Because . . .' he began, but stopped, the words unspoken and the haunted look back in his eyes. He indicated the right portion of the coffer, and eased along slightly so that there was room enough for her to be seated without having to touch him. 'Sit down, I'm not going to eat you . . . please.'

Not without misgivings, Linnet did so, not for his asking, but because she no longer trusted her legs to support her. She sat down on the very edge, her hands clasped rigidly together in her lap.

'When your son comes of age and I have to yield the lands, I will still have your dower estates near York and rights to a lead-mine in Derbyshire,' he resumed. 'And if I serve the Justiciar well, other rewards will come my way. Why jeopardize a comfortable future for the sake of a few years of extravagance?'

Yes, she thought. My lands, my rights, myself. 'And a life on the tourney circuits qualifies you for such a post?'

This time he did not shout, and his anger was all the more potent because of it. He contained it, the tension apparent in the taut eyelids and the line of his mouth. When he spoke his tone was stilted and icy. 'I've lived on crumbs and I've lived on largesse, depending on my fortunes, but I have never been reduced to begging in the gutter. Early on I learned to pace my income and not live beyond it. You will find me well qualified to govern.'

She could feel his gaze on her, heavy and possessive, almost like a physical touch. 'What advantage is there to me in becoming any man's wife when I can remain Giles's widow?' she asked, her stomach churning with apprehension.

'De Luci will still have to appoint a warden for your son. And your dower lands will cause men to seek you in marriage, perhaps by force.'

'Richard de Luci would never permit that to happen!'

He shook his head. 'Possession is nine-tenths of the law and money the other. If the Justiciar decides that you are difficult because you rejected my suit, he'll be far less inclined to sympathy on the next occasion – he might well choose to levy a fine and turn a blind eye.'

She looked at her hands and consciously held them still so that her agitation would not be displayed to his miss-nothing stare. She studied the walls of her trap for a means of escape. There were doors to her cage but, as she examined them, she saw that they only led into other cages, smaller and meaner, without even the room to turn and chase her own tail.

Circumspectly, she looked at Joscelin through her lids. He had been kind to Robert, she thought, and he had twice the patience of Giles, but that by no means made of him a saint. Like Giles he was strong-willed, determined and ambitious; she had no reason to associate those traits with her own personal happiness and security. And yet what was the alternative? The thought of men such as Hubert de Beaumont filled her veins with ice.

'What would you have done if I had not overheard you talking downstairs?' she asked curiously.

'Approached you in the morning.' A tired smile lifted

his features and took her completely by surprise. 'Probably on the turf seat in the orchard after mass with Stephen playing his lute behind the wall and me on my bended knees.'

She had to swallow an answering, treacherous smile. 'Then I would have refused you indeed.'

'And do you refuse me now?'

Linnet glanced around the current setting – a bed-chamber at night in shadowy rushlight with a curious audience a mere curtain away and the bed itself, its satin coverlet gleaming like horsehide, inviting the wild ride and the nightmare. How she hated it. Throughout her life it had been a symbol of betrayal, pain and death.

She inhaled deeply. 'I do not refuse you,' she capitulated.

A spark leaped in his eyes. 'And you are willing?'

'I give my consent,' which was not the same thing. 'And I want to observe three months of mourning for Giles in the proper manner. I owe him that duty at least.' The last sentence was uttered softly, more than half to herself.

She saw him stiffen as he registered the tone and content of her reply. His own gaze on the bed, he said quietly, 'I doubt you owe him any kind of duty at all.' Then he looked at her and shrugged wryly. 'Still, it's as close as I'm going to get for the nonce, and the prize is worth the compromise.' Making no attempt at physical contact, he rose to his feet. 'Will you agree to plight troth in front of witnesses tomorrow before we leave the city?'

Linnet hesitated. She had bowed her neck for the collar. Now came the leash. Mutely she nodded acceptance.

'You'll have no cause for regret, I swear,' he said earnestly.

She recalled that Raymond de Montsorrel had said those same words once, whispering, coaxing. He had lied, oh Christ on the Cross, how he had lied as he destroyed her soul.

Joscelin paused, but when she did not respond, her face averted, he sighed and went to the door. On the threshold he stopped and, snapping his fingers, whirled round to face her. 'You were going to suggest something about the security of the strongbox earlier?'

Linnet rose unsteadily from the coffer. She had been silently praying for him to leave, but obviously she was not a good enough Christian. It would be easy to put him off by saying that it was nothing, a feminine foolishness that could wait until the morning. She knew that he would not argue, for there were tired shadows beneath his eyes and he still had his vigil to keep at the bier of the soldier who had died. But by the morning there would be too many other considerations to snatch at her time. Nor was her idea foolish. To the contrary, it was eminently sound.

And so she told him, and was rewarded by a look of admiration and a dark chuckle. 'I'll set it in motion straight away, before I go to prayer,' he promised and, when he left her, his tread was buoyant, as if he saw her willingness to cooperate with him where the silver was concerned as a willingness on all other levels. She might have hated him for it, but was aware, instead, of a strange glow of satisfaction.

CHAPTER 11

I N THE WARMTH OF a midsummer afternoon, Joscelin approached Rushcliffe by way of the ancient Fosse Road that ran through the undulating wolds to the east of the River Trent and the city of Nottingham, and then turned on to the frequently used pack pony route which linked Rushcliffe to Southwell and Newark.

Leaning against him, tucked into his cloak, was Robert de Montsorrel. Joscelin had taken the child on to his saddle to give Linnet and her maid a respite and, besides, he had a paternal responsibility to the little boy now. An empty space within him seemed a little less barren for the comfort of the warm weight against his ribs.

He smiled down at Robert's drowsy blond head, imagining Ironheart's response could he but witness the scene. His father would snort and say that he was storing up trouble for the years to come; he would say that people would consider him soft and afford him less respect. A child's place was with its mother and its mother's place was at the hearth if a man had any sense. Joscelin's smile became wry and dark. He had never claimed to be sensible where women and children were concerned.

Rounding a bend in the dusty road, the castle of Rushcliffe came into view, filled his vision, and momentarily took his breath. Limewashed a brilliant white to protect the stones from the weather, the keep thrust a hundred feet of pride into the sky, a monument to the power and lust of the Norman lords of Montsorrel. A warm feeling of possession came upon him, but he did his best to hold it down. Rushcliffe was only on loan to him until the child in his arms should come of age, and it was unwise when faced with a banquet after years of privation to attack the rich food voraciously. For his own sake he had to consume sparingly.

A small town had grown up in the security of the keep's towering shadow and, as they rode down the narrow main street and negotiated the market cross, folk emerged from their daub and wattle dwellings to watch the procession of soldiers and the funeral cortège. Dogs, chickens and children scampered from underfoot. An enormous spotted sow held up their progress while she was persuaded to leave the middle of the road where she had been lying in a puddle suckling her litter.

Women with children at their skirts and babies in their arms watched from their doorways. A carpenter, bare-chested and powdered with sawdust, stood outside his workshop, wood-shavings curling from the plane in his hand. Joscelin was quickly aware of cold eyes and unsmiling mouths. One or two people crossed themselves as the coffin filed past, but most just stared and a belligerent little old woman outside the alehouse was even bold enough to spit and shake her fist.

Joscelin guided his tall chestnut into line beside Linnet's roan mare. 'Giles was not a popular lord,' he commented wryly.

Linnet pursed her lips. 'They hated him,' she said quietly. 'He wanted their respect, but never understood it was an entitlement he had to earn. He taxed them to the hilt; he abused their rights and refused to listen to their complaints.'

'Did you hate him too?' He gave her a searching look.

She lowered her gaze. 'He was my husband. I have said too much already.'

'Very dutiful.' He pulled a face.

Colour stained her cheekbones. 'Do you have a complaint?'

'Only that I would know your true thoughts, not what you think you ought to say.'

She gave him a startled look.

93

Joscelin shrugged. 'I'm used to the women of the barracks and the camps. Propriety never stands in their way, and better so I think.'

She considered this for a moment and he saw her hands clench on the bridle, but when she spoke her voice was steady and cool. 'By all means, let us be candid, but I do not want to talk about Giles.'

Joscelin was enough of a strategist to know when to draw in his horns. From the set of her jaw he judged that persistence would only meet with stubborn hostility. He looked down at the sleepy blond head pillowed in the crook of his arm. 'Then let us talk about this young man instead. As soon as I've an opportunity, I'll find him a pony of his own. It is past time he began his training.'

She nodded with alacrity and immediately brightened, as if she had been released from a trap.

In murmured conversation so as not to wake the child, they rode past the watermill which was responsible for grinding the corn for both village and castle. Arcs of silver water cascaded from the rotating wheel steps and tumbled to be churned round and up again. The roof of the mill building was being rethatched and stooks of reed were laid up against the south wall. The miller's family and employees had clumped together outside the door of their dwelling to watch the company ride past. A small boy of about Robert's age stood beside a buxom young woman. He had a leather sling in one hand. Beneath the uneven hem of his tunic, his legs were bare and his knees earth-streaked. His hair was copper-blonde and his bones strongly Norse like those of the obese, red-bearded miller, but his eyes and thin-lipped mouth bore mute testimony to his Montsorrel blood.

Joscelin glanced curiously at the boy and beside him felt Linnet's renewed tension.

'Your husband's?' he asked, wondering how on earth it was going to be possible to avoid the subject of Giles de Montsorrel when reminders of his presence were all around them.

She shook her head. 'One of Raymond's.'

'Yes, he did have a certain reputation.' Joscelin's eyes narrowed with amusement as he remembered several bawdy tales and jests that had done the rounds of the Nottingham barracks. 'How many more are there?'

'I do not know,' she said coldly, making it obvious that the subject was distasteful to her. 'Giles and his father quarrelled several years ago and after that we lived on my dower lands.' Her gaze travelled over him with hostility, and when she spoke again, it was in a tone of challenge. 'Do you claim any bastards, Sir Joscelin?'

'When you are one yourself, you think twice about begetting others.' He shifted in the saddle and added bleakly, 'Sometimes you think twice and still take the risk because you need the comfort, but as far as I know I have no living offspring.' *Not any more.*

They rode in uncomfortable silence after that until Robert roused from his doze and had to be set down to relieve his bladder. They were among the trees now, coppices of birch and hazel belonging to the lord who sold the villagers the right to collect firewood and forage for nuts in the autumn. Beyond the woods lay rich meadowland on which grazed the castle's dairy herd. Further up the slope, closer to the keep, sheep and geese kept the grass nibbled to a springy turf.

Robert returned to his mother and sat across the saddle in front of her, his small hands grasping the rectangular pommel. Dusty sunlight turned his hair to white gold and lightened his eyes to the palest grey-blue, making of him a radiant faerie child.

From somewhere on their left at the far side of the coppice they heard the chunk of an axe on wood. Joscelin's bones began to feel uncomfortable within his skin. The coppiced trees looked like giant hands, deformed fists with fingers sprouting from the knuckle joints. He looked over his shoulder at the pall-covered coffin. The wain on which it lay creaked and jarred over the ruts in the track and Joscelin had an irrational expectation that they were going

95

to jolt into one rut too many and awaken the dead. Icy chills started to crawl up and down his spine like large spiders.

'What's the matter?' Linnet asked anxiously.

'Oblige me by riding in the centre of the men, my lady,' he said. Lifting his helm from the saddle, he donned it, slipping his shield from its long strap on his back and thrusting his left arm through the two shorter hand grips to bring it into battle position.

Linnet stared at him, her mouth open.

'Skirmish formation!' he turned in the saddle to alert his men. 'Malcolm, stay with my lady!'

'Aye, sir!' Red hair bushing irrepressibly from beneath his helm, the young Galwegian took Linnet's bridle and guided the mare into the heart of the troop.

The path through the coppice remained innocent and sunlit but the soldiers took up their positions, weapons bared and shields raised.

'Did you see something, sir?' asked Milo de Selsey, riding abreast of Joscelin.

Joscelin felt the curiosity in his adjutant's grey stare. 'Intuition,' he said. 'A soldier's gut as my father always says. Have you noticed how still it is – no birdsong?'

De Selsey's saddle creaked as he shifted and looked over his shoulder into the trees. He narrowed his eyes and nodded in wordless acknowledgement of Joscelin's concern.

As they rode onwards, Joscelin felt as if his eyes and ears were out on stalks. Every tiny hair on his body was upright. Beneath him, Whitesocks pranced nervously as he absorbed his master's mood.

They approached the end of the coppice, the track running narrow and straight. It bore the prints of foresters' carts and old hoofmarks and the occasional heap of stale dung. A soft breeze hissed between the reaching branches. The path divided like a snake's tongue, but a fallen log blocked the wider route, and the troop had to narrow down to two abreast.

A glint of silver flashed in the trees, dazzling Joscelin's eyes as he turned to look, disappeared, then flashed again closer. He heard a terse command and the rapid thud of hooves as a troop of horsemen moved to block the way out of the coppice. The leading knight was whirling a hand axe above his head, the sunlight gleaming along its edge. Then he stopped, caught it by the rounded base of the haft and used it as a baton as he bellowed the command to attack.

Within seconds the enemy troop was upon Joscelin's, but the advantage of surprise had been lost and the first impetus of assault was not as devastating as it might have been. Nevertheless, the odds were not in Joscelin's favour, for he was outnumbered and, having two baggage wains and a coffin cart to protect, he was also unable to manoeuvre.

Two of the attacking soldiers hacked their way through the guard surrounding Linnet and Robert. A bay destrier drew level with Linnet's roan and its rider seized the bridle to bring the small mare around. Robert was torn screaming from her arms.

She shrieked at the full pitch of her lungs for aid. Malcolm struggled valiantly to respond but he was engaged in a fierce battle with an opponent on either side of him and it was impossible for him to break free and help her.

A chestnut whirlwind surged into the midst of the attempted abduction. The downswing of Joscelin's sword took off one man's arm clean through the shoulder joint, thus freeing the restraint on Linnet's bridle. Howling, the knight toppled from his saddle. Joscelin spurred Whitesocks around Linnet, thrust his shield into the sword stroke of the second knight, heaved the blade off and counter-struck. The knight doubled over and fell from the saddle. Joscelin caught Robert and hauled him to safety.

'Here, take him,' he gasped to Linnet.

She closed her arms convulsively around her child, and then, seeing the blood, recoiled. Feverishly she dabbed at where it was thickest with a fold of her cloak, trying to gauge the extent of his injury.

'God's death, woman, it's not his!' Joscelin snapped. 'You'll have wounded aplenty to tend without fussing over trifles!'

She inhaled to shriek at him that Robert's near capture and rough handling were no mere trifles to her, but he had gone, spurring Whitesocks towards one of the wains which had been captured. Joscelin's driver was sprawled face down on the coppice floor, and in his place a young knight was making a competent effort at turning the horses. He had set his shield down while he handled the wain. The device of a golden firedrake on a cobalt-blue background could not be mistaken by Joscelin whose own shield bore the same emblem, scored over by the black bend-sinister of bastardy.

'Ragnar!' he bellowed furiously. His sword blade was caught by the under-curve of the hand-axe wielded by a paunchy knight, who was powerfully muscled in arm and shoulder. Joscelin tightened his thigh against the saddle to hold his seat and turned his wrist to free his weapon. In the moment he disengaged, he locked eyes with Hubert de Beaumont and knew that this time there would be no backing down.

Beaumont swung the axe. Joscelin ducked. The blade sang past his ear and caught his shoulder a glancing buffet. It did not break the links of his hauberk, but it was enough to rock him back against his cantle. Beaumont took advantage and leaped, his axe dangling from a leather loop on his wrist to leave his hands free to drag Joscelin out of the saddle.

With the right timing, Hubert de Beaumont would have killed Joscelin, but the move went awry and Joscelin, taught to fight in the routier camps of Normandy and Flanders, was no lamb to the slaughter. Even as they fell together, he kept hold of his sword and twisted, so that Beaumont's fifteen stone weight, augmented by another thirty pounds of armour, landed beside and not on top of him. As Joscelin hit the ground, he rolled over and struck. It was a short, haphazard blow with the top edge of the blade close to the hilt, but it bought him sufficient time for a second, true stroke.

Panting, his vision marred by fluctuating black stars, Joscelin straddled the body of Hubert de Beaumont and watched the baggage wain containing the Montsorrel strongbox disappear down the track in the direction of the Nottingham road, escorted by a dozen hallooing, jubilant soldiers.

Blood trickled down his arm where his mail had been pierced. Feeling as if he had been crushed by a mill grindstone, Joscelin removed his helm and went to catch Whitesocks.

'Shall we ride after them, sir?'

He looked up at Milo. His adjutant's grey had minor wounds, but the cuts welled brightly upon the white coat. 'Jesu, no, let them go. We're outnumbered and damned fortunate to escape with the mauling we got.' His smile was stark and brief. 'Let Ragnar savour his victory for the small time it is his. Safer I think to ride for Rushcliffe before he takes it into his head to look at his prize.' He stared round the battle site. 'Put our dead across horses. The men too badly wounded to ride can use the funeral wain.'

'Yes sir.' Milo turned away and began shouting commands.

Joscelin watched the uninjured men in his troop begin the grisly, depressing task of tying their lifeless companions across spare horses like slaughtered deer at the end of a day's hunting. Six dead in all, and four too injured to ride with competence – almost half his troop. He picked his way among the men, talking, helping, until he came to Linnet, who was bending beside one of the sorely wounded, comforting him while he waited his turn to be lifted on to the wain.

'Malcolm?' Joscelin crouched beside the young merce-nary and looked at the bloody spear gouge that had ripped open the milky, freckled skin from collarbone to bicep.

'I wasna fast enough, sir . . .' Malcolm's teeth clenched

in a rictus of pain. Tears oozed from his eye corners and trickled into the red hair fluffing above his ears. His Scots accent thickened. 'There were two o' the deils right and left o' me. I couldna stop them.' He stared wildly from Joscelin to Linnet, who was holding his blood-soaked shirt in her hand. 'I'm going tae die, aren't I?'

'Of course not!' Joscelin replied a little too heartily.

The frightened eyes registered disbelief and Malcolm started to gasp and thresh in panic. New blood filled the wound cavity and dribbled over the ragged lips of skin.

'It's a nasty tear,' Linnet's voice was firm as she bent over him, 'but it can be stitched, and if you do not take the wound fever, you'll live. See, it's only a flesh tear, no vital part has been touched.'

Beneath her calm authority, Malcolm's breathing eased. 'Ye mus' think I'm a bairn!' he lamented.

'No worse than any man,' she remarked wryly. 'It's going to hurt when they lift you but, God willing, you'll soon be comfortable in a bed.'

As Malcolm was gently raised by two soldiers and taken to the wain, Joscelin laid his hand upon Linnet's sleeve. 'Thank you,' he said quietly. 'You have the gift.'

'It was the truth. If he does not take the stiffening sickness and if the wound stays clean, he'll survive with barely a scar.'

Her pragmatic tone sat completely at odds with her earlier hysteria over her son, but Joscelin knew only too well how fierce the bond between mother and child could be. A glance showed him Robert cuddled in the maid's arms, his basket of coneys clutched tightly to his breast, and his eyes as huge as moons in his thin, pale face.

'It was wrong of me to shout at you,' he said as he turned to mount up. 'In the heat of battle everything happens so fast.'

She shook her head and smiled ruefully. 'You made me so angry that you killed my terror.'

He briefly returned her smile, then sobered. 'Hubert de Beaumont was leading them, so obviously they were acting on Leicester's orders.' His mouth tightened. 'My brother Ragnar was with them too.'

'I'm sorry, it must be a grief to you.'

He snorted impatiently as he gained the saddle. 'Not really. I have never known Ragnar as anything but my enemy. The grief is all my father's.'

'They took the strongbox,' she said.

He met her grey gaze and it was as if they were connected by an invisible line of understanding. 'Yes, they took it,' he replied with an arid smile. 'And five casks of vinegar and two of scouring sand for cleaning mail. Nothing of value.' The hangings and tapestries, household goods and trinkets were stored at Nottingham and would arrive later that week down the Trent by slow barge. Grimacing, he pulled himself into the saddle. 'Nothing of value,' he repeated, 'but the lives of six good men. And the life of Hubert de Beaumont is scarcely adequate recompense.'

Waiting impatiently for the ferry on the wooded banks of the Trent, Ragnar looked over his shoulder, his ears straining for the sound of pursuit, but all he heard was the harsh gasp of his own breathing. The horizon remained innocent. He turned to stare at the sullen sheet of grey water. The ferry was a dark wedge half a mile away on the other side of the river and the two ferrymen were taking their own good time about pulling their craft across.

Ragnar bit his nails and muttered nervously. He could still see Hubert de Beaumont's eyes, wide open in disbelief as Joscelin's sword stabbed down, could still see the blood and hear the brief, choking sounds that Beaumont made as he died. The memory made him cold and queasy.

He glanced round at the baggage wain. His instructions had been to capture Montsorrel's strongbox and deliver it to the Earl of Leicester, its rightful owner. Success should have elated him, but he was aware of a nagging feeling of doubt. Something stank. He eyed the strongbox where it stood squat and stolid amid various casks and barrels. Joscelin had been entrusted with its safety and it was more than his hide was worth to lose it. So why had he not pursued?

The doubt became a sickening suspicion. Ragnar drew his sword from his belt and ducked inside the canvas covering. Iron bindings gleaming malevolently, the strongbox mocked him, the seam between lid and base a smiling mouth tightly closed upon its secrets. He could not bear it and struck at the hasps. They were stoutly made and held fast. Sparks flashed in the dim light and the sound of his blade on the iron was loud enough to waken a corpse. It brought the other men running, demanding to know what he was doing.

Sobbing with effort and frustration, Ragnar took one last swing. The hasps shattered, but so did his beautiful, lovingly honed sword. A sliver of metal flew from the blade and lodged in his browbone. Blood streamed from the wound, blinding him, and it was one of the other soldiers who opened the violated strongbox and discovered that the scuffed leather money pouches within held not silver pennies but small, round stones, smelling pungently of river and weed.

CHAPTER 12

ARMAND DE CORBETTE, Rushcliffe's seneschal, folded his hands inside his silk-edged sleeves and rocked back and forth on his gilded leather boots. Heel and toe, heel and toe, restless with anxiety. Eyes narrowed against the wind scurrying in and out of the crenels of the east tower wall walk, he stared towards the approaching troop. A messenger had brought him advance warning of the new lord's arrival, together with a parchment bearing the seal of the Justiciar ordering him to yield the castle into the hands of Joscelin de Gael and offer him every cooperation.

Corbette focused upon a rangy liver-chestnut stallion and the man sitting confidently astride. William de Rocher's bastard, a man of repute in some circles and reputation in others; hand-picked by the Justiciar. Corbette knew him by sight as part of the Nottingham garrison. This new position was a step up indeed. Obviously the Justiciar had selected de Gael for his ability, a thought that was most unwelcome and made Corbette ease his finger around the gilded neckband of his tunic as if a noose were tightening there.

Halfdan, the serjeant in command of the keep's garrison, thrust out his wet lower lip. 'Why can't we just keep the drawbridge up and tell 'em to piss off?' he demanded belligerently.

'Oh, you want to end up in the forest as an outlaw,' Corbette mocked. 'If you had brains, you'd be dangerous. It is not just a piddling matter of someone's lackey presenting a writ of authority at our gates. It is William de Rocher and Richard de Luci; it is King Henry himself!'

103

He shook the parchment beneath the Anglo-Dane's nose like a curse. 'Jesu, don't you understand?!'

Halfdan stared at him blankly. Corbette growled through his teeth with exasperation. 'Look, just keep your mouth shut and stay out of the way. Let me do all the talking. You don't want to end up doing a gibbet dance from the battlements, do you?'

Puzzled but obedient, Halfdan shambled off down the stairs. Corbette breathed deeply in and out. Old Lord Raymond had liked to display Halfdan for his visitors. The idiot's muscles were as impressive as his wits were lacking. Occasionally, for entertainment, Raymond had organized fights between Halfdan and other mercenaries, sometimes to the death, with money laid upon the outcome. Corbette had found the enormous Anglo-Dane useful for keeping awkward castle retainers in line after Raymond's death, but the change of master had rapidly altered that perspective.

Descending to the bailey, Corbette could feel the sweat ice-cold in his armpits, staining through his shirt to his expensive blue silk tunic.

The chestnut stallion paced over the drawbridge and entered the courtyard and Corbette hastened forwards to bend the knee at the new master's stirrup. 'Welcome, my lord, and gladly so.' He made very sure to emphasize the title.

De Gael's fist moved slightly on the reins, curbing the horse. 'And who might you be?' he enquired frostily.

'Armand de Corbette, at your service, my lord – I am the seneschal.'

There was a moment's hesitation while the air grew more frigid still. 'Get up,' said de Gael, and Corbette shivered. The hazel eyes were as clear and hard as green agates. Every nuance and gesture spoke of hostility and suspicion. 'Why did you permit armed men to lie up in the coppice on the Nottingham road?'

Eyes downcast, Corbette straightened. He had known that this question was coming – de Gael's messenger had told him what had happened, but finding an excuse for sheer laziness was difficult. 'I did not know they were there, my lord. Some of our soldiers were in the village yesterday, but they made no mention of . . .'

De Gael gave him a look of utter contempt that boded nothing but ill, and stiffly dismounted. He swept the bailey with a disparaging gaze that took in its state of untidy filth and hurled it at Corbette's gilded leather feet. 'Your business is to know everything that pertains to the security of this keep, especially in times of rebellion and war.'

Corbette cleared his throat. 'Lord Raymond was a difficult master to serve in his last year and Lord Giles only came into the inheritance at Easter . . .'

'I am not interested in excuses. The evidence before my eyes is enough to prove to me that you're as incompetent as your previous masters.'

'My lord, I'm not seeking to absolve . . .' Corbette began, and broke off with relief as a roan mare entered the bailey, pacing daintily beside a wain which bore a pall-covered coffin and several wounded soldiers. He could grovel when necessary, but it was not his favourite occupation. 'My lady,' he murmured, inclining his head and silently thanking God for the timely distraction.

'Corbette,' she acknowledged with a cool nod. 'Will you fetch the priest and make sure that the bower has been prepared to receive the wounded.'

Corbette leaped to obey with an alacrity that would have been commendable had he not been so obviously desperate to escape.

Joscelin eyed his retreating figure and confirmed Corbette's fears by murmuring to Linnet, 'More than dust is going to fly in this place before I'm finished. The first priority, I think, is a new seneschal.'

Linnet looked up from the row of pallets occupied by the men of Joscelin's troop too sorely wounded to return to their duties and saw their commander standing in the doorway. It was late. Dusk had fallen and rush dips

105

flickered in the gloom. The tallow in which they had been dipped was so coarse and salty that there was more sputter and smoke than flame, and the room was filled with the stink of burning mutton fat.

'I thought you were not coming.' She turned away to pick up her shears.

He moved stiffly into the room, and unlatching his belt laid it across a bench. 'I've been inspecting the keep. The stonework's sound, but the rest is little better than a butcher's shambles.'

'Giles's father had no wife to keep the place in order.' She turned the shears over and over in her hands, watching the dull gleam of the tempered iron. 'After he and Giles quarrelled, we did not visit to see how he lived . . . not even when Raymond was on his deathbed.'

'What about Corbette's wife? I assume he has one?'

'Oh yes.' Linnet wrinkled her nose. 'The lady Mabel. She was always conspicuous by her absence whenever there was work to be done, and I doubt that she's changed. I haven't seen her in the sickroom once, nor her daughter, but the moment the dinner horn sounds, they'll be first at the trough.'

'In my troop, the men who don't work, don't eat,' he said grimly, and went to the row of wounded men to address each one in turn and speak words of comfort.

Linnet could see from the manner in which he carried himself that he was tired and in pain, but he did not skimp his duty. He lingered at Malcolm's pallet and she heard their low exchange of words and then wry laughter. Joscelin was still grinning broadly and shaking his head when he returned to her.

'Malcolm says I'm nae to fash myself, you've a touch like an angel,' he declared in appalling mimicry of a Galwegian accent, and sat down on the frayed tapestry-work cover of a clothing chest.

Linnet opened and closed the shears and smiled. 'Did you believe him?'

'He's a notorious liar, but I reckon you're bound to be

106

gentler than Milo who'd act the chirurgeon otherwise.' He started to remove his surcoat, but desisted with a gasp of pain.

Quickly Linnet moved to help him, easing the garment over his shoulders. The mail coat proved a little more difficult, for it was bulky, not pliable, and the sleeves fitted closely over the padded undergarment. The intimacy was disturbing; the heat of his body, the acrid male smell of battle sweat and the very proximity of his flesh made her feel stifled and panicky. Memories throbbed within this room, sweet with corruption, and it was with not a little relief that she finally succeeded in divesting him of hauberk and gambeson, and was able to step away.

His head was bowed, his breathing harsh with pain. When it eased, he looked up at her through sweat-tangled hair. 'Is there any wine before we go further?' he asked haltingly.

Linnet laid his garments down on the coffer and fetched a glazed pitcher and cup from a trestle by the window embrasure. 'It's last year's,' she apologized, pouring him a cloudy measure. 'It tastes more like verjuice than wine, but it's all we have immediately to hand ... according to Corbette's manservant. I will check myself when I have time.' She gave the cup to him and tried to conquer the feeling of oppression that had come upon her as she helped him remove his garments.

'It doesn't matter.' He took several fast swallows and paused, gasping. 'Jesu, that hurt.'

His shirt was glued to his shoulder wound by dried blood. Linnet started to soak it away with firm, careful strokes, watching his face for indications of excessive pain. 'You're fortunate it wasn't much worse,' she murmured. 'It looks as if you've only cut a surface flap of skin, and the rest is heavy bruising.'

'What did Giles and Raymond quarrel about?'

Linnet ceased bathing his wound and turned away to wring the pad out in a bowl of pine water. The drop-lets plinked over the surface and were absorbed into the

107

shimmering golden whole. Her fingers started to hurt as she twisted the linen. Her womb, her lights, the centre of pleasure in her loins were twisting too. By asking her a question to take his mind from pain, he had inadvertently torn open her own invisible wounds.

'Giles and his father were always disagreeing one way or another,' she said, resuming her ministrations. 'Giles could never do anything right. Raymond criticized him at every turn, told him how much better he could manage things . . . and of course he could. Giles never had a chance. There, ease your shirt off now so I can take a proper look.'

'And?' he prompted.

Linnet drew the shirt over his head and pulled it off down his uninjured arm, making herself busy, so that she would not meet the shrewd clarity of his stare. 'You come from these parts yourself. Did you know Raymond de Montsorrel?'

'Not well. Occasionally he and my father would go hunting together, but they were uneasy neighbours. Raymond de Montsorrel had a high opinion of himself – born of the noblest blood in Normandy, if you can call it noble. He tended to look down on my father because of the Danish taint in our bloodstock. Mind you,' Joscelin added wryly, 'he wasn't niggardly in his endeavours to improve the breeding of those less gifted; his lechery was a legend far and wide.'

Linnet felt as if her heart had plummeted into her stomach. She drew a constricted breath and put his bloodstained shirt on the coffer, looking anywhere but at his face while memory and guilt assaulted her.

It had happened in this very room. Raymond de Montsorrel, touching her hair, his wine-soaked breath at her throat, hoarsely whispering, *'If my son had any steel in his sword, I'd have a grandchild by now. You need a real man to quicken you.'* And then the heat of his mouth on hers and his hand stroking between her thighs with delicate, perfect knowledge. It had been wrong, it had been revolting, but pinned against the wall by his suggestively thrusting hips, for the first time in her life she had felt exquisite twinges of pleasure stabbing through the other emotions.

A shudder ran down her spine and threatened to buckle her knees. She was aware of Joscelin's scrutiny and sought frantically for a way across the pit that had opened up beneath her feet. 'Raymond baited Giles once too often and too far,' she said, swallowing. 'Swords were drawn and Giles slashed his father across the face and had to be dragged off by the guards. We left the same day and we did not return until Raymond was dead.' She darted a glance at him and saw that he was frowning, his eyes narrow and thoughtful. Quickly she broke the wax seal on a clay pot of salve and dipped a trembling forefinger. 'You have few scars to show for a man of your trade,' she said to change the subject. Men liked to talk about themselves and by appealing to his vanity she hoped to divert him from a subject that was fraught with danger.

'You learn fast or you perish.' His thoughtful expression persisted as she daubed the ointment on his shoulder. 'And not all of the scars are visible. I . . . ah!' He broke off and gripped the coffer edge.

'I'm sorry,' she said breathlessly. 'That's the worst part over now.'

He had clenched his lids against the pain, but now he opened them and caught her gaze with his. 'I know what happens when you don't bury the past and let it go. My father has grown old on bitter grieving for my mother, and I too have had my share of folly.' His expression grew bleak and he stared beyond her into the shadows behind the sputtering rush dips. 'The problem with burying the past is that you keep on stumbling over unquiet graves,' he added softly.

Linnet wiped the ointment from her fingers on a piece of softened linen which she then used to bandage his shoulder. Not graves but corpses, she thought, as she used a cloak-pin to hold the dressing in place. The living dead.

Their fingertips touched, the barest involuntary meeting as Linnet secured the pin. Eyes examined. Hunger flared in

109

his and he extended his hand to possess hers. A maid came into the room with a pile of linen sheets over her arm and the moment was broken. Linnet withdrew and Joscelin lowered his hand to pick up his half-finished wine.

'Do you remember your mother?' she asked.

'Only in fragments. I was younger than Robert when she died. I know that she had long, dark hair and that she used to scent it with attar of roses.' He looked beyond her. 'I remember the ends of her braids hanging at my eye-level when I stood at her side. She used to decorate them with ribbons and little jewelled fillets. Perhaps because she had lived such an uncertain life before she took up with my father, she was fond of dressing lavishly.' He swirled the drink in the cup. 'Truly, if I look back to my childhood, my comfort wears the face of my Aunt Maude. She had no children of her own and, since I had no mother, she decided that we could each fulfil the other's need.' His eyelids crinkled. 'The wonder is that I'm not as fat as a bacon pig and still have all my teeth the way she used to stuff me with sweetmeats!' Then he added softly, 'Maude's care meant a great deal to me. It still does.' His gaze had been idly following the linen maid's progress towards the door, but now it stopped and widened. Linnet had been about to say how much she liked Maude herself but, seeing the look on his face, turned round instead.

A young woman hesitated on the threshold of the room and looked around. The expensive salmon-red velvet of her gown encased a voluptuous figure that stopped just short of being plump. Her skin was milk-white and she had glossy raven braids a full handspan thick. Her roving gaze lit upon Joscelin and she drew a deep breath that served to increase the munificence of her breasts. His eyes widened. Smiling, she ran her hands over her body as if to smooth her gown, the motion holding more than a hint of provocative sensuality, and, undulating over to Joscelin, she knelt at his feet.

Linnet stared, indignant rage growing within her. The young woman's pose meant that Joscelin was being granted a more than generous view of cleavage down the unfastened neck opening of the velvet gown. And he was taking full advantage, his eyes plundering avidly.

He looked dazed as he came to his senses enough to lift the girl to her feet. She laid her hand over his, her long fingers enhanced by several fine gold rings and tipped by nails that were elegantly manicured talons. Lifting her head, she favoured him with a look through almond-shaped eyes, hot and dark as coals. Her gaze was first innocent, then feral as it ranged over his naked chest and shoulders. She slowly licked her lips.

'Your shirt, Sir Joscelin,' Linnet said icily, thrusting the garment at him, then rounded on the girl. 'Where were you when you were needed earlier?'

'I'm . . . I'm sorry, Madam. I was paying my respects to Giles. . . Lord Montsorrel in the chapel. His death was a terrible shock to us all, and so soon after Lord Raymond's, God rest their souls.' She looked pathetically at Joscelin, the moist lower lip drooping.

'I am sure it was a shock.' Linnet retorted sarcastically, and added for Joscelin's benefit, 'This is Helwis de Corbette, our seneschal's daughter. She and her mother have been responsible for the housekeeping here these five years past.' A damning indictment considering the domestic chaos that held sway.

The girl shot Linnet a malicious look, then moved closer to Joscelin. As she helped him don the shirt her voice was low and intimate. 'My lord, I will strive to perform anything you desire of me to your . . . satisfaction.' The final word was embellished with promise.

Linnet stifled a sound in the back of her throat. The words slut and hussy burned the tip of her tongue. Joscelin's eyes were very bright and his complexion slightly congested. Lust was a tangible aura in the room.

'Then do this for me,' he grated, his voice suddenly a harsh echo of William Ironheart's. 'Get out of my sight now and return to your devotions. Since you were so concerned for your lord's soul as to avoid your duties up

111

here, you can spend from now until retiring in further vigil.' He stepped away from the greedy touch of her fingers.

Helwis de Corbette gaped at him as if he had spoken in a foreign language.

'Out!' he snarled like a wounded bear.

She uttered a gasp, stared between him and Linnet, then whirled and ran from the room.

'Giles's solace in the time he was lord here, and yours if you want her, judging from her behaviour just now,' she said contemptuously, her eyes hostile.

'You think I'd follow my father's folly and take a mistress beneath my own wife's roof?' he demanded angrily and, before she could move or cry out, he had set his arms around her waist and drawn her hard against him, his mouth descending over hers.

At first Linnet was too shocked to move. Images of herself and Raymond de Montsorrel embracing in this room were overlaid by the scratchy force of Joscelin's kiss, the heat of his touch, the pungent odour of his sweat. If she had felt stifled earlier, now she felt well and truly engulfed.

He swept his hand down her spine in a slow, powerful stroke until he cupped her buttocks and pressed her closer to him. Her back strained. Against her belly she felt the vigorous surge of his manhood. Releasing her lips, he gasped words of need and pleasure, nibbled her ear lobe and the angle of her jaw. Then he took her hand and slowly, slowly, guided her down to his swollen shaft. As her fingers brushed over the bulge in his chausses, he swallowed a groan.

Linnet knew what to do. Raymond had shown her once, his hand over hers, guiding her into the hot layer of his breeches to stroke the quivering, blind monster within. Oh yes, she knew. The quicker the release, the sooner she would be free, but not here, witnessed by her conscience, four wounded knights, two maids, and quite possibly her son, should he wake from his slumber in the wall chamber beyond.

She snatched her hand away as if he had burned her, and tried to free herself from his grip. 'Let me go, oh please let me go!' she cried, struggling against him. When he did not respond except to tighten his hold instinctively, his lips questing blindly, she began to panic, fearing rape. She succeeded in wriggling one arm free and hit him on his freshly bandaged shoulder with as much force as her position would allow.

That reached him. He yelped and his hold slackened. She tore from his embrace and faced him, panting and wild-eyed.

Joscelin stared at her, then cursed and sat down on the coffer, his breath hissing through clenched teeth, his good hand clutching his injured shoulder.

Linnet gnawed her lip and, still poised for flight, watched him with fear and apprehension.

His breathing became less harsh and he looked at her through tangled spikes of dark hair. 'That was stupid,' he said.

Linnet gave him a look of pure disgust, and he quickly shook his head, his expression appalled.

'Jesu, I didn't mean you.' He extended his hand. 'For what it's worth, I've been on too tight a rein recently and that girl . . .' He broke off and grimaced. 'I give you my word of honour it won't happen again.'

Linnet eyed him warily. Her stomach was turning over and over. She knew that he could have beaten her for defying him, that the incident could have ended in rape upon the floor rushes. She should think herself fortunate, but could manage no more than a wan thread of remorse. 'You frightened me,' she said. 'I didn't mean to hurt you.'

'Nor I you. I don't want to live in a household like my father's.' He did not elaborate, but after a moment sighed heavily. The act of drawing and releasing a deep breath caused him to wrinkle his nose. 'Is there a bathtub in this place? I stink to high heaven.'

'There should be one in the laundry; I'll find out.' Linnet relaxed slightly as their conversation started to flow over the difficult moment. 'What about the silver?'

His glance flickered to the great bed and the mattress that had recently been unloaded from beneath the coffin and thrown across the rope frame. Safe among the layers of goose down stuffing were nestled fourteen small leather bags, each containing five marks of silver.

'Leave it where it is for the nonce until I've had time to commission a new strongbox from the carpenter and the locksmith.'

'Will you be sleeping on it?' As she asked the question, she felt heat sweep into her face. Until that moment she had not given any thought to their respective sleeping arrangements during the official period of her mourning.

His smile was wry. 'That would be like inviting a fox to share a chicken coop. I'd never resist the temptation if I had to dwell in your bower. Stephen's organizing a bed for me in the wall chamber near the chapel to keep me in a state of grace until Michaelmas.'

'And you trust me with the coin?' she was driven by a devil to challenge.

'You would not cheat your own son. Yes, I trust you.' His tone held mild rebuke as if he suspected her of deliberately needling him.

After he had gone, Linnet wandered to the bed and sat down upon it. It would have eased her conscience if he had taken the money into his own keeping, or not stated his trust in her with so clear a gaze. No, she would not cheat Robert, he was all her life, but for his sake she had cheated Joscelin. She and Maude had sewn the fourteen money bags into the mattress that night in London, but there had already been another thirty marks stitched into one corner, money that she had sequestered from the strongbox in secret on the night Giles died. This was her security for the future, a secret hoard of her own.

She had made her bed and now she had to lie on it, lumps and all.

CHAPTER 13

'FOR JUST HOW MUCH is Corbette responsible in the keep and on the estate?' Joscelin asked Linnet at table that night. The main dish was mutton. It was tough as saddle leather and in places charred black, revealing an inattentive hand at the spit. Joscelin swallowed a final mouthful by resorting to a liberal gulp of wine and abandoned the meat in favour of a dish of shrimps and mussels steamed in their shells.

'I do not know. I haven't dwelt at Rushcliffe since . . . since the quarrel.' Linnet looked at him from the corner of her eye. He was acting as if nothing had happened between them a few hours ago, but she could remember the texture of his mouth on hers too vividly to follow his lead.

He had made thorough use of the bathtub that had been found and he now exuded a scent of coarse laundry soap that stung her nostrils and made her want to sneeze. Time she thought and past time to set to work with the maids and manufacture something less caustic for personal use. Time would also have to be found to make Joscelin some more tunics. The one he was wearing tonight was the brown wool from the horse fair and it was beginning to look more than just hard worn. Perhaps it would ease her guilt about the thirty silver marks if she sewed for him and made of herself a model, industrious wife.

He grimaced at the sourness of the sauce in which he had dipped a shrimp and again reached to his cup. Then he said, 'Corbette appears to have a wide-ranging authority. It seems that he has become steward of Rushcliffe as well as seneschal. Every time I have wanted a key to a coffer or to ask a question I am informed that Corbette has it or knows the answer, and that worries me. He has his own little kingdom here and everyone is trapped in his web.' Wiping his fingers on a napkin, he reclined in the chair and studied Corbette through narrowed lids. Linnet too looked at the seneschal. He was deep in conversation with a stout man clothed in a maroon wool tunic that made his corpulent torso look like a ripe plum. As Corbette spoke to him, his pouchy gaze darted nervously in the direction of the high table.

'Who's that?' Joscelin murmured.

'Fulbert, the senior scribe,' Linnet identified.

'What's he like?'

She frowned, her head tilted slightly to one side as she sought to be impartial. 'He's pleasant and courteous and writes a fine fair hand, but he's as soft as unfired clay.'

Joscelin nodded thoughtfully.

The words between Corbette and the scribe were becoming heated. Fulbert shook his head, his glance flickering towards Joscelin with fear. A woman leaned between the two arguing men and spoke sharply. Rolls of fat strained at the seams of her blue and silver gown. Her bosom surged like an incoming tide, her throat bulged against a necklet of amber beads, and the dainty features of her face were swamped in a mound of suet-pudding flesh.

Despite her annoyance, Linnet's mouth twitched. 'Giles bought that blue velvet she's wearing because he wanted a new court tunic, but when we left at the time of the quarrel it went missing. I don't think Giles could ever have graced the stuff the way it now graces Mabel de Corbette.'

'*That* is Corbette's wife?' Joscelin said in astonishment.

She watched him stare from Corbette's lean, aristocratic profile to the woman's blowsy over-abundance and try without success to reconcile the two. 'I am told that she was once as beautiful as her daughter Helwis,' she added wickedly.

'Is that a warning?'

'I would not presume so far, Sir Joscelin,' she said archly. 'Besides, I trust to your common sense.'

He snorted with sour amusement and his regard travelled outwards again. 'That velvet will have to last her a lifetime. She'll find herself beggared of all but homespuns from this day forth.'

She directed a servant to fill his empty cup and Joscelin swiftly set his palm over the top. 'Would you have me so gilded that I spend the night under the trestle in a stupor?'

'I thought that was your intent since you swallowed the last three with a swiller's skill.'

He smiled bleakly. 'I'd not have eaten my dinner else. We have enough tosspots in this hall already to drink an alehouse dry.' He stared derisively at Halfdan Siggurdson, who was arm-wrestling with another guard, lighted candle stubs set to either side of their straining wrists. Halfdan was using his free hand to raise a leather cup to his lips, egged on by his cronies, not one of them sober.

Abruptly Joscelin rose to his feet and, leaving the dais, set out to mingle with the people gathered in the hall. It was not a conventional move and earned him glances of suspicion and hostile surprise as well as those of approval and curiosity. Raymond and Giles de Montsorrel would have retired to the private rooms on the floor above, leaving their senior servants to deal with affairs in the hall. But then, for the moment, the new lord was a gardener in diligent search of weeds to uproot and plants to nurture. And, being a mercenary, the subtleties of what was correct to rank and breeding went largely ignored.

Joscelin passed close to Corbette. The seneschal had now ceased his vehement conversation with the scribe and bowed most properly to his new lord. His wife also made her obeisance to Joscelin and batted her lashes at him but, being twice as old and heavy as her daughter, the effect devastated Joscelin in a quite different manner. Biting his lip, he moved rapidly on to the keep's fletcher and immersed himself in a conversation about the possibility of making arrows to fit the Welsh longbows he intended introducing into the keep's armoury.

The shouting of the soldiers watching the arm-wrestling

contest drowned out the fletcher's reply. Frowning, Joscelin lifted his head and stared down the long trestle to the chanting men. Halfdan was about to press his victim's knuckles into the molten tallow of the burning candle end. Fists pounded on the board in unison with the chanting. The wood vibrated. Mugs leaped up and down. The flame wavered and was extinguished as Halfdan applied a last burst of pressure and seared his opponent's wrist into the hot wax. Then he held him there as if branding a beast. The other soldier gasped through clenched teeth. A miasma of tallow smoke thickened the surrounding air as a grinning Halfdan released his victim and scooped up his winnings to unanimous cheers. No one wanted to be on the wrong side of the huge Anglo-Dane. Flexing his powerful shoulders, posing, he stared round the ring of fixed smiles and saw beyond them, Joscelin, unsmiling.

'Want to challenge me?' Halfdan extended a meaty paw. His wrist was braceleted by tattooed blue runes. 'Or are you afraid, Norman?'

A silence fell, a silence as loud as the shouting that had preceded it, and charged with tension. One by one the smiles fell away.

'You've more words than wits, man,' Joscelin said with quiet contempt. 'It's the drink in you talking; you'd not last a minute against me.' He turned his back and started to walk away, his shoulder-blades menaced by the weight of Halfdan's stare.

'Ergyaskr!' Halfdan roared.

There was an audible gasp from the assembled company. Halfdan was asking for more than just a contest of arm strength by accusing Rushcliffe's new lord of cowardice.

Joscelin paused, weighing up the risks. He could pretend ignorance of the old Norse tongue; he could display superior contempt. He was tired and sore, and did not relish a confrontation tonight with a man of Halfdan's massive bulk; yet if he passed it over, there would be repercussions. He was being tested and he knew that he could not be found lacking. Slowly he turned round and walked

118

back down the hall towards the danger.

Halfdan grinned like a delighted gargoyle. His companions were notably more circumspect. One of them relit the candle stubs from a table rushlight, and then made himself scarce in the shadows outside the designated arena.

Joscelin seated himself opposite Halfdan. 'You have a death wish,' he said softly. *'Duatha-mathr.'* He held out his hand.

Halfdan was visibly perturbed by Joscelin's confident manner and his knowledge of the old tongue. He wiped his hand down his chausses and fortified himself with another drink of ale, adding to the gallon he had already consumed, and, planting his elbow solidly on the scuffed oak board, he clasped Joscelin's hand within his enormous fist.

Joscelin resisted as Halfdan started to push, and smiled into the soldier's red, freckled face. He was no stranger to this game himself for he and his uncle Conan had often played it on campaign, sometimes for stones when there was no money. There was a skill to it, brute force alone was not enough, and Joscelin knew that Halfdan's reactions must be impaired by the amount of ale in his belly.

Their forearms remained at the starting point. Halfdan's great muscles tightened and bulged with strain, but he moved Joscelin scarcely an inch towards the candle. Struggling, he held his breath and pushed with all the force of a woman in the last throes of childbirth. His efforts bore no fruit and as he expended the last of his breath on a sob and drew more air, Joscelin began to apply slow, inexorable pressure of his own, bearing down smoothly. Halfdan grimaced, then he howled, his whole arm rigid and shaking with the effort of keeping his pride out of the molten wax. Flesh and flame made tenuous contact. It was too much for Halfdan to endure and, with a bellow of rage, he tore himself free of Joscelin's grip and towered to his feet.

'Bastard spawn of a whoring bitch!' he roared and, throwing himself across the trestle, grabbed Joscelin by the throat. Joscelin felt the pressure on his windpipe, and knew

119

that the berserker would snap his neck as easily as he would snap that of a barnyard fowl. He jerked his knee hard into Halfdan's groin, freed the boot knife that no self-respecting mercenary was ever without, and drove it upwards and forwards with all the strength in his body.

Halfdan buckled and sagged forwards, following the knife as Joscelin withdrew it, his life-blood a red, salty gush. Halfdan struck the trestle like a wild boar crashing down at the end of a hunt, staining the board, rolling upon the reed dips, extinguishing their flame, and thudding at last on the floor rushes.

'My lord, are you all right?' Milo reached Joscelin, his own dagger in his hand.

Joscelin stared down at the lifeless, still twitching hulk at his feet and nodded brusquely. His neck might be twisted and his sore shoulder pulsing heavily with pain, but he was still alive and he had made a lasting impression on the boggle-eyed witnesses. They would not dare to challenge his lordship now that their champion had been sacrificed across his own profane altar.

'Get rid of this,' he commanded, pushing Halfdan with the toe of his boot. 'The men can dig a grave in the morning.' Pivoting on his heel, he returned to the dais, making sure to stalk disdainfully, although in truth every step gave him pain. He sat down in the lord's chair, propped his dagger boot on the edge of the table in fine vagabond style and stared out over his domain. Conversation started again, raggedly at first, but rapidly gaining volume. Halfdan's corpse was dragged from the hall by its heels like a carcass fit only for the hounds.

'They'll be searching his belongings already for what they can scrounge,' Joscelin muttered, his expression one of scowling distaste that caused several guilty consciences to hunch their shoulders and pay determined attention to their ale.

'You should not have ventured below the salt,' Linnet remonstrated as he surreptitiously rubbed his neck. 'You were almost killed.'

'There was need.' This time he did not refuse when she directed a servant to replenish his cup. 'To know Rushcliffe, I must know its backbone and root out any canker lurking there. If I am known as a man who does not stand on ceremony, I become more approachable and my task is made simpler.'

'You also become known as a man who carries a dagger in his boot,' she said wryly.

'A man who plans for adversity, and has the wit and will to overcome it,' he answered, his tone light, but the words themselves weighted with conviction. He smiled at her and raised a toast. 'You're a woman of a similar breed yourself. Here's to our wedding bed, all seventy marks' worth.'

Linnet blushed becomingly, not entirely for reasons of modesty, as she lifted her own cup.

CHAPTER 14

THE FIRST BUSINESS of the morning was Giles's funeral. It was a short, unpleasant affair, for the weather was warm and, despite having been well salted and divested of internal organs, the corpse had defied attempts at preservation and was riper than an overhung pheasant. The chapel enclosed the mourners like a shroud, smothering them in the taint of death. Perfumed smoke rippled from the censers and mingled in sweet, sickening waves with the stench of rotting meat.

Helwis de Corbette fainted and had to be carried out. Linnet suspected that it was a deliberate ploy on her behalf to avoid the stink. Indeed, she doubted that Helwis had been anywhere near Giles's coffin yesterday, but had feigned piety in order to shirk her other duties.

The ceremony was hastily concluded by the ashen-faced family priest, Father Gregory, and the coffin was borne away to the crypt and placed beside the tomb of Raymond de Montsorrel. Father and son were together in death as they had never been in life, Linnet thought and shivered, feeling as if a bony finger had pressed upon her spine. As soon as it was decently possible, she made her excuses and went to attend to her patients in the bower.

She swore to herself as she changed dressings and administered possets that she would expunge every trace of Giles and his father from the living core of the keep. That involved, however, pacifying the dead with a show of duty. After she had reassured herself of the condition of her charges, she left them in the hands of the maids. Retiring to a corner of the bower near the window, she sent for Fulbert the scribe and, when he arrived with his quills, ink and parchment, set about composing a letter to a noted Nottingham craftsman in alabaster. She would have effigies carved and set upon the tombs in stiff white splendour. Let no one accuse her of a lack of respect. She would pay to have prayers said too. God knew there was a need.

Below, in the courtyard, Joscelin studied the men drawn up before him. On first sight they appeared to be a flabby collection of dregs and gutter sweepings, sullen, defensive and afraid. Watching them shuffle and mutter, he wondered whether he ought to dismiss them piecemeal and ride into Nottingham to recruit anew. But then, he reminded himself, even the best troop in the world could suffer from bad leadership and he could not spare the time just now to go picking through Nottingham's rag heaps for likely men.

Legs apart, hands on hips, he delivered a brief lecture on what he expected of the gathered soldiers, what they could expect of him in return, and what would happen should they break the strict codes under which they would now be living.

'You have a month to prove yourselves,' he said. 'After that, any man who has shown himself worthy is guaranteed employment for the rest of the year. Those who fail to reach the standard will be dismissed. Any questions?'

When he left them in Milo's tender care, their eyes pursued him. Some men remained sullen and defensive, but among others there were glimmers of interest and reawakening.

'When I'm talking you pay attention!' Milo roared, striding forward to fill their vision, a six-foot ash spear brandished in his fist. 'Anyone know what this is? No, it's not for leaning on while you fall asleep or oggle a kitchen maid's tits! You, stop grinning and come here. Show me how you'd beat down a sword attack with one of these.'

Smothering a grin of his own, Joscelin left his captain in full flow and went inside the keep to the small chamber off

123

the hall where the vellum account rolls, tally sticks and exchequer cloths were stored. Taking the key that Corbette had most reluctantly given to him the previous evening, he unlocked an iron-bound chest, removed the top layer of parchments, the tally bag and abacus, and bade a hovering manservant bring him a waxed tablet and stylus.

'Shall I fetch Sir Armand to attend you, sir?' enquired the man as Joscelin loosened the drawstring on the tally bag and tipped the notched sticks it contained on to the trestle.

'I'm quite capable of deciphering these without the seneschal's aid.' He searched among the parchments and, glancing from beneath his brows, gave the servant a wintery smile. 'A pitcher of ale would be useful though. Doubtless there's a recent brewing if the state of the men in the hall last night was any indication.'

'Yes, sir.' The young man hurried out, his manner one of cheerful alacrity that was very refreshing after the dull indifference that Joscelin had generally encountered thus far.

The servant returned promptly with the requested articles and poured Joscelin a horn beaker full of viscous golden-brown ale. 'You'll get none better between Newark and Nottingham, my lord,' he announced with pride. 'And I doesn't say that just because me aunt's the brewster.'

Joscelin took a deep swallow of the ale, and immediately appreciated the bitter, malty flavour. 'You're right,' he said with a smile and a toast of the leather mug. 'My compliments to your aunt. She's a highly skilled woman.' Idly, he ran his finger along the smooth wooden beads strung on linen thread across the abacus frame.

The serving man, who had yet to be dismissed, eyed him quizzically, then cleared his throat. 'Do you really know how to use one of them things, sir?' He indicated the abacus.

Joscelin shrugged. 'There is no mystery once you have learned the principle. I was taught by the monks at Lenton when I was a boy. We used to count the flocks when they came in for shearing.'

'But you're a fighting man, sir!' The servant screwed up his face in perplexity.

'Does that mean I cannot have more than one string to my bow? It is useful to have someone else to do this for me, but my knowledge of letters and ciphering means that I can check their honesty if the need arises. How else will I know if I am being cheated?'

The man hesitated, shifting uncomfortably from foot to foot as if the floor were hot. 'Sir, I know it ain't my place to speak, and I saw last night as you could look after yoursen, but the seneschal's mighty vexed at what you're doing.'

This volunteering of information was precisely what Joscelin had been hoping for. 'He's going to be more vexed yet,' he said tartly and leaned against the carved chair back. 'What's your name?'

'Henry, sir.' Given encouragement, there was no stopping his naturally garrulous nature. 'I was born the year the King came to the throne and me mam had me christened to honour him.' He added with a note of pride, 'Me dad's head groom here and me older brother's following him on. I serve in the hall with me mam and two sisters.'

Joscelin flicked his forefinger against one of the creamy polished beads and watched it spin and vibrate on the thread. 'So you must see and hear a great deal of what goes forth?'

'I do, sir, more than some would like.' He glanced darkly towards the hall. 'But I ain't a gossip; I know when to keep me mouth shut.'

Joscelin studied him with thoughtful amusement. 'I'm sure you do,' he said, 'and it occurs to me that you might be suited to act as a mediator between myself and the people here. They are nervous of Milo, and while I would welcome their direct approach to me it's not always going to be possible or practical.'

'Like a reeve you mean, sir?'

125

'If you like, but tied to the castle, not to the land. I'll pay you eight pence a day, the same rate as for a footsoldier.'

Henry's ingenuous freckled face shone but, although his reply glowed in his eyes, and his quivering body was not large enough to contain his delight, he took a moment for consideration and, in doing so, rose again in Joscelin's estimation.

'Me mam'll be that proud,' Henry said huskily.

Joscelin smiled. 'Which one is she?'

'She tends the big soup pot, sir, and airs the pallets by the fire.'

'Ah yes.' He grinned as his mind was filled with the image of a beady-eyed little stick of a woman poking all two brawny yards of Milo away from her precious cauldron armed with nothing more than her ladle and her razor-sharp tongue. That was the kind of spirit he had to nurture in order to obtain a harvest from his ambition.

After Henry had departed, bursting with his news, Joscelin's grin faded and with a sigh he set to work. Gradually he began to frown. Several times he erased his own calculations and began again. The abacus beads shot viciously back and forth; his frown deepened and his mouth compressed.

Thirty hogsheads of wine delivered last week, so the vellum stated, and only eight left. The lord not being in residence, that left only a skeleton household of servants and retainers to maintain, half of whom would only drink ale or cider. And yet over a thousand gallons had been consumed. Someone, it seemed, had found a fatted calf and stuck in their knife with a vengeance.

Leaving his calculations, Joscelin took a lighted wax candle and descended into the vast, vaulted undercroft beneath the great hall, intent on checking matters for himself.

Near the door, standing against three casks of cider, he found the hogsheads of wine, the barrels stamped with the mark of their Angevin producer. There were seven of them. He had passed the eighth in the hall where one of

126

Henry's sisters had been filling flagons from it for the high table. The evidence before his eyes agreed with the tally.

Holding his candle on high, Joscelin prowled forwards. There were barrels of salt beef and pork, herrings and mackerel. Cured sausages and hams dangled from the ceiling together with bunches of herbs, strings of onions, and three Easter buns which had been hung up to dry so that, when required, pieces could be broken off and crumbled into cider or wine to cure the ague. There were crocks of honey, firkins of tallow, ash staves, hides, bundles of rushes for weaving and floor-strewing, a broken cart-wheel. Obviously Rushcliffe's wheelwright was not a master craftsman. Neither was its chatelaine to judge by the higgledy-piggledy state of the undercroft. Sins had been swept in here out of view and it had been used without the supervision of a diligent storekeeper.

Staring around the arc of candlelight, his stomach contracted as he realized that if this place were tidied up and everything that was useless were discarded, it would be nigh on empty.

A keep was built to hold supplies, to be self-sufficient for long stretches of time. As a mercenary he knew just how vital that principle was. Run out of salt beef, stock fish and wine, and you ran out of morale. Run out of bread and you were finished. Cursing under his breath, he picked his way across coils of rope and a broken eel trap to the stores of winnowed grain. It appeared to be plentiful and of a high quality. He examined all the bins, thrusting his arm well down into the golden harvest to make sure that it was not just a thin layer of whole grain poured on top of chaff. All appeared to be well until he stepped back and realized that it in no way tallied with the written accounts. Standing there, staring at yet more evidence not only of mismanagement, but also of treachery, he remembered the previous evening in the hall and Corbette's urgent conversation with Fulbert the scribe. His temper ignited and he stormed from the undercroft and up the turret stairs to the bower.

127

His wounded soldiers gaped at him in astonishment as he strode past them without a word.

'Someone's in for it,' muttered Malcolm. 'I've never seen him look sae fashed before.'

Joscelin strode across the bower to the corner where Linnet and Fulbert were working on a parchment. His expression was one of blazing anger, as he hurled the most damning of the evidence across Fulbert's lectern. The pot of goose quills flew across the room to smash against the laver and the ink tipped over, ruining the exquisitely formed letters on the vellum.

'What's wrong?' Linnet stared at Joscelin in astonishment.

'Ask this turd here!'

Fulbert's jowls wobbled. His neck reddened against the fine white Cambray shirt. He put his plump hand to the gold braid at the throat of his tunic as if an invisible noose were already tightening there. 'I do not know what you mean, my lord,' he said, his gaze sliding off Joscelin's as though it were a sheer glass wall.

'These accounts are in your hand, I presume?'

Silence.

Joscelin slammed his good fist down on the lectern, causing the remaining sheets of vellum to leap in the air and then slide off on to the floor. 'Answer me!' he thundered.

'I'm only a poor scribe, my lord!' Fulbert gibbered. 'I write what the seneschal tells me, and the rest is none of my business!'

Joscelin clutched a fistful of Fulbert's thick velvet tunic and hauled the scribe up to face him, nose to nose, eye to eye. 'Your clothes sing a different tune, scribe. You dress more finely than King Henry himself!' Unleashing the power in his bunched arm, he shoved Fulbert away from him as though the man's deceit had physically soiled his hands.

The force of the thrust sent Fulbert to his knees. He did not rise, but curled his hands over his head and wept, a snail without a shell. 'I had no choice my lord!' he blubbered. 'If I had protested, Corbette would have set Halfdan Siggurdson upon me and my family. Lord Raymond was not in his right wits at the end and no one could make him understand what was happening . . . And where Corbette's influence didn't run, his daughter's did, if you take my meaning.'

'In God's name, will you tell me what is happening?' Linnet demanded, rising to her feet.

Joscelin's attention flickered over to her impatiently. 'Thievery on a vast scale. The undercroft's near empty and, if I'm not mistaken about the grain tally, about to be emptier still.'

Her eyes met his, appalled, then skimmed to the weeping Fulbert.

'Summon your men, I am guilty,' the scribe sobbed, curling more tightly into his fetal ball.

Joscelin breathed out hard. Looking down at Fulbert's pathetic, snivelling form, his anger dampened into disgusted irritation. He remembered building castles of mud as a child and then pissing on them from a height to watch them collapse. 'Oh I know you are,' he said in a quieter, almost normal tone, 'but I doubt marching you down to the cells is going to be of benefit to anyone, including myself. I'm very tempted to swing you from the battlements, but there are things I need to know.' He rubbed his thumb along his jaw. 'Perhaps you would like to barter your hide for the answers?'

'I'll tell you anything, anything you want to know. Don't hang me, I beg you. I've a wife and four children, the youngest is only a babe in arms. Oh Jesu, please!'

Joscelin stepped back to avoid being embraced around the ankles as Fulbert crawled towards him across the rushes. 'You should have taken thought of that earlier,' he said icily. 'Where is the stolen stuff sold?'

'Corbette has a relative in Nottingham who's a merchant. The goods go to him downriver or on pack ponies every now and again. Good my lord, I beg you, give me my life! I'll serve you faithfully, I swear it!'

'As well as you served your two previous lords?' Narrowing his eyes, Joscelin scrutinized the spineless blob at his feet. He had every right to hang him. At the very least he ought to have the fool stripped, flogged and put in the stocks for a week without sustenance, but as he stared, an idea came to him, one that might yet save the man from himself.

'You're of no use to me,' he shrugged. 'For your own safety and my peace of mind I cannot keep you in this household, but I know that my father, William de Rocher, is in sore need of a scribe at Arnsby. He can read and write after a fashion, but he's not fond of the quill and his eyesight is not what it was. You'll go to him under escort, giving him your full history and a letter of recommendation from me.'

Fulbert gave a loud, mucous sniff and looked at Joscelin in abject misery.

'It's either that or the gibbet. Make your choice quickly before my forbearance comes to an end.'

'Wh . . . when do I have to leave, my lord?'

'As soon as you can pack your belongings.'

Fulbert sat up. He was still shivering but the tears had ceased and he stared grimly at the wall as if it carried a vision of his future.

'Serve William de Rocher honestly and you'll have nothing to fear,' Joscelin said curtly. 'Go now and, as you value your reprieve, say nothing to anyone.'

'On my mother's grave, I swear I will not!' Whey-faced, Fulbert bowed out of the room.

Joscelin's breath hissed out through his teeth. He began collecting the scattered tally sticks and replacing them in their drawstring bag with an untoward gentleness that spoke of rigidly controlled temper.

Linnet picked up the sheet of vellum he had thrust beneath Fulbert's nose. 'I still don't understand. What do you mean the undercroft's empty?'

'Corbette's been diverting the keep's vital supplies elsewhere to his own profit and Fulbert's been falsifying the accounts to make everything seem normal at first glance. Come, I'll show you.'

On their way to the undercroft, Joscelin paused in the hall and spoke to two of his off-duty troops who were engaged in mortal combat over a merels board. 'Leave your game,' he said quietly. 'Go and find the seneschal and bring him to the solar. I want him kept there until I'm ready to deal with him.'

'With pleasure, sir.' Guy de Montauban flashed a white grin and rose, keen to be about his errand.

'What will you do to Corbette?' Linnet enquired as once more Joscelin lit his candle and together they descended the stone stairway into the darkness of the undercroft.

'String him up. Village or bailey I haven't decided yet. Village probably. His corpse will serve notice that I'm not to be duped and that my justice is swiftly meted.'

'And his wife and daughter?'

'They've aided and abetted him, they deserve it,' he said, looking at her sidelong. Her tone had tried to match his neutrality, but he had heard the hint of censure. 'Would you plead for their lives?'

She dropped her gaze. 'You must do as you see fit,' she murmured, 'but if you hang women, you will lose much respect and support I think. Men will see the beauty of Helwis de Corbette as she stands before the gibbet, and afterwards they will see what the rope has done to that beauty and they will blame you.'

'Yes, I'd come to that conclusion myself.' He rubbed the back of his neck. 'Besides, I'm not sure I'd be able to bring myself to give the order – too soft a marrow my father would say.'

'Then what will you do?'

'Put them out of the keep to make their own way. There are enough troops in Nottingham to assure them of employment. As long as I never see them again, I don't care.'

They reached the foot of the stairs and he took her arm to guide her into the depths of the undercroft. He was

131

aware of the scent of her, the closeness of her body, and felt an echo of yesterday's havoc ripple through him. Jesu, it was going to be hard to keep his distance for the required three months.

He raised the candle on high and showed her the dark, vaulted storeroom, its state of disarray sure evidence of sloppy housekeeping. She clicked her tongue and walked ahead of him, staring round.

'What about supplies elsewhere?' she asked him.

'I've included them in my estimations, but even so we're woefully short.' Drawing her between the pillars, he showed her the wine casks, the salted meats and the grain. 'See how the barrels are spread out? Close them together and you have next to nothing.'

Linnet lifted her gaze quickly to his. Unspoken between them lay the knowledge that a war was at hand and they were woefully unprepared to face it. No supplies, a sparse, demoralized garrison and villagers who were either hostile or indifferent.

Footsteps grated on the undercroft stairs and the light from a torch swirled around the walls. Joscelin turned quickly. 'Who's there?' he demanded sharply.

'Henry, my lord. I knew as you was down here; I saw you unlocking the door.' The servant rounded the corner of the newel post and peered down anxiously. 'There's a messenger arrived, says he's come from the Ju . . . Justiciar?' He stumbled over the last unfamiliar word. 'My sister's given him somat to drink and settled him at the high table.'

'Did he give his name?'

'Yes, sir . . . Brien FitzRenard?' Henry stared around the undercroft, absorbing every detail.

Joscelin nodded and moved towards the stairs. 'Prove that I can trust you and you'll be well rewarded,' he said to Henry, the arch of his brow more eloquent than the tone of his voice.

'I ain't seen or heard a thing, sir.' Henry was swift to take the hint and held the torch on high to light the way

132

up the stairs. 'We're always short o' supplies this time o' year.'

Henry was trying too hard, Joscelin thought, exchanging a brief glance over his shoulder with Linnet, but he let it pass, recognizing the man's underlying anxiety to please.

FitzRenard had left the dais where Henry's sister had served him hot wine, and was restlessly prowling the hall. His garments were powdered with dust and there was a grim set to his mouth, but when he saw Joscelin he relaxed enough to smile.

'I'm sorry to take you from your toil,' he said, nodding at Joscelin's tunic.

Glancing down, Joscelin brushed perfunctorily at the cobwebs and smears of old mortar festooning his garments. 'I've been hunting rats in the undercroft – two-legged ones.'

'Ah.' FitzRenard nodded with understanding sympathy. Dishonest household officials were an all too common hazard in large baronies, particularly one such as this where a guiding hand had not been secure on the reins for the past two years at least.

'What brings you to Rushcliffe?' Joscelin took the cup of wine that Linnet offered him.

'You know that Robert of Leicester was sailing for Normandy with an aid of money and men for the King? Well, Leicester's done what we half-suspected he would do and turned rebel. Instead of joining the King, he's ridden straight for his own lands and declared for Young Henry. The shore-watch has been alerted, the shire levies are being called up, and every baron is required to swear his loyalty to the King. Those who do not are by default rebels and their estates forfeit. I'm riding north with the Justiciar's writ commanding the oaths of fealty and serving notice to stand to arms.'

'Anyone who trespasses on these lands will be taking the short road to hell on the edge of my sword,' Joscelin said, his voice quiet, his tone saturated in possessive vehemence.

FitzRenard eyed him. In the five years he had known

133

him, Joscelin had never seemed to care that he was a landless bastard, forced to live by his weapons and his wits. His attitude had always been one of shrug and smile, but perhaps it was a shield behind which ambition and resentment had simmered with silent intensity. Being himself the fourth son in a potent Welsh Marcher family, his own position was similar to Joscelin's in that he had had to earn rather than inherit a living, and he understood how keenly the desire to succeed could bite.

'Is my father still in London?'

'No. Actually we rode part of the way here together; he was escorting his womenfolk back to Arnsby.' Brien gave Joscelin a shrewd grey glance. 'Your brothers were not with him, apart from the little one, and it was more than my life was worth to enquire after them. From what I did glean, they've joined Leicester's rebellion.'

'Yes, they have,' Joscelin said shortly and changed the subject. 'Are you resting here the night, or are you bound elsewhere?'

'I've to go on to Newark, but I was hoping for a bed tonight and a fresh horse in the morning. My grey's got a leg strain. I can collect him and reimburse you on the way back south.' Brien sent a slow, perusing glance around the great hall. 'I had no inkling that Rushcliffe was so large. You have landed on your feet indeed.'

'I have landed,' Joscelin retorted, 'up to my neck in dung.'

Undeceived, Brien smiled. Despite the complaint, he had heard the note of proprietorial satisfaction in Joscelin's voice and seen the glance he cast at his bride-to-be.

A soldier entered the hall from the forebuilding, looked around, and strode rapidly towards their group. Joscelin's head came up like a hound scenting the wind. 'What is it, Guy?'

'Corbette's gone, sir,' Montauban panted, pressing his hand to the stitch in his side. 'The gate guards say he and his family rode out an hour since.'

'And the guards did not see fit to stop them?'

'No, sir. They assumed you had ordered Corbette to leave because all his belongings were loaded on three pack ponies and all the men knew that there had been strong words between you already.'

Joscelin swore through his teeth. He could not blame the guards for their action. He had given them no instructions to detain the seneschal until now and their reasoning was only logical. 'All right, Guy. Tell the grooms to saddle up the horses. We should still be able to pick up their trail.'

'Yes, sir.' Montauban saluted and hurried away.

Brien cocked an enquiring brow. 'Trouble?'

'The seneschal's been bleeding Rushcliffe white for the past year and a half at least. He knows I'm wise to him, so he's run, doubtless with his pockets crammed at Rushcliffe's expense. I should have arrested him last night, not waited until I had positive evidence.'

'Lend me a horse and I'll come with you.' Brien put his glazed cup down on the nearest trestle.

'Be welcome,' Joscelin said with a brisk nod, then turned his attention to Linnet, who was looking at him with dismay. 'What's the matter?'

'You're as battered and bruised as a tiltyard dummy!' she cried. 'What of your shoulder? If you are pulling yourself in and out of a saddle and controlling a war-horse, you'll tear the wound open again. Even now it should be in a sling.'

He gave her a left shouldered shrug. 'It will hold up for what needs to be done.'

'Surely Milo could go in your stead. He has not a mark on him,' she pointed out.

'The responsibility is mine. Some things I can delegate elsewhere, but not this. I promise to be careful,' he added soothingly.

Her eyes narrowed and her jaw tilted stubbornly. 'Then let me at least add some more padding to your bandages – for my peace of mind if not yours.'

Joscelin drew breath to deny that he required any such tending, but Linnet was quicker.

'You have to come to the bedchamber anyway to put on your hauberk, and it won't take a moment.'

His lips closed, and then slowly curved in a smile. He inclined his head in amused capitulation, realizing himself outmanoeuvred. 'If you were a swordsman, you'd be deadly,' he said admiringly.

Linnet went pink and turned away to the stairs.

'You've seen some fighting already then?' asked Brien.

'A skirmish.' Once more Joscelin shrugged, his eyes following the sway of Linnet's hips. 'I'll tell you about it while we ride.'

CHAPTER 15

FINDING CORBETTE'S TRAIL was a simple matter for a seasoned troop of mercenaries who were accustomed like wolves to hunting in a cooperative pack, their senses sharpened by the proximity of their prey.

Corbette could only have taken the one road, and all that Joscelin had to decide was whether to pursue it to Newark or Nottingham. The latter led through the village, and since Corbette was heartily disliked there, Joscelin sent Guy de Montauban to question the people. Henry accompanied the soldier to reassure the villagers and translate the local tongue, Guy having few words of Anglo-Dane. A bag of silver went with them too, to loosen reluctant tongues. Following his own suspicions, Joscelin took the road towards Newark at a rapid trot.

Within two miles those suspicions were confirmed when they came across a lame pony grazing among a flock of sheep. It still wore a rope pack bridle and there were cinch marks branded in sweat on its belly. When it saw the soldier's horses, it nickered and limped eagerly to greet them. The pony bore a distinctive star marking on his forehead and Joscelin recognized it as one of the sturdy Clevelands that had carried supplies on the journey between London and Rushcliffe.

The wind ruffled the grass. A small shred of colour fluttered upon the spikes of a young hawthorn bush growing against a crumbling stone wall. Dismounting, Joscelin went to investigate and discovered a blue silk headshawl and nearby a linen bolster stuffed with women's clothing.

'They've had to lighten their load,' he commented to Brien with satisfaction. 'We're on the right track. Jean, go back to the village and fetch Sir Guy.' Joscelin remounted and strapped the bundle to his crupper.

A mile further on, a narrow cart track branched off the road to give access to one of the minor farmsteads beholden to Rushcliffe. Thick woodland lay to one side of the track, open fields to the other. Nestling in the sheltered corner of a dip in the undulating wolds stood the farm buildings – a longhouse in the old Saxon style, together with a barn and outbuildings.

The main building was on fire.

The breeze backed and eddied and the smell of smoke obliterated the perfumes of summer greenery. Ripples of heat zigzagged and shimmered, giving the burning farm the illusion of being under water.

'It doesn't look as if someone's just been careless with their cooking fire,' Brien unstrapped his helm from his saddle bow.

Joscelin heard the tension in Brien's voice. The thought of Leicester's rebellion was uppermost in everyone's mind, but surely it was too soon for this kind of trouble . . . unless this was concerned with the skirmish on the road yesterday. Perhaps it was done by way of petty revenge. He hesitated briefly, then shook the reins and urged Whitesocks onwards.

As he drew closer to the farmstead, the eddies of smoke strengthened and the stallion pranced nervously beneath him. He almost lost control of him when they came upon the body of a horse stretched across the rutted track. It was a palfrey this time, a dainty black barb mare. One foreleg was broken and, because of it Joscelin assumed, someone had cut her throat. A thick cloud of flies buzzed on the blackening blood at her muzzle. Of harness there was not a sign, although her hide still bore the impression of bridle and saddle.

Feeling cold, the hairs prickling at his nape, Joscelin steadied Whitesocks and rode on. The smell of burning was now woven with the crackling noise of feeding flames. In places all the flesh of the farm building had been devoured, and the wooden bones were enveloped in greedy red tongues of fire. Beside the track, face down in the grass, was a body.

Armand de Corbette had been stripped of his fine garments and was clad in nought but his linen braies. Three diagonal slashes were carved across his corpse as if he were a mackerel newly prepared for griddling. One eye glared. The other was concealed against the bloodied earth. Joscelin dismounted and, holding the reins fast in one hand, crouched to touch the edges of the gaping wounds.

Brien's face twisted. 'What are you doing?'

Joscelin rubbed the wetness of blood between his thumb and fingertips. 'Seeking answers. Look at these cuts. Whoever did this had a good sword and some useful weight behind his swing. These are sword blows. An axe would have left a broader, deeper wound. A scram would not have caused as much damage as this.'

Brien shrugged. 'So why does it matter how he was killed?' He averted his gaze from the layers of underlying creamy fat glistening in the light.

Joscelin stood up and drew his own sword. 'It matters because only a man of wealth or long fighting ability would own a sword.' Raising his own, he turned it with a flick of his wrist. 'And only a man who sells his services would strip a body of clothing. I've done it myself in winters past when an extra cloak means the difference between living and freezing.'

'So you think this is the work of mercenaries?'

'Probably.' Joscelin began to prowl in the direction of the palisade that surrounded the burning farm buildings. A stifled sob close on his left made Whitesocks throw up his head and snort with alarm. Joscelin calmed the horse and stared at the reeds and sedge bordering the muddy ditch at the foot of the low palisade slope. 'Come out where I can see you,' he commanded.

Two women, one young and heavily pregnant, the other in her late thirties but still handsome, emerged from their hiding place in a clump of feather reeds. Their gowns' hems were mud-stained and heavy with water. The younger woman was hysterical, wailing and clutching her gravid belly. Her companion, however, chose attack as the best form of defence now that they had been discovered.

'You'll not be laying your filthy hands on us!' she screamed, brandishing her chopping knife at the startled men. 'Heathen whoresons. Get back to the hell you came from!'

'No one's going to harm you,' Joscelin said rapidly in the native tongue. 'I am Joscelin de Gael, appointed by the Crown to be your new lord. What has happened here? Where are your menfolk?'

The woman stared at him over the haft of the raised knife. The blade was stained as if she had recently been cutting vegetables. Her gaze pointedly absorbed the bare sword in his hand before slashing over the troop of rough-looking soldiers surrounding him, of whom only Brien looked fit to be respected. 'Rushcliffe has had many new lords lately,' she said. An expression bordering on contempt flickered in her pale eyes.

'For good or ill, I'm here to stay. If it is to be good, then I need your help,' Joscelin said, hoping that her disillusion was not too deeply entrenched.

Neither eyes nor expression thawed, but after a silence while she pursed her lips and sucked her teeth she chose to speak. 'Men came with weapons. Their tongue was foreign, but not French like they speak up at the castle. We saw them coming: we heard them too, the bastards, because they was chasing the seneschal and he was screaming like a trapped coney. Our menfolk have gone to the mill to get some of our corn sheaves ground into flour, else they'd be dead too.' She put her arm around the younger woman whose anguished wails had diminished to snuffles and sobs.

'Me and Meg was outside feeding the poultry when we heard the commotion, and when we looked up the track we saw the seneschal and his family being attacked and robbed by these foreign soldiers. I made Meg drop everything straightaway and we ran to hide in the ditch.' She shuddered. 'We could hear them yellin' and boastin'. Madam Corbette was screaming and swearing, calling 'em all the names under the sun, and they was laughing. I was sure they'd discover us, the sounds was so close.' The woman's eyes glittered with angry, unshed tears. 'Next thing we knew the farm was on fire. How are we supposed to live now with the rent due in two months' time and all our stores gone?'

'You needn't worry about that,' Joscelin said impatiently. 'I'll see to it that you're not destitute. How many soldiers did you see?'

'I don't rightly know, only got a couple o' glimpses.' She counted laboriously on her fingers. ''Bout a score I suppose, but only half of them had horses. They took the seneschal's destrier, and Madam's palfrey. They'd have had our old cob too if Rob and Will hadn't taken him to the mill this morning.' Bleakly, over her companion's head, she surveyed the burning buildings. 'This was my father's place, built it from wasteland with his own hands, he did. We'd heard rumours o' trouble, of course, but we thought it was all ale-talk. King Henry won't stand for no nonsense from his sons we said.' Her chin wobbled and she fiercely compressed her lips and glared bitterly at Joscelin.

'I will go surety for the King's justice on all Rushcliffe lands,' Joscelin said firmly. 'If there are bands of reavers at large of whatever faction, I will deal with them and swiftly.'

'Yes, my lord.' Her tone was sceptical. Anger stirred within him, but he held it down. The local population were descendants of the old communities of the Norse Danelaw and had more reason than most to hate their Norman overlords. A hundred years ago the Conqueror had purged the region. Every native-born male over the age of fifteen had been slaughtered and every home razed to the ground. During the slow years of recovery the people of Rushcliffe had endured the arrogant dominance of four generations of the Montsorrel family, Raymond and Giles being less than scions of their illustrious house. It

141

was easy to rule the demesne from the saddle of a war-horse and kick aside anyone who obstructed your path.

'Go to the castle,' he told the women. 'Ask for Lady Linnet and tell her that I sent you. Henry will escort you there.' He gestured at the wide-eyed manservant.

The older woman stared at him long and hard, then nodded brusquely, the closest he was going to get to approbation. And then her eyes changed, focusing on something beyond him, and the pregnant woman shrieked, her knees buckling.

Joscelin whirled round and saw a motley assortment of horsemen and foot soldiers advancing towards them from the direction of the woods. The leading horse was the seneschal's handsome piebald stallion, and the warrior astride it had the raddled face of a fallen angel. A scar running from left mouth corner to mutilated left ear tilted and creased his grin, transforming it into a leer as he drew rein before Joscelin.

'Greetings, nephew,' said Conan de Gael, performing a mocking salute with the hilt of his drawn sword.

'We heard in Nottingham that the Rushcliffe honour was yours.' Conan shook his head, the grin still in place, and reclined on one elbow in the grass. 'Lucky bastard – no offence intended.'

Joscelin was not deceived by his uncle's air of relaxed affability. The hazel-green eyes were as hard as stones and although the mercenary had removed his sword in token of goodwill, he would still have a knife in his boot and another up his sleeve. 'I could be forgiven for disbelieving you,' he replied, nodding at the smoke still choking out from the farm building. An ox that had been slaughtered in the earlier mayhem had been carved into chunks and was now roasting over a purpose-built firepit. The two peasant women had retired to a distance, but Joscelin could feel their hatred boring into his spine together with their belief that he was a worse devil than the two previous lords of Rushcliffe had ever been.

'Ah, come now Josce, that wasn't my fault.'

'Wasn't it?'

Conan drew his meat dagger from his belt and, rising, went to the firepit and tested a lump of meat to see if it was cooked. The women glared at him. Conan saluted them, the tip of his knife holding a sizzling, bloody chunk of their plough ox. 'We bumped into your seneschal and his family on the road. Course, I didn't know he was yours then and a man has to have the money to eat and clothe himself – you know that. If a fatted calf walks up to you dripping in wealth, it's just begging to be sacrificed. It was obvious he was on the run with some very ill-gotten gains.' The mercenary tore a shred of blackened meat off the edge of the beef portion and chewed vigorously. 'The two women with him ran like headless chickens into the longhouse and barred the door against us. One of them must have caught her gown in the hearth, because next thing we knew the place was on fire, and the flames too fierce for any of us to get near enough to rescue either of them, more's the pity. The younger one was a tasty dish.'

Joscelin eyed Conan narrowly. 'I saw my seneschal's body,' he said. 'In the old days you'd not have mutilated the dead.'

Conan spat out a knurl of gristle. 'That was Godred's work.' He jabbed his head in the direction of a young bearded soldier sitting close to the firepit, moodily prodding the glowing embers with a stick. 'He's not fond of Normans at the best of times, and the way we were treated in Nottingham was bound to have repercussions.'

'What do you mean, the way you were treated in Nottingham? What were you doing there in the first place? I thought you were in Normandy.'

'We sailed in the late spring, just before Pentecost. Trouble was brewing and men of our trade have to sell our swords where we can ... unless we land ourselves an heiress.' He flashed Joscelin a mocking glance. 'We took employment with Robert Ferrers, the great Earl of Derby and Lord of Nottingham town.' He spat another piece of gristle into the grass. 'Ever worked for him, Josce?'

'No. He might have several fiefs in Nottingham, but the castle itself belongs to the Crown. My employer was always the sheriff, FitzRanulf.'

Brien said thoughtfully, 'I have heard that Ferrers is a haphazard paymaster?'

'Haphazard? Hah! If we saw four shillings a week between us we counted ourselves fortunate. When I tackled him about it, he threw us out, said that he could get Flemings for half as much as he was paying us and that we were lucky he hadn't thrown us in his dungeon for presumption. Arrogant, soft-cocked wind-bladder! he's lucky I didn't slit his gizzard to silence him.' He wiped his bloody knife blade on the grass.

'Instead you slit my seneschal's,' growled Joscelin.

'You didn't want him, did you? You ought to be grateful.'

Joscelin snorted. 'I don't see why.'

'Did Ferrers hire you for any particular purpose?' asked Brien.

'No, just building up his troops in the area. When we were in Nottingham, we were billeted in some ramshackle houses of his near a stinking marsh with tanneries right next door. I've seen better cesspits.'

'But he said he was going to replace you with Flemings?'

'Flemings, Brabants, whoever he could get the cheapest,' Conan said with a shrug. 'Of course, like us, they'll have to cross the narrow sea. Be quite an invasion, eh? If you ask me, they'll come piecemeal, rounded up by those rebellious earls of yours and sent over here with promises of riches beyond their greediest imaginings. Mind you, most of 'em won't be professional soldiers – jobless weavers and dyers for the most part.'

'But you are not part of the vanguard?' questioned Brien.

Conan narrowed his eyes suspiciously. 'You want to know a mortal great deal.' His blond brows drew together across the bridge of his strong, straight nose.

'Brien is the Justiciar's adjutant and messenger,' Joscelin explained, and was amused by the look of consternation that briefly flickered in Conan's eyes. 'It is his sworn duty to discover as much as he can about the doings of the rebellious barons.'

'Well don't look to me,' Conan grumbled. 'I can tell you more about the latrine habits of Nottingham tanners than I can about the doings of William Ferrers. All he said was that he was going to replace us with Flemings, but he didn't disclose their source. And we're not part of anyone's vanguard, although there's hiring aplenty going on across the narrow sea.'

Joscelin regarded Conan with a mixture of exasperation and curiosity. 'What are you really doing in England when Normandy is your true field?'

Conan sucked his teeth and eased a fingernail between the front two to loosen a tag of meat. 'I'm not getting any younger – eight and forty next Christmastide, although I know I don't look it. One day experience won't be enough to save me from some youngster's sword and I'll be glad to die. But before that happens, I've to attend to some personal family business.' He looked pointedly at Brien, who was swift to take a hint and, rising to his feet, went to cut himself some meat from the ox.

When he was out of earshot Conan said, 'I have come to make my peace with your father . . . and Morwenna.'

'You might find that difficult,' Joscelin said. 'My father never talks about her. If I bring up the subject he looks at me as if I have deliberately stabbed him.'

Conan grunted. 'When your mother died it tore him apart. He begot on her the child that killed her. He wasn't there to catch her when she tripped on the hem of her gown and fell down the stairs. You'll never reason it away from him. God knows I tried in the months after her death, and in the end he kicked me out because he wanted to wear his guilt like a hair-shirt for the rest of his life.'

'He has made a shrine of his guilt now,' Joscelin said tonelessly. 'Near his hunting lodge in Arnsby woods there

145

is a chapel of white Caen stone built to house my mother's remains. He has masses said for her every day and candles lit, and there is a tomb of the finest Chellaston alabaster.'

Conan shook his head and stared dumbly at Joscelin, as if unsure whether to be pleased or appalled.

'The first time I saw the white chapel I wept,' Joscelin confessed. 'He had it built after I ran away to become a mercenary. In part I think it was a shrine for me too. He never thought to see me again.' He looked at the ground and stirred the grass with the toe of his boot.

'He probably wouldn't have either, if it were not for me!' Conan chose to remind him, his voice loud and over-hearty. 'You were greener than the grass stains on a whore's gown when you arrived in my camp!'

'I was, wasn't I?' Joscelin glanced sideways at his uncle, not in the least deceived. Conan was deeply affected by what he had just been told and, rather than flounder a reply, had taken refuge in coarse bantering.

'You grew up fast though.'

Joscelin arched his brow. 'I had no choice.'

Conan gently massaged his disfiguring scar with two fingers. 'Nay, I don't suppose you did,' he said in a gentler tone. 'I saw your woman, Breaca, the month before we sailed. She gave me board and lodging in Rouen for two nights.'

'She's not my woman any longer,' Joscelin said and returned to stirring the grass. He watched the shiny, stiff stems bend and spring upright. Then he glanced at Conan. 'Is she happy?'

'Merry as a nesting sparrow with three fine fledglings to show to the world – two little wenches and a baby boy in the cradle. She told me to wish you well the next time I saw you, and to say that you and Juhel are constantly in her prayers.'

Joscelin bit the inside of his mouth. After Juhel had died, he had been unable to hold Breaca. She had been at a crossroads age, craving a roof over her head and more security than he could provide. In the year of grieving

146

determination it had taken him to become a competent, tough soldier, standing on his own merits and paid accordingly, she had ceased following the mercenary road from one war to the next, and settled down with a tavern-keeper from Rouen. 'She is in my thoughts and prayers too,' he said softly. 'And if she has found what she wants, then I'm glad for her.' There was an ache behind his eyes and a tightness in his throat. He changed the subject. 'Are you seeking employment now?'

The older man eyed him suspiciously. 'Why?'

'I'm short of troops. Indeed, I was thinking of riding into Nottingham to hire men, but since you've already lined your purse with Rushcliffe's silver, perhaps you and your men would like the position?'

Conan stared. He grasped the drawstring pouch at his belt and waggled it at Joscelin. 'What do you mean? See, it's as empty as a hag's tit!'

'You're not going to tell me that my seneschal rode into your troop wearing nothing but his drawers?' Joscelin scoffed. 'If those woods behind us are searched, I warrant they'll yield up more than just the odd fallen bird's nest!'

Conan continued to stare. Despite his best effort his lips twitched and in a moment he was lost to a full grin. Joscelin himself was similarly afflicted, the compression of his lips owing more to amusement than anger, and his hazel eyes bright with laughter.

'You are your father's son,' Conan growled by way of capitulation.

'And my uncle's nephew,' Joscelin retorted.

CHAPTER 16

'LOOK MAMA, WHAT ARE they doing?' Robert wriggled upright on the saddle to point at the cage of scaffolding confining Arnsby's tall, octagonal keep. Men stood on platforms, or toiled on the ground, caparisoning the monstrous stone beast in white summer plumage.

'They're giving it a fresh coat of limewash to protect it from the weather,' Joscelin said over his shoulder and slowed his courser so that Linnet could join him. 'We've to do the same to Rushcliffe before the winter comes.'

'Why?'

'To protect the stone from the bad weather and keep it strong.'

Robert sucked his underlip while he considered the reply. Linnet had watched her son gain rapidly in confidence during the weeks following Giles's death. Given space to breathe without being slapped, glared at or found lacking, Robert had begun to emerge from his shell – tentatively at first, with much drawing in of horns, but growing bolder by the day. Joscelin had put him on an ancient pack pony in the tiltyard and had begun teaching him to ride. He had fashioned a small, blunt-tipped lance for him and a wooden sword. Conan de Gael, Joscelin's uncle, had played at knights and outlaws with Robert and conceded defeat with dramatic death throes much to her son's consternation and delight. And Robert, so silent and withdrawn before his father's death, had started asking questions. One after another they tumbled out of him, queuing up to trip off his busy tongue. Why is the sky blue? Why don't people have fur like coneys? How does Job the shepherd know when it's going to rain?

Where does the sea go when the tide is out?

'Why are we here?'

'I told you; to visit Sir Joscelin's father.' Linnet kissed Robert's fair hair.

'Why?'

'Because I need to talk to him,' Joscelin said. 'Here, come and sit on my saddle and stop bedevilling your mother with questions. You can guide Whitesocks if you want.'

The words were no sooner spoken than accomplished. Robert scrambled with alacrity from his mother's arms into Joscelin's and settled there as if they had been his security since birth.

They approached the open gateway, the horses' hooves thudding on the solid drawbridge planks. The huge iron pulley chains were speckled with limewash and there were splashes of it like enormous bird droppings on the bridge itself. Robert's small hand pointed and he chirruped a question. Joscelin bent over him and responded with patient good humour. A pang cut through Linnet to see them thus – the familiar sensations of guilt and love and a deeper, primal twisting of heart, gut and womb.

'Ach,' said Conan softly as he joined her on the draw-bridge, 'Give him a child and he turns to butter.'

There was a strange note in the mercenary's voice that caused Linnet to raise her head and look at him curiously. 'Certainly my son has taken to him,' she replied. 'And in London, I met him in the company of his youngest brother.' She looked thoughtfully at the mercenary. He was wearing a somewhat garish tunic of northern plaid and riding Corbette's piebald stallion. Bracelets of copper and silver jangled in abundance on his tattooed forearms. The word disreputable came easily to mind. And yet he had helped ungrudgingly with his own war-scarred hands to rebuild the farmhouse and paid good silver to have masses said over the two women who had died. 'You must know Joscelin very well.'

Conan shrugged. The fur-edged cloak he wore made his

149

shoulders look broad and powerful. 'Yes and no, my lady. He came to me when he was fifteen, stubborn, proud and half-starved.' A sardonic grin curled his scarred lips. 'I took him in and I took him on, taught him the bare fist and teeth side of fighting, the kind that keeps you alive.'

'Like a knife down your boot?' she asked, her mouth curving.

Conan chuckled. 'Never be without one.' He regarded Joscelin as he was swallowed by the darkness of the port-cullis arch and emerged again into the bright sunshine of the courtyard. 'His own lad was about Robert's age when he died,' he added quietly. 'It's a hard life for a mother and child in a mercenary baggage train. It is a good thing that Joscelin has a place of his own to settle now, and a family. There's as much hunger in his soul as there is in his damned father's.'

They entered the darkness themselves, emerged into light. Linnet was unaware of blinking in the brilliance, nor did she feel the warmth of the sun, for a chill had run down her spine. 'You are telling me that he was married once?'

'They never had a priest say the words over them or witness borne to their handfasting – Breaca wasn't one for fuss or ceremony, but they were together for more than five years and she bore him a child. After the lad died, she wandered with us for a little longer, but it was finished between her and Joscelin. She married a widower in Rouen and settled down with him to run a hostelry.'

Linnet swallowed, feeling dizzy, and Conan leaned closer, taking her upper arm in his strong calloused hand. 'I'd prefer you to keep it to yourself, lass. Not even his father knows the tale, and Josce would kill me if he thought I'd been interfering in his private concerns. But I thought it was something of which you should be aware.' Releasing his grip, he leaped lightly from his mount and stood at her stirrup to help her down.

Linnet thought that he deserved killing, to spring some-thing like this upon her at a moment when she needed all her social skills to be polite to her betrothed's unpleasant father. She shivered, feeling queasy as she wondered how many untold secrets would scrabble and whisper in the dark beneath their marriage bed, feeding and growing on the guilt until one night, darker than the rest, they would rage out and destroy everything in their path.

Robert's hand clasped in his, Joscelin appeared at her side. She saw his glance flicker to Conan's blandly innocent expression. 'What has he been saying to you?'

He spoke lightly and there was a smile on his face, but she was still reminded of Giles, who had been suspicious of her every conversation with another man. 'I . . .' The words stuck in her throat and her mind went blank with panic.

'I was just giving her some friendly advice on how to be a dutiful wife to my nephew,' Conan said smoothly. 'If she is lost for words it is because she cannot repeat what I told her without being indelicate.' He winked at her, slapped Joscelin hard on the shoulder, and turned to face the keep. 'Hasn't changed a stone in twenty years! I always liked this place – good and solid, a gem to defend against siege.'

The horses were led away to the stables. Linnet pressed her damp hands against her cloak and regained her composure. Just another lie to live, she thought, and not even the greatest of them. She shut her new knowledge in the darkness where the other lies fed and multiplied on their abundant supply of guilt and fear.

Agnes de Rocher pushed the weft through the narrow shed of the wool braid she was weaving, knocked down the twisted threads into the pattern, and stared at her work with dissatisfaction. The tension was uneven, dictated by her mood at the different times she had sat down to the work and the braid snaked broad, thin and slantwise by turns like the unruly river of her thoughts. The colours were supposed to be autumnal – gold, brown and soft green, but they looked sallow, without enough contrast to make them interesting.

She laid down the wooden weaving tablets on the trestle and secured them with another piece of completed braid. Her hands were smooth and adorned with gold rings as befitted a baron's wife. They were also fat and clumsy, her flesh puffing around the gold like half-risen dough. She had never regained her figure after Martyn's birth and her body was slack and soft, a worn-out vessel. She was glad that William had not offered her the luxury of a gazing glass as he had offered one to his mistress. Agnes knew that if she should see her own reflection warped and distorted in polished steel, the real Agnes de Rocher would step from the quivering surface of the mirror and show the world hands that were steeped in blood to the wrists.

Her secret had been concealed for almost twenty-five years now and was like an unborn child that still kicked beneath her heart, causing her pleasure and discomfort. Despite the fact that each year its enormity grew, she had no pressing urge to deliver it into the arms of a priest. To her husband perhaps, ripped out and bloody with the triumph of revenge, but thus far she had resisted temptation.

Sometimes in the corner of her eye she would see for an instant the insubstantial form of Morwenna de Gael, luxuriant brown hair rippling down her back, the hem of her green velvet gown trailing the floor rushes, and her body ripe with the promise of new life never to come to fruition. Agnes often heard Morwenna's last scream when she set her own foot on the stairs that twisted down to the level of the great hall. Morwenna, the bitch and the whore, not content with just sharing William's bed, had taken everything from him that she could – his honour, duty and affection, and made sure that there was nothing left for his rightful wife. Indeed, Morwenna had been so greedy as to swallow it all into that faultless white crypt he had built for her. Agnes curled her fingers around her embroidery shears and scored the trestle, gouging a narrow white scar.

Her mind was far less free to wander when her sister-in-law was in attendance. Maude's cheerful, inquisitive nature, her sheer garrulity, left little space for Agnes to brood. But Maude had found the excuse of visiting a pensioned-off servant at a convent close to Newark and would not be back for two days at least. Agnes knew that Maude found her company a trial and was always eager for moments of escape.

A small sound in the doorway caused Agnes to jump and conceal the shears within her hand. She narrowed her eyes the better to focus on the young woman and child standing in the doorway behind her maid. Surely she knew them, and recently so?

'Lady Linnet de Montsorrel,' announced the maid and stepped aside so that the visitor could enter Agnes's private sanctum. William had his own room on the opposite side of the castle and would not come to this one unless forced. The coven, he called it, not entirely in jest – a refuge for hags.

Agnes's thick eyebrows shot up, then came down hard in a frown. She remembered now. Maude had been asked to take care of Linnet de Montsorrel in the days immediately following the husband's death as the result of being rolled upon by a mad horse at Smithfield Fair. That she was Giles de Montsorrel's widow was a matter of supreme indifference to Agnes. That she was betrothed to the whore's bastard and brought with her a marriage portion to elevate him at one stride from hired soldier to baron of the realm, made her blood simmer with bile.

'This is indeed an unlooked-for pleasure,' she said through stiff lips and carefully laid the shears back down on the board, covering the jagged scratch she had made. 'Will you sit down?' A peremptory gesture sent another maid hurrying to plump the cushions of a box chair. Agnes looked Linnet coldly up and down. The wimple of pale blue silk was secured by a plaited circlet in a darker shade, both giving emphasis to the fine grey-blue eyes. Her cloak of double-lined Flemish twill was cut in the English style to show the soft grey overgown and undertunic of flax-blue linen. From her gilded belt hung a purse and an exquisitely tooled ivory needlecase. The hem of the over-gown was trimmed with tablet-woven braid such as Agnes was making, but of a far superior quality to the effort lying on the table. Her antipathy increased. It would have been easier to offer the semblance of hospitality to Linnet de Montsorrel had she been plain of feature and dressed less immaculately. Agnes had never felt anything but distrust and revulsion for women who possessed style or beauty.

'Thank you, Lady Agnes.' Linnet approached the chair, Robert hanging back reluctantly and looking over his shoulder at the door.

'Have you come alone?'

The maid went to a cupboard standing against the wall and took out a pair of handsome glazed earthenware cups.

'No, my lady.' Linnet hesitated, feeling uncomfortable beneath Agnes's cold, almost fishy stare. 'You must know that Joscelin is here to see his father.'

Agnes nodded contemptuously. 'I knew it wouldn't be long before he came prowling to Arnsby like a starving wolf after a pen of sheep. And he was bound to bring you – his prize.'

'It was a matter of courtesy that he brought me,' Linnet replied, matching Agnes's glacial tones, and sat down on the edge of the offered chair. Robert climbed on to her knee and wrapped his arms tightly around her neck. 'I see now that it was a mistake.'

'Oh, no mistake on *his* part,' Agnes sneered. Her skirts swished upon the rushes as she turned, and her fists clenched and unclenched spasmodically. 'Nigh on thirty years I have lived with the humiliation. My sons count for nothing in William's eyes and yet he'd move heaven and earth for the bastard of that conniving whore! I well know why Joscelin is here.'

'I think you are overwrought, Lady Agnes.' Linnet was shocked by the older woman's bitterness. 'Joscelin is here to talk to his father about borrowing supplies for Rushcliffe.'

'Doubtless that is the excuse he would mouth to anyone gullible enough to believe such a lie. He has come because his brothers are involved in Leicester's rebellion, and he thinks to secure Arnsby's inheritance for himself.'

'You malign him, Lady Agnes. Even if Joscelin did desire Arnsby of his father, you still have another son at home, and I know that he loves Martyn dearly.'

'Martyn is a child, not yet nine years old,' Agnes snapped. 'He's hardly a threat.'

'Even so, I know that Joscelin is not here with the intention of disinheriting his brothers,' Linnet defended and then, unable to prevent herself, added waspishly, 'they are quite capable of accomplishing that feat themselves.'

Agnes made a clucking sound, her face scarlet.

'The only other reason we are here is that Joscelin has brought his uncle, Conan de Gael, to make his peace with Lord William.'

The red wattling of temper faded from Agnes's face, leaving it the skull-white of pure rage. The limp edges of her wimple trembled and her hands grasped and flexed at the air. 'You dare to come here to my private chamber and utter the name of that hell-begotten, swindling pimp?' She was so full of fury that she could hardly force the words out.

Linnet sprang to her feet, afraid that Agnes was going to assault her physically. The maid, who had been about to present Linnet with a cup of mead, hastily sidestepped to avoid spilling it. Taking Robert in her arms, Linnet went purposefully towards the door. 'I think it best if I leave,' she said with as much dignity as she could muster.

'I will have my say first,' Agnes snapped. She took three steps towards Linnet. The loose sole of her shoe caught in the hem of her undergown and sent her sprawling heavily to the floor. Her wimple tumbled off and her sparse, brownish-grey braids dangled against her neck like rats' tails. Her shriek sliced the space remaining between herself and Linnet like a boning knife.

The maid, a look of horror on her face, quickly put the

155

cups aside and stooped to her mistress. Linnet hesitated on the threshold of the room, desiring nothing more than to make her escape, but prevented by her conscience. Supposing Agnes had broken a bone or was having a seizure?

She set Robert on his feet. 'Do you think you can go down to the hall and find Conan and Joscelin?'

Robert looked up at his mother. 'You come too.' He tugged on her hand.

'I cannot. Lady Agnes needs help. Find Joscelin and stay with him until I come. Yes?'

Robert nodded, his underlip caught in his teeth.

'Good boy. Go on then, quickly.' Linnet hugged him and shooed him gently on his way. It was astonishing how swiftly Joscelin's name had become a talisman to the child. Mention it and a hundred doors opened where doors had not even existed before. Here he was in a place he did not know, turning from the security of her skirts because Joscelin was the prize.

Giving brisk orders to the frightened maid, Linnet checked Agnes for broken bones. Thankfully there were none and Agnes was able to rise and be helped to her bed. The sheets had a stale smell and there were smears and crumbs upon the counterpane. Linnet urged a cup of mead upon Agnes. Grey-faced, the woman obediently sipped, and in a few moments her colour began to return.

Her eyes cleared and she focused lucidly on Linnet. 'Dear Christ, how I envy your innocence,' she said wearily. 'I too was innocent once. I can see it in your eyes; you think I am mad, don't you?'

'I think certainly you are ill,' Linnet said, pity softening her attitude.

Agnes sniffed and looked bleakly at the wall where a plasterwork scene depicted two lovers seated at a merels board in a garden. 'William wants to lock me up in a nunnery. I'm past child-bearing now and naught but a burden to him.' She narrowed her eyes. With her grey hair hanging down, she reminded Linnet of an old female wolf. 'But I want him to carry his burden until it kills him, and then may he rot in hell with his precious whore!'

When Linnet rose to leave, Agnes did not try again to stop her, but rocked gently back and forth in her bed, cradling the mead cup as if it were an infant, and muttering softly to herself.

It had been more than twenty years since the last encounter between William de Rocher and Conan de Gael. On that occasion William had taken his sword and fought Conan from tower to tower, room to room, across the ward and out of Arnsby's gates. Then he had slammed them in the mercenary's face and ordered him never to return on pain of hanging.

Now, face to face, eyes on a level, blue to hazel, they confronted each other.

'Going to string me up then?' Conan enquired in his usual cocksure fashion and lounged upon his sword hip.

William sucked a sharp breath through his teeth as if he had been fisted in the gut. 'Don't tempt me,' he growled, and seizing hold of his belt, proceeded to throttle it as if he wished it were Conan's throat. 'Why are you here except to cause trouble?'

Conan clicked his tongue against his palate. 'You do me an injustice William, but then what has changed? You always have believed my motives to be the worst in the world. Don't worry, I do not intend lingering beneath your salt for long. I've about as much taste for your company as you have for mine.'

William glared at the mercenary.

'He's working for me,' Joscelin said calmly. 'I need seasoned men at my back with the trouble that's brewing, and Rushcliffe's garrison is as magnificent a collection of oafs and lack-wits as ever graced a fool's banquet.'

'And you must be a fool indeed if you're hiring him!' William snapped.

'Not so much that I would cut off my nose to spite my face,' Joscelin retorted, fixing his father with a hard stare. 'Would you rather he sold his sword to the rebellion?'

Ironheart ground such teeth as remained to him.

Conan smiled, the creases at his eye corners deepening with genuine amusement. 'I think he would,' he said to Joscelin. 'I could keep my eyes open for Ragnar then, couldn't I?'

Joscelin threw him a warning stare and made a short, chopping movement with his right hand. Unperturbed, Conan continued to smile, his scar turning his expression into a leer.

'Is he really your uncle?' asked Martyn, who had attached himself to the three men without being noticed until now. He looked upon Conan with the same bright curiosity he had given to the bear at Smithfield Fair.

Joscelin laughed and tousled his younger brother's cropped brown curls. 'I'm afraid he is, but don't let his appearance deceive you.' He raised his eyes to Conan. 'Although he's a liability when there's no one to fight, there are few people I'd rather have at my back on the battlefield.'

Conan raised a sardonic eyebrow. 'Kind of you to admit it,' he growled, but Joscelin could tell he was pleased.

'Why aren't you at sword practise?' William demanded roughly of his youngest son, laying a heavy hand on his shoulder.

Martyn looked fearlessly up at his father. 'Sir Alain sent me to get another sword. The old wooden one I was using broke.'

'And you are on your way now?'

'Yes, Papa. But I thought it only courteous to stop and greet our guests.'

William's lips twitched. With an effort he kept them straight. 'I doubt that it was courtesy that bid you stop. A long, inquisitive nose is nearer to the truth. Go on, hurry now, before you find yourself answering to Sir Alain for your tardiness.' He gave the boy's shoulder a swift shake and released him.

No sooner had Martyn gone, than Robert appeared, running down the hall, his blond hair gleaming. Panting, he flung himself at Joscelin, who swung him up into his arms.

'Where's your mother, does she know that you are here?'

Robert nodded and burrowed his head against Joscelin's throat, his arms tightening. Joscelin could feel the rapid pitter-patter of the child's heartbeat beneath his fingers. 'She sent me to stay with you,' Robert said. 'The lady we went to see wasn't very nice. I didn't like her, but she fell over and Mama stayed to help her get up.'

Joscelin looked across the boy's fair head at William.

'Agnes has been very difficult of late,' his father said with an impatient shrug and a look of distaste. 'She spends all her time brooding about Ragnar and Ivo and plotting ways to see them back into my favour.'

Joscelin cuddled Robert and said nothing. What could he say? It had always been Agnes's obsession to see Ragnar's star firmly established in Arnsby's firmament. And he himself had always been the comet that threatened to outblaze his half-brother. Given the present political circumstances, it was small wonder if Agnes spat venom to know that her eldest son's rival was here.

'In the spring, once Martyn has gone for fostering in de Luci's household, I'm going to buy her a corrody and settle her with the nuns at Southwell,' William added.

'Should have done it years ago, man,' Conan said bluntly. 'I've always thought she only had one oar in the water.'

William's mouth twisted. 'She is my penance,' he said. 'I have worn her presence like a hair-shirt for more than half my life.'

And she had worn his too for the sake of her sons, Joscelin thought, and was unlikely to agree to enter a nunnery while their future remained in doubt.

'I saw another lady on the stairs,' Robert piped up as his hero's attention strayed. 'A nice lady. She smelled like flowers.'

'Did she?' Joscelin said, not taking much notice.

'Her hair was longer than Mama's, nearly to her knees, and she was wearing a pretty green dress with dangly sleeves,' Robert babbled.

159

His words were like stones dropped in a pool. Ripples of silence expanded from them and drowned the men in shock. William's face turned the colour of ashes.

'Jesu!' muttered Conan and, crossing himself, stared at the child, a visible shudder lungeing down his spine.

'Did she speak to you?' Involuntarily Joscelin looked towards the dark entrance of the tower stairs, then raised his head to study the long walk of the gallery and the double row of oak rails. Sunlight from the tall windows above the dais gilded the spear tips impaling the family banners above the hearth. They stirred in the updraught from the flames. He could feel the erratic hard thud of his own pulse against the pressure of the child's body.

Robert shook his head. 'No, but she smiled and walked down the stairs with me so I wouldn't be frightened of the dark. She's gone now.'

The men looked at one another, not daring to voice what was shouting across their minds.

'No,' William said hoarsely, 'it cannot be true.'

'Belike it was one of your maids,' Conan said, his heartiness far too hollow for conviction. 'Or perhaps the lad has overheard something and embroidered it with his imagination.' His gaze went as Joscelin's had done to the dark tower mouth where they had found his sister unconscious, tangled in the folds of her green gown. He closed his eyes and did not open them again until he had turned to face William Ironheart. 'You asked me why I was here. I never did pay my respects at Morwenna's tomb. You threw me out, and said you would hang me like a common felon if I so much as set foot on Arnsby land. But that was a long time ago. We're old men now. I want to make peace with the past before it is too late for all of us.'

'There is no such thing as peace,' William replied hoarsely, his own eyes riveted on the tower entrance.

CHAPTER 17

THE CHAPEL DEDICATED to Morwenna de Gael stood on the edge of the forest, close to the village of Arnsby, but separated from it by the millstream which was crossed by means of an ancient hump-backed stone bridge. In front of the chapel, sheep cropped the grass, keeping it nibbled to a short turf starred with daisies and pink clover.

Linnet studied this shrine to Joscelin's mother. The white Caen stone wore a golden reflection of the afternoon sun. Arched windows eyebrowed with intricate stone-carved patterns viewed the world from dark irises of stained glass. A solid wooden door, handsomely decorated with barrings of wrought iron was wedged open, and a path of sunlight beckoned the eye over the stone flags of the threshold and into the nave. Beautiful and tranquil, she thought, so unlike the restless spirit that walked Arnsby's corridors in the minds of its occupants.

She glanced at Robert, whom Joscelin was lowering from his crupper on to the springy turf. Joscelin had told her what her son had said. 'He scared us half to death,' he grimaced wryly. 'Conan says it was probably one of the maids and we're all clinging to that belief but . . .' Then he had shrugged and spread his hands. 'It is strange all the same, very strange.'

Linnet watched Robert kneel in the grass and cup his hands around a ladybird. The sunlight made a numbus of his hair and his face was open and bright with pleasure. Whatever he had seen or absorbed on that stair had done him no harm. Any darkness had settled on the adults long ago and was probably of their own making. She thought of Agnes de Rocher with mixed feelings of pity and revulsion. The woman was a victim of her own bitterness and hatred.

Joscelin was waiting at her stirrup, and he held up his arms to lift her down. 'Why the frown?' he queried.

'Nothing.' Her brow cleared and she shook her head. 'I was thinking of your father's wife and there but for the grace of God . . .' She descended into his arms, twisting slightly to avoid hurting his wounded shoulder.

'She upset you, didn't she?' He set her on the ground, but his hands remained lightly at her waist.

She felt the pressure of his palms and fingers, and a weakness went through her, as if he had touched not her garments, but her naked skin. She was aware of the wool of his overtunic beneath her own hands where she gripped his sleeves, of each measured breath he took, and the brightness of his stare.

'More than a little,' she admitted breathlessly, her colour high, and tried to concentrate on what he had said rather than the effect his closeness was having on her senses. 'She said that you had deliberately visited Arnsby to remind your father that he still had a loyal son of full age, and to show me off as a trophy of your success.'

He pursed his lips and tilted his head a little to one side, his hand busily drawing light, lazy circles in the small of her back. 'And is there anything wrong with either of those?'

'It was the way she spoke of your motives, as if you had come to take what advantage you could.' She shivered as his thigh brushed hers.

'Jesu, but she doesn't know how close to the truth she was,' he muttered with obvious double meaning, and closed the distance between her mouth and his.

Swept into the heady sweetness of his kiss, Linnet clutched him for support. She felt him move back on his heels to keep his balance as she swayed against him, and in that moment Robert thrust between them, eager to show off his ladybird and jealous of their embrace. Joscelin

162

staggered and released her. Linnet stumbled one pace after him, almost tripping over her son before she steadied herself. Robert stared up at the adults out of shining light grey eyes.

'Look, mama!' he cried, holding out the ladybird on the palm of his hand. The beetle opened its glossy wing cases and whirred into the air. 'It's gone!' Robert dashed across the grass, squinting into the blue.

Joscelin drew a slow, deep breath and clamped his hands around his belt, in unconscious imitation of his father. 'Sometimes,' he said, 'honour is a hard sacrament to preserve. Yes, I've considered laying claim to Arnsby. If it weren't for Martyn, I might even have discarded my integrity to do it.' He smiled with more pain than humour. 'And if it weren't so important to you that this three months of mourning be observed, I'd have laid claim to your bed long ago.'

Linnet quivered, her spine dissolving in the brooding look he gave her. She was sorely tempted to say that the three months of mourning were far less important than they had been, but she held back. He knew that Giles had not trusted her and she did not want to give him cause to wonder if Giles had been right. Let him see that she could resist temptation. And on a level far deeper and fraught with guilt, she had to prove it to herself.

'It is not that I am unwilling but I would rather wait and make sure that I am not carrying Giles's seed,' she murmured quickly. 'And people must see that you are the Justiciar's true representative, not just some adventurer who has snatched me from across my husband's coffin and dragged me before the nearest priest.'

Joscelin sighed. 'People will always see what they want to see,' he said, but stood aside to let her walk up the path to the open chapel doorway.

She could feel his eyes burning upon her spine like a physical touch. Shivering, she forced herself neither to quicken her pace nor to look over her shoulder. She heard Robert cry to Joscelin that he had found another ladybird, and Joscelin's distracted reply. And then the solid walls of the chapel interior cut off all sounds from outside, and she found herself immersed in a tranquillity of pale stone arches rising in two tiers to a ceiling patterned with curves and lozenges of chiselled stone.

Linnet's breathing slowed as she absorbed the atmosphere of somnolent peacefulness. Kneeling, she crossed herself, then rose and walked slowly down the nave, until she came to the tomb of Morwenna de Gael.

The sun threw solid diamonds of red and purple and green from the stained windows to tip Linnet's shoulder and the drapes of stone that clothed the plinth. She touched the smooth alabaster pleats of Morwenna's robe. White, with a hint of translucence, Ironheart's mistress lay in stone state above her mortal remains, her slender hands clasped in the attitude of prayer. In the crook of her arm was the swaddled baby she had died bearing. Someone had recently crowned the pristine stiff wimple with a chaplet of threaded marigolds and they cast an amber shadow upon the smooth, white brow. The face was patrician, with romanesque orbits and straight, severe nose – the usual stonemason's work and unlikely to resemble the subject entombed. The mouth, however, wore the faintest shadow of a smile, probably attributable to a slip of the chisel or a moment's absent-mindedness, but the effect gave the face a depth of individuality.

Deeper into the church, before the altar, a pyramid of small votive candles burned in vigil for Morwenna's soul. Ironheart and Conan knelt side by side, facing the rood. A priest must have lit the majority of the flickering beeswax tapers, but he was not here now to intrude on the silence. Tall candles, thick as a warrior's wrist, stood like spears on the altar, and between them rose a Byzantine cross of garnet and silver-gilt, a crusading legacy of a former de Rocher. Wealth was here, but only as an understated backdrop to the flawless white tomb.

Quietly Linnet joined the men and lit a candle of her own. Her lips moved in silent prayer for the soul of

Morwenna de Gael. Then she said a prayer for herself, asking silently for courage and forgiveness. When she genuflected and rose, she noticed that William de Rocher's hands bore a dusting of pollen, as if he had been gathering flowers.

CHAPTER 18

September 1173

I T WAS RAINING outside and pitch-dark. Joscelin cursed as he surfaced from sleep and heard the water spattering against the shutters. He pushed down the sheepskins that had been cocooning him and, shivering, sat up. The night candle had gone out. Groping, he found the coffer and, after a moment, the tinder box on top of it. By the time he had managed to coax a light from the two flints and the small pieces of shaved wood, a yawning Henry had appeared with a sputtering taper in his hand.

'I'm sorry, my lord. You woke before I did,' he apologized, kindling a steadier flame from the night candle. 'My mother's boiling up some pottage for the men to eat before you ride out. You'll need something hot inside you this morning.'

Joscelin grimaced. There had been other times like this in his days as a mercenary – foul, pre-dawn mornings when any sane man would bury his head beneath the covers and hibernate. Even packed in waxed linen for travelling, chain mail, helms and weapons would be rusty within hours, and the chill of steadily falling rain would seep through garments into flesh and permeate bones. Unfortunately, with the Scots over the border in force and heading rapidly south, granted free passage by the treacherous Bishop of Durham, there was no alternative but to ride out and intercept their ravages. The command from de Luci had arrived yesterday noon with the instruction that Joscelin was to take his men and join a preliminary muster at Nottingham.

Henry's teeth chattered as the rain threw itself full force against the shutters. 'Can't say as I'm sorry to be staying here, my lord,' he said. 'Do you reckon they'll get as far as Derby?'

Joscelin drew a waxed linen gambeson over his shirt and tunic and topped it with a shepherd's leather jerkin. 'If we act now, I doubt it. But the Earl of Leicester is massing troops across the narrow sea for an invasion. It would be inconvenient if he were to strike at the same time as the Scots. That's why de Luci said we had to move as fast as possible.'

'I'll pray for your safekeeping and victory, my lord,' Henry said fervently, crossing himself for good measure.

When Joscelin arrived in the great hall, his men and Conan's were crowded blearily around the fire, sipping bowls of broth, tying cross-garters, fastening belts, yawning and scratching. Not particularly hungry, but knowing he must eat something if he was to survive a long, wet day in the saddle, Joscelin went to claim his own portion of soup from Dame Winifred.

'God send you good fortune, my lord,' she said, presenting him with a steaming bowl. Her bright black eyes fixed on him until he had taken the first sip and assured her that it was good. The crone at the cauldron, Milo called her, but only because she guarded its contents jealously and would not permit him to go sampling them as and when he chose.

Joscelin moved among the men, speaking a brief word here and there. Conan eyed him sidelong, concealing a smile in his greying fair beard. 'Seems not a moment since I was giving you the orders,' he remarked.

'More than five years,' Joscelin said sharply.

Conan raised a defensive hand. 'Pax, you pay my wages. As long as your head doesn't swell so much that you can't fit it through your tunic neck, I'll not interfere.'

'And as long as you keep your tongue behind your teeth, I'll not be tempted to cut it out!' Joscelin snapped. 'When you've finished your broth, you can give the order to mount up. I want to be on the road by first light.'

Conan pursed his lips. 'You always were a grouchy sod in the mornings,' he said, but began to drink down his broth.

Joscelin narrowed his eyes, but let the comment pass. A tug on his gambeson hem made him look down to find Robert standing before him. The child's hair was still sleep-ruffled and his tunic had been put on back-to-front and inside-out. Juhel had often stood thus, but his hair had been black and he had had the dark, narrow eyes of a faun.

Joscelin crouched. 'Shouldn't you still be in bed, young man?'

'I wanted to see you – to tell you not to go.'

Joscelin took Robert's icy hands in his, then drew the shivering little boy into the circle of his arms and perched him on his thigh. 'We spoke about this last night, didn't we?' Joscelin said gently. 'I have to leave for a short while at least. The man who asked me to take care of you and your mother needs my help.'

'But if you go to him, you won't be here to look after us.'

'Milo is staying. You know Milo; he won't let anything happen to you. And Malcolm will be here too. His wound's almost better, but not quite enough for a long ride. I won't be gone long, I promise.'

Robert was quiet for a moment, but not in acquiescence. Joscelin could almost see his mind working like the machinery inside a flour mill. 'Mama doesn't want you to go either,' he said, clenching his jaw stubbornly.

'But she knows that I have to.'

'She was crying last night. She thought I was asleep but I heard her. She told Ella she did not know what she would do if you were killed.' Robert flung his arms around Joscelin's neck in a throttling grip. 'I don't want you to die.'

Joscelin swallowed and held him close. 'I'm not going to die. There's too much to live for.'

The boy trembled and shook his head. 'I don't want you to go,' he repeated.

'Look,' Joscelin delved inside his various layers of clothing and pulled out a leather thong upon which was threaded a small cross of carved olive wood. 'I've had this since I was sixteen. It was given to me by someone very special, and I've not taken it off once. It protects me in battle.' A lie, since Joscelin relied on nothing in battle except his own skill and the speed of his responses. But the child had need of magic and talismans. Breaca had given the cross to him as they lay on a goatskin rug beneath the stars on the road to Falaise. A piece of the True Cross she had said, her mouth both scornful and tender.

Robert touched the dark, crudely carved wood and seemed to derive some comfort from it, for Joscelin felt him relax slightly. 'Does it truly protect you?'

'I swear it,' Joscelin said solemnly. 'But it will help its power if you pray for me too, every day after Mass.'

Robert nodded and wriggled slightly, his attention wandering now that his fear was subsiding.

'And when I return, I expect you to be able to canter your pony round the tiltyard all by yourself.'

'I can nearly do that now!'

'I know, but I won't be gone long. Now then, you had better go and find some warmer clothes if you're coming out to see us on the road.' He gave Robert a final hug and set him on his feet. Then he rose to his own as Linnet and her maid entered the hall. Ella immediately took Robert in hand, scolding him gently as she led him away to be dressed properly.

Joscelin tucked the old wooden cross back down inside his tunic, and looked at Linnet. There were shadows beneath her eyes as if she had not slept well, and she was pale, her colour not improved by the undergown of undyed wool she was wearing. Neither veil nor wimple covered her head at this early hour and her hair was confined in a simple, thick braid. He thought about what Robert had said and wondered how he should go about calming her fears. It was hardly politic to do as he had done with Robert and show her Breaca's cross.

The men were drifting from the comfort of the fire and their now empty bowls. Joscelin was aware of time trickling all too rapidly through his hands. There was so much to say and the words all stuck in limbo.

'I've still got a knife in my boot,' he smiled, 'and Conan riding at my left shoulder.' Reaching out he touched her honey-brown plait. 'In another week the three months of your mourning will be over. When I come home, we'll hold a wedding celebration. Take some silver and make yourself a fine gown.'

She bit her lip. Beneath his hand he felt her heart leap and begin to thud rapidly, as if he had frightened her.

'Linnet?'

Her colour rose. She met his eyes and then looked quickly away. 'I already have some silver – thirty marks to be precise.'

'What?' He had been about to set his arm around her waist, but stopped in mid-motion. 'Where from?'

She drew a deep breath. 'The strongbox . . . no, wait, hear me out. I took the money in London between the time when Giles died and Richard de Luci gave you custody of the coin. When you and he counted it, I had already removed the thirty marks. I did not know what was to become of myself and Robert. It was his inheritance and I wanted to secure some of it at least.'

Joscelin did not know whether to be angry or amused. Certainly he was unsettled. Such cleverness would bear watching. 'Why tell me?' he asked warily. 'You could have said nothing, and I would never have suspected anything.'

'I know you enough to trust you now.' She looked up at him through her lashes. 'You would not do anything to diminish Robert's inheritance.'

In his mind, Joscelin swore softly with admiration at the way she had disarmed him. And her timing was superb. He had no opportunity now to rail at her in righteous indignation, and by the time he returned the matter would be half-forgotten, its cutting edge blunted. 'I don't think I would dare,' he said wryly.

'Then you are not angry?'

'I didn't say that.' He drew her into his arms and kissed her long and deliberately.

Behind them, Conan loudly cleared his throat. 'Do you want me to instruct the men to bide awhile?'

Joscelin lifted his head and glanced round at his grinning uncle. 'No, tell them to mount up. I'm coming now.' He kissed Linnet again, hard as the rain that was sweeping down outside.

'God keep you safe, my lord,' she gasped as he released her. Her lips were full, her eyes very bright, holding the suspicion of unshed tears.

It was the first time she had ever afforded him that title and it was not yet his right. Perhaps it was a placebo aimed at smoothing his ruffled feathers, but he did not think so. Her response to his kiss had been too fierce and spontaneous. 'If ever there was a reason to hasten home in one piece, I'm looking at it now,' he said as he swept on his cloak and headed towards the door.

CHAPTER 19

'CHRIST'S NAILS', IRONHEART wheezed before his voice was robbed from him by the innocuous-looking clear liquid in his cup. 'What is this stuff?'

'Don't tell me you've never sampled usquebaugh before!' scoffed Conan, sloshing a liberal amount into his own drinking horn and passing the flask to Joscelin. It was part of the meagre spoils bludgeoned from a party of Galwegians earlier in the day as the Scots retreated over the Tees, pursued by de Luci's hastily mustered army.

Ironheart rubbed his throat. 'God, it's barbarian!'

Conan grinned. 'Give it time, William. Their usquebaugh's like their women – rough at first, but soon your blood's so hot that you don't notice.'

'That depends where you keep your brains.'

'Same place as yours.' Conan straddled a camp stool, copper bracelets jangling on his braced, tattooed forearm. 'I saw you eyeing up that laundry wench when we were setting up camp.'

Ironheart made a disparaging sound and took another tentative sip of the fiery pale yellow brew. This time his throat did not burn quite so much. A warm glow was spreading from his stomach into his veins, comforting him against the chill of the evening. Autumn was on the horizon and came earlier in the north. Up here on the Scots border, the leaves and bracken were already beginning to turn golden. He stared into the heart of the fire until the heat made him blink and acknowledged that he was becoming too old to go on campaign. His body ached with the effort of keeping pace with younger men and his mood was tetchy. Knowing his limitations did not make accepting them any easier. Perhaps he ought to lie the laundry wench on his cloak and comfort himself with her softness, except that he had an aversion to the women of the camp, an aversion rooted in deep fear. He raised his cup to his lips, took a full swallow this time, and told Joscelin to pass the flask.

His son darted a look at Conan, but handed it over without comment.

'What's wrong, don't you believe I can handle my drink?' Ironheart snapped. 'Good God, the night you were whelped, Conan'll tell you I drank him under the trestle and walked away damned near sober.'

'Usquebaugh is not wine, Papa. You'd not even be able to stand up if you drank that flask to the dregs.'

William was tempted to prove the opposite, but resisted. Joscelin had spoken with the conviction of experience. 'Where did you learn that, as if I didn't know?' he scowled at Conan.

Joscelin's eyelids tensed. 'In a disease-ridden camp on the road to Rouen,' he said. 'It bought me oblivion for a time.' Rising to his feet he left the fire and went to check their horse line. Ironheart watched him pause at a captured Galloway pony tethered beside the pack horses and destriers. It was a young but sweet-natured mare with a fox-chestnut hide and silver mane and tail. Ironheart knew that Joscelin intended her as a mount for Robert de Montsorrel; he knew everything and more than he wanted to know about the woman and child because Joscelin talked of nothing else – a besotted fool. The usquebaugh burned in Ironheart's stomach like a red-hot stone, or perhaps it was bitter envy mixed with the corrosive lees of memory.

Sparks hoisted themselves into the darkness on ropes of smoke. A soldier softly played the mournful tune of 'Bird on a briar' on his bone flute. Conan took out his darning kit and began to mend one of his hose. Nearby two soldiers played dice, gambling for quarter-pennies. Joscelin returned to the fire, threw on a couple more faggots, and sat down.

William drank from his cup and raised one wavering forefinger at his son. 'It was on a night like this that I met your mother – has Conan ever told you the tale?'

'You're drunk,' Conan said sharply. 'Whatever you say now, you'll regret it in the morning.'

William answered the question himself. 'No, he hasn't.' His lip curled. 'But I wouldn't expect him to boast his part abroad.'

'So help me God, William, I've made my peace with you and her. I'll not have you drag it out of the tomb again because you cannot hold your drink!' Conan said hoarsely. 'What good will it do?'

William hunched his shoulders and, ignoring Conan, faced Joscelin. 'I was sitting at a fire like this one, drinking some poison from Normandy that dared to call itself wine, and eating coarse peasant bread, when a young Breton mercenary approached me and begged for employment. Begged,' he emphasized, eyes narrow with malice.

Conan sat very still. In the light from the campfire a groove of muscle tightened in the hollow of his cheek.

'Papa, if you want to speak about this, do it tomorrow when you're sober.'

Ironheart looked down at the restraining hand Joscelin had put on his sleeve. 'I won't want to talk when I'm sober. No, you sit here and listen; it's time that you knew.' He shook off Joscelin's touch and raised his cup in toast to Conan. 'As it happened, I needed men and decided that if he was useful with a sword, I would hire him. In the meantime, soft fool that I was in those days, I let him sit at my fire and share my supper. Imagine that. I might as well have invited a wolf to dinner!'

'You were as glad of my company as I was of the warmth,' Conan said, quietly angry now. 'And when I asked if you had employment for my sister too, you immediately jumped to the conclusion that she was a whore.'

'It was the way you asked, and the way she came to the fire with neither wimple nor veil to cover her hair.'

'She was a virgin; she didn't have to wear a head covering to be respectable.'

Ironheart's laugh was caustic. 'God's toes, I'm not stupid. No man in his right mind would allow his sister to walk around an army camp with her hair uncovered, especially if she were a virgin. It would be an incitement to rape if ever there was one. You knew what you were about Conan. You thought you'd use Morwenna to make sure of your position in my retinue. A nice, clean "virgin" would be certain to appeal to a man who was finicky about using the camp sluts and had been a long time from home. It's the truth, isn't it?'

Conan chewed the inside of his mouth. 'She *was* a virgin,' he said thickly. 'And it was her own idea to remove her veil, not mine. We had argued about it earlier. She said that she was sick of traipsing the mercenary route never knowing where the next meal was coming from and that she intended finding herself a provider. I came to you genuinely seeking employment, hoping that we could settle somewhere for a while and that she could work as a laundry maid or in the kitchens, but Morwenna wanted more.'

Ironheart gulped the last mouthful of usquebaugh. 'You didn't stop her when she loosened her braids, and you didn't refuse the silver I paid you for her maidenhead.'

'No,' Conan bit out. 'You're right. I was enough of a whore myself to sell her to you. Would to God that I'd kept away from your banner that night.'

'Amen to that!' Ironheart snarled and looked at the son he had begotten on that long ago campaign. Morwenna's clear, beautiful eyes watched him across the firelight. He remembered her laughter, her wilfulness and impudence that sat so at odds with his ideal of women. He remembered her hair in his hands, dark and heavy and cool; the predatory demands of her body that took his own by surprise, although she had indeed been a virgin. And suddenly all the usquebaugh in the world would not have been enough to grant him oblivion. His eyes burned and filled with

175

moisture, and his chest and throat tightened. In the distance a wolf howled and he lurched to his feet and staggered towards the mournful sound as though it were calling him.

Conan put his face in his hands for a moment, then lifted his head and looked at Joscelin. 'I should never have taken the usquebaugh from that Galwegian,' he said bleakly.

The prow of the longboat climbed a wave and plunged down the other side like a bucking horse. Salt water sprayed her rigging and deck. A brisk wind cracked her square striped linen sail, driving her towards the hazy East Anglian shoreline. It was good sailing weather for September, so the vessel's Flemish master said, amusement gleaming in the creases of his leathery face. The crew grinned and agreed with him. The soldiers they were being paid to transport across the narrow sea from Flanders to England huddled miserably in what shelter they could find and either cursed or prayed, depending on their state of grace.

Ivo did neither; he was too ill to care. He hung over the side and retched. There was nothing left to bring up. The spasms tore his stomach muscles and roughened his throat. He kept his eyes closed so that he would not see the water pitching and heaving beneath him like a muscular serpent. The times that he snatched respite from the sickness in sleep, his dreams were haunted by scenes of drowning and of slimy sea-monsters that sucked the marrow out of him in the same way that the tossing of the ship was dragging him slowly inside-out.

'Ah Christ, still puking?' Ragnar demanded scornfully, lounging beside his suffering brother.

Ivo gulped and suppressed a heave. Ragnar had been sick too at first, but had made a rapid recovery. He was tanned and vigorous, and with his sandy-gold hair in need of barbering and a ruddy beard hugging his jawline, his Norse ancestry had never been more in evidence. The same ancestry ran in Ivo's veins, but he knew that Ragnar had been given double measure, and if a pinch existed in his own, he had yet to discover it.

'Look there,' Ragnar pointed. 'The coastline's in view. We'll be beaching before nightfall.'

Ivo groaned softly. *Before nightfall.* Ragnar might as well have said before next week. Opening his eyes, Ivo glanced across the hummocky swell and saw a distant smudge of what might have been land, or just stormclouds descending to the surface of the sea. 'I'm never leaving dry land again.' The last word was lost in a fresh bout of retching.

Ragnar gave up on his brother and turned away. To the side and in front of them were ranged other longboats and galleys of varying sizes and sea-worthiness. Some, like their own, carried the soldiers with which Robert of Leicester intended to wrest England from King Henry. Others were laden with horses and supplies. The army had been promised succour by Hugh Bigod, Earl of Norfolk, and these were his shores that the longboats were approaching.

Leicester's campaign had not fared particularly well in Normandy. His Breton allies had been defeated and his fellow magnate Hugh, Earl of Chester, had been captured and ignominiously thrown in prison at Dol. At one point it had seemed that Henry and his sons would agree to a truce, but the talks had broken down. In the wake of renewed dissent, Leicester had decided to change his field of operation to England.

Ragnar had been involved in sporadic skirmishes on Norman soil, had blooded his sword on several peasants and a runaway pig, had known the exhilaration of looting, raping and destroying, and the aftermath of feeling sick and sullied. The only cure was to seek that exhilaration again and forget.

A beacon fire had been kindled on the dunes to guide the ships safely in to shore. Small fishing boats were putting out to welcome them. Ragnar watched their approach, and tasted the sea spray on his lips, salty as blood.

CHAPTER 20

Q UIVERING WITH EXCITEMENT, Robert stood at his mother's side in the dank September evening while Rushcliffe's courtyard filled with men and horses and laden baggage wains.

'Mama, there's Joscelin!' he pointed vigorously at the familiar liver-chestnut with its distinctive stocking marks.

Linnet quivered too, her heart fluctuating between her throat and her stomach. For three weeks they had heard nothing, apart from occasional frightening rumours that came down the Humber and the Foss road with Nottingham-bound traders. They had been told on different occasions that the Scots had reached Yorkshire and were marching on York itself, that the Scottish army was thirty thousand strong, and every man a skin-clad savage. Both Milo and Malcolm had scoffed at such exaggerations.

'Three thousand perhaps,' Malcolm had said, as Linnet smeared soothing ointment on his scar to prevent it from itching. 'I'm no saying they willna be doughty warriors, and gey savage, but they'll be more lightly armed – out for what they can loot. They'll nae hold fast against mounted Normans. I should know. I was born Galwegian masel'.'

Linnet had taken what comfort she could from his confidence and gone about her normal business as if the castle's force were out for the day hunting deer, and not hundreds of miles further north engaged in the far more dangerous pursuit of hunting Scots tribesmen through the heather. To keep herself from brooding, she had taken up needlework with a vengeance. Not only was her wedding gown of Lincoln scarlet with charcoal trim finish, but she had also made Joscelin two shirts and a woollen tunic of deep forest green. And beside her, Robert was resplendent in a new tunic of that same green, his garment mirroring in miniature the one she had made for Joscelin. In Robert, the colour admirably set off the blond of his hair. In Joscelin, it would heighten the green in his eyes.

He was home to wear the tunic now, but not for long. Four hours ago, at noon, Brien FitzRenard had arrived in a state of near exhaustion, craving food and lodging for the night and a fresh horse in the morning. He had staggered to the pallet she had hastily arranged for him in a wall chamber and fallen asleep almost immediately, but not before telling her that he had orders for Joscelin the moment that he returned. Orders that she knew with a coldness in her stomach would only send him somewhere else to fight.

She watched Joscelin light down from the saddle and noted with relief as he came towards her that he moved easily, without any impediment to suggest injury. Robert danced from one foot to the other like a hound straining on a leash. The man's lips twitched. Linnet stooped, murmured in her son's ear, and gave him a gentle push. With a pang she watched him run to his hero.

'I prayed every day like you said, and I can gallop my pony now and, guess what, one of the coneys has had five babies, and they've got no fur!' Robert gabbled out in one, long breath, then shrieked with delight as Joscelin swept him up in his arms.

'And he has learned to write his name too!' Linnet added, laughing, and, coming into the curve of Joscelin's free arm, received a hard, scratchy kiss. 'I've set the laundry tubs boiling, so you'll be able to bathe, and there's mulled wine in the bower.'

'You'll turn him soft, wench,' said a harsh voice, and Linnet turned on Joscelin's arm, her eyes widening with a dismay she was not quite swift enough to conceal. William de Rocher's presence was a shock. Only having had eyes for Joscelin, she had not realized until he spoke that his father was with him. Heavy lines drew down the older

179

man's features. Surrounding the flint-grey irises, the whites were bloodshot.

'I doubt it, my lord.' She found an icy civility entering her tone. William de Rocher set her teeth on edge with his arrogance and superiority. He looked at her like a merchant eyeing up a doubtful piece of ware. And he was soon to be her father-in-law. 'Surely it is the duty of any chatelaine to offer her lord such comforts on his return.'

Ironheart grunted, unimpressed. 'You've learned duty since midsummer then?' he growled sarcastically.

'And I didn't even have to beat her,' Joscelin said, putting himself between his father and Linnet. 'Don't you want a goblet of mulled wine and a hot tub to take away the aches of the road? I know that I do. And if that's turning me soft, then I can live with it.'

'Pah!' snapped Ironheart and, without being invited, stalked towards the hall, his gait marred by a noticeable limp.

'Pay no heed,' Joscelin said. 'The damp weather's given him the ague in his joints and a temper worse than a mangy bear. If his pride weren't so touchy, he'd accept everything you offered.' He shrugged and sighed. 'It has not been the easiest campaign. Conan and my father haven't really made their peace and I won't become embroiled in their battle to blame each other for what happened almost thirty years ago.' He looked at Linnet and then at the child in his arms, and changed the subject.

'That's a fine new tunic to greet my return,' he admired.

'It was supposed to be kept for our wedding,' Linnet said, 'but he wanted to wear it, and today is a day of celebration. Who knows when the next one will be.'

'Why do you say that?' he asked sharply.

'Brien FitzRenard rode in earlier with parchments for you, and they do not bode well, I think.'

Joscelin groaned softly, and turned to walk into the hall. On the threshold, while they were still alone, he turned to Linnet. 'Marry me now,' he said, 'today.'

His words sent a ripple of shock through her, but the

after-effect was one of pleasant warmth. 'If that is your wish, then it is mine too,' she said demurely, but knew from the look on his face that he was not deceived by her very proper response.

'The Earl of Leicester has landed an army on the east coast,' announced Brien FitzRenard grimly, and drew his stool up to the edge of the large, oval bathtub. 'Bigod of Norfolk is giving him all the aid he requires.'

'Bigod? He must be seventy if he's a day!' Joscelin rested his arms along the sides of the tub. The water contained crushed salt to ease the aches of hard riding and was deliciously hot, almost unbearable.

Brien tiredly pinched the bridge of his nose. 'He's a perennial rebel. If there's a brew of trouble, you'll find him taking a turn at stirring it. I've got parchments in my baggage for you to read . . . and you too, my lord de Rocher.' His glance went to Ironheart, who was sitting on a coffer condescending with bad grace but with a copious thirst to drink Linnet's mulled wine. 'Hugh de Bohun the Constable is mustering an army to prevent Leicester striking across the Midlands to join his allies. You are commanded to respond as soon as you can.'

Joscelin sipped the hot wine and watched Linnet and a maid warming towels at the hearth and laying out clean garments for him to wear. Linnet stopped in the act of unfolding a shirt and stared his way, a look of dismay on her face.

'The horses are in no fit shape,' Ironheart snapped. 'We've pushed them up hill and down dale these past three weeks chasing Galwegian arses! What do you want, blood out of a stone?'

'If we don't stop them now, it will be worse later,' Brien's voice was laden with weariness. 'I need not remind you, my lord, that Arnsby and Rushcliffe will be prime targets for Leicester to attempt should he gain a solid footing in the region.'

Ironheart tossed off the wine and stalked across to the

hearth to replenish his cup. Robert skipped nervously out of his way and ran to the side of the bathtub. Joscelin gently tousled the boy's thistledown hair. He could not remember the anarchy of King Stephen's reign, since he had only been a small boy himself when it had ended, but he had heard enough from his father and seen the lasting effect of its ravages to have a healthy fear of a like situation ever occurring again.

'Give me a night and a day to get married and I'll put the troops on the road,' Joscelin sighed to Brien. 'As my father says, the horses need to be rested, but I daresay I can commandeer some fresh mounts round and about.'

Brien looked from Joscelin to Linnet and spread his hands in a gesture of apology. 'I know it is a lot to ask, but if we can break Leicester now, then I do believe we have a chance of peace.'

When Brien had gone below to the hall, Joscelin looked at his father. 'If you want to stay behind, I'll take your men,' he suggested.

'I'm not in my dotage yet!' Ironheart snapped. 'All right, I would rather not go chasing across the country, but Ragnar and Ivo are with Leicester, and it is past time they weren't. I have given them free rein to no avail. Now let them feel the weight of my displeasure.'

Joscelin bit his tongue and attended to his ablutions, knowing that his words would only be wasted on his father's current mood. To Ragnar and Ivo the weight of Ironheart's displeasure would probably seem little different to the way he usually treated them.

Drying himself, Joscelin stepped from the tub and donned the new clothes that Linnet had laid out – a shirt of softened linen, an undertunic also of linen in a mustard colour, and a tunic of dark-green wool. All were new, and while there had been no time for Linnet to do any embroidery, they were embellished with braid and far finer than anything he had owned before.

'Fine feathers,' Ironheart grunted.

'Very fine,' Joscelin said softly, with a smile for Linnet.

Ironheart scowled heavily at both of them and, with an impatient sound, turned away and shrugging off his cloak, began unlatching his belt. 'There's no point in wasting this bath water, it's still hot enough to boil an egg. Lay me out some fresh towels will you?'

Beside him, Joscelin felt Linnet stiffen. Her eyes narrowed. Oblivious, Ironheart continued to tug off his clothes and toss them on the floor. Linnet drew herself up. In a quiet, cold voice, she told her maid to see to the towels and find fresh clothes for Ironheart to wear. Then, on the pretext of checking that the dinner arrangements were all going smoothly forward, she excused herself.

Ironheart scowled after her. 'She's a wayward wench,' he said.

Joscelin eyed his father with no small degree of irritation. 'I think she had had enough of you,' he said. 'To have played bathmaid, as duty insists, would have been too much. She might have drowned you. I know I certainly would.'

'Where's Mama gone?' Robert sidled nervously around Ironheart.

Joscelin picked him up. 'To talk to the cook. Do you want to come to the stables and see what I've brought you all the way from the north?'

Robert nodded his head vigorously.

Ironheart shook his and, naked, went to the hearth to pour another cup of hot wine before stepping into the tub.

It had been September when Linnet had married Giles, hot, sultry weather, the harvest new in the barns and golden motes of chaff hanging permanently in the air above the threshing floor. She had worn a chaplet woven with ears of grain as a fertility charm. The ploughing of the virgin soil and the scattering of seed in hope of abundant harvest.

It was September again and the grain was stacked in the barns, although the weather this time was grey and damp, and she had deliberately omitted to weave herself a bridal chaplet.

183

On the high table set out with Rushcliffe's rescued silver plate, Linnet sipped from the magnificent engraved loving cup. She had toasted her first marriage in its depths as now she was toasting her marriage to Joscelin.

The ceremony itself had been short, very similar to that of a betrothal. Father Gregory had borne witness for the Church that both parties were willing participants. All Joscelin and Linnet had to do was pledge themselves to each other, and seal the pledge by the gift of a blessed ring. The sign of the cross had been made over them, and they were man and wife. The entire ritual had taken less than a quarter-notch on the candle clock. Tonight came the final bonding that meant nothing save death could rend them asunder. And tomorrow Joscelin was riding away to flirt with that death. She pushed the thought away, but it hovered on the periphery of her mind and taunted her.

Henry, resplendent in a new tunic of green fustian, leaned between herself and Joscelin to refill the loving cup from the pitcher in his hand. When he moved on down the table, she was faced by the full, bright hunger in Joscelin's eyes. His look was like a hot handprint on her bare skin.

She swallowed nervously. Giles had been drunk and fumbling on their wedding night, full of terse instructions and curses. *Open your legs, damn you. Wider, higher. Don't just lie there like a cabbage. Stop screaming, it doesn't hurt.*

Joscelin placed his hand over hers and with the other lifted the refilled loving cup to drink from the place where she had set her own lips. A drink of libation before the ploughing. *It doesn't always hurt. There is pleasure in sin.*

She became aware of Conan watching herself and Joscelin with benign amusement. He raised his cup in toast and murmured something sidelong to his table companion, Brien FitzRenard. The Justiciar's man laughed and looked teasingly at bride and groom. Linnet wanted to snatch her hand from beneath Joscelin's but knew that it would only occasion further teasing. It was, after all, their wedding night, and Conan was doing his best to preserve the

184

traditions. Now and then Ironheart would raise his head from the stupor of wine fumes to mutter about duty.

'Use her well in bed,' he slurred, his eyes focusing independently of each other. 'Girl children're what you want.' His head nodded as if too heavy for his neck. 'When they marry you can choose your sons. Won't be lum . . . lumbered with idiots.'

Joscelin cast an exasperated glance in his father's direction. 'God, how much longer before the drink poles him silent?' he muttered to Linnet.

Linnet gave a small shudder of revulsion as she watched her father-in-law's behaviour sinking further into boorishness with the diminishing level of wine in his cup. She laid her hand urgently along Joscelin's sleeve. 'I know that we are indebted to your father for the restocking of the keep,' she murmured, 'but I cannot bear to sit here and listen to him.' Her fingers tightened as she fought panic. 'And duty or not, I know I won't be able to strip myself naked before him at the bedding ceremony.'

'There is no need for us to stand unclothed before witnesses,' he soothed, laying his hand over hers. 'You have seen me naked before and been able to judge that you are not getting damaged goods, and I would have to be mad to repudiate you because of some unseen physical flaw. Besides,' he added with a rueful glance at Conan, 'do you think I relish the thought of being stripped naked and drunkenly commented upon? A man has more to conceal than a woman. Stiff or limp, I'll be cause for all manner of bawdy jests.'

Linnet felt a weak surge of relief. 'Thank you,' she swallowed. 'I think when I married Giles, the bedding ceremony was the thing I hated most about my wedding night. It was as if I were being shut in a cage with a wild animal, and all the guests were grinning onlookers.'

'You have nothing to fear from me.'

'Yes, I know.' She crumbled a sweet honey cake set on the platter beside her trencher. 'It is not you I fear.'

He pursed his lips for a moment, then leaned closer to

speak softly, 'Look, there's only one more course to be served, and we've eaten ourselves stupid anyway. Make the excuse that you're going to check that Robert has settled down, and remain above. I'll sit here and make idle conversation for a while to disarm their suspicions, then I'll take a casual stroll to the latrine. By the time they realize what has happened, we'll have the bedchamber door bolted in their faces.'

She nodded and rose to her feet as the final parade of food from the kitchens began arriving – sweet frumenties and tarts, pressed cheeses, small pasties, and bowls of fresh green herbs. She was aware of the salacious glances following her, of men imagining how she would look unclothed, her hair loose. She heard the bawdy remarks shouted to Joscelin, and his good-natured rejoinders. Her face flamed and her heart began to thump. Glancing over her shoulder as she reached the tower entrance, she saw that Joscelin was unconcernedly helping himself to a slice of nutmeg tart and bandying words with Conan, lulling him into a false sense of security. Gratefully Linnet started up the concealing twists of dimly lit stone stairs.

Joscelin dropped the bar across the door. 'They might rattle at the latch,' he said, 'but I doubt they'll go to the trouble of fetching an axe to see tradition upheld.'

Linnet sighed with relief. 'I am sorry, but I could not have endured the bedding ceremony.'

'Once must be penance enough for anyone,' he said wryly and sat down in the chair before the hearth. He knew what he wanted. He also knew that to take it with the directness that was now his right would be a grave mistake. As he began slowly unwinding his cross-garters, he wondered why she was so frightened of his father. Certainly Ironheart was not particularly personable at the best of times, but he was no worse than many other barons and surely far less of a threat than the men who had previously occupied her life.

'Was Robert asleep?' he asked mildly.

186

'Indeed yes.' Her face brightened. 'I think he was thoroughly exhausted by all the excitement. He's head over heels in love with that pony you brought.'

'I thought they would suit,' Joscelin said with satisfaction, and felt a glow, remembering the joy in Robert's small face as he was given the Galloway mare.

'Do you know what he's called her?'

Joscelin shook his head.

'Giles once remarked that Leicester's wife had the teeth and backside of a mare. Robert must have been listening. He's named her Petronilla after the Countess.'

Joscelin choked. Petronilla de Beaumont did indeed resemble a horse, although her colouring was more iron-grey than chestnut, and on balance he thought the Galloway pony the more attractive. Petronilla, what a mouthful. 'I don't know whether the horse should be insulted, or the Countess,' he grinned.

'Is it true that she girds herself like a man and rides into battle at her husband's side?'

'More or less. She's with him now for certain.' He looked at her from under his brows. 'Not thinking of following her example, are you?'

'Perhaps it would be easier than to sit here waiting,' she said, and looked at him across the firelight as she unbound her braids.

Leaving the chair, he took her ivory comb from her coffer and sat down beside her on the bed. 'Give me your hair,' he coaxed. 'You don't want to unbar the door to summon your maid and I've done this many times before.'

She had tensed at his approach, but now she relaxed and gave him a quizzical half-smile. 'Is that by way of reassurance or confession?' she asked mischievously.

'Which do you want?' he responded in a similar tone and, taking her hair in his hands, started to brush out the twists of braid. The firelight caught the ripples that the plaiting had left behind, gilding the soft honey-brown with golden-red lights. The scent of rosemary and chamomile rose from the slow movement of the comb and delicately assaulted his senses. 'If you think I've led a debauched life of bedchambers and broken hearts, you are sadly mistaken.'

'And you a tourney champion?' Her voice was pitched low as her head yielded to the gentle passage of the comb. He watched the movement of the sinews in her slender throat, the soft hollow above her collarbone and the memory of Breaca hovered bitter-sweet in the shadows.

'I do confess to plucking the occasional ripe fruit from a tree overhanging someone else's orchard wall, but if not into my hand it would have fallen elsewhere.' He brushed in contemplative silence for a moment. Her hair crackled and glowed with light as if it were an extension of the fire. 'Besides,' he added, 'for a long time I had a woman of my own and no inclination to go filching forbidden apples. Breaca would have gelded me for certain.'

She turned her head and looked up at him. 'Conan has made mention of your past,' she murmured.

'I thought he might. Probably he believed you would feel sorry for me and your heart would melt.'

'He was watching you and Robert together. I think he spoke because he was pleased for you, and he said very little. Only that your son had died and that you and his mother had drifted apart.'

How distant it sounded, spoken softly in this chamber alone with his new beginning. 'Dysentery,' he said. 'It can hit the cleanest of camps and he was only four years old. Breaca nearly died too. He is buried in a churchyard on the road to Rouen and it cost all the silver I had to bribe the priest to let Juhel lie in consecrated ground – a mercenary's unshriven bastard child.' Setting the comb down, he gathered her hair to one side and started unfastening the back-lacing of her gown. 'It hit me hard. For a time I was wild; I didn't care. The summer Juhel died was my most successful ever on the tourney route. I earned back all the silver I had paid to the priest, and enough to employ my own troop of men instead of traipsing in Conan's wake.'

'Your son's name was Juhel?'

'It's Breton, the name of Breaca's father.' He felt her quivering beneath the touch of his fingers, or perhaps it was his hand that trembled with the effort of controlling all that was within him. 'He was small like his mother, but quick and bright as a pin.' He shrugged. 'It's eight years now.'

Again she turned to look at him, her brows arching this time in startled question.

'I was a little short of seventeen when he was born.'

'And Breaca?'

The lacing undone, he slipped the gown from her shoulders. She stepped out of it, and then her undergown, and stood before him in her shift.

'She was two and thirty – old enough to have been my mother,' he added with a hint of self-mockery.

'Why are you telling me this?'

'You think it would stay a secret long with Conan in the same household? He would let you have it piece by little piece and I would know from the way you looked at me which occasions he had chosen to enlighten you. Now it is told, it no longer lies between us.'

Her throat moved. Her lashes swept quickly down, making feathery shadows on her cheekbones.

'Or does it?' Frowning, he tilted her chin on his fingertips.

'No,' she said huskily, 'it doesn't.' But other things did. She was not brave enough to give him the sword of her own past to break across his knee.

He cupped her shoulders and slipped the chemise slowly off them. She stared at the rushes while his gaze devoured her.

'Jesu,' he whispered, and through the trembling of his hands, she felt his urgency and his restraint. She shivered as the cold air played over her body. Her nipples grew hard and tight and her flesh rose in goosebumps. Weathered brown upon white, his hand stroked her skin, and his mouth sought hers.

The minutes passed, the casual questing of first intimacy

189

yielding to a more determined assault on the senses. The last of the spiced wine from earlier was consumed, Joscelin's garments were tossed on the floor and were joined by Linnet's garters and hose. Gestures became bolder, more explicit as pleasure and tension mounted. Perspiration dampened Linnet's brow. She was no longer cold. The hot pressure of Joscelin's body pinned her to the feather mattress. Against his ribs she felt the driving thud of his heart. Her palms slid upon the textures of wet skin, smooth muscle and striving grooves of tendon. She stroked the engorged heat of his manhood where it lay upon her thighs, teasing him a little as he had earlier been teasing her.

He broke the kiss and groaned with pleasure, thrusting against her hand, pleading in her ear.

Relenting, driven by her own surging need, she guided him home.

Someone banged on the door with what sounded like one of her best silver-gilt cups. 'Joscelin, open up, you spoilsport!' Conan bellowed furiously. 'You haven't been properly bedded yet!'

Linnet stifled a scream and stared over Joscelin's shoulder at the shuddering door, hoping that the bar would hold.

Joscelin muttered an oath through his teeth.

'Joscelin!' The door quivered beneath the repeated hammering. Then there was a curse of pain. Milo de Selsey's voice came muffled through the thick oak, and Henry's too, trying to cajole Conan away from the barred door. 'Not fair! 'Snot tradish . . . tradishnal!' Conan bewailed.

Henry murmured enticingly that a new cask of wine was about to be broached. Footsteps staggered and scuffled. 'That's it, Sir Conan,' Linnet heard Henry say. 'It's much better down in the hall than up here on a draughty landing.'

'Spoilsport!' There was a final thump on the door; sounds retreated and silence reigned again. Joscelin sighed and pressed his head into the curve of Linnet's throat. 'Conan in his cups is a fiend straight out of hell,' he muttered. 'It's because we've come out of one battle to go straight to another. Drink and women, the mercenary's sovereign remedy.'

She heard the self-mockery in his tone and touched his sweat-damp hair. 'Then lose yourself,' she whispered.

He was quiet for a moment, then he lifted his head and breathed soft laughter. 'Conan was right,' he declared. 'I haven't been properly bedded . . . yet.'

He was still within her, although somewhat diminished, but now she felt his surge of renewed eagerness.

'Do you think he'll come back?' she asked, tightening around him.

'I doubt it,' he said breathlessly. 'I'll kill him if he does!'

Linnet strained her ears, wondering if anyone was listening outside the door, but all she heard were the intimate sounds of love-making – the growing harshness of Joscelin's breathing, the movement of skin on skin, her voice pleading. Independent of her mind, her loins were stretching and filling with a pleasurable tension so huge that she knew she was going to burst.

Joscelin's lips were upon her breast, his head butting the angle of her jaw. She clenched her teeth, trying not to make a sound, but the cries came anyway. Against the curve of her breast, Joscelin moaned, his voice rising and breaking. His spine arched, his head came up. She closed her eyes and gripped him, absorbing his tremors through her own.

As his breathing eased, he returned his attention lazily to her breast, her throat and jaw. Linnet shivered, savouring the sensations even while the edge between this tender nibbling and Giles's sated wet fondling shone as keen and narrow as the edge of a blade. One slip and she would bleed to death. She did not want the memory of other occasions to mar this one for her and she pressed herself hard against Joscelin's bulk, hiding her face in his sweat-salty skin, her fingers tightening in his hair as she sought the sharp sensations that would bring her oblivion.

CHAPTER 21

MAUDE DE MONSART shook out her crumpled riding gown of heavy Flemish twill. 'Has there been any news, my dear?' she asked Linnet as the placid bay ambler was led away by a groom to be watered and rubbed down. The two soldiers who had escorted her from Arnsby were already on their way to the guardroom to wait out her stay before the comfort of a stoked brazier.

Linnet sighed and shook her head. 'Not since last Tuesday. Joscelin sent me some hides he'd bought at a bargain price from a tannery on Leenside, and wrote that he was leaving Nottingham the next morning, but that was all. What about you?' She drew Maude across the bailey and up the forebuilding stairs into the great hall.

'William sent a messenger over to fetch his thick cloak and waxed linens. That must have been about the same time that Joscelin wrote to you. My brother never communicates well even at the best of times.'

'No,' Linnet said wryly, thinking of her wedding day.

Maude looked at her curiously.

Linnet told her about Ironheart's ungracious behaviour. 'And then he had the gall to soak in the tub until the water was nearly cold!' she said indignantly. 'Nor did he object when I gave him Giles's old fur-lined bedrobe to wear afterwards while he was barbered, the hypocrite!' Then she laughed reluctantly. Recounting it now, she could see the funny side.

Maude's eyelids creased with amusement. 'William has a reputation to maintain. He's not as hard as people think. That myth grew out of the time just after Morwenna died

192

when no one could approach him without getting his head bitten off.' She smiled warmly at Linnet. 'Look at it this way, my dear: he chose to stay here at Rushcliffe before leaving to rendezvous with the Constable's troops, rather than riding on to Arnsby.'

Linnet nodded. It was a dubious sign of favour, she thought, and one that she could easily have forgone.

Maude lifted her eyes to the high windows. 'I cannot blame him either. This is a beautiful keep.'

Linnet looked up too. The proportions of this, Raymond's lair, were surprisingly elegant, displaying strong, pure lines that picked up and carried the Romanesque curves of windows and supporting arches like embroidery on a beautifully cut but austere gown. 'Giles's grandsire went on Crusade and captured an emir. He put all the ransom money into stone,' she said and led Maude up the stairs to the bower.

Panting somewhat from the climb, Maude nevertheless looked around with avid curiosity. 'Arnsby is downright squat and ugly compared to this,' she declared as she surveyed the large, sun-flooded bower, its whitewashed walls decorated with Flemish hangings. 'Oh, it's lovely! Just look at the size of this fireplace, and a stone canopy too!'

Linnet was silent as Maude examined and enthused over the bower. At length the older woman plumped herself down heavily on a lavishly padded chair – an oriental piece brought back on the baggage wain of the Crusader Montsorrel. Something of Linnet's mood must have communicated itself to Maude, for she cocked her head inquisitively. 'Do you not like living here, my dear?'

Linnet frowned unconsciously and looked around the warm, bright room. 'It is the memories I do not like,' she said after a hesitation. 'My marriage to Giles, and what came after.'

Maude nodded and pursed her lips. 'But that is over now. You are a new wife, and you have new memories to make. I trust Joscelin is treating you well?'

Linnet blushed and sat down on the other end of the couch. 'I have no complaint to make. He has been very good to me.'

'More than that to judge from the colour in your cheeks!' Maude chuckled.

Linnet smiled, but without her entire heart. Yes, he had been very good to her, but perhaps he would cease to be if she told him about herself and Raymond de Montsorrel. It had been on the tip of her tongue as they lay entwined in the afterglow of a second coupling, but her first tentative words had been met by the indifferent mumble of a man already three-quarters asleep, and her courage had failed her. Why tell him at all? It was in the past, finished. And all the time, at the back of her mind, a small voice was crying *You would not love me if you knew what I had done.* Not even to a priest had she ever confessed her sin. She would go to hell when she died, and assuredly meet Raymond there.

Maude's humour faded and, leaning over, she gently touched Linnet's knee. 'Is there something troubling you?'

Linnet blinked a veil of moisture from her eyes, and swallowed. 'No,' she lied. 'Nothing.'

The curtain across the bower doorway billowed and bulged, then was flurried aside by a giggling Robert who was running away from Ella.

'Just you come here this instant, master Robert, and wash those muddy hands!' the maid cried and, catching him, tickled him into a state of helpless submission and swept him across the room to the laver.

Distracted by the intrusion, Maude craned round to watch the child complain and grimace at being scrubbed. 'I never had infants of my own,' she said wistfully. 'William's brood have been my family.'

Linnet looked at the sad, smiling warmth of Maude's homely face, at the generous lap that was just made to nurse small children. 'Robert has no grandparents,' she said. 'Perhaps you would like to become one to him?'

Maude stared at Linnet as if she had just been offered a

place in heaven and her small, pouchy eyes filled with emotion. 'There is nothing that would give me more pleasure.' Her voice quavered with joy. 'Martyn's leaving Arnsby after Christmas to become a squire to Richard de Luci and I'll miss having a child about the place. To know I can visit here and be special to Robert – thank you. It is a gift without price.' She embraced Linnet fervently.

'It is as much for my sake as yours!' Linnet responded, her own voice suddenly weak. Her nostrils were filled with the smell of stale lavender and almond paste. 'My mother died when I was nine years old. I've never had another woman to talk to – except Richard de Luci's wife sometimes and the Countess Petronilla.'

'That's the name of my horse!' Overhearing, Robert skipped up to them, his demeanour chirpy as a squirrel. 'But she's called Petra for short. Malcolm's been teaching me to jump her over logs.' He leaped in the air, demonstrating. 'Joscelin says that he's going to show me how to tilt at the quintain when he comes home, and he's promised me some bridle bells too. Joscelin's my papa now.'

'Yes, my love, I know, so that makes you and I relatives,' Maude said, and produced from within her cloak a small box containing squares of a sticky date sweetmeat which she gave to the child. 'Don't eat too many at once or you'll make yourself sick and your mother will be cross with me.'

Robert was more taken with the carvings on the little sweetmeat box than he was with the contents. Maude helped him to eat one of the glistening dark pieces and enquired after the coneys.

'They're grazing in the pleasaunce,' Linnet said. 'The carpenter has fashioned a special run to keep them from harm, or from doing harm to the salat crops.'

'The baby ones were all pink and blind at first, but they've got black fur now,' Robert announced, somewhat stickily. 'The messenger said he'd like a coney-skin cloak, but Malcolm told him my coneys were special pets.'

'What messenger, sweetheart?' Linnet grasped Robert's arm.

'The one who arrived when we were unsaddling Petra. He was all covered in dust and his horse was foamy. Henry's sister gave the man a drink.'

Linnet rose to her feet, her mouth dry and her heart pounding. She had taken only two steps towards the chamber door when she heard voices on the stairs and Malcolm appeared on her threshold with Milo. They flanked a travel-stained, dishevelled, and obviously exhausted young soldier.

Linnet clenched her fingers in her gown and stood straight and still, her face ashen. She looked at the men. 'What news?' she demanded. 'Tell me.'

The messenger advanced and bent his knee. He was one of Conan's Bretons, a stocky young man scarcely out of adolescence, with a downy haze of beard lining his square jaw. 'There is no need for fear, my lady, the news is excellent,' he said as she gestured him to rise and face her. 'Our troops met Leicester's close on Bury St Edmunds, hard by a place called Fornham. All swampy the land was and no fit place to fight but we forced them to a battle nevertheless and cut them to pieces. Them as we didn't get, the peasants did with pitchforks and spears. The Earl himself has been taken prisoner and his Countess with him.' Rummaging in his pouch, he withdrew a crumpled, waterstained packet. 'A letter from my lord. He says to expect him the day after tomorrow, all being well.'

The colour flooded back into Linnet's face as she took the packet from the mercenary's blunt fingers. 'And is he whole? He took no injury?'

'No, my lady.' The young man grinned, revealing a recently lost front tooth. 'Mostly it was like spearing fish in a barrel. In the end we fetched up pitying the poor bastards that were left and let them run away into the marshes.' He shrugged his broad shoulders with sanguine indifference. 'Not as that'll do 'em any good. Like as not they'll drown or be picked off one by one by the eel fishers and fowlers round about.' His voice gave out and he began to cough.

196

Maude quickly poured him wine from the pitcher on the sidetable and brought it to him. 'Do you know what happened to your lord's half-brothers, Ragnar and Ivo de Rocher?' she asked anxiously.

The mercenary took two rapid swallows. 'No, my lady. All I can tell you is that they weren't taken with the Earl and his wife. Sir William has offered a reward for their safe delivery into his custody and he's stayed behind at Fornham to see if anyone turns them in. Lord Joscelin says as Sir William ought to come home, the damp's not good for him, but he won't be swayed. Says he don't care whether his sons are alive or corpses, they're still coming home.'

Linnet unfolded the smooth, creamy vellum and gazed upon the firm brown ink-strokes. Joscelin wrote almost as good a hand as a professional scribe, although the flow was a little too open and generous of vellum for a true craftsman. She imagined him seated at a table, one hand thrust into his brown hair, the other busy with a quill. It was a satisfying image and she deliberately enlarged upon it to banish the other one of him astride Whitesocks, dripping sword on high.

'My heart bleeds for them,' Maude had said to her when the messenger had gone. 'William and my nephews both. What if Ragnar and Ivo are dead? How will William live with the burden of knowing he might have killed them? They might look like grown men, but really they are still jealous little boys.' And she had dabbed at her eyes with the trailing end of her sleeve.

Robert had taken Maude to the pleasaunce to look at his coneys. She had willingly accompanied him and dissuaded Linnet when she rose to come too. 'Stay here and read your letter,' she said. 'I know how few and far between moments of peace can be.'

And so Linnet had taken the vellum to the window embrasure and sat down. A puddle of late September sunshine warmed her feet through her soft leather shoes. The only sound was the muted conversation of two maids weaving braid by the hearth.

197

As a child, Linnet had received basic tuition in reading and writing from the household priest – enough so that she could understand, but she was not particularly fluent. Painstakingly, she picked up each word of Joscelin's and consigned it like a jewel from page to memory.

> *Joscelin de Gael to my lady and before God mine own beloved wife, greeting.*
>
> *As you will know by the time you read this, I am coming home to you unscathed from our army's meeting with the Earl of Leicester. A truce has been agreed with the rebel forces until the early spring and so we will have time to say and do the many things that were before but unspoken yearnings.*
>
> *We should reach Nottingham the day after tomorrow. I will lodge there the night in my father's town house, and ride on home to you as soon as I have concluded business with the sheriff. Until then, I give you keeping of my heart.*
>
> *Written by mine own hand this tenth day after Michael-mas, year of our lord eleven hundred and seventy three.*

Beloved wife. The words warmed her as much as the splash of sunlight and foolish tears blurred her vision. Not since childhood had affection been hers to command except in Robert's eyes. Once she had made the mistake of believing that Raymond de Montsorrel was fond of her, that the gentle hands and persuasive voice were indicative of his concern, but it had all been a game to him, a bolster to his prideful boast that no woman, lady or whore, had ever refused him. She knew the difference now.

The sunlight blazed on the vellum as she folded it tenderly, her fingertips lingering on the strokes that bore the mark of Joscelin's hand.

CHAPTER 22

'WE'RE LOST, AREN'T WE?' Ivo snivelled.

Ragnar clenched his fists on the damp, slippery reins and turned in the saddle to scowl at his brother. 'God's eyes, will you cease your whining!' he snarled through his teeth. 'You're still alive, aren't you?'

The rain had been falling steadily since dawn, making of the forest a permanent green twilight. Water sluiced down Ragnar's helm and soaked through the twin layers of his cloak. His hauberk bled gritty rust and his thighs chaffed against the saddle pads with each stride of his tired horse.

In heavy drizzle, Leicester's army had struck across the country towards the Earl's Midland strongholds and had been met by their doom on the marshy ground near the village of Fornham. Earl Robert had relied too heavily on his Flemish recruits – weedy men and boys who were mostly unemployed weavers by trade – and Hugh de Bohun's knights had smashed them. Filled with rage and fear, Ragnar had hacked out an escape route, dragging a terrified Ivo in his wake. Now the forests surrounding Bury and Thetford stretched for miles, punctuated only by the occasional charcoal burner's dwelling or verderer's settlement. And outside of their gloomy green protection, for all Ragnar knew, Hugh de Bohun's army was waiting to finish off anyone who had not died by the sword or drowned in the marshes.

'My horse is going lame,' Ivo complained. 'Do you think we'll come to shelter soon?'

Ragnar closed his eyes and swallowed. In a moment he was going to offer Ivo shelter – six feet deep with a cosy counterpane of leaf mould. The idiot was about as much use as a punctured waterskin. Couldn't fight, couldn't think. A dead haddock would be better company. He did not answer but urged his own horse to a faster pace. If Ivo's mount truly was going lame, then perhaps he would fall behind and give Ragnar some blessed space.

The forest dripped around him like a giant open mouth waiting to swallow whatever was foolish enough to ride over the drawbridge of its mossy tongue. The smell of mildew and fungus was almost overpowering.

His eyes stung and his vision became a green blur. He was a rebel, an outcast, shivering to death in a lowland forest. The first spark of rebellion that had led him in fellow sympathy to join Young Henry's cause had been doused. The desire to wound his father and at the same time to prove his own worth was still a growling emptiness in his gut. He hungered for respect and admiration, and the more they eluded him the more hungry and desperate he became.

'Ragnar, wait!' Ivo's forlorn cry came muffled through the grey-green downpour.

Viciously he jabbed the stallion's flanks. The beast stumbled on a tree root then shied as a woodpecker dipped across the path, uttering harsh warning cries. Ragnar gripped the pommel to steady himself in the saddle. One shoulder struck a treetrunk and he cursed at the crunch of pain. He curbed the sidling horse and with resignation listened to the beat of approaching hooves as Ivo made up the ground between them.

'Ragnar . . .' Ivo said miserably.

Ragnar inhaled to bellow at him, but the breath solidified in his breast and his diaphragm went into spasm, for Ivo was held at spearpoint by a smiling English warrior, who was one of a group of half a dozen armed men.

'If your hand is going to your sword, I hope it's only to surrender it,' said the Englishman in thickly accented French. 'Give me one small excuse, Norman, and I'll have your guts to banner my spear.'

Ragnar shuddered, more than half-tempted to give the

soldier the very excuse he needed. It would be so simple. One thrust and everything would be finished. But was there any guarantee except a priest's prating assurance that the afterlife was any better? Slowly he grasped the hilt of his borrowed sword and drew it from its wool-lined scabbard.

'Ragnar, for Jesu's sake, give it to him!' Ivo croaked, eyes huge with alarm. 'You'll find us worth the ransom,' he gabbled, eyes darting around the tightening circle of soldiers. 'We're the sons of William de Rocher, known as Ironheart . . . his heirs in fact.' He licked his lips.

Ragnar sent Ivo a glare of utter scorn and threw the sword down into the thick leaf mould at his destrier's forehooves as if he were tossing a coin to a beggar.

The Englishman grinned. 'The sons of the great Ironheart, eh?' The relish in his tone scoured deep. 'I wonder how much your illustrious sire is willing to pay for the return of his two little lost black sheep? Better hope it's more than your true worth, or I might be tempted not to go to the bother of ransoming you.'

'He'll pay anything you want,' Ivo assured the Englishman anxiously. 'He will Ragnar, won't he?'

Ragnar narrowed his light brown eyes. 'Oh yes,' he muttered. 'He'll pay.'

It was a wet evening on October's brink. A bitter wind herded a wet fleece of clouds northwards and blew into the face of William de Rocher as he and his men drew rein outside the village alehouse to which their English guide had brought them.

'Is this the place?' William demanded, a paradox of hope and sinking despair making his tone harsh and angry.

'Yes, my lord.' His guide looked at him sidelong. 'It might not look much, but there's a mighty stout apple cellar under the main room floor.'

A muscle flickered in Ironheart's jaw. 'My sons are in the apple cellar?'

'Safest place for 'em. If they weren't worth good silver, they'd be feeding the ravens of Hallows Wood by now.'

201

'Watch your mouth,' Ironheart warned as the English soldier nimbly dismounted. 'Just because you have something I want, do not think you can take liberties with me.'

The younger man looked him up and down. 'I wasn't, my lord. I thought you were known as a man of plain speaking, and I have told you nothing but the truth. Many of Leicester's troops have not lived to see their ransoms paid.'

William glared at him and felt a goutish envy for the lively arrogance and fluid grace of youth. Slowly he swung his stiff right leg over the cantle and dismounted. The ground was soggy underfoot with a mulch of dead leaves. They twirled from the elm trees across the green like souls fleeing into the darkness, some of them falling by the wayside at his feet. Rain spattered into his face, forcing him to narrow his eyes. Puddles gleamed in the dips and hollows of beaten mud that made up the village street. Noisy laughter drifted from the alehouse and a raucous voice bellowed an English ballad about a virgin and a blacksmith. A well-lubricated villager staggered out of the withy doorway and away up the street towards a cluster of dwellings huddled around the green.

'They're still celebrating their victory over Leicester's army,' said his guide with a tolerant smile. 'It'll be the talk of the parish for generations to come – how Grandpa beat off hoards of Flemings with nowt but a pitchfork.'

'My sons,' said Ironheart icily, 'I want my sons. Now.'

The smile dropped from the soldier's face. 'Of course,' he said neutrally. 'This way, my lord.' He flourished towards the alehouse doorway like a servant ushering a great lord into a magnificent hall. It took all of Ironheart's control not to send him teeth over tail into the mud.

Ragnar was dozing, the nearest he could come to sleep in his cramped, cold prison. They had handled him roughly, goaded by his lack of response and the contempt in his eyes. The places where they had kicked him had stiffened and, since there was virtually no room to move, he had set.

202

In his shallow dream there was a witch who wore the face of a lovely dark-haired woman with shining green eyes that exactly matched the shade of her velvet gown. But then she changed. The face began to melt of flesh until it was a hideous skull. The hand reaching out to curse him was a white filigree of bone. The skull whispered *Look at me*. Terrified, but forced to obey, he raised his eyes to the cavernous orbits and saw the eyes of his mother staring out at him.

Ragnar jerked awake, his breath ragged in his throat and his heart thundering against his ribs like a runaway horse. The sweet smell of apples cloyed the darkness, hinting that they were soon to be over-ripe – rotting. Slumped against him, Ivo whimpered in his own sleep. They had not abused Ivo as much for there had been no challenge in taunting such easy game.

Above their heads the sound of the world outside was a muffled cacophony of footsteps, voices and raucous laughter. They were celebrating with a vengeance. Ragnar thought about the mistakes he had made and how, when he got out of this pit, he would go about rectifying them. Groping in the darkness he found the loaf they had lowered down earlier. Help yourself to apples, his captors had said, laughing. He set his teeth in the coarse brown sawdust and thought of the moist, golden honey bread that his aunt Maude would always bake on feast days. The thought of it brought moisture to his mouth and at least he was able to chew the excuse for bread that was his current sustenance.

He swallowed hard, then stopped chewing and raised his head, suddenly attentive as the general noise subsided and the heavy trestle bench standing over the cellar trap was scraped to one side. 'Ivo!' he whispered urgently and nudged his brother. Ivo jumped and then demanded in a frightened voice to know what was happening.

The bar on the trap was unfastened and the door was flung back to reveal by dingy rushlight a rectangle of blackened ceiling beam festooned with three coils of sausage

and a bundle of besom twigs. These were almost immediately blotted out by the human shapes that bent over the
entrance and peered down.

'Safe and sound, just like I told you,' declared the smug
voice of the English soldier responsible for Ragnar and
Ivo's capture and their current ignominious situation. 'Snug
as apples in a barrel.' A snort of amusement followed.

'Ragnar? Ivo?' Ironheart's voice sounded as if his larynx
was fashioned of rusty chain mail. 'I've come to fetch you
home. God knows, neither of you are worth the ransom,
but at least I know the duty owed to my blood.'

Duty! Ragnar almost gagged as he heard the word.
How often it had been rammed down his throat like a
medicine to cure all ills. By God, he would show his father
duty!

'Papa?' he said, and inching gingerly to his feet, looked
up at the broad shape covering the rectangle of light. 'I
was trying to reach you, but these gutter sweepings took
me and Ivo for ransom and threw us down here.'

'Less of the gutter sweepings!' growled the English
soldier. 'We could have left your butchered bodies in the
forest for the foxes and ravens to eat.'

'With your own for company!' Ragnar spat, fists
clenched. Then he took a deep breath and steadied himself.
'Papa, you were right about the Earl of Leicester and
Young Henry. They're not worth the spit of any man's
oath.'

Ivo struggled to rise, and even in the bad light, Ragnar
could see that his eyes were as round as candle cups. 'But
you said ... Oooff!' Ivo collapsed as Ragnar's elbow
found his midriff.

'What's the matter with him?' Ironheart demanded as a
wooden ladder was brought and slotted down through the
trapdoor.

'Belly gripes,' Ragnar said. 'He's been eating too many
apples.'

Ivo groaned and retched as Ragnar climbed slowly up
the ladder. His limbs felt like struts of rickety wood and

when his father stretched down his hand and pulled him out into the light, he did not have to feign the grimace of pain that crossed his face. After the darkness of the apple cellar, the rushlit main room of the alehouse appeared as huge and bright as a palace, although the courtiers wore the appearance of disreputables and beggars. And his father was king of the beggars in his water-stained, shabby garments, his grey hair showing wild wings of white and the flesh untidily loose upon the gaunt, powerful bones.

Shock hit Ragnar like an actual body blow. Christ, he was looking at an old man, not the granite-thewed god of his childhood and adolescence.

'I knew you'd come to your senses,' Ironheart said, his upper lip disdainfully curled. 'Pity it took so long and cost so much.'

'Yes, Papa.' Ragnar gazed at the ground while he recovered himself.

'Don't think you can pull the wool over my eyes. It's no more in your nature to be meek than it is for a wolf to turn into a lap dog! Look at me!'

Ragnar raised his head and stared his father in the eyes. Defiance flickered; there was nothing he could do to prevent it, but it brought a wintery smile to Ironheart's lips.

'That's more like the truth. I know you're not spineless.' He turned his regard upon Ivo who had emerged unaided from the cellar. 'If it had been your brother here, I could well have believed it,' he seized Ivo by the scruff and dragged him forward into the light. 'He's always had curd for guts!'

Hunched and shivering, Ivo stood like an ox outside a slaughter pen and made no defence. There was a tightness in Ragnar's throat and rigours shook his jaw. He had never felt such hatred in his entire life, but knew that it would transmute into an explosion of love and remorse if his father offered but one word or gesture of affection.

Hard-eyed, Ironheart said, 'Go outside and wait for me. There are saddled horses and an escort waiting.'

205

The ale-wife, a smirk on her fat face, handed over two meagre peasant cloaks. The fine fur-lined ones in which the brothers had arrived had been put away against her daughter's dowry.

'Are we under guard?' Ragnar asked huskily.

'No,' Ironheart said.

'Then we are free to leave?'

'Where would you go?' Ironheart untied two heavy pouches of silver from his belt and handed them to the soldier standing near the firepit. 'A nomad life on the tourney circuits for the price of a crust? Walk out on me now, Ragnar, and you might as well be dead. I'll not seek you out a second time. Why should I when I have a son at home and another whose loyalty I do not doubt?'

Ragnar clenched his teeth and by a supreme effort of control, prevented himself from either answering his father in the manner he deserved or storming out. He had learned all about cutting off his nose to spite his face. Taking the cloak from the woman, he swept it around his shoulders. The ragged hem hung drunkenly at knee-level and the pin was fashioned out of a chicken bone. 'I know where I stand, Papa,' he said, his voice quiet but intensely bitter. 'I hope to God that you do.' And went into the dark, rainy night to the waiting soldiers.

CHAPTER 23

THE WEEKDAY MARKET in Nottingham was almost as busy as London's Cheapside Joscelin thought as he threaded his way through the crowded butcher's shambles of Flesher gate and Blowbladder lane, and headed up the hill to the shops and booths that crowded along the road to St Mary's church and Hologate. Cheek by jowl, squashed together like herrings in a barrel, the stall-holders cried aloud the merits of their wares, or sat at their trade behind tables cluttered with their tools.

At a haberdasher's booth, Joscelin purchased a small set of bridle bells, thereby fulfilling his promise to Robert. They jingled merrily on their leather strap as he stowed them in his pouch. He remembered Juhel's dark eyes wistfully admiring such bright trinkets dangling from a trader's stall in Paris. In those days money had provided the luxuries of bread and firewood. He thought about a gift for Linnet. The coins in his pouch were not part of Robert's patrimony but his own property, courtesy of his prowess against Leicester's men. Withholding a death blow and claiming a ransom instead was by far the most profitable way of conducting warfare and he had indeed made an excellent profit.

There were gold and silver merchants aplenty to offer him cunningly worked rings and brooches, earrings and pendants. He knew that Linnet possessed little jewellery, but what he saw did not appeal to him. It was too commonplace. Every woman of means had a round brooch with a secret message carved on the reverse – *Amor vincit omnia* or *Vous et nul autre*. He had bought Breaca one in cheap bronze when she first became pregnant, and the memory was still so poignant that he had to avert his eyes from the stall. One goldsmith offered him a reliquary cross in which, amidst a confection of silver and rock crystal, was set a sliver of bone from the blessed Virgin herself, or so he was assured. Shavings of pig bone from the cesspit dug out of the sandstone rock at the bottom of the merchant's yard was the more likely source, Joscelin thought, and found no difficulty in declining the bargain.

What he did purchase finally was a small, beautifully carved wooden comb, the grip inlaid with mother-of-pearl. Its seller, Gamel, was an ex-mercenary who now eked a living carving dice and trinkets for members of the garrison to which he had once belonged. A sword had sliced off his leg at knee-level. He had survived the wound fever and now stumped around on a peg-leg, ungainly but determined. Just now the wooden limb was lying beside his bag of tools on the rushes of The Weekday alehouse as he thirstily accepted the piggin of ale that Joscelin had bought for him.

'God bless you, sir.' His eyes were bright with pleasure as he took a long drink, his scrawny throat bobbing up and down.

'How's the leg?' Joscelin sat down beside him on the cramped trestle. A pang of nostalgia ran through him as his senses were assaulted by the smoky, noisy atmosphere of the dingy little tavern. He had not known Gamel when the man had two sound legs, but the wound had only been a few months old when he first met him sitting in the guardroom at the castle, carving a cradle for a retainer's infant daughter.

'Not bad, not bad. Mustn't grumble or you'll not bother to keep me in ale,' Gamel grinned. 'Mind you, I had a close escape last month. The landlord's new hound took a fancy to chew up me old peg while I was resting here. Regular mess he made of it – huge great teethmarks, you shoulda seen 'em.'

'I've seen the dog,' Joscelin said sympathetically. Chained in the yard was something that appeared to be a cross between an alaunt and a wolfhound, but bigger than both and certainly looking more bite than bark.

'You'll not see it for much longer if I have me way,' Gamel muttered and took another long drink of ale. Then he looked at Joscelin from the tail of his eye. 'Rumour roundabouts says that you're a titled man now.'

Joscelin smiled at Gamel's nosy expression and spread his free hand wide. 'Who am I to deny rumours?'

Gamel sucked his teeth. 'They're fine, fair lands you've got yourself.'

'And a fine, fair wife.' Joscelin looked down at the comb between his hands. He had wanted to give Linnet a personal gift, and this, with its evocations of their wedding night, was perfect.

'God grant you many fine, fair children too,' Gamel toasted, and when he had finished drinking, lifted his empty cup on high and signalled to the serving woman. 'Cradle carving's my special talent . . .' He broke off as four soldiers swaggered into the alehouse and made loud demands to be served. One of them apprehended the woman who was on her way to Gamel and Joscelin.

'C'mon sweetheart, soldiers first, cripples c'n wait,' he sneered, grasping her arm and turning her round.

Joscelin opened his mouth, but Gamel quickly nudged him silent. 'Leave be. It's best not to tangle with Robert Ferrers's men, 'specially when they're drunk.'

'You let them get away with it?' Joscelin eyed the raucous soldiers with disfavour. He knew the type. Put a sword at their hips and they thought they had a licence to bully everyone they encountered. Give them ale to drink and the result was volatile. Looking at them, he judged that they had already consumed a good skinful.

'Too many of 'em to do otherwise. Town's been overrun with 'em recently. There's no peace to be had in any alehouse this side o' Sneinton.'

Joscelin rubbed his jaw. Robert Ferrers, Earl of Derby, was a known ally of Leicester's. Had Leicester's army of Flemings reached the Midlands, Ferrers would have leaped to join him, of that there was no doubt. Despite the fact that the Ferrers family owned substantial lands in Nottingham, the city had remained staunch to the Crown and showed no sign of wavering – a probable reason for the intimidation. With Leicester imprisoned and truces agreed until spring, there was bound to be a corked-up surplus of frustration and bad feeling.

Gamel shrugged. 'They'll not be here much longer. With all the King's men like yoursen coming into the city, it won't be as safe for them to do their mischief.'

'Can't the garrison deal with the troublemakers?'

'Oh aye, we've seen some rare old street battles and it goes quiet for a while, but then the trouble starts again. Earl Ferrers turns a deaf ear to all complaints. That's why the landlord's got hissen that dog in the yard.'

The muttering serving woman approached Joscelin and Gamel to replenish their cups. One of Ferrer's men tried to trip her up, but she avoided him, her lips compressed. Two tradesmen drank up and left. Joscelin decided to do the same.

'Strap on your leg,' he said to Gamel. 'I'll take you back to the castle.'

The old man reached down for his peg but, before he could grasp it, one of the soldiers had darted forward and snatched it away. 'Look what I got, lads!' he crowed. 'A lump of firewood!' He approached the firepit, tossing Gamel's stump from hand to hand.

Joscelin stood up. 'Give it back, now,' he said quietly.

'What if I don't?' The soldier threw the leg in the air and deliberately refrained from catching it until it was almost too late. Joscelin looked at the clusters of adolescent spots on the young man's face, at the erratic individual hairs sprouting on his chin and began to feel very angry indeed.

'You won't live to grow up.'

The young soldier's face reddened. He thrust out his bottom lip and dropped Gamel's leg into the flames.

All hell let loose. Joscelin leaped upon the soldier, and

his three companions leaped upon Joscelin. Gamel crawled across the floor to the firepit to rescue his peg before it became too badly charred. The serving woman ran outside screaming for help and encountered the landlord who had just returned from buying provisions in the market. He immediately unchained his dog and, fist wrapped around the broad leather collar, plunged into the dark interior of the alehouse. He was followed by Conan in search of Joscelin. For five frantic minutes, the pandemonium redoubled. The dog snarled and bit indiscriminately at anything it could get its teeth into. The landlord belaboured the soldiers with a quarterstaff which Conan seized from him and with his greater bulk and experience, wielded to far better effect. Joscelin emerged from the heap of flailing arms and legs with his fist firmly upon the scruff of a youth who was spitting blood, teeth and curses. He was the first of Derby's men to sprawl in the street outside, and his companions quickly followed. Nor did they stay to hurl invective. The dog made sure of that.

'Just like old times!' Conan declared with relish, leaning on the quarterstaff to regain his breath.

Gasping, clutching his bruised ribs, Joscelin gave him an eloquent look, and turned to Gamel who was blowing on his wooden leg and scrubbing at the worst of the charring with his sleeve. 'How bad is it? Can it be saved?'

'It'll do, until I can carve mesen a new un',' Gamel shrugged. He did not seem particularly perturbed, indeed, a grin slowly spread across his leathery features. 'It were almost worth it, just to see 'is face when you went for 'im, the little swine.'

Joscelin sat down on a bench and gratefully took the mug of ale the landlord served him. Several inquisitive customers braved entering The Weekday now that the danger had gone and Gamel became an instant celebrity.

'Is everything ready to leave?' Joscelin enquired of Conan. He had left his uncle in charge of loading the wain for the last stage of their journey home.

'Well, that's what I was coming to tell you.' Conan

rubbed the back of his neck. 'There's a split axle on the front wheel of the wain. It might last until we reach Rushcliffe, but then again it might break miles from anywhere. I've taken the cart down to Warser gate to get a wheelwright to patch it up, but it won't be ready until this afternoon at the earliest.'

Joscelin swore at the news, and then swore again, cursing Rushcliffe's wheelwright for a cross-eyed incompetent mash-wit.

'Does this mean another night in Nottingham?'

'It means travelling by moonlight if necessary,' Joscelin said. 'Come fire or flood, I'm sharing my wife's bed tonight.'

Conan flashed his brows and chuckled. 'A touch impatient, eh?'

'More than that.' He smiled wryly at his uncle. 'These have been the longest eight days of my life.'

The landlord's dog trotted into the alehouse, tail carried high with the pride of a job well done. It sniffed curiously at Gamel's leg, but the charred smell put it off, and having cocked its leg disdainfully against one of the trestles, it loped out of the back entrance to its kennel in the yard.

CHAPTER 24

MATTHEW THE PEDLAR unfastened his pack and, spreading a cloth of woven orange wool on the floor rushes, proceeded to lay out his wares for the inspection of his potential customers. Every Michaelmas and Easter for the past ten years Rushcliffe had been a point on the circumference of his regular trade route between Nottingham and Newark. He was a sturdily built, red-cheeked man in his early thirties and usually enjoyed the rudest of health. Recently, however, he had caught a cold he could not shake off and today he felt like death warmed up. A tight band of pain seemed to be slicing off the top of his skull and his limbs felt as if they were made of hot lead. Shoulders jerking, he fought to subdue the spasms of a racking cough, knowing that it was extremely bad for business.

Fingers shaking, he reached inside a leather pouch and brought out a selection of ring and pin brooches, some plain bronze, some enamelled. Another sack contained heavy glass and ceramic beads for women to thread on waxed linen string to make their own feast day necklaces.

One of the keep's laundresses stopped by with her little girl to watch him setting out his wares and started haggling with him over a small pair of sewing shears in a tooled leather case. Her astonishment was boundless when Matthew scarcely bothered to argue over the price of the shears and accepted her second offer with a wan smile. Emboldened, she also purchased half a dozen millefiore beads to make a necklace for her daughter.

'Lost your killer instinct, Matthew?' Henry asked as the laundress walked off, a gleam of triumph in her eyes, the

213

little girl skipping excitedly at her side.

The pedlar rumpled his hair and sniffed loudly. 'I'm not feeling too good to tell the truth. Must have picked up an ague at the last place I stayed.'

'I'll get me Mam to make you some hot cider and honey,' Henry offered. 'Or Lady Linnet might even have some mulled wine if I ask her nicely.'

Despite his savagely throbbing head, the pedlar did not miss the proprietorial note in Henry's voice. The dapper cut of Henry's tunic and the gilded belt embracing his hips had not gone unnoticed either. 'Taken a ride on fortune's wheel, have you?'

Henry's smile described a half-circle punctuated by two dimples. 'I'm Lord Joscelin's understeward these days. It's my task to see that everything runs smoothly and that grumbles get aired rather than fester in dark corners. Lord Joscelin says it's no use having a head if there's no backbone to support it and legs to make it walk.'

'He's a better master than the last two, then?'

'Make up your own mind. He'll be home by compline tonight.' Henry rubbed the side of his small, pugnacious nose. 'You landed on your feet arriving when the men are due back in triumph from battle. They'll all have money in their pouches and women they'll want to spend it on. And there's to be a fine feast tonight. It's not every day you get to sample marchpane fancies and roast swan with chaudron sauce, eh?'

Matthew gagged. Chaudron sauce was made from the bird's blood and entrails. It was considered a delicacy, but at the moment even the mention of ordinary food was enough to make him heave. The image of the dark, almost black sauce was too much for his quailing stomach.

'Best go and lie down,' Henry said, his smile fading as he took a proper look at Matthew. 'Your customers aren't going to run away in a day.'

Matthew nodded, suddenly not having the strength to argue. Wretched and as limp as a worn-out dishcloth, he began clumsily to replace his wares in his pack. Henry

214

stooped to help him, then jumped and spun round at an unholy whistling sound immediately behind him.

'Henry, look what Cook gave me!' Robert waved a bone flute under the servant's nose. 'Father Gregory says he's going to teach me to play a tune!'

'Sooner rather than later, I hope,' Henry winced and decided a serious word with Saul the Cook was long overdue since the man's nature appeared to have taken an irresponsible and sadistic turn.

'Oh yes, before Papa comes home, then I'll be able to play it for him.' Robert gave the flute another excruciating twiddle, then stopped, his head cocked on one side. 'What are you doing?'

'Matthew's too sick to sell his wares today; I'm helping him put them away.'

'Can I help too?' Before Henry could answer, Robert had knelt down on the tradecloth and had reached for a small heap of crosses carved of bone.

'Better, I think, if you leave me and Matthew to it, master Robert,' said Henry as the child returned the crosses to their leather pouch, pulled the drawstring tight and handed them to the pedlar. If Matthew was exuding evil vapours, then this was the last place Robert ought to be. Although the child had grown in stature and girth this summer he still looked as if a puff of wind would blow him away and his mother would roast anyone who put him in danger.

The pedlar reached for the bag of coloured beads but fumbled and knocked them over. Robert, attracted by the bright colours and millefiore patterns, ignored Henry and leaned over to pick them up. Matthew was taken with another bout of coughing. Spasms ripped through him and, although he covered his face with his cloak, sputum still sprayed into the immediately surrounding atmosphere.

'Go now,' Henry commanded Robert, his voice sharp with anxiety.

Robert jutted his small chin mulishly. Henry stared him out. The boy's eyes flickered away and landed on Matthew,

215

who was loudly wiping his nose on his sleeve. Robert pulled a face. 'Don't want to stay anyway,' he said and, turning on his heel, he scampered from the hall, the shrill notes of the bone flute alerting everyone to his passage.

It was very late and Joscelin had still not arrived. Linnet paced the bedchamber beset by niggling fear. The distance between Rushcliffe and Nottingham could easily be covered between dawn and dusk in the early autumn and he had said he would be here today.

She reached beneath her garments and drew out his letter on its leather cord. Clutching the folded vellum she walked to the hearth and crouched shivering before the glowing logs as her imagination conjured up all manner of horrible accidents that might have happened to Joscelin on his way home.

The wind moaned in the chimney and the flames gusted upon the logs. Otherwise there was a suffocating silence. Below in the hall the household was settling down for the night, the arrival hour of compline but a memory. The tables had been cleared of their fine linen cloths and golden glazed earthenware. Food had been returned to the kitchens – congealing roasts and ragouts, limp salads glistening with oil and vinegar, pears in hippocras syrup. All for nothing. How difficult it had been to make a pretence of eating and enjoying the several courses when she was feeling sick with anxiety. Robert had picked at his food and whined, demanding to know when Joscelin would be back. At length her patience had snapped and she had shouted at him. He had thrown a tantrum and been put to bed.

Rising from the fire, she went to look at him. He was curled in a fetal ball on his small truckle bed, his thumb in his mouth and his breathing easy and regular. She gently touched his cheek. It was flushed, but he did not appear overly warm and she decided that it was just a residue of his earlier tantrum. Linnet felt like screaming herself. She paced back into the main room and caught sight of herself in the distorted gazing glass that was hung upon a bare section of wall. It was another heirloom of the Crusader Montsorrel and she had always hated it but had never had the courage to take down and get rid of such a rare and valuable item.

Her face wavered at her, ghostly and pale, all eyes. The candlelight had darkened the colour of her gown from a soft, rich blue to something that a nun might wear. Raising her arms, she unpinned the brooch holding her wimple in place, removed her circlet and pulled the pale blue linen rectangle from her hair. A little better, she thought, and unwinding her braids, shook out the soft, honey-brown twists to frame her face. She studied the effect critically then, with an irritated sigh, covered the hated mirror with the wimple and turned away to continue her preparations for sleep.

The sheets were cold as she drew them around her naked body. She thought of Joscelin's warm bulk and the comforting security of his arms, and a fresh wave of anxiety assaulted her. Perhaps she ought to send a messenger to Nottingham to find out where he was. Her common sense told her not to be so foolish. Only for a dire emergency would a messenger be sent out in the deep of the night, not for an emotional whim.

She tossed restlessly, beset by feelings of helplessness and frustration, but at last, clutching the letter, she fell into a light, troubled sleep.

A dream came to her, shockingly erotic in content, and vividly real. She was lying on top of the bed dressed in the green samite wedding gown of her first marriage. A man was teasing her, his hand beneath her skirts and his hot, slow kisses draining her will.

'Does that feel good?' he whispered against her mouth.

'Joscelin,' she murmured, arching towards him. She raised her hands to bury them in his thick, dark hair. Instead she encountered thin wisps receding from a broad, bony forehead. Her eyes flew open and met the lustful gaze and cruel smile of Raymond de Montsorrel, and she screamed. Candlelight blossomed in her face and she shot

217

bolt upright in bed, scrabbling backwards in terror from the brightness.

The light flickered rapidly sideways as its bearer placed the candlestick on the coffer. She saw the glitter of raindrops on a wet cloak, the flash of metal on brooch and belt, dark hair curling around a worsted Phrygian cap. Her heart flopped over and over like a struggling landed fish.

'I didn't mean to startle you,' Joscelin said. 'I thought you'd be long asleep.'

She became aware that she was exposed to his stare, and that it was both admiring and avid. Kneeling up among the bedclothes, she took her bedrobe from the coverlet and put it on. 'I've not long retired, and then to a nightmare. I have been so worried, wondering where you were.'

'We didn't leave Nottingham until late.' He tossed his hat and cloak carelessly over the coffer. 'I was using that old baggage wain of Giles's and a wheel axle broke.' He drew her against him and cupped her face for a long, exploratory kiss.

Linnet closed her eyes and melted against him. His lips and hands were cold, but warmth spread through her from their touch. 'Do you want to eat?' she murmured between kisses.

'Only you.' He pushed aside the bedrobe to cup her breast. She uttered a small gasp that was silenced by another kiss. Her knees weakened.

'You're all wet!' she giggled as his lips followed the touch of his fingers, and spikes of hair struck cold against her throat and chest.

'That's because it's filthy weather outside,' he answered in a muffled voice as they fell together across the bed. She revelled in his weight, the hard pressure of his hips upon hers. She found her way inside his braies and softly rubbed. He was hot and hard, tight to bursting and she could not bear it she wanted him so much. 'Oh please, now!' she half-sobbed against his mouth in a fever of urgency, positioning herself to receive him and make herself whole.

The prickle of damp wool against her skin, the thrust of

hot, smooth flesh, the grip of his cold hands, lent exciting contrasts of texture and sensation to the experience, and within moments she was threshing on the crest of a wild climax as Joscelin drove to his own.

'God send me this kind of homecoming every time!' he chuckled as he began to recover and, having kissed her tenderly on each eyelid, he sat up and removed the rest of his clothing. Linnet eyed his physique by the glow of the candle. He was not heavily muscled and broad like Conan, indeed he carried more than a hint of his father's wiriness. Here and there were minor scars, reminders of his life as a mercenary, but she could see no new ones to worry about.

'Now do you want to eat?' she asked, conscious of other wifely duties. Coupling had always given Giles a voracious appetite and she knew that, despite his lean frame, Joscelin could put away vast amounts of food.

'Again? Give me time to rest, woman!'

'You know what I mean!' She nudged him, then smiled impishly. 'Besides, you might have difficulty in managing a second time without sustenance.'

'Would you care to wager?' His eyes gleamed.

Linnet lay back on the bed and raised one thigh. He looked at it gleaming through the slipped fold of the bedrobe and snorted.

'All right, I cry quarter. Go and bring me some food!'

'We heard about the battle,' Linnet said later as she watched Joscelin tuck into thick slices of cold roast swan and manchet bread. 'And all sorts of rumours have arrived with merchants and pedlars. Will there be peace now, do you think?'

Joscelin swallowed and shook his head. 'Hard to tell. The King and his sons are still wrangling in Normandy. At least there's a truce until the spring. Once the grass stops growing there is not enough provender for the destriers. I've known winter campaigns before, but if they can be avoided, they usually are.' He cut another slice from the side of swan breast and there was silence while he devoured it. Then he wiped his hands on a napkin and picked up his goblet. 'I know that the Earls of Leicester and Chester are imprisoned but there are still plenty of troublemakers left – Norfolk for one, Ferrers for another. His men were all over Nottingham making nuisances of themselves.'

Linnet waited until he had finished drinking and then refilled his cup. Robert Ferrers she had met on occasion – a strikingly handsome young man, although somewhat short of stature and possessed of the belligerent sharp-cornered aggression that so often characterized men who lacked height. He was one of Nottingham's main landholders and she knew that it was a source of anger and jealous envy to him that he did not also own the castle which was firmly in the hands of the Crown.

'That was another reason I was late,' Joscelin said. Rising, he dusted crumbs from the fresh tunic he had slipped on and went to the bed where his hastily removed belt still lay, his knife and purse hanging from it. Joscelin pulled open the drawstring of the purse, removed an item and returned to her. 'I went to The Weekday tavern and met up with an old acquaintance from my garrison days.'

'You were late because you were gossiping in a tavern?' Linnet pursed her lips and narrowed her eyes.

'He was being made fun of by a group of Derby's ne'er do wells. I persuaded them to leave with a little help from Conan, the landlord and his dog. And then I took Gamel back home. I bought this off him for you.' He laid an intricately carved wooden comb case in her hand. The comb within was fashioned of polished beechwood and inlaid with narrow bands of mother-of-pearl.

'I thought it was appropriate,' he said softly. 'A token of our wedding night.'

Linnet's annoyance at the thought of him drinking merrily in a tavern while she was worried sick for his safety was quickly overtaken by remorse. She turned his gift over and over in her hands, and felt the pressure of tears at the back of her eyes. 'It's lovely,' she said a little unsteadily. Giles had never thought to give her gifts, apart from the occasion of their betrothal and the belt of woven thread-of-gold had been to impress her guardian, not her. 'He's a member of the garrison, you said?'

'Used to be. He lost his leg in a sword fight and had to turn to wood-carving to earn a living. He has a small booth on the Weekday market up at the St Mary's end towards Hologate.' He grinned. 'Gamel even carves his own legs now.' Resuming his seat, he prepared to assault a dish of raisin honey cakes. 'I've commissioned him to put the carving on two new chairs for the dais, and he has promised to make us a cradle when the time comes.'

Linnet was about to enquire if they could afford such luxuries, then remembered what the messenger had said about the battle of Fornham. 'Did you take many ransoms?'

He gave her a look of irritated amusement. 'Do you want me to show you a tally of the keep's accounts? I assure you, I haggled a good bargain out of him – although not as good as yourself, I do admit, having seen you at work in London.'

She blushed a fiery red, but nevertheless held his gaze steadily. 'Well, did you?'

Joscelin sighed. 'Enough to keep Conan and his men until Easter. Enough not to have to raise the villagers' rents. Enough to pay for two new chairs and a set of bridle bells for my stepson's pony.' He dusted crumbs from his fingers and finished the wine in his cup, and added softly, 'And enough to repay my father for what he lent to us in the summer. He has need of coin and comfort now.' He frowned and shook his head. 'I never thought my prowess with the sword would lead me to contribute to my brothers' ransoms.'

Linnet ran her forefinger across the wooden teeth of the comb. Although she disliked Joscelin's father, she was slowly coming to understand that his brusque arrogance was the blazon on a battered shield of pride behind which lay the accumulated years of loneliness and pain. 'Will he find them, do you think?'

Joscelin shrugged. 'I expect so, unless they're at the bottom of a bog. The battle was fragmented chaos, but we held the better ground and the spine of Leicester's army was made up of untried Flemings – out-of-work weavers with spears. Once they broke and ran it was all over. Some of the locals pulled the Countess Petronilla out of a ditch half-drowned. Leicester was on the other side of the ditch but his horse had jumped it badly and strained a foreleg, so he was easily taken too.' He pushed his hands through his hair which had now dried in rough whorls. Leaving the hearth, he drifted into the bedchamber.

'I helped Papa search among the dead and the prisoners the next day, but there wasn't any sign of Ragnar or Ivo. If they escaped the killing and there is any sense in their skulls, they'll try and make their way back to Norfolk's lands.' He turned to face her as she rose from the stool by the hearthside.

'If we ever have sons other than Robert, God forbid that I should ever raise them the way my father raised us. I thought his face was going to crack beneath the strain of keeping it blank when we were looking at all the bodies laid out. Do you know, the only time I've ever seen him weep, the tears were made of usquebaugh.'

He held out his hand and Linnet came to him across the dimness of firelight and wrapped her arms around him.

CHAPTER 25

DRAWN BY THE SOUND of childish squeals of glee, Linnet left her sewing and went to look out of the unscreened window into the area of greensward between the inner and outer baileys. Joscelin and Robert were playing a chasing game, a romp of duck and dodge, catch and cuddle. Her heart filled with an ache of love that was almost too much to bear and tears prickled her eyes.

Beyond the keep walls the forest was an ocean of gold and russet leaves tossed by a frisky wind and it was with delight that she watched the tints ruffle and surge. She had Joscelin to herself for all of the long autumn and winter. No campaigning, no dangerous separations, just time to gain fulfilling knowledge. She was not in the least dismayed by the thought of short, cold days and even colder long, long nights. Their chamber faced south to catch the best of the light, it had a fire and they could always pile furs upon the bed if their body heat was not enough. She smiled at the thought, warmth settling in her loins.

The sound of a throat being cleared made her jump and turn quickly round.

'I'm sorry to disturb you, Madam,' said Henry, from the doorway, 'but you know Matthew the pedlar, the man you looked at last night – well, he's worse and I think Father Gregory ought to be fetched to him. Me mam gave him that willowbark tisane like you told her, but he just spewed it back up and his fever's worse than ever.'

'Is he so bad?' Linnet said with anxious concern.

'I fear so, my lady.' Henry tugged at one ear lobe in a worried manner. 'When me mam looked at him there were red spots all over his chest and belly, the size of silver pieces. She reckons as it's probably spotted fever.'

'I'll come down at once, and, yes, you had better send for Father Gregory,' she said, and hastened to follow Henry down to the hall, her joy evaporating like morning mist.

On inspecting the sick pedlar, Linnet's fears were both increased and diminished. Matthew did indeed appear to be close to death. His breathing was ragged and harsh and the only colour on his face was provided by the two bright red fever streaks on each cheekbone and the smudged dark caverns of his eye sockets. A glance at the spots Henry had mentioned, however, revealed that they were not pus-filled and angry as was usual in cases of the deadliest kind of spotted fever. If a victim survived they were nearly always left with scarred, pitted skin. These blemishes were pustule-free, more of a rash.

There was nothing to be done for him except to keep him lightly covered with a blanket, isolate him in a corner of the hall, and try to make him drink brews of feverfew and willowbark to keep the fever down.

'I must warn Robert not to go anywhere near him,' she said to Henry as she left the pedlar to Father Gregory's spiritual care. 'Obviously he is surrounded by evil vapours.'

Henry bit his lip and looked away, knowing that it was probably too late for the warning to be of any use.

The pedlar's fever did not abate; his lungs continued to fill with fluid and he died at dawn the next morning. The words *spotted fever* spread from mouth to mouth like a plague. Women gathered herbs to burn to ward off the sickness. Rushcliffe's village wise woman suddenly found herself inundated with worried customers. So did Father Gregory. Confessions poured into his ears by the bucketload, quite glueing them up. Holy relics and badges competed for space on people's belts with nosegays and pommanders. Lurid stories of previous epidemics were related by sundry generations of survivors.

224

On the day that Matthew was buried in the churchyard, the laundress and her daughter complained of feeling ill, and by the evening of that same day both were huddled upon their pallets with high fevers and blinding headaches. A report arrived via a pack train from Newark that the spotted fever was raging there too, and that several villages between the town and Rushcliffe had also been struck. The only good news was that most victims appeared to be recovering from the disease and that it was only dangerous to the old, the very young, or those already sick. Matthew had been suffering from a chest ague before he contracted the spotted fever, and Linnet believed that each must have worsened the other to the point of fatality.

Feeling tired and apprehensive, Linnet sent Ella away to bed, and sat down on the couch in the bedchamber to finish sewing the hem of a new tunic she was making for Joscelin. He was in the antechamber talking business with Milo, Henry, Malcolm and Conan, the men who were fast becoming the nucleus of Rushcliffe's administration. Conan was present in a military capacity, being responsible for the garrison and patrols. Milo straddled a bridge between the duties of seneschal and steward, with Malcolm as his adjutant and Henry ensuring that all went smoothly on a practical level.

The arrangement appeared to be working well. It was less than six months since Joscelin had taken up the reins of government, but there was already a marked difference in people's attitudes. They had a sense of purpose now, and knew that if they took pride in their work that their new lord would take pride in them and reward them accordingly.

The men left and Joscelin came into the bedchamber, arms stretched above his head to ease a stiff muscle. 'My brothers have been ransomed,' he announced. 'Apparently they were captured in the forest not far from the battlefield and held by some enterprising villagers in the apple cellar of the local alehouse.' Lowering his arms, he set them around her from behind and kissed her cheek.

'What happens now?'

'The usual,' he said and she felt his shrug before he released her and sat down on the great bed. 'They'll all snarl at each other but my father will snarl the loudest and Ragnar will be forced to back down – for a while at least. As soon as he sees my father's attention wandering, he'll up and cause mischief again, and Ivo will follow him.'

Linnet yawned and, leaving her sewing, followed him to the bed. Her limbs felt heavy and she was a little cold, as if it was the time of her monthly flux, although that was not due for another week at least. Her mind upon the relationship of Joscelin, his father and his brothers she asked, 'Why did you run away to Normandy when you were fifteen?'

He paused in the act of unlacing his boot. 'Because if I hadn't,' he said slowly, 'either I would have killed Ragnar or he would have killed me. Our father used to intervene – he put us in the dungeon once, in different cells, and left us there for three days. But that only made us hate him as well as each other. Running away was the only means of breaking the chain. When I came home, it was on my terms, not my father's, and I had outgrown Ragnar.' He pulled off one boot, then the other and leaned his forearms upon his thighs. 'Ragnar's still trying to break his chain, but his struggles just bind him all the more tightly.'

'And if he breaks loose?' Linnet asked.

Joscelin's lips compressed. 'Then God help us all,' he said, then turned his head at a sound from the curtain that partitioned Robert's small truckle bed from theirs.

'Mama, my tummy feels all funny and my head hurts,' Robert whimpered, wandering into the main chamber like a little ghost. Linnet gasped and started forwards, but Joscelin reached the child first and, picking him up, brought him to the bed.

'He's as hot as a furnace,' he said to Linnet, and they looked at each other in dawning horror.

'It's all right, sweetheart,' Linnet soothed, gathering his small body into her arms. 'Mama will give you something to make you better.'

226

Even as she spoke, Robert began to shudder with chills. 'I saw Papa, my old Papa in a dream and I was frightened.'

Linnet flickered a glance at Joscelin. 'Hush, there's nothing to worry about, dreams cannot hurt you,' she crooned, kissing her son's flushed brow. 'Sit here with Joscelin while I fetch you something to drink. It won't taste nice but it will help your poorly head.' Easing Robert into Joscelin's arms, she left the bed and went quickly to the hearth.

Joscelin felt the rapid throb, throb of Robert's heartbeat against the fragile rib-cage and heard the swift, shallow breathing, and knew as he had known in the past how terrifying it was to be helpless.

In the bleak darkness of a wet October dawn, Joscelin fitfully dozed in the box chair at the side of the great bed. Beneath the covers, Linnet and Robert slept, the latter tossing and moaning in the grip of high fever.

The rain drummed against the shutters, but in his mind the sound became the drumming of horses' hooves on the hard-baked soil of a mercenary camp in the grip of burning midsummer heat.

He sat astride a bay stallion, a horse past its prime with a spavined hind leg. The harness was scuffed and shabby, so was the scabbard housing his plain battle sword. With the eyes of a dreamer he looked upon his own face, seeing the burn of summer on cheekbone, nose and brow, the hard brightness of eye, and the predatory leanness that showed an edge of hunger.

A woman ran to his stirrup and looked up at him. She was slender and dark-eyed, her fine bones sharp with worry beneath lined, sallow skin. He tasted wine on his tongue and knew that he had been drinking, although he was not drunk. Dismounting, he followed her urgings to a tent of waxed linen that bore more patches than original canvas. As he stooped through the opening, the foetid stench of fever and bowel sickness hit him like a fist. Overwhelming love and fear drove him forwards, instinct pegged him back.

227

The child on the pallet still breathed, but he wore the face of a corpse; the dark eyes he had inherited from his mother were sunk back in their sockets, his mouth was tinged with blue. He turned his head and looked at Joscelin. 'Papa,' he said through dry, blistered lips. The woman uttered a small, almost inaudible whimper and she, too, looked at Joscelin with dead eyes before slowly turning her back on him.

'No!' he roared, and jerked awake to the sound of his own voice wrenching out a denial.

Linnet raised her head from the pillow and looked at him hazily.

'A bad dream,' he said, struggling to banish the image of Juhel's waxen face. It faded but remained at the back of his head, a small, haunting shadow. 'How is he?'

Linnet leaned on one elbow to look at her child, and set her palm against his neck. 'The willowbark has held the fever, but not taken it away. He'll need another dose soon. I must try and get him to drink.' She sat up and pushed the hair out of her eyes, then pressed her hands into the small of her back.

'I'll fetch him something – apple juice from the press?' he suggested, knowing that the trees had been recently harvested and that cider brewing was underway.

'Yes.'

Joscelin hesitated, perturbed by the dull tone of her voice and unable to see her face because of the tangled screen of her hair. 'Linnet?'

She turned towards him and folded her arms across her breasts, not in modesty, but in a gesture of shivering cold. 'It will be for the best if you give the apple juice to Ella and do not come back,' she said through chattering teeth. 'She has had the spotted fever before.'

Fear flashed through Joscelin's veins like a sheet of fire and flared into terror. 'What are you saying?'

'I think you know.'

Hard-burning, stubborn anger joined Joscelin's other emotions. 'Then you will also know that you cannot command me to something like that.'

'Then I ask it.'

'No!' he said violently. 'You ask too much. Breaca sent me away when Juhel was dying. She said that it was a woman's domain, that I should be out earning silver to keep us in firewood. And when he died and she took sick with the bloody flux, she would not let me near her.' His voice became ragged as old scars were torn into new wounds. 'Christ on the Cross!' he choked. Striding to the bed, he seized her in his arms and crushed his mouth down on hers in a long, hard kiss, absorbing her sweat and fever-heat.

'There!' He parted from her gasping and darkly trium-phant. 'I'm irrevocably committed now. I'll go and bring the apple juice and the willowbark tisane, and you won't gainsay me again!'

CHAPTER 26

IS LEFT FOOT presented, Ragnar leaned into his shield and hammered his sword hilt lightly against the rawhide rim in a steady litany of challenge. The blade was fashioned of whalebone and his opponent was Hamo, one of his father's knights who had agreed to a practice bout in a corner of the bailey.

All the pent-up anger and tension within Ragnar came seeping to the surface. He found himself wishing that it was for real, that he could strike and see blood flow. From the perimeter of the battle circle that had been roughly marked with a charred stick, soldiers, knights and retainers shouted advice and encouragement. Ragnar could smell their anticipation. A rapid glance upwards showed him that his mother and aunt were watching from the bower window. He would give them what they wanted, show them the kind of warrior he truly was. But desire for their admiration was not the spur that drove him. That particular goad was in the possession of the badger-haired man who had reined in his grey horse and, hand on hip, was watching the encounter thoughtfully.

As wary as a stalking beast, Ragnar started to circle Hamo, seeking a weakness, an opening to exploit. He lunged. Hamo twisted and quickly parried with his shield.

'Come on, Ragnar, get him!' shouted someone in the crowd. Two or three others added their voices and Ragnar noted them with grim pleasure. For all that he had been in disgrace for joining Leicester's rebellion, he was still the heir. His father had pardoned him and accepted him back into the family fold. It was believed in some quarters that William Ironheart was beginning to fail and Ragnar had

230

done nothing to disabuse that notion. Only let them look to him as Ironheart's natural successor.

Hamo wove and dodged and managed to strike the occasional good blow on Ragnar's shield, but the effort it cost him was told by his scarlet complexion and whistling breath. Ragnar remained on the balls of his feet – light, elegant and deadly.

'Get yourself out of that corner, Ham, or he'll have you!' A knight in the crowd yelled, his own sympathies with the older, heavier man.

Eyes blazing golden with exultation, Ragnar sprang like a lion and made a triumphant killing blow. Hamo dropped sword and shield and fell to his knees, conceding defeat. Ragnar's howl of triumph rang around the bailey, raising hairs on scalps and spines. The whalebone sword lifted on high, he pivoted in a slow circle, accepting the adulation of the women in the window splay. Eyes hot with joy, he sought his father's gaze. But his father's attention was not upon him. Ironheart's back was turned and he was listening to the mercenary Conan de Gael, who had just dismounted from a foam-spattered courser and was talking rapidly.

Ragnar's exultation transformed into bitter rage. He spat over the side of his raised shield, and broke through the circle to advance upon his father and the mercenary.

'It is very important that you come . . .' Conan was saying, but broke off and turned to look Ragnar up and down. 'Learning to fight?' he said pleasantly.

Ragnar wished that his whalebone sword had a true steel blade. He looked at his father, but the old man's expression was so stiff with control that it might have been carved of rock. Not a word of defence for Ragnar emerged from between the hard, thin lips, but then in the barren waste of his soul, Ragnar had expected no other response. 'I already know how to fight, but if you want me to teach you a lesson?' he sneered and raised the whalebone sword suggestively.

Conan lifted his brows. He, too, glanced at William, but receiving the same stony response, he shrugged his powerful shoulders. 'Why not?' he said. 'I've to wait while a fresh horse is saddled and a man gets rusty without regular practise. Besides, it won't take long.' He left William and went to Hamo. 'May I?' He took the whalebone practice sword from the knight and tested its balance, the bracelets on his wrists clinking together.

Ragnar quivered with rage at the mercenary's light, nonchalant tone. The man was near his father's age, with more scars than an old tomcat. His blond hair was receding and the suggestion of a paunch bulged his quilted surcoat. It was obscene that Conan de Gael should even be allowed within Arnsby's courtyard.

A larger crowd was gathering now, drawn by the scent of drama. Martyn pushed and wriggled his way to the forefront of the audience. Conan saw him and winked and grinned. Martyn winked back and then cheekily stuck his tongue out at Ragnar.

It was the final insult and Ragnar attacked without warning, fast and savage, a howl forcing itself through his teeth. Conan was flung backwards by the flurry of blows, but after the first undignified leap, he kept Hamo's shield high to absorb the violence of Ragnar's attack and set himself to play a defensive role until he had worn the edge off the younger man. Again and again Ragnar came at him, full of vicious aggression, determined to make a kill. Conan parried and heard the howls of derision from the watchers, the yells encouraging Ragnar to finish him off.

'Come on, you whoreson, yield!' Ragnar snarled through his teeth as he pressed Conan to the edge of the charcoal circle.

'Don't waste your breath, boy!' Conan retorted. 'That's one of the first rules.'

Ragnar redoubled his efforts. Although he still moved gracefully, his face was pink and streaked and his chest thrust rapidly up and down. Conan, sweating and red himself, did not neglect to notice the signs. He waited his moment and then made a deliberate, almost clumsy feint at Ragnar's legs. Ragnar immediately lowered his shield to counter the intended blow, but Conan straightened and changed direction with lightning rapidity, and the blade of the blunt sword came down across the back of Ragnar's unprotected neck.

'You're dead,' Conan panted, lowering his guard and standing back.

An uneasy silence descended, and Conan knew that the onlookers were not quite believing what they had seen, it had been so quick. Ragnar quivered, muscles tense to renew the attack. 'Don't make a fool of yourself,' Conan said quietly out of the side of his mouth. 'Part of learning is knowing how to take defeat.'

'I don't need a lecture from vermin like you!' Ragnar spat and, tossing down his sword, shoved his way out of the circle, making sure that his shoulder barged Conan's in passing.

Conan returned the whalebone sword and shield to the knight from whom he had borrowed them and thoughtfully watched Ragnar stride towards the hall. The spectators started to disperse.

'He let his hatred cloud his senses,' Conan said to William. 'Otherwise he's an accomplished young man.'

'You didn't exactly encourage him to be rational,' William answered coolly as a fresh horse was led out for Conan.

The mercenary set his foot in the stirrup. 'Neither would an enemy,' he retorted. 'He's wound up as tight as the pulleys on a loaded mangonel. Just make sure that when he lets fly you aren't standing in the way.'

Ironheart grunted. 'I don't need your advice on how to handle my own son. Ragnar doesn't like you. I don't entirely blame him.'

Conan sighed deeply, seeing the wide rift that still lay between himself and William. Perhaps even in Morwenna's time it had never been otherwise.

William scowled at him. 'Anyway,' he said shortly, 'why send for me? What makes you think I am going to be of any comfort to Joscelin?'

'If the woman and child die, he will need you. You have known the grief. I do not want to see him ruined as you and I were ruined. I've always had the lad's best interests at heart, whatever you think of me. After all, he is my kin. The de Gael's were not always mercenaries and ne'er-do-wells. My grandfather had lands and a proud bloodline, but he was brought low by taking the wrong side in a dispute. I want Joscelin to succeed; I want him to have a better life than either you or I have done.' Conan paused and sucked a breath through his teeth, his complexion dusky with high feeling and a dawning embarrassment. 'I have said more than I should, but perhaps it is not the time for holding back.'

They rode out of the keep in silence, a normal state for William but not for Conan, who was usually as bright and brash as a jay.

'The woman and child are mortally sick then?' William asked after a long time.

'I do not know,' Conan said wearily. 'As few people as possible are going near them lest they breathe in the evil vapours – Lady Linnet's instructions. I only know that Joscelin has scarcely eaten or slept since they took ill and this morning he sent for Father Gregory.'

'Does he know you have come to fetch me?'

Conan shook his head. 'I do not think he knows anything but the mortal peril of his wife and stepson.'

William compressed his lips. 'He's only been wed to the wench since harvest time,' he growled. 'You're not telling me he's heartsick beyond all healing.' And without waiting for Conan's contradiction, rode on ahead, making it clear to the other man that he did not wish to communicate at all.

Joscelin looked down at the congealing bowl of soup that Stephen had brought to the bedchamber half an hour since. Small circles of fat were forming at the edges, encrusting the pieces of diced vegetable sticking out of the liquid. His stomach, normally robust enough to accept any form of sustenance without demur, clenched and recoiled at the mere suggestion of food. He abandoned the bowl on the hearthstones, an untouched loaf beside it, and reached for the flagon of wine that Stephen had brought with the soup. That, at least, he could swallow without retching.

With dragging feet he returned to the bed and sat down in the box chair that had become his prison and his prop during two lonely nights of vigil, or was it three? Time had lost all meaning as he watched the contagion invade and consume.

Father Gregory had visited mother and child, and used the opportunity to shrive them. A precaution and a comfort he had said, but it had been small comfort to Joscelin. To shrive them was to acknowledge that they might not recover.

His eyes felt hot and raw with lack of sleep, but he knew that if he closed his lids, if he relaxed his vigil for one moment, that death would come robbing on swift, stealthy feet and take Robert and Linnet from him as it had taken Juhel. And if death stayed away, the dreams would not.

He stared at mother and child, sleeping together in the great bed. Perhaps Robert was breathing more easily since the last dose of feverfew, or perhaps it was just the fancy of his aching mind. Linnet tossed and moaned softly, her hair darkly damp, her face and throat marked with the red blotches of the fever. She pushed at the covers and began to mutter. Her body arched and bucked and she licked her dry, pale lips.

Joscelin leaned over her, grasping her hot hand in his, stroking her forehead.

Her glazed eyes flew open and she stared directly at him, but he knew she could not see him. 'Raymond,' she panted. 'Raymond, someone will come, please don't.'

'It's all right, Raymond's not here,' he murmured, and turned briefly away to wring out a cloth in cold water and then lay it across her brow. 'You're dreaming.'

'No.' She frowned, weakly fighting him. 'Not a dream.' Her body moved beneath the damp linen sheet, arching sinuously as if receiving a lover. 'No, please, it is too dangerous. I . . . ah!' A spasm caught her, leaving him in no doubt that her imaginary lover had entered her body. Prickles of cold shivered down Joscelin's spine. His gut churned as she twisted and cried out, for the sounds, despite the torment of fever, were of pleasure, not pain. Raymond de Montsorrel. He was being cuckolded by a phantom in his own bed.

'Linnet, in God's name, he's dead!' Joscelin cried and knelt on the bed to hold down her thrashing body. 'Christ, wake up, I cannot bear to listen to this!'

She fought him, her muscles rigid, her lips drawn back from her teeth in something that was part-snarl, part-sob, then she gasped and went limp.

Almost weeping himself, Joscelin slowly released her. 'Oh God,' he said weakly, and put his head in his hands.

'It will be safer if you let me pleasure you in the other way,' she said in hoarse, pleading whisper, her gaze darting upon the ceiling as if she could see moving pictures there. 'If Giles were to find out he'd kill us both. I know you like it when I do this.'

The urge to crush his hand over her mouth and silence her almost overpowered him. He sprang to his feet and strode into the antechamber while he still retained the control to do so. Pressing his temple against the cold stone wall, he fought his gorge. He remembered the bawdy barrack-room gossip in Nottingham. Raymond de Montsorrel's appetite for futtering had been legend. The man himself had been nothing to look upon – balding with bowed legs from a life in the saddle, and an enormous, bulbous nose, but that had never spoiled his attraction as far as women were concerned. His talents were all tucked away inside his braies, or so the gossip went. One of the garrison whores had boasted that Montsorrel had taken her up against the wall of St Mary's church on Ascension Day, and that the size of his manhood would have put a bull to shame. And Linnet had let him . . . Joscelin ground his fist against the wall, not feeling the pain, and tried to think with his head, not his lurching gut.

It was no different to himself and Breaca, he told his recoiling instincts. She had been twice his age, amused and experienced in the ways of lust, and he had had no sense of guilt or sin at the time. He had no right to cast stones and he was deeply chagrined to find them lying at his feet anyway, tempting him to pick them up and hurl. Good Christ, Linnet was fighting against death and all he could worry about was the fact that she had lain with Raymond de Montsorrel. Self-disgust filled him and he turned round to go back to the bed. The sight of his father standing in the doorway prevented him.

'Conan told me,' Ironheart said and stepped over the threshold. 'And for once he was right to open his stupid big mouth. Stand aside and stop glowering. I've had the spotted fever, both kinds.' He pointed to a series of small, pitted scars on his chin. 'Nearly died myself, so they say, although I don't remember. I was only four years old at the time. Where are they, through here?'

Joscelin nodded. His head felt muzzy and he sensed one of the incapacitating megrim headaches lurking on the borders of his consciousness. Damn Conan, he thought, and at the same time felt a tight swelling of relief in his throat and behind his eyes. Unsteadily, he followed his father into the bedchamber.

Ironheart stood at the bedside. Joscelin heard the low mutter of Linnet's voice.

'What is she saying?' He hastened to his father's side in alarm.

Ironheart looked sidelong at Joscelin, his grey eyes bright with speculation. 'That you cannot lie with her any more because she is with child.'

'What?'

'Is it true?'

'I . . . I don't know. She didn't say anything before the fever struck.' Joscelin sat down on the chair at the bedside and clasped his hands. 'It is too soon I think, and there have been very few opportunities.' How many opportunities had there been with Raymond de Montsorrel? His eyes flickered to the little boy. The fever flush had faded from his brow and he appeared to be sleeping deeply and calmly. He resembled his mother, scarcely any Montsorrel traits to be seen lest it be in the slant of cheekbone and jaw. Did it really matter which Montsorrel? An exquisite pain was beginning to throb through his skull, making rational thought impossible. Behind his closed lids, small specks of colour performed a wayward dance and he groaned softly.

'You need to sleep,' Ironheart said giving him a sharp look. 'You'll do more harm than good by driving yourself so hard. There is nothing you can do that a maidservant cannot. Go to.'

Joscelin was horrified. The thought of what Linnet might gasp out to a maid or his father in her fever was enough to make him shake his head in vehement denial of the suggestion. And there was also the memory of how he had lost Juhel and Breaca, one in the flesh, the other in spirit. 'I cannot!' he said hoarsely.

'You must.' Ironheart laid his hand on Joscelin's shoulder and stared him in the eye. 'I do not know how loyal your men are, but if necessary I will give the order for you to be taken and bound. Milo and Conan for sure will not hesitate.'

'You would not dare!' White-faced, the first waves of nausea rolling over him as the megrim attacked, Joscelin returned his father's glare.

For reply, Ironheart removed his hand from Joscelin's shoulder and headed towards the door, his breath indrawn to bellow.

'For Jesu's sake, you do not understand!' Joscelin cried after him, his voice breaking. The effort of forcing his shout through the tightness in his throat increased the viciousness of the band of pain pulsing across his forehead. 'I had a woman and child once before and I lost them. I wasn't there when it mattered!'

Ironheart winced as if the raw anguish in Joscelin's voice had been a physical blow. Turning, he took two paces back towards his son, then stopped. His fists opened and closed and his throat worked. When the words came they were heaved out with effort as if they were enormous stones. 'I wasn't there for your mother,' he said. 'That was the worst part of it. When I arrived from their summons, she was dead, but still warm enough for me to have believed she still lived.' He gave a choked laugh. 'They said I tried to kill myself for love of her, but it wasn't true. It was for hatred of myself.' Clamping his hands around his belt, he drew a shaken breath and asked, 'The woman and child you mentioned, this happened on the tourney circuit in your missing seven years?'

Joscelin nodded, his pain too great for him to be amazed that his father had voluntarily spoken of his own hidden guilts and griefs. 'Breca took me under her wing and then into her bed. She bore Juhel in the winter of '63. Your grandson would have been ten years old by now.'

'What happened?'

'Camp fever.' Joscelin bit his lip. 'He wasn't strong enough to survive it. When he died, so did the fire between his mother and me . . . or perhaps it was already out. I don't want to lose Linnet and Robert too.' He bowed his head and closed his eyes. Even the candlelight was almost too much to bear as the headache invaded and wrecked his every faculty.

'You won't lose them,' Ironheart said gruffly. 'The child looks to be over the worst from what I saw just now, and the woman's got a stubborn core of steel.'

'No, Papa, I'm losing her too. Everything has changed.'

'Don't talk such drivel. All that has changed is your ability to think. I can tell by your voice that you're suffering a megrim.' His harsh features suddenly softened and he breathed out heavily. 'Conan thought I'd dredge up some wise words from somewhere to comfort you, but I fear he overestimated my ability. All I can say is that I am here. You have to trust me. Give me the care of your wife and stepson for tonight, and I promise I won't let them down.'

Joscelin wanted to deny his father, tell him it was

239

impossible, but the pain that had been toying with him like a cat with a mouse now sheathed its claws in his skull and the world became a seething red agony. He was only dimly aware that the words emerging from his mouth were not the ones he desired to say.

Ironheart went to the door and shouted for the servants.

Linnet felt something lying on top of her. Hot and smothering, it pinned her to the mattress making it impossible to breathe. She struggled to push it off, but it responded by tightening its grip. She thought she could feel cruel fingers digging into her flesh, and the bowl of her pelvis cramped as if she had been invaded. Choking for air, she opened her eyes and at first saw only the darkness of the night illuminated by the one lonely flame of the night candle beside the bed. Sitting in the chair she could just make out the figure of a man. He started to rise and bend towards her and as he did the weight on her chest became leaden.

'Don't fight me,' whispered the voice of Raymond de Montsorrel. 'You cannot win.'

She tried to scream, but there was no breath in her lungs and, as she opened her mouth, it was possessed by a hungry, wet kiss, raspy with beard stubble. A whirling darkness engulfed her. Her eyes were blind, but she could still hear voices. Raymond whispering in her ear with the darkness of lust, Giles raging, calling her a harlot. Joscelin . . . Joscelin saying *Christ, wake up, I don't want to listen to this.* Another voice, closer, harder with frustration.

'Come on, woman, damn you, breathe! Do you think I'm going to do this all night!'

She felt the force of breath driving into her lungs. The weight on her chest eased and the darkness ceased to whirl. The voices faded and her lungs shuddered, filling with cold air. She tasted usquebaugh on her lips as she drew another breath.

With a tremendous effort she forced her lids apart. The same lonely night-candle flame illuminated the room, and the figure was still leaning over her, eyes darkly gleaming.

Silver-grey hair and brows, gaunt bones, their hollows sketched with shadow drew her to slow recognition of William de Rocher. He stretched out a calloused palm and laid it on her brow in a surprisingly gentle manner. She tried to flinch, but her weakness was too great. Indeed, her eyelids were too heavy to hold open and after a brief struggle she had to let them flicker down.

'Hmph, still hot,' she heard Ironheart say, 'but steadying down I think. It was the angle of her head on the bolster, shut off her breath. You girl, see to your mistress.'

'Yes, sir.'

Linnet heard the trickle of water in a bowl and in a moment a blessedly cool cloth was laid across her forehead. The bedside chair creaked as Ironheart sat down again. Why was he here, she wondered vaguely, and where were Joscelin and Robert? It was too difficult to think. Sleep was claiming her in a soft, deep blanket and she welcomed its embrace.

Ironheart watched Linnet sink into sleep as the maid lightly wiped her down. Dawn was still several hours away, late because of the encroaching winter, but he judged that the worst of his night vigil was over. Would she have started breathing again by herself if he had just moved her head? He was not sure. The technique he had used was one shown to him by his grandfather who had picked it up from a Greek physician on the long march from Antioch to Jerusalem. Once before William had used it. One of his squires had gone swimming in the Trent, had got into difficulties, and had been dragged out blue and unbreathing. William had given him the gift of breath and in the end, the youth had revived and been none the worse for his ordeal.

He wondered if Joscelin had had a premonition that Linnet might slip away tonight. Morwenna had possessed a touch of the second sight, although not enough to save herself, and there was much of her in Joscelin. Morwenna had suffered terribly with bad headaches. He remembered that the priest had wanted to exorcise her, claiming that she must have demons dwelling in her head. Agnes had said outright to one of her maids that she believed Morwenna was a witch. It was the only time she had ever voiced that opinion, for William had sworn to cut out her tongue if she ever spread such lies again.

It had not prevented her from thinking them, he knew. Perhaps the unenlightened would have called what he did just now witchcraft, the giving of the breath of life. It was so close to the taking of it, the way cats and evil spirits were supposed to do to infants.

'Call me if there is a change in your mistress,' he said to the maid, and went stiffly into the antechamber where Joscelin was sleeping with Robert on a makeshift pallet. The child was visibly improving. Probably by the morning he would be complaining of hunger pangs. A thin, small waif of a thing he was, the illness having sapped him to pallor and shadows, but he also possessed the tenacity of a clinging vine.

Ironheart turned his attention to the man against whom Robert was curled. Even in sleep, the marks of the megrim pain were etched between Joscelin's dark brows. He remembered his son's earlier words. *A woman and child on the tourney circuits*. The thought that had been held on the surface by other considerations now began to seep into every level of his being. Ironheart stooped to the hearth to pick up the flagon of usquebaugh-laden wine. Seven missing years in which, unaware, he had become a grandfather and then been bereaved. Joscelin was so much like him that he almost felt cursed.

CHAPTER 27

Christmas 1173

A PIG'S BLADDER football sailed through the air and struck the dais with a solid thump, dislodging a branch of evergreen and a pair of antlers pegging the foliage in place. The bladder bounced off the decorations and squelched into a dish of tripe on one of the lower tables. A diner fished it out of the tripe and hurled it back the way it had come. Blazing a comet trail of white, sticky lumps, the bladder curved across the dais and landed on the floor at Father Gregory's feet. A look of intense revulsion on his fine-cut features, the priest nudged the football away with the edge of his boot.

With considerably more enthusiasm, a lyme hound surged from beneath the table to lick at the remnants of tripe still clinging to the bladder. When a servant approached with the intention of rescuing the missile, the dog wrinkled its muzzle and snarled, then secured the bladder firmly between its forepaws and bit at the knotted end. There was a loud explosion. The remnants of the football shot into the air and came down on the dog's back. Whining, ears flat, the lyme hound retreated beneath the table and knocked Father Gregory off the trestle.

Conan leaned down and flexed his massive forearm to haul the unfortunate priest off the floor. Howls of mirth and appreciation were hurled in their direction by the unruly crowd below the dais.

'Church always does take a tumble on Twelfth Night!' Conan laughed, roughly setting Father Gregory back on the bench. 'Never fear, you've got all year to take your revenge in tithe payments, Peter's pence and penances. Isn't that right, Josce?'

'If you say so.' Joscelin, resplendent in a tunic of dark-red wool trimmed with gold silk braid, toasted his uncle in mead. The garment was a Christmas gift from Linnet. Robert had one exactly the same and could not be persuaded to wear anything else.

Conan made a rude face at Joscelin's indifferent tone of voice. 'God, you're getting to be as sour as your father!' he declared. 'Where's your Twelfth Night spirit?'

'Wearing thin,' Joscelin said as one of the cook's apprentices capered past the dais wearing a woman's gown, a wimple set askew on his yellow curls. Twelfth Night was never any different – short of murder, everyone was given license to behave as outrageously as they desired, and the rules were always stretched to their limit. Usually Joscelin would have joined the merriment, if not with alacrity, then with a reasonable degree of grace, but tonight, although he knew he should be rejoicing, he just could not find the spirit. It was as though a dark cloud were hovering above his head. The residue of yet another megrim burned behind his eyes. They came upon him frequently now; there was seldom a week when he was not dogged by flickering colours and violent headaches.

There had been no real peace since October's end, since Linnet had almost died of the spotted fever and shown him in her delirium what he did not wish to see. And she had no recollection of her illness beyond the first day of fever; she did not know what she had said, and what had changed. He had tried to behave in a normal manner while he battled his demons, but from the bewildered, almost hurt way she looked at him sometimes, he knew that he had failed.

'Oh come on, Josce! Don't be . . . don' be miserable!' Conan's words were starting to slur under the powerful, sweet influence of the Welsh mead that Brien FitzRenard had sent to them as a Christmas gift in thanks for Joscelin's aid earlier in the year. 'Let's . . . let's have a game of hoodman blind!' He pushed himself to his feet, took a step backwards and then steadied himself. 'I'll wear the blindfold first if you want. Henry, lend me your hood!'

Joscelin opened his mouth to say that he did not wish to play hoodman blind or any other boisterous, stupid game that his uncle had lurking up his sleeve, but the good humour surrounding him and the look of bright anticipation on Robert's face made him close it again and yield to Conan's jovial bullying.

A space was cleared in the well of the hall. Conan, blindfolded by Henry's blue fustian hood, which he had donned back-to-front, was placed in the centre of the space, turned round and round several times to disorientate him, then given a vigorous push. The basic plan of the game was for the hoodman to try to capture someone to take his place, and for others to poke and prod and tease him without being caught themselves.

Conan made several wild, bear-like swipes and embraced only thin air. He growled like a bear too. Giggling, Robert ran in beneath the mercenary's clutching arms and struck him on the leg. Conan lunged, Robert evaded and, shrieking with glee, ran to the safety of Joscelin's arms.

'Papa, did you see?'

Conan struck rapidly towards the sound of the child's excited voice. Joscelin spun Robert out of the way. Conan's fingertips touched the soft red wool of Joscelin's sleeve. Joscelin twisted sideways, grabbed hold of a laughing Milo and flung him straight into Conan's path. The mercenary's arms closed on his prey. Now all he had to do was guess who he had caught.

'Not a wench,' he muttered, spreading his hand across the bearded face. 'Not unless she's standing on her head.'

'You'd be surprised what a wench will do on Twelfth Night, Sir Conan,' Milo said, affecting a falsetto voice that had an appreciative audience doubled up with laughter.

'Reckon I would. In fact I'd be downright buggered!' Conan retorted, feeling lower across shoulders and chest until his fingers happened upon the ornate silver-gilt cross that Milo wore on a cord around his neck. 'I'd know this anywhere. It's bigger than anything Father Gregory's got!' the mercenary crowed ambiguously. 'Has to be you, Milo de Selsey!' He pulled off the hood and gave a hoot of triumph.

The game progressed, becoming rough and more boisterous. People swapped clothing to confuse the hoodman, although when Robert was captured by Henry and had to wear the hood everyone gentled their performance, and Joscelin allowed Robert to catch him, although not too quickly for the sake of the child's pride.

As the hood was secured around his head, Joscelin discovered that he was actually enjoying the sport. It was like the tourney field where all thought was bent upon controlling the body in order to survive and no space was left for introversion and brooding.

'Now then,' he rubbed his hands, entering the bawdy spirit of the game. 'To catch me a coney!'

He felt a push low on his leg and heard Robert's squeal. The hood had a smell of wool and sheep-oil and very effectively blocked out the light from the sconces and candles. He tried to blot out the calls and countercalls of disguised voices, ignored the pushes and buffets as best he could, and gave his instinct free rein. The megrims he suffered were a bedevilling nuisance, but they had the side-effect of sharpening his senses, including the sixth one. He began to turn towards the nudges and blows before they were made; he began to know whose voice it was on the first word.

Twice he almost captured Milo, then Henry. He deliberately missed Robert, who spun away, shrieking with glee. Conan was very nearly his victim and only escaped by sheer, brute strength. Joscelin staggered, unbalanced. To one side of the dais, the musicians struck up the tune of the lover's carol.

> *A young man came with heart aflame*
> *Into the north country*

And there he met a maiden yet
As fresh and fair as he
When this bachelor was come to her
He kissed her lovingly
And looking down in her bosom
He said I do love thee

A softness brushed against him and a hint of summer herbs and rose petals invaded the wool smell. Turning quickly, he grabbed and pulled, and suddenly there was a slender body in his arms and the summer scent was much stronger. Before he could begin a litany of bawdy suggestions and guesses, his victim snatched off the hood and stood on tiptoe to kiss him on the lips.

The audience cheered and whistled.

'Yuk,' said Robert, screwing up his face.

Linnet and Joscelin looked at each other with a mutual combination of merriment and sparking lust, and kissed again.

He said 'Dear maid, be not afraid
But trust thyself to me
The power of love down from above
Does now inspire me
thou can'st give relief without a grief
As love tells unto me
And we can meet and fully greet
Each other nakedly.'

Flushed, laughing, a little giddy with the mead she had drunk, Linnet hung against Joscelin, returning him kiss for kiss, then flopped on to their bed, her eyes soft with desire, with wanting and the hope that tonight had broken the mould of the past two months.

Ever since she had almost died of the spotted fever, Joscelin had been different – not towards Robert, he still doted on the little boy. If anything, the bond between man and child had deepened; the change was in Joscelin's attitude to her. He treated her now in the cautious fashion that had characterized the days in London when he had been a mercenary with a reluctant duty to perform and she had been a lady of high birth beyond his reach. Now and then she would find him looking at her, his expression one of frowning, almost angry bewilderment, but when she asked him what was wrong, he would shake his head and smile, and pretend that he had not been brooding. She had learned not to push the point.

But now he was neither brooding nor remote, his eyes bright with laughter and desire. Whatever was troubling him had been banished for the nonce at last, and she intended it to remain that way. Reaching up, she unpinned her wimple and shook free her braids, then leaned forward, letting him inhale their herbal scent while their lips met and parted, met and parted. He buried his hands in the heavy coolness of her hair, then slowly slipped them down her body.

Below in the hall where the Yule celebrations still continued, the revellers danced to pagan tunes that wore only the barest dressing of Christian decency.

Naked, Linnet pressed herself shamelessly against Joscelin, offering him her breasts, the willow slenderness of flank and thigh, the soft mound of her womanhood. He poised over her and she arched herself to receive him, her eyes closed, her lips parted. The pause extended and anticipation became impatience. A cold draught whispered between their bodies. Joscelin muttered a soft oath and, lifting himself off her, rolled on to his back.

Linnet opened her eyes and stared at him in worried astonishment. 'What's the matter?' Her gaze darted over him. His manhood, which had been quiveringly eager a moment ago, was now rapidly becoming flaccid. The look on his face told her that he was well aware of the fact and that he was angry.

'Nothing,' he said stiffly, and moved to cover himself with the sheet and counterpane. 'I'm tired and I've drunk too much mead.'

Linnet did not for one moment believe that the effects of drink and exhaustion had suddenly attacked him at the crucial moment. She tried to look into his eyes, but he avoided the contact and stared silently up at the cobalt-blue ceiling with its dusting of silver-painted stars.

Her body clenched with pain. Tears filling her eyes, she left the bed and went to take a comb from her coffer so that she could tidy and braid her hair for sleep. It was the comb of polished beechwood he had brought her from Nottingham that she picked up. The mother-of-pearl inlay gleamed with a white, rainbow lustre as she raised it and drew it down through her hair. Joscelin had only performed the task once or twice since giving it to her, and she had been too proud to ask him of her own accord.

Rapidly she plaited her hair and secured it with a strip of soft leather, then returned to bed. He was still lying on his back, but he had closed his eyes. 'Is it something I have done or not done?' she asked, her throat tight. 'In God's name, tell me. I would rather you took your belt to me than treat me like this!'

The silence dragged out for so long that she thought he was not going to respond, that whatever was troubling him had eaten so deeply inwards that he was unable to bring it to the surface, but at last he turned his head on the pillow and opened his eyes. 'Raymond de Montsorrel,' he said wearily. 'In this very room on this very bed.'

Linnet gasped as if he had indeed struck her, and for a moment the room spun around her and she thought she was going to faint. She clutched at the bedclothes. Her stomach heaved. 'Who told you?' she asked weakly.

'Who else knows, you mean? Oh, I assume it's a well-kept secret since I've heard no rumours within the keep itself.' His eyelids tensed with pain. 'You told me yourself while you were wild with fever. No, that's wrong,' he amended grimly, 'you acted out a scene before my very eyes, begging him not to with your voice but wantonly offering your body at the same time. And then you said it was really too dangerous and you offered to satisfy him by

249

other means which you didn't specify, but I could well guess at.'

'Oh dear Jesu,' Linnet whispered brokenly and hung her head, her whole frame shuddering. 'I thought it was finished, buried. If I could undo it, I swear I would.'

'So it is true?' His jaw clenched. 'I would have asked you before, but while I was ignorant at least I could cling to the hope that it was a delusion of your fever.'

Linnet wrung the sheet and coverlet until her knuckles were white. 'Yes, I lay with him.' Her breath caught on a sob. 'He was so kind and gentle compared to Giles. I . . . I thought he really cared for me but all he wanted to do was prove to Giles that he could better him in everything, that he could even have his wife just for the crooking of his little finger.'

'You lay with him because he was kind to you?'

Linnet swallowed, but the choking lump in her throat just grew larger. 'Yes, I mean no . . . I don't really remember.' Panic surged through her as she saw a look of disgust flicker across Joscelin's face. This was more horrible than she had ever imagined. Certainly far worse than the beatings she had endured at Giles's hands. 'Giles was away,' she said. 'Probably jousting in France, I don't remember the reason, only that he was not here at Rushcliffe. Raymond was good to me – spent time with me and did not shout or become impatient. How was I to know that he was baiting his trap? I was not even fourteen years old. One evening he came to my chamber – to talk about a feast he was planning for when Giles came home, so he said.' Linnet clenched her lids as if in pain. 'He brought a flagon of wine with him – not the ordinary household stuff, but a mixture of Burgundy and Ginevra with spices. I can still taste it now.' She heaved and almost retched. 'By the time I realized what he was about, it was too late and I was incapable of stopping him, nor did I wish to, God help me.

'When I came to my senses in the morning, I had a dreadful headache. He was not there beside me, but I knew what we had done.' Shivering, she risked a glance at

Joscelin's face, but his expression was as unreadable as stone. 'I ordered the maids to prepare a tub and almost scrubbed my skin off, but it didn't do any good. I dared not confess my sin to Father Gregory, so I kept it to myself, but it wasn't the end of the matter by far.' She rose jerkily from the bed and, pulling on her bedrobe, began to pace the room as if it were a cage. In contrast, Joscelin remained as still and watchful as an icon.

She rubbed her palms together, feeling them slick with cold sweat. She would far rather have faced physical torture than the mental torture of revealing her shame to Joscelin. As she passed the mirror, her distorted reflection caught her gaze, showing her a wild, frightened creature with doom in its eyes, and she knew that she would remember that image for ever. 'Raymond said that if I didn't let him have his will whenever he wanted, he would tell Giles about what had happened in his absence. I was so afraid. I knew that Giles would kill me.'

A grimace crossed Joscelin's face. 'How long did you endure this?'

'A little over a year I think – until my pregnancy started to show. He left me alone then. Corbette's daughter Helwis was becoming a woman and he had started to notice. He had a new innocence to corrupt then.'

The question, unspoken, loomed between them like an enormous coiled serpent. She felt it take and squeeze her until she could not breathe. 'I am almost certain that Robert is Giles's,' she said. 'Raymond was away much of the month when I conceived, and the times he did pester me I managed to persuade him that other ways could be just as rewarding.'

Joscelin grimaced again.

'I was trapped, don't you understand!' she cried at him and thumped the counterpane in frustration. 'If it had not been a mortal sin, I would have thrown myself off the battlements! How can you sit there and judge me when you know nothing of the abuse I suffered!'

He shook his head. 'I know that you were Raymond de

Montsorrel's victim. The lack is within me. I keep seeing you with that vile lecher; I wish my inner eye was blind.'

'As blind as my own not to imagine you and the woman you had before!' Linnet rallied enough to retort, stung by the unfairness.

'Yes, I know, I know,' he snapped irritably. 'Do you think I have not reasoned with myself over and again these last weeks? I tell myself it doesn't matter, the past should be buried – I don't have to look further than my own father for proof of that. If it was something I could govern, then I would.'

Linnet bowed her head and began to weep. 'You loathe me now,' she gulped.

Joscelin's heart wrenched as she broke down before him. Unable to bear her anguish, he pulled her against him and enfolded her in his arms. He could not tell her that it did not matter, because obviously it did. He was as susceptible as Giles to the torments of jealousy, suspicion and pride. But holding her now, he vowed that they were not going to ruin his marriage. 'No,' he said gently, 'I love you. My heart was lost that first day on the road when you faced down Giles and me for the sake of your child and I saw your courage.' His eyes suddenly narrowed, and his lips tightened. 'I'll be damned if Raymond de Montsorrel is going to defeat us from beyond the grave. Tomorrow I'll burn this bed and all that has gone before, and commission a new one that will be ours alone.'

Linnet raised her tear-streaked face and upon it he saw hope and doubt mingled.

'For tonight you can sleep like a true mercenary's woman,' he added, 'on skins by the fire.' Without more ado, he tugged the coney fur coverlet from the bed, and his cloak from his clothing pole. Catching her hand in his, he pulled her to the banked hearth. It was the work of moments to spread his cloak upon the floor, lie her down upon it, and cover them both with the coneyskin canopy.

Her body pressed against his, seeking reassurance and comfort. He curved his arm around her waist. The warmth of her breath fluttered at his throat. Beneath his hand, her skin was like silk and, against the softness of her thighs, he felt the welcome throb of desire. He blotted all thought of Raymond de Montsorrel from his mind and thought instead of a summer night beneath the stars, of the champing of destriers at the horse lines, and the mournful sound of a soldier's bone flute. His hands moved in slow tandem with his thoughts. Linnet's breath quickened, but she remained very still. He could feel her tension, the inner coiling of her body in response to his touch. He parted her thighs, kneeling up as he entered her, teasing her with his thumb until her reticence was broken and, arching, she cried out. Her pleasure rippled the length of his shaft and, with a cry of his own, he thrust fully home, claiming her forever from Raymond de Montsorrel.

CHAPTER 28

R AISING HIS HEAD, the buck sifted the wind, ears
and eyes alert, jaws moving rhythmically on birch
bark strips. Something had disturbed the deep
forest atmosphere, but he was unsure yet as to what it was
and whether it was dangerous. His breath vapourized in
the frozen February air and beneath his dainty cloven
hooves the ground was dusted with snow. Tiny flakes,
needle-sharp, fell from a flat blanket of grey cloud making
it difficult for the buck to absorb any scent and he remained
nervous, facing the east where the light was brightest and
from which direction he sensed the disturbance came. The
other bucks in the herd had stopped eating now too and
were staring eastwards with flickering ears and restlessly
switching scuts.

With a sudden pitter-patter of footfalls a group of does
skittered past the bachelor stags, paused briefly as one to
look over their tails towards the east, then whisked away
through the trees. Faintly, but clear and true on the breeze,
threading through the particles of snow, the buck heard
the knell of a hunting horn and scented the rank, terrifying
odour of dogs and men.

Within seconds the clearing was empty as the bucks
bounded into Sherwood's dark heart, but their slots
remained and the snow was falling too softly to cover them.

Chest heaving with the exertion of the chase, eyes bright
with the lust of having witnessed the death of the magnificent fallow buck, it took Ragnar a moment to realize he
was being addressed, and by Robert Ferrers, Earl of Derby,
a young man you did not ignore when it was his hunt

254

you were attending, having invited yourself because you happened to be a drinking crony of one of his knights.

'I'm sorry, my lord, I was still caught up in the wildness of the chase.'

'So I see,' Ferrers said, amusement curling his narrow lips. He had narrow eyes too, forest-dark, and his features were pointed and elfish. 'I asked how your lord father was these days?'

'He is well, my lord,' Ragnar answered somewhat stiffly, well on his guard now. Robert Ferrers was not the kind who made small talk with relative strangers.

Ferrers nodded and toyed with a loose thread on his saddlecloth. 'He seems to have emerged from last year's troubles gilded with honour.'

Ragnar shot Ferrers a look that was half-angry, half-questioning. Was he being baited or courted?

The kennel-keepers were whipping the dogs into order and two bearers were tying the buck upside-down to a carrying pole. 'Ride with me awhile,' Ferrers commanded and reined his horse out of the ring of trees where they had brought the buck to bay. The snow had all been trampled away, leaving churned soil and bloody leaf mould. When his squires made to follow, he gestured them to stay back.

The forest closed around them, the light a strange, luminous grey filled with small stinging barbs of ice. The heat of the chase began to seep from Ragnar's veins, leaving him aware of how numbingly cold it was becoming. Weather like this always cursed the borders of spring.

Ferrers regarded Ragnar with pursed lips. 'You and Sir William are reconciled, so I am led to believe?'

'Yes, my lord,' Ragnar said warily.

'And your half-brother, the one who married into such good fortune? Are you and he on speaking terms?'

Ragnar swallowed. Beneath him his horse paced smoothly, his hoofbeats thud-thudding like his heart. 'I haven't seen him since we met in London last summer.'

Robert Ferrers grunted. 'It is a pity your father did not try to obtain Linnet de Montsorrel for you instead of him,' he said, watching Ragnar closely. 'I would have thought it was the natural thing to do, you being the heir.'

Ragnar said nothing. He might hate Joscelin and feel scalding resentment for the way their father had favoured his precious bastard over his legitimate sons, but his rebellion had taught him caution. Hearts and hatreds were not to be worn on the sleeve and he could play as cagey a game as Ferrers.

'Perhaps your father has a wife in mind for you also?'

'I do not know, my lord.' Good God, was he going to be offered Ferrers's sister or some such? His gut churned.

Ferrers sighed down his thin, sharp nose with the beginnings of irritation. A huge silver deerhound lolloped to his mount's shoulder and jogged with them through the trees. The snow was falling with determination now, the flakes penny-sized and dry, the kind that was likely to settle and remain on the ground for weeks unless it thawed. 'I can understand your suspicion,' said the Earl, 'and I suppose being locked in an apple cellar for two days and nights by a hoard of ignorant peasants must have knocked some of the stuffing out of you, but there is no need to be on tenterhooks with me.'

There was every need, Ragnar thought, but his curiosity must have shown on his face, because Ferrers smiled and leaned intimately across his saddle. 'The winter truces end soon. Robert of Leicester might be in prison, but he was only one wave on a huge floodtide. What will King Henry do when France, Flanders and Scotland take up arms against him in the spring? What was won can soon be lost.'

Ragnar looked into the gleaming, narrow eyes – weasel's eyes, predatory and lustful. What was won can soon be lost? He looked over his shoulder. Men were riding along the path behind them, fellow guests, equerries, beaters and foresters, keeping their distance, but obviously concerned by the increasing heaviness of the snow. 'What do you want of me, my lord?'

Ferrers smoothed his mouth corners between forefinger and thumb. 'I believe we might be useful to each other in

256

the future. Running to my banner as you ran to Leicester's would be downright foolish, and a waste of time to us both . . . but if you were lord of Arnsby, matters might be differ ent.'

'You mean if my father were to die?' Ragnar's voice suddenly cracked with dryness. What was Ferrers suggesting? Rapidly in his mind's eye he saw a vision of himself waiting in a dark stairwell with a dagger in his hand, or tipping a vial of poison into a flagon of wine.

Ferrers saw him balk and laid a hand quickly on his sleeve. 'In the fullness of time, of course,' he soothed, but his eyes told a different story.

Ragnar looked at Ferrers, both drawn and repelled by what he was intimating. It was like the time in Leicester's camp when he had raped a woman – the excitement of the struggle and the subjugation, the final tremendous thrust, and then the revulsion and self-disgust.

'We'll talk again later,' said Ferrers, and turned his horse around to join his companions, the dog turning faultlessly with him. Ragnar sat where he was until the bearers came past him with the body of the deer. Snow fell, making new spots on its fallow hide and was melted away by the residual body heat. Blood dripped in slow, black clots from its muzzle and stained the forest floor. Ragnar gasped and spurred away from the sight of death to join his fellow huntsmen, seeking their company and their loud, trivial banter to take the bitter darkness from his mind.

'A nunnery!' Agnes said through her teeth to Ragnar. 'I'll see him in hell first!' Her tone was pitched low and the hatred with which it smouldered was made all the more venomous. Her maid, who had become accustomed to the low muttering these past few days, did not respond to it except to make herself as inconspicuous as possible.

Agnes left the window splay where she had been sitting to watch William and his entourage ride away in the direction of the Nottingham road. 'He cannot force me. I'll not be put aside like a worn-out dishclout.' She faced her son who was here in her chamber to be fitted for a new tunic. He was standing somewhat impatiently for the seamstress who was taking note of his measurements by making knots in lengths of string.

'No, Mama,' Ragnar said, a glazed look in his eye, and stretched his arm horizontally to be measured from armpit to wrist.

Agnes regarded his broad, handsome strength, the gleam of light on his red-gold hair and his powerfully moulded bones. William wanted to obtain a wife for Ragnar and was looking around for a suitable girl. Agnes feared that she understood his reasoning. Martyn was soon to be a page in Richard de Luci's household and her nest would be empty of chicks. She was of no more use to him. He would fill her place in the household with Ragnar's young wife. Jealousy and fear gnawed at her vitals. If she were placed in a nunnery, she would not be able to keep an eye on the girl – as she had kept an eye on Morwenna.

With an irritated sound, she grabbed the string from the seamstress and waved her away. 'I'll do it myself!' she snapped. 'Go and look in the coffers to see what fabric we have.'

'Yes, Madam.' The woman curtseyed, her eyes devoid of emotion.

Agnes moved in closer to Ragnar's pungent, masculine warmth. She knew that he had been out in the village last night, gaming in the alehouse and wenching. A residue of his indulgences still clung to his skin. 'You would not put me away in a nunnery if you were master here, would you?' she wheedled.

He recoiled slightly and looked at her sidelong as if she had said something shocking. 'Of course not, Mama.'

Agnes smiled and kissed his cheek, feeling the prickle of beard stubble under her lips where once his skin had been smooth and silky. 'I knew you would say that, you're a good son.'

A slight shudder ran through him. At first, dismayed, she thought it was because she had touched him, but then he said abruptly, 'Nottingham is going to be raided by Robert Ferrers.'

Her hands fumbled with the string and she stared up at him, a red flush creeping from her lined throat into her face. 'When?' She moistened her lips.

Ragnar shrugged. 'Today, tomorrow, the day after. I don't know exactly, but it will be while Papa is there. I was brought a warning by one of Ferrers's own men last night. That's why I went to the alehouse. I have been in contact with the rebels since I went to Ferrers's Candlemas hunt. They are going to hit the town, and, if all goes well, the castle.' He folded his arms and leaned against a decorated stone pillar, his eyes golden with hunger. 'There is an understanding that were I suddenly to become master of Arnsby there would be a handsome reward for the person who put me in that position.'

Agnes's wits were dull, but she possessed an innate craftiness and it did not take a scholar to unravel what Ragnar was implying. 'You've employed someone to kill your father?' she whispered, fear and exultation mingling in equal proportions.

'It is more of an unspoken understanding. If I had wanted, I could have stopped him from riding out just now, but why should I?' He gave her a challenging, moody stare. 'He has never taken the time to stop for me lest it be to bawl his disapproval. Arnsby is mine now, every stick and stone and beast in the field.' He ran a possessive hand over the blood-red chevrons decorating the pillar.

Agnes bit her lip and drew the knotted string through her fingers. 'What if your father returns unharmed?'

'Who's to know – will you tell him?'

Agnes sniffed scornfully. 'What reason would I have after the way he has treated me all these years? You have my support and always will. One thing I will say to you – do not mention anything of this to Ivo. He is a weak reed and not to be trusted.'

'I can deal with Ivo,' he said softly.

'What about the bastard and his wife?' she said after a

moment. 'I heard William say that he was meeting them in Nottingham?'

Ragnar smiled, but it was not a pleasant expression. 'I also let it be known that the lord of Rushcliffe was a thorn in my side and I would pay handsomely to have him plucked out. The woman and child won't be harmed,' he added magnanimously. 'I've no grudge against them and they will make valuable pawns since I will be kin to the deceased with a family interest in what happens to the lands.' Turning to the window he set his foot on the stone seat in the niche, and rested his arm across his knee.

Agnes had never heard him speak like this before, in so controlled and calculated a way. She did not doubt that he would deal with Ivo, and anyone else who stood in his way, and she realized with a disturbing jolt that her love for him was tinged with an undercurrent of fear.

CHAPTER 29

WILLIAM IRONHEART OWNED three houses in Nottingham on the hill that meandered down from the Derby road at Chapel Bar towards the merchants' dwellings on Long Row, the Saturday market and the Poultry. The second house was leased to a wine merchant. The third was currently empty, although soon to be inhabited by the merchant's son and new daughter-in-law as soon as the marriage had taken place in her hometown of Lincoln.

Ironheart's own residence was maintained by a man and wife in late middle age. Jonas kept the house in repair and ran his own small odd-job business from the premises. Tillie took in laundry from the well-to-do merchants further down the Row as her own sideline and there was always a huge cauldron full of linens and steaming lye suds in the back yard.

From the doorway Linnet watched the pungent steam billowing skywards and felt queasy. Inside the house it was no better, the air being humid with the odour of boiled cabbages and onions from the second cauldron that bubbled over the firepit in the main room. These last three days her stomach had been unsettled. Indeed, only this morning before they set out she had almost been sick when Stephen had laid a dish of hot smoked herrings on the table in front of her. Usually she enjoyed such fare, but she had scarcely been able to swallow a morsel of bread without retching.

She had begun to toy with the suspicion that she was with child but, since it was indeed no more than a suspicion, she had said nothing to Joscelin. Her flux was scarcely more than a week late, and in her previous marriage she had been slow to conceive. She smiled through the nausea, thinking of the new bed that now occupied the main chamber, with its coverings of linen, sheepskin and northern plaid. All ostentation had been consigned to the pyre of wood in the bailey. Together she and Joscelin had watched the burning of the Montsorrel family bed and the construction of one that would honour the name of de Gael.

Joscelin was up at the castle visiting acquaintances from his garrison days and had intimated that he would not be home until well after noon. Robert had been thoroughly upset because he could not go too, but Joscelin's promise to take him round the market booths on the morrow had somewhat mollified the little boy.

In a corner of the yard he now played with a young ginger cat that Tillie had bought at the Weekday market up by St Mary's to deal with the endemic rat and mouse problem. Linnet watched her son tenderly. He loved animals of any sort, although those with the thickest, softest fur were the most popular. She and Joscelin had been forced to share the bower with an injured squirrel Robert had discovered on a pony ride. Only last week he had rescued a dormouse from the cook who had intended to serve it up, baked in its skin, as a delicacy for the high table. That too now dwelt in the bower, its wicker cage hung beside that of the squirrel in the alcove where Robert slept. No mention of dormouse as table fare had been made since.

She was just turning to go back inside the house when Ironheart returned from his own errand to a wool merchant who lived at the top of Organ Lane close by the city wall.

'Daughter,' he greeted her with a gruff nod.

Linnet inclined her head in response and went dutifully inside the house to offer him wine if he so desired it. Since her illness in the autumn, their relationship had subtly altered. She knew that Ironheart had been present at the crisis of her fever for Joscelin's sake and that he had remained at Rushcliffe until it was certain that she would recover, his support silent, but solid as rock. Somehow she no longer thought of him as a threat nor did she have to stiffen her spine in his presence to control her fear. Yes, he had his flaws, some of them deep and ugly, but beyond them was the rock, and to that she trusted.

For his part, Joscelin's father had tempered his aggression towards her and sometimes seemed almost on the point of awkward tenderness. He had ceased speaking darkly to Joscelin of beating and bedding, and while she and Ironheart seldom held prolonged conversations, at least they could communicate with each other without bristling up like cat and dog.

'Joscelin not back yet?' Ironheart asked. His long nose wrinkled at the smell of the steam from Tillie's cauldron. 'You can never tell whether it's Tillie's washing or the dinner in here,' he commented.

'No, he said he might be late.'

'Gossiping with his old cronies I daresay.'

'Yes.' She gave him a wan smile.

Ironheart eyed her from beneath his brows while rubbing his hands together. 'You're as green as a new cheese,' he said abruptly. 'Is something the matter?'

'No, Father.' Linnet moved further away from the bubbling cauldron. 'A slight stomach upset, nothing more.'

'Hah!' He continued to eye her, not in the face but up and down.

Linnet blushed and quickly put her hand to her belly to reassure herself that it was flat, showing only the natural slight curve of former child-bearing, but the gesture itself gave her away.

Ironheart, however, did not press the point. 'You need to go and rest then,' he said mildly. 'Dry bread and sweet wine are good for such an ailment.' He jerked his head. 'Go on, get you to the loft for an hour. I'll watch the boy.'

Linnet hesitated for a moment, but another pungent waft of steam from the cooking pot caused her stomach to lurch and she accepted the offer with a grateful smile.

★

263

'I don't like it,' said Ranulf FitzRanulf, sheriff of Notting-ham, and stared out of the high tower window. Spread before his view was Nottingham's immediate southern hinterland – the rivers Leen and Trent holding between them the broad green flood plain of The Meadows, and beyond them the villages of Briggford, Wilford and Clif-tun. 'There are too many of Ferrers's men in the city and they are bent upon mischief.' He ground his teeth upon his thumbnail which was already gnawed down to the quick.

Standing beside his former paymaster, Joscelin too looked out on the scene of pastoral tranquillity. The trees lining the riverbank wore new mantles of tender green and the meadowland was a lush carpet of flower-starred grass dotted by grazing cattle. Smoke was twirling in lazy grey wisps from the roofs of the tanneries on the banks of the Leen, and a supply barge was wending its way upriver towards the supply wharf at the foot of the castle rock. 'I noticed a lot of Ferrers's soldiers when I was here in the autumn,' he said.

'Around the time of the battle of Fornham?' FitzRanulf turned to look at Joscelin out of watery light blue eyes. The left one had a slight cast so that FitzRanulf never seemed to be looking directly even when he was. It was an illusion, for the sheriff of Nottingham was the most direct of men. 'They were vultures waiting their moment to strike, but it never came. When news of Leicester's defeat arrived, they gradually melted away.'

'And now they are back.'

'The winter truces are at an end.' FitzRanulf examined his bitten thumbnail. There was nothing left to chew and he turned his assault to a forefinger. 'I have men enough to defend the castle, but not the town. Ferrers has too much influence there. If anything serious happens, the citizens will have to fend for themselves. How long are you staying?'

'We're only here to buy provisions. Two, three days at the most, although my father will probably leave guards at his house since it's so near to Ferrers's.'

264

'Your father's here too?'

'On different errands and likely to be here a couple of days more than myself. I know he intends to call on you.'

FitzRanulf nodded, then he gave a humour-filled scowl. 'It was the worst turn the Justiciar ever did me when he gave you Linnet de Montsorrel to wife,' he grumbled. 'I lost the best group of soldiers I ever had. Still, it's an ill wind. At least I can rely on Rushcliffe's loyalty now. When the Montsorrels had possession, getting them to cooperate on anything was like trying to turn water into wine. Old Raymond could be as difficult as they come.'

'Yes, I know.'

FitzRanulf cocked his head, his expression curious, but Joscelin had no intention of divulging the particular 'difficulties' that Raymond de Montsorrel had bequeathed to him. 'I have to return to Rushcliffe,' he said diverting the conversation, 'but I can leave some of my men here if you want – trained mercenaries with full battle kit.'

'At whose expense?' enquired FitzRanulf, revealing himself to be as shrewd about money as he was about everything else.

'They have a contract with me until midsummer. All you need to do is feed and house them. They are within a day's march if I have need of them at Rushcliffe.'

'Fair enough,' nodded FitzRanulf. 'I know a golden goose when it waddles over my foot. If there's anything I can do for you in the future, let me know.'

Having visited the sheriff, Joscelin repaired to the guard-room to pay his respects there and was furnished with a piggin of the castle's justly famous ale and some bread and new cheese. One of the guards, Odinel le Gros, so named because of his enormous gut, leaned his elbows on the trestle and moistened his lips salaciously. 'Hey, Josce, is it all really true about Raymond de Montsorrel then?'

Joscelin's mouthful of bread and cheese suddenly seemed too enormous to swallow. He chewed, took a drink of ale, and shrugged, affecting bored indifference.

'Aw, come on, stop teasing. You know what I mean.

265

They say he tupped every woman on the estate between the ages of thirteen and fifty. I bet everywhere you ride you see little bastards made in the old man's image!' Odinel sniggered, his dark eyes glistening. 'Don't you remember that wench we brought in here who was futtered by him against St Mary's wall. She said his pizzle were bigger than a bull's! I reckon it should'a' been preserved when he died, just like wi' a saint's fingers!' He stared round the room, seeking approbation.

The words ran on in an obscene torrent. Joscelin heard the laughter of the other soldiers, but it was fuzzy, as if it were coming from a far distance. A red mist was before his eyes and the sweat sprang on his body. And yet he did not leap at Odinel and tear his voice out of his throat, for to do that would be to acknowledge that Raymond's ghost still had a hold on him. As far as Joscelin was concerned, the burning of the bed had been the end of the matter.

'You have a high imagination,' he said when he could trust himself to speak. 'Raymond de Montsorrel was a common lecher, and whores will always tell exaggerated tales of any high-born client who passes between their thighs. It gives them a feeling of importance and makes people listen to them,' he added pointedly.

Odinel blinked uncertainly. There was a short, uncomfortable silence. Joscelin wondered what on earth he was truly doing here in the guardroom. His title was a barrier as tangible as the gold silk braid hemming his tunic and the beryl and amber brooch pinned high on the shoulder of his fur-lined cloak. Although he had not deliberately willed it, the situation had changed and he had become an outsider, one of 'them', and because of his past status, viewed with both admiration and resentment. In his absence they would talk about him as they talked about Raymond de Montsorrel. And it was not fair to stay.

Joscelin took his leave of them quickly, with relief on both sides. As the guardroom door closed behind him, the soldiers breathed out and relaxed as if they had been standing to attention all the time he had been in the room.

266

And on the other side of the door, Joscelin closed his eyes, and inhaled deeply like a prisoner released. His only dilemma, as he started down the hill towards the Saturday market, was where to go. Not back to Linnet, not yet, with Odinel's words still sliding across his mind like a slime trail.

In the end, he turned his feet in Conan's direction, which he knew of old would be The Weekday tavern across town near the market cross. He wound his way through narrow streets and alleys into the dip of Broad Marsh, then up the other side. The stream running down the middle of Byard lane was blocked again, this time by a dead dog, and various residents of the cut-through were conducting a lively argument as to who was responsible for clearing the obstruction. Joscelin picked his way through the sludge at the side of the lane, easing past dark doorways that gave entrance to cramped dwellings with central firepits and smoke holes in the roof. At one point, near the top of the hill, there were steps cut down to a series of habitations carved out of the soft sandstone rock upon which the city was built.

A cordwainer sat outside his home, a small trestle set up to hold his tools and the cut pieces of leather he was making into shoes. Next door to him stood a small dyehouse and, as Joscelin walked past, its proprietor paused as he pummelled a cloth in a cauldron of bright orange water to watch him. Beside the dyeshop and next door to The Weekday alehouse was a booth belonging to Rothgar the swordsmith, and Joscelin paused here to examine a long poniard.

'Best Lombardy steel, sir,' said the proprietor, laying down his tools and coming forward.

Joscelin had know Rothgar since childhood, when Ironheart had brought him in wide-eyed delight to this very same booth. Rothgar's wife, dead now, had fed him sugared figs and made a fuss over him, and Rothgar had let him handle the weapons.

The poniard he was handling today had a nine-inch

blade, sharp on both edges, and a haft of plain, but pleasing to grip natural buckskin. His own poniard, which had served him since his early days as a mercenary, was wearing out. It had already been fitted with several new grips and the blade was thinning and would not hold an edge for longer than a week.

'How much?'

'Eight shillings,' Rothgar immediately responded and wiped his wrist across his full moustache. 'The materials alone cost me four, and there's my time and skill on top.'

'I'll give you five,' Joscelin said, testing the sharpened edge against the ball of his thumb. 'That's how much I'd pay on the road in Normandy.'

Rothgar clicked his tongue. 'Normandy's closer to the Lombards and the steel costs less because of it. It's a mortal long way to go to get a bargain.' The smith tugged on the thick, silver-salted hairs on his upper lip. 'Tell you what, being as you and your father are good customers here, I'll let you have it for six and a half.'

'Six,' said Joscelin, 'and I'll commission a blunt sword for my stepson while I'm here.'

Rothgar continued to tug at his beard. 'You drive a hard bargain, my lord, but I reckon it fair enough if you are going to put more business my way. Six shillings it is.'

'On the nail,' Joscelin said, putting the coins down on top of the post used for that purpose.

Rothgar counted them and swept them into his cupped palm. 'You'll need to bring the lad into the shop to be measured.'

'This afternoon?'

'Aye, that'll do.' Rothgar started to unlatch the toggle on his beltbag, but paused and lifted his head. 'What's that rumpus?'

Joscelin ducked out into the street. At first he was blinded by the brilliance of daylight after the earthy darkness of the shop. From the direction of the Hologate road he could hear shouting and the clash of weapons. Then louder shrieks of terror and dismay, and the bright blossoming of flame.

'God's eyes, what's happening?' Rothgar peered over Joscelin's shoulder, his forging hammer in his fist.

'I can't tell, except that it's trouble. Best shut up shop and make yourself and any valuables scarce. As a weapons smith, you're a prime target. I'm going to The Weekday, my mercenary captain should be there.'

Rothgar nodded dourly and, without further ado, bellowed for his apprentice and began gathering his wares together.

Joscelin moved quickly across the narrow, muddy street and started up the hill towards the alehouse. Folk were emerging from their shops and houses, exclaiming, looking anxious, demanding to know what was happening. Other townsfolk were beginning to pour down the hill away from the market-place, fleeing in panic.

'Reavers!' a panting merchant paused to cry warning. Tucked under his arm, a fat goose wildly paddled its orange feet. 'Derby's men, save yourselves!'

Joscelin thrust himself against the tide of panicking humanity, shouldering through them until he reached The Weekday. The evergreen bush that was usually suspended on a horizontal pole from the gable advertising the place as an alehouse was trampled in the mud outside the door and smoke was billowing in choking clouds from the burning floor rushes which had been kicked across the firepit to set the tavern alight. The yard at the back was silent, there was no sign of the landlord's guard dog, only its kennel and the length of bear chain that was used to confine it.

Joscelin went back into the street. People were streaming away from the market-place, heading for the sanctuary of the churches. Smoke was rising from a row of merchant's houses on the King's road leading to St Mary's. Fire crowned the thatch in sudden licks of flame, but no one stopped to organize a bucket chain. With life and limb at stake, houses could burn.

Joscelin stood still and was buffeted like a rock in the middle of a turbulent sea by the crowds milling around him. Then he saw the soldiers. Reflections of fire from the torches they held glinted on their helms and mail. In and out of houses and shops they darted like fireflies, setting alight thatch and straw, kicking apart hearths, scattering embers to consume homes and businesses in the fury of flame.

Joscelin came across two dead bodies sprawled in the street. One of them was a town whore, her gaudy yellow gown splashed with blood. The other, his arm still across her body where he had been trying to protect her, was Gamel. His bag of carpentry tools were scattered across the street, and his wooden leg stuck out at an awkward angle.

Appalled, Joscelin crouched and quickly discovered that they were both beyond help. He made the sign of the cross over them, closed Gamel's staring eyes and rose to his feet. He was filled with fear and anger. Where in God's name was Conan?

The church bells were clamouring from all quarters. His thoughts leaped to Linnet and Robert and his gut churned. With his father absent on business and just a few servants in the house, they were extremely vulnerable. His father's town houses stood almost on top of Derby's. That might protect the dwellings from fire, but it also meant there would be a high concentration of Derby's men in the area.

He began to run, forcing his way along the narrow street which was full of people hurrying towards the safety, they hoped, of St Peter's church. The ground underfoot was muddy and he slipped and skidded. Behind him there was panic as a barrel of pine pitch in a carpenter's workshop exploded, showering the crowd with flaming debris. A globule landed on his hand and sizzled well into his flesh before he was able to brush it off. He was pushed and jostled, almost forced by the surge of humanity to enter St Peter's church. Finally, however, he managed to duck aside and thrust his way across the street to a narrow, stinking passageway that progressed in crooked, dog-leg fashion to the backs of the houses lining the Saturday market square.

Here, too, there was chaos, and Joscelin realized with a

270

renewed leap of fear that the assault on the city was widespread.

Surrounded by the sounds of looting and burning, he crouched for a moment in the garden of one of the houses to recover his breath. He wondered if the sheriff would send any men down into the city, or just hold fast to the castle and hope that Ferrers's attack was more an act of spite and bile than an attempt to subjugate city and castle to his will.

His hand on his new poniard, Joscelin straightened and moved up through the garden. With a sudden thundering of cloven feet, ears flapping over her small eyes, an enormous black sow galloped around the corner of the building and almost bowled him over. He leaped rapidly to one side and found himself confronted by two footsoldiers, their own long knives to hand for the purposes of pig-sticking. The sow snorted away down the garth, wallowed across the damaged wattle fence at the foot, and disappeared into the noissome alley beyond.

The footsoldiers and Joscelin appraised each other over their poised weapons.

'I have no quarrel with you,' Joscelin said. 'Let me go my way in peace, and I will let you go yours.'

The men exchanged swift glances, and returned their scrutiny to Joscelin. He became intensely aware of the gold braid edging his tunic, the quality of his cloak and the very fine clasp – temptations far greater than a prospective haunch of roast pork that was already half-way to Broadmarsh by now.

'We wouldn't rightly want to quarrel with you neither,' said the older of the two men, 'but we'd like you better if you was to hand over that cloak and pin as a sign of goodwill.'

'Your purse and belt too,' added the second, whose quick, crafty gaze had not missed the promising roundness of Joscelin's money pouch and the gilding on the tooled leather belt.

One soldier moved right, the other left. Joscelin ran at

the latter, dagger lifted to strike. His attack was blocked as the man grasped his knife hand. Joscelin responded in a similar manner by grasping his opponent's wrist, and used their grip on each other as leverage to hurl the man hard to the right, fouling the other soldier's path. Having broken free, Joscelin ran. He heard the sound of rapid footfalls in pursuit, but he had a start on them and, being faster into the bargain, reached the market square well in front.

Here, too, houses were being looted and put to the torch. Across the square Joscelin could see soldiers rolling wine barrels out of the cellar of a vintner's house while the vintner and his family looked on helpless and horrified. A soldier in a hauberk sat astride his war-horse conducting operations, a long whip dangling from his clenched fist.

Behind Joscelin there was a triumphant cry. 'There he is, the whoreson, get him!'

Flashing a glance over his shoulder, Joscelin saw the two soldiers he had just evaded running out of the doorway of a house on Cuckstool row. Joscelin took to his heels, knowing full well that if he were caught he would be killed.

The market square was a shambles of overturned booths and stalls, the looters picking among them like scavengers at the scene of a wolf kill. Joscelin sought the shelter of these booths, dodging in and out between them, weaving from one to the other across the square towards Organ lane. Near the low wall that separated the cornmarket from the rest of the stalls, a looter threatened him with a short knife, but backed off the moment he saw the gleaming length of Joscelin's poniard and went in search of easier prey. Joscelin was so occupied in watching the looter that he did not see the body sprawled behind one of the raided booths until too late. He measured his length across the corpse and lay upon it, momentarily too winded to move. When he drew his first breath, he almost choked, for the stench emanating from the dead man's garments proclaimed that he had been wearing his working clothes when he died and that he was employed in one of the

272

numerous tanneries down by the Leen bridge. Essence of excrement mingled with that of putrefication, rancid mutton fat and the metallic tang of tannin. The stink was so powerful that Joscelin retched. In the distant background, but coming nearer, he heard his pursuers. In a moment they would round the corner of the booth and discover him lying at their feet, an easy sacrifice to their knives.

Without thinking about it, because if he had he would have balked, Joscelin tore off his own mantle and gilded tunic. Stuffing them beneath the trestle in the booth, he rolled the corpse over, dragged off its cloak and stained tunic and dressed himself in the foulsome rags. A greasy, louse-infested hood fastened with a toggle and a knobbled quarterstaff completed the ensemble – and not a moment too soon. As Joscelin started to walk away from the corpse, the two reavers ran panting round the side of the booth.

His fall, had he but known it, was greatly to Joscelin's advantage. Being still winded, he did not stride out as he might have otherwise done, which would have given him away immediately. Instead he moved with a slightly shuffling walk far more reminiscent of a peasant.

'Ho!' cried one of the soldiers. 'You there, have you seen a noble running this way? Tall, wearing a dark red cloak?'

Joscelin shook his head and mumbled a reply in the rustic Anglo-Dane of the countryside. At the same time, he gestured with his arm so that the dreadful stench of his garments wafted towards the men. Neither of them, he hazarded, would want to move in as close as it would take to kill him.

'Ah God, he stinks as if he's been dead a week!' declared the other soldier. 'Can you tell what he's saying?'

His companion shook his head, equally as baffled. 'His accent's really heavy even for a native. Come on, we're wasting our time, and I'm going to puke if I have to stand here a moment longer. Let's search round the other side.'

Cold sweat clasping his body, Joscelin watched them walk rapidly away. He breathed out hard, then in again.

The smell from his garments did not seem so bad now that he had grown accustomed to it. Quite probably it had saved his life. Turning, he cut his way across the market-place and up towards the town gate at Chapel Bar. The looted houses of Long Row gave the market-place a ragged border of fire. Joscelin held out the forlorn hope that because his father's houses were so close to Derby's they would not be torched. Horrible visions writhed in his mind as he hurried up the muddy thoroughfare.

From a dark alleyway that ran down from the city wall to the market-place, a band of hurrying soldiers emerged like wine running from an open flask. They spilled over Joscelin before he could avoid them, and then they drew back, exclaiming at the stench of him.

Joscelin took them in at a glance and his hand relaxed on the grip of his dagger. 'Conan!' he roared. 'Where in God's name have you been?'

His uncle set his hands on his hips and stared Joscelin up and down. 'I might ask the same of you.' His scarred lip curved lopsidedly towards his left nostril. 'Christ's buttocks, but you stink worse than a three-week-old battlefield!'

'I had to exchange clothes with a tanner's corpse to keep myself from being skewered by two routiers,' Joscelin said shortly. 'I thought you'd be in The Weekday.'

'And so we would, except that Godric's uncle has an alehouse on Cherry Tree lane. We were paying our respects there when a brawl of Derby men came by and started causing trouble. We got rid of them soon enough, then realized it was more serious than our little disagreement. We're on our way back to your father's house even now.'

'There's no time to waste.' Joscelin began hurrying up the hill again. 'I don't think Derby's men will harm Linnet and Robert – they're too valuable, but I don't want them taken into his care.'

'Surely your father's knights will protect the house?' Conan said, trotting beside him, his face still wrinkled in response to the stench of Joscelin's garments.

'My father had business with a wool merchant up Organ

lane, and he gave most of his men leave to go round the town, the same as I gave leave to you,' Joscelin answered. 'As far as I'm aware, only the servants are there.'

Joscelin and Conan arrived at Ironheart's three houses to find them standing deceptively silent and tranquil. A cook-shop across the road was on fire, but otherwise this quarter of the town had seen less damage. But the suggestion that all was well was an illusion. The front door of the first house hung drunkenly on one hinge and on the floor in the passage were the plundered bodies of Ironheart's squire and Tillie's husband, Jonas. The rooms were all empty. Everything of value had been stripped and no one answered Joscelin's shout. He went out into the yard. Tillie's laundry cauldron lay overturned, a mess of torn, crumpled linens spilling on to the dirty ground. Ears flat to its small skull, Tillie's kitten hissed and spat at him from beneath a wooden trestle. A bowl of water containing some strips of softened rawhide stood on the bench beside some of his father's weapon-mending tools. His father's blue and gold shield lay on the ground, a great split running from a damaged section of rawhide right through to the centre boss. There were blood smears on the ground where bodies, injured or dead, had been dragged away.

He picked up a pair of blacksmith's pincers and squeezed the grip until the pressure brought pain. He could not be too late. It was impossible; he would not allow it to happen.

And then he heard the sound of shouting from the gardens backing on to the other side of the narrow alley, and a woman's scream.

Dropping the pincers, he grabbed hold of his father's shield by the short hand straps, and began to run.

CHAPTER 30

As soon as Linnet had retired to the sleeping loft on the second floor of the house, Ironheart fetched his tools and his shield and brought them outside to the bench leaning against the yard wall.

Bracing the shield against his leg, he took up a small pair of blacksmith's pincers and began to pull out the tacks that held the shield's narrow rawhide rim in position. A section near the top was damaged and needed replacing. It was something he had meant to do in the winter, but had kept putting off, and now the truces had all come to an end and there was no time left.

Robert ceased playing with the kitten and ambled across the yard to watch Ironheart at work.

'What are you doing?'

'I'm going . . .' said Ironheart between grunts of effort as he pulled the tacks out of the wood, 'to replace . . . this damaged section at the top . . . with a new piece of rawhide. See.' He pointed with a calloused forefinger. 'That's the mark of a Scottish short sword. Nearly got me, the whoreson.'

Robert nodded, grey eyes large and impressed. 'Can I help?'

'I don't see why not,' Ironheart said gruffly. 'You see that jar over there; bring it here, will you? I've had a piece of rawhide soaking in it overnight, so it should be soft enough to cut and nail by now.' He watched Robert carefully lift the yellow glazed jar and bring it to him, a look of intense concentration on his small face. A pang went through the old man, so warm and sweet that it made a mockery of the barriers he had erected against the

276

world a quarter of a century ago. Thus had Joscelin learned the art of caring for his weapons, a small child against Ironheart's knee. Those had been the springtime years. Now, in the cold approach to winter, he could smell the spring again, and wanted to weep because he had missed the summertime completely and was aware of the last leaves of autumn drifting from the tree.

'Now what do we do?' asked Robert, bringing him firmly back to earth.

'Take the rawhide out of the jar and squeeze it as hard as you can.'

'Like this? Yuk, it's all slimy, and it stinks!' Robert screwed up his face in disgust, and a chuckle rumbled up from the depths of Ironheart's chest.

'You can't nail it on when it's hard,' he said, and looked at the child's tendons standing out on the bony wrist. There was nothing on him, he was like a skinned coney, but there was a powerful underlying tenacity. Still chuckling, Ironheart rummaged in his tool kit and discovered that his shears were missing.

'Leave that now, you've squeezed out most of the water. Go inside to Tillie and ask her for a pair of shears.'

Robert scampered off. Picking up the crumpled piece of rawhide, Ironheart gave it a final wringing with his own powerful, scarred hands. He was just drying them on a piece of rag, when Tillie's shriek and Robert's even louder scream brought him rapidly to his feet.

The little boy shot out into the back yard, the shears clutched in his hand, his eyes huge with terror. Tillie raced after him, stumbling on her skirts. 'Soldiers, sir!' she gasped. 'Soldiers with swords coming this way from Ferrer's house! They mean mischief, I know they do!'

'What's happening?' asked Linnet in bewilderment. She stood at the foot of the loft stairs, her face flushed with sleep and no head-dress covering her golden-brown braid.

Ironheart opened his mouth but, before he could speak, the front entrance of the house was darkened by three soldiers clad in the boiled leather armour of regular troops.

Two brandished scramaseaxs, the other wielded a Danish hand-axe.

Linnet screamed, then cut the sound off rapidly against the palm of her hand. Ironheart seized his sword and shield from the bench and faced the intruders.

'Get out of my house or, by God, I'll kill you!' he snarled.

One of the soldiers laughed. 'You're a foolish old man,' he said, advancing with a heavy, deliberate step. 'And God's asleep.'

Linnet backed away. Never taking his eyes off the soldiers, Ironheart side-stepped so that Linnet could squeeze past him. 'The cellars next door,' he muttered from the side of his mouth. 'It is your only hope.'

Linnet cast a frightened glance over her shoulder, then ran into the back yard. Grabbing Robert's hand, she pulled him across the yard at a run and out of the back gate into the communal narrow entry running behind the houses. Tillie and Ella panted behind her. She reached for the iron ring on the gate of the house adjoining Ironheart's and twisted. The door did not move. She thrust her shoulder against it until her flesh bruised and her bones hurt, but to no avail. The door's hinges had dropped at some time and its base dragged the dusty ground. Tillie and Ella joined her, kicking and pushing, fear lending them strength, and finally, reluctantly, the door scraped open enough for the women to squeeze through into the yard of the vintner's house.

Wheezing, Tillie unfastened the hoop of household keys from the belt at her thick waist and found the one to the solid rear door of the building.

'Lord William said we should hide in the cellars,' Linnet panted, looking round the empty back yard with wide eyes and thinking that at any moment they would be caught. From the direction of Ironheart's house they heard a loud bellow and the shriek of steel meeting steel, then a high-pitched scream of pain. Tillie fumbled the key into the lock and twisted and pushed.

278

The house was dim and had the musty odour that settled on places when they had not been occupied for a number of weeks. The walls were bare, for the merchant had taken all his portable goods with him and only the plainest of furniture remained. An empty iron cauldron stood over the firepit which had been cleaned of rubbish and new kindling laid to hand.

'The cellar's this way,' gasped Tillie and disappeared behind a wooden screen into the storeroom. Bunches of herbs and smoked hams hung from hooks hammered into strong wooden beams that supported the floor of the sleeping loft above. Two buckets stood on the floor beside an old pair of pattens and several cooking pots were laid out on a trestle. There was an iron candle pricket standing on the trestle too, with a complete beeswax candle rammed on the spike. Tillie pounced on this and kindled a flame with shaking hands from the tinderbox laid beside it. Holding the light on high, she hurried to a low doorway at the end of the room and told Ella to pull back the heavy iron bolts. Linnet ran to help the maid. The bolts, although stout, had been kept well oiled and were fairly easy to draw back. The oak door swung open and the candle flame danced, making huge shadows on the roughly cut sandstone stairs that led down into a throat of darkness.

Robert hung back. 'I don't want to go down there,' he whimpered and clung tightly to his mother. 'I don't like the dark. Monsters might get me!'

'You cannot stay up here.' Crouching, Linnet gave him a cuddle. 'And there are no monsters. Sir William wouldn't allow them to live in his cellar, would he?' Over Robert's shoulder, she gestured the other women to continue down the stairs. Tillie gave her the hoop of keys, holding out to her the cellar one, and started downwards to the dark horseshoe arch where the first room opened out.

Linnet smoothed Robert's hair. 'Look, I'll carry you, and you can hide your face against my shoulder.'

Robert still resisted, a whine of fear escaping between his teeth, but Linnet scooped him up in her arms. She did not have the time to cozen him further and could only hope that he would not begin to scream.

A scraping sound came from the direction of the yard entrance, and almost simultaneously the women heard the thump of weapons upon the street door.

'Quickly, my lady!' Tillie hissed, beckoning from the foot of the stairs, her eye-whites gleaming.

Linnet started down the steps, Robert clinging to her like a limpet. She began to close the cellar door with the hand not supporting him, but stopped as Ironheart staggered into the storeroom, his mouth twisted in a grimace of effort and pain. She widened the door again. He was too breathless to speak, but gestured her away down the stairs. Wordless herself because she had seen the blood glistening on his shoulder, she gave him the key and hastened down after the other women. As she reached the cave, she heard the front door crash down and the iron key grate in the cellar lock.

The darkness closed around them like a tomb, musty and cold. Tillie had discovered a candle lantern standing upon a wine barrel and, having kindled it, brought it over to light Ironheart's way down the steps. He leaned heavily on the rope supports hammered into one side of the wall, and when he reached the bottom, collapsed against a row of casks, his breathing harsh.

'I haven't given you away,' he panted. 'We killed the first three, me and Jonas . . . and the two who came after . . .' His eyes squeezed shut and he put his hand to the wetness at his shoulder.

'Where is Jonas?' Tillie asked. Her hand trembled as she set down the candle lantern.

Ironheart swallowed. 'I'm sorry, Tillie, there was nothing I could do. There were two of them at me and I could not reach him. I tried, God knows I did. Then one of the bastards ran into this yard after you and I gave chase. I got him . . . but he got me. You think you're safe enough in your own house not to bother with mail.'

'Let me have a look.' Kneeling, Linnet reached to examine the wide split in his leather jerkin, tunic and shirt.

280

'No time,' he gasped. 'They will be looking for loot, and in a vintner's house that means the cellar.'

Linnet withdrew and looked at him askance. 'Then why tell us to come down here in the first place?'

Ironheart swallowed. 'The cave runs the length of all the houses and then some more. There is a passage branching off beneath the entry where there used to be a meat store. We had a dispute with the old basket weaver across the alleyway – he cut a room for his workshop that broke through into my cellars. As far as I know, the hole has only been boarded over. It should be possible to crawl through. Give me your arm, girl.'

Linnet was almost dragged to the floor by Ironheart's weight as he levered himself to his feet and leaned briefly against the casks.

'Here, boy,' he commanded Robert who was holding tightly to Linnet's skirts. 'Carry my sword for me, be my squire.' He held out the weapon. The candlelight flashed upon the blade edge and up the tendons of the man's rigid hand.

Tentatively, Robert did as he was bid, his own small hand inadequate on the braided grip.

At the top of the stairs, the door suddenly rattled vigorously on its hinges.

'Locked,' said a gruff voice. 'Use the axe, Greg.'

'This way,' Ironheart said urgently, and began weaving a path through the casks. The cellar door shook beneath the blows of an axe and they all heard the sound of splintering wood.

Linnet did not like the way Ironheart was breathing, and from the size of the wound as she had briefly seen it she was sure that it would need attending very soon if he was not to bleed to death.

They rounded a corner and had to stoop as the roof of the cave suddenly dipped and seemed to come to an end. The lantern light illuminated the chisel marks on the walls where the cave had been cut. To their left the shadows seemed blacker than elsewhere, and it was towards these that Ironheart headed. In a moment the shadows resolved themselves into a narrow, dark connecting passageway. Gazing over her shoulder, Linnet saw only blackness, but the hammering sounds went on, and there was a cry of triumph as the soldiers split through the door.

'I wish Joscelin was here,' Robert said forlornly to his mother as they crouched along the passage and into the storage cave of the house next door. 'Will he come and save us, Mama?' He, too, looked back with the wide eyes of a hunted animal. The heavy sword was making his wrist droop.

'If he is able to, I know he will,' Linnet said. She knew he had gone to the castle. Probably the alarm had not even been raised there yet and, by the time it was, it might well be too late. 'But for now, sweeting, we have to use our own wits.'

'Mama, why can't we . . .?'

'Hush,' she admonished quickly. 'They will hear us!'

They could not see the soldiers' torchlight, but suddenly they could hear their voices in the first cellar and the grate of footsteps on the sandy cave floor.

' 'E don't have much wine stored down here to say he's such a busy merchant,' complained a rough voice. 'Hold the light closer, Greg, I want to see the mark on this barrel. Hah, Rhenish!' A glint of greedy pleasure entered the voice and there were various unidentifiable clinking, scraping sounds followed by the trickle of wine into some sort of vessel. Everyone in the tunnel held their breath. Tillie shielded the light of the candle against her cupped palm and turned away from the first cellar. Ironheart silently removed his sword from Robert's hand.

'You reckon there's anything upstairs worth a look?' asked one of the looters between swallows.

'We'll have a look in a minute. By Christ's toes, this is good stuff.'

Footsteps scuffed in the direction of the passageway and Ironheart tightened his hand around the grip of the sword.

'Hoi, Thomas, look at this. There's a passage here, bring the torch!'

282

In the moment while the refugees deliberated between fight and flight, another voice, angry and imperative, filled the first cave.

'I might have expected you two tosspots to find the wine!' it snapped, and there came the sound of a blow and a pot smashing on the cave floor. 'Get upstairs now. The men I sent to de Rocher's house are all dead and there's no sign of the old fox or the woman and child. I want them found, is that understood?'

'Yes, sir. We was only investigating the cave. They could be down here for all we know!'

'Oh aye,' said their captain sarcastically. 'I presume you were drinking all the barrels dry to make sure they weren't hiding in them. You must think I was born yesterday and blind. Go on, get out of here and find Simon; he's coordinating the search parties.'

'Yes, sir.'

The sound of running footsteps retreated and the captain's voice, softly cursing, followed them, boots crunching upon the shards of broken pottery.

Linnet released her breath and sucked air into her starving lungs. Ironheart groaned and slipped slowly down the wall. His grip loosened on the sword and it clattered sideways. A single blue spark flashed along the edge of the blade and was quenched in darkness. Linnet crouched beside her father-in-law. His eyelids flickered.

'Go on,' he croaked. 'I won't be able to keep pace with you.' A wry smile barely curved his lips. 'I doubt I'm even able to stand up. Fetch help if you can. If not . . . guard yourself. Take my sword. I still have my dagger.'

Linnet bit her lip, considered briefly, then nodded. 'Give me the lantern,' she said to Tillie and, when the older woman handed it across, set it down beside the wounded man.

'Leave me alone,' he growled. 'You have no time.'

'Time enough to make you comfortable,' she retorted. 'I won't be gainsaid. You saved my life once. At least let me redress the balance a little.'

Ironheart snorted. 'I didn't save it for you to indulge in this kind of folly,' he said, but after a brief attempt to push her hand away, he allowed her to have her will.

Linnet raised her skirt and undergown to reach the good linen of her shift. Taking the hem in both hands at the side seam, she tore it upwards and then hard across. The fibres resisted and she had to use her belt knife to finish tearing off a long, wide strip. This she used as wadding and bandage to cover Ironheart's wound, securing it with her own belt of plaited, soft fabric. Ironheart's tougher leather belt she took and bound around her waist, setting her knife in the empty poniard sheath.

'It will hurt you badly, but you must press down hard on the bandage to staunch the bleeding,' she told him. 'I don't think you are losing as much blood as you were. This stop seems to have slowed it.' She picked up the lantern from his side and returned to the first cave, picking her way over the shards of broken pottery and the dark glimmer of splattered wine. There was a small ledge carved into the wall and on it stood two more pitchers of a similar design to the one that lay in pieces on the floor. Lifting one down, she filled it from the broached keg of wine and brought it to Ironheart, setting it down at his good side.

He regarded her with grim amusement. 'What's this for, to drown my sorrows?'

'To dull the pain and replace the blood you have lost,' she replied, her tone sharp.

Ironheart hefted the pitcher and took a shaky gulp of the wine from the cracked rim. '*Waes hael,*' he toasted with irony. 'Go on wench, get you gone. There's nothing to be gained in watching a drunkard die.'

Linnet blinked hard. 'Get as drunk as you want,' she said, 'but don't you dare die!' Bending over him, she kissed his cheek fiercely, then straightened and gestured brusquely at Tillie to lead on.

Ironheart watched their small light disappear in the direction of the third cellar and raised the pitcher to his lips again. He was indeed inordinately thirsty with loss of blood. He was tired too, and could feel the chill of the cave floor seeping up through his bones. How long did it take to die? He closed his eyes, then remembered he was supposed to drink the wine. The pitcher was so heavy. He raised it, swallowed, choked, swallowed, and lowered his aching arm.

The meat store in the fourth cellar had a fatty, strong aroma, and this despite the cool temperature of the sandstone vaulting. Linnet's stomach churned and fluid filled her mouth so that she had to turn aside to spit. Tillie's wavering candle illuminated the boarded-up hole, the source of the dispute between Ironheart and his neighbours.

'We need something to prize off these planks,' said Tillie. 'It ain't safe down here. They'll be down after us soon enough, the scavenging vultures. My poor Jonas . . .' Her double chins quivered.

'Tillie, I'm sorry . . .' Linnet began, knowing that whatever she said would be inadequate, but the older woman cut her off short.

'Nay, mistress Linnet, 'tis kind of you to offer comfort, but it ain't much use. It'll not bring him back, will it?' Tillie compressed her lips and blinked vigorously. 'He's dead. 'Tis our own lives we must save.'

Linnet bit her lip and nodded, recognizing the older woman's brusqueness as a bulwark against the onset of grief. On a stone slab jutting from the wall lay the carcasses of two skinned sheep and she had to swallow several times before she could speak. 'We could try the sword,' she suggested.

'You will break the blade, my lady.'

'I don't think so, not if we put the hilt under like this.' She lodged the pommel which was shaped like a flattened fist, beneath one of the wooden planks and pushed downwards. For a moment nothing happened. Linnet raised her foot and braced it against another strut for more leverage. With a loud creak and then a sudden splintering sound, one of the holding nails flew out of the wood and tinkled on the ground. Tillie took hold of the loosened plank in her strong, laundry pummeller's hands and ripped it away from the hole.

''Tis mortal narrow,' she pronounced, peering dubiously through and running her hands over her ample curves.

Linnet loosened some more boards and Tillie and Ella pulled them free. The women held their candle up to the hole and saw that it led through into a small, dusty cellar full of bundles of rushes and withies, of woven baskets and trugs, some completed, some half-finished, and beyond them, stairs leading up to a shadowed doorway.

'Old Andrew's workshop,' Tillie said. 'The door comes out in his garth, under his grapevines.' Her plump face wrinkled. 'There's no telling it's going to be any safer there, save that his cellar door's well hidden beneath all the greenery, and he's not a rich man – nowt worth looting.'

But it was not loot alone they were after, Linnet thought, remembering the exchange of words between the soldiers in the first cellar. She, Robert and Ironheart were sought and for God alone knew what purpose. Anger at their helplessness flashed through her like fire and renewed her courage.

'Hold up the candle,' she commanded Tillie. 'I'll go first and you can pass me Robert through. Here, sweetheart, take the sword for me.'

The gap was like a lightless window set in the middle of the wall and she had to drag her skirts through her belt so that she could clamber through the aperture. The air on this side was thick with the chaffy residue of old Andrew's trade and made her sneeze. She stifled the sound against her hand, but it still seemed to echo resoundingly.

'Pass me through the sword,' she called to Robert. 'Hilt-first, it's very dark in here and I don't want to cut my fingers.'

There was a scraping, grating noise. Using the haphazard gleams of Tillie's lantern, Linnet located the braided grip and pulled the sword through into the new cave. Robert

286

followed it through, agile as a small ape. As she helped him down, she could feel him trembling, but he neither spoke nor whimpered.

Then, without warning, without time to run or hide, Andrew's cellar door was flung open and bright daylight flooded down the dozen stairs, blinding Linnet and Robert.

'I told you, I ain't got no valuables hidden away!' whined an elderly, cracked voice. 'See for yourselves. This here's me workshop!'

'Nothing valuable? Oh come now, I wouldn't say that. Looks to me as if you've got two little birds nesting in your straw.'

Linnet's eyesight began to adjust and she saw a broad-shouldered leather-clad soldier standing at the head of the stairs grinning down at them. An old scrawny man dangled from the soldier's fist by the ripped edge of a brown fustian hood.

'I nivver seen 'em before!' the old man squeaked with an incongruous mixture of fear and indignation. 'They're nowt to do wi' me.'

'Good, then you won't be wanting a share in the reward for finding them,' said the soldier cheerfully, and dropped him. Turning, he shouted, 'Lads, come and look at what I've found!' And grinning broadly, he started down the stairs. Linnet saw his look intensify as his eyes settled on the dark hole in the wall behind her and Robert. She licked her lips, knowing that he would investigate and quickly discover the two serving women and Ironheart. It was too late to distract him from what he had seen and deduced.

Robert was shivering violently, his eyes widening with each footfall of the approaching soldier.

'My lady,' the man said, 'you will yield yourself and the child into my keeping.' His left foot scraped the bottom step. Linnet wrapped both hands around the sword grip and attacked him. The blade swung in an arc and hit his lower bicep and elbow. Although the blade did not bite

287

flesh, he was bruised and knocked off balance. Cursing her, he began to straighten up and reach for his own sword, but Linnet struck again, this time catching him against and beneath the curtain of his loose leather neck coif.

He screamed and clutched at his throat, blood squirting between his fingers. Linnet dropped the sword, picked up Robert, and thrust him at the wall. 'Go back!' she commanded. 'Stay with Tillie and Ella until I come for you.'

Without waiting for the women on the other side to pull him through, Linnet began feverishly piling up baskets and stacking rushes against the hole, concealing it, while in front of her the soldier died, his eyes full of frightened disbelief.

Four more soldiers arrived at the top of the stairs. 'Found some treasure have you, Rob?' one shouted. The laughter left his voice and his eyes widened incredulously as he took in the scene below him. 'Rob?' he croaked. 'Jesu, you bitch, what have you done to him?'

Linnet backed away from them, side-stepping the body so that their eyes followed her to the far wall, not the one that concealed the opening behind the precariously balanced trugs and baskets. 'I am the Lady Linnet de Gael, daughter-in-law of William Ironheart,' she said as they advanced down the steps, clubs and swords raised menacingly. 'It will go ill with you if I am harmed.'

She saw the looks they exchanged. The soldier who had spoken reached the foot of the stairs and crouched beside the dead man to check him for signs of life. His fingers came away bloody from the slashed throat and he looked at her across the corpse, his face twisted with revulsion. Linnet returned his stare. 'Soldiers killed my father-in-law,' she said. 'I took his sword to defend myself.'

He jerked to his feet and, crossing to her in two swift strides, struck her across the face. 'You lying whore!' he snarled raggedly. 'Rob would never have attacked you. Soft as mutton fat he were with women!' He raised his hand to strike her again, but one of the other quickly caught him back.

'Steady Alex, Lord Ferrers said he'd pay good money for her and the brat. And he can be mighty peculiar. It's nothing to him to thrash a woman to death, but if we bring this un' to him in any kind o' state, he'll have us on the gibbet for sure — and that'll be all four of us dead because of her, and no profit.'

The soldier called Alex resisted the hand clamped on his wrist for a moment longer, then shrugged free and pushed his way out of the cave.

'Where's the boy?' demanded the soldier who had prevented him from trying to strike Linnet twice. His face was stone-hard and without compassion. He would do whatever was in his own best interests, Linnet could see.

'At the castle with his stepfather,' she lied, looking him straight in the eyes. 'You'll not get your hands on him.'

He scowled, obviously displeased by her reply, but believing her. 'Get her out of here,' he said to the other two. 'Take her to Lord Ferrer's house. Alex and I will follow with Rob's body.'

Linnet was seized by the elbows and dragged up the stairs into the full daylight of the basketmaker's back yard. They tied her hands behind her back with a piece of leather thonging and knotted a rope leash through her belt with which to pull her along. Linnet put up a token struggle, enough for them to jerk her roughly a couple of times, but she did not engage in any spirited resistance. The sooner they were away from the cellar the better.

They dragged her towards the back alley. Of the old man there was not a sign, for he had taken to his heels while the soldiers were distracted in the cellar.

As Ferrer's men pulled Linnet out of the yard, some other soldiers came running up the alleyway from the direction of Ironheart's house, their swords drawn. Linnet dug in her heels and stared. Her heart started to pound in swift hammerstrokes. 'Joscelin!' she screamed. 'Joscelin, Conan, help me!'

The soldier holding the rope cursed and raised his sword hilt to strike her. Linnet kicked him as hard as she could in the testicles. She was only wearing soft indoor slippers, but his gambeson was on the short side and did not offer full protection, and he grunted and hunched over.

Unbalanced because of her tied hands and the rope at her waist, the force of her kick toppled Linnet and she sprawled on her face in the alley's filth.

Before Linnet's captor could straighten and turn to defend himself, Joscelin struck a killing blow. Linnet screamed and rolled away as his body crashed down next to her. The reddened sword slashed down again, severing the rope that bound her to the shuddering body. She struggled to her knees. Joscelin pulled her the rest of the way to her feet and freed her wrists, and then she was in his arms.

She clung to him, shaking, as the sounds of battle died away. One man had fled up the alley towards Organ lane, the others lay dead. Linnet could smell their lifelessness as though they were already putrefying. The stench invaded her nostrils and descended to her stomach bringing on a lurching nausea. Then she realized that Joscelin's garments were the source of the stink and that they were naught but infested rags.

'Are you all right?' He held her a little away to study her face. His hand gently touched the swollen bruise where the soldier had hit her. 'Where are the others?'

Linnet nodded jerkily. She was far from being all right, but for the nonce she could cope because she had to. She compressed her lips as the smell of his garments continued to agitate her stomach. 'We hid in the house cellars. The others are still there. Your father's been wounded – badly I think. It was very hard to tell in the dark. The soldiers . . . they had orders to hunt us down, I heard them talking.'

'They are everywhere,' Joscelin said, stroking her dishevelled hair. 'Once they've done looting and burning, they'll turn on anything that moves, and even the size of Conan's troop might not deter them. We have to reach the castle as quickly as we can.'

Linnet swallowed and swallowed again. 'I'll take you to

your father. We had to leave him in the passageway between the caves – he could go no further. I bandaged him as best I could and left him a pitcher of wine to ease his thirst and his pain. He gave me his sword and I used it to kill a man. No, do not comfort me or I will be sick.' She pushed herself out of his arms and, averting her gaze from the corpse at her feet, stumbled towards the vintner's back yard.

Joscelin followed her, pausing only to give Conan orders and send a soldier in search of a hand cart to carry the wounded man.

CHAPTER 31

'IF I'M GOING TO die,' Ironheart grumbled, 'I'm going to do it at Arnsby in the bed where I was conceived and born, not on some poxy borrowed pallet in this Godforsaken place!'

Linnet eyed him with exasperation as she wiped clean the razor with which she had just finished shaving him and went to empty the laver bowl of scummy water down the waste shaft. '*This Godforsaken place*' was a comfortable private room in the tower of the castle and had been vacated by the sheriff at some considerable inconvenience. The bed, far from being poxy or a pallet, was a sumptuous affair, large enough to hold six people, and boasting crisp linen sheets and the finest Flemish coverings. In the three days since he had been placed there, Ironheart had gone from grey-faced docility to this state of febrile crabiness where he was impossible to please.

'You're too lively to think of dying, Father,' she said wryly. 'If you would only keep still and cease complaining, the wound would pain you less.'

'It's the pain that makes me realize I'm still alive!' he retorted and shifted irritably against the pillows. His left arm was caged in a leather sling, and beneath it he was padded with swathes of linen bandage. Linnet had stitched the wound as best she could and the sheriff had sent his own physician to attend Ironheart. According to the good doctor, Ironheart was suffering from an excess of choler and the wound had only served further to unbalance his humours. Linnet had had to bite her tongue on the comment that her father-in-law's humours had always been out of balance. Fortunately the physician had owned the good sense not to suggest bleeding as a remedy, otherwise she would have been bound to speak up since, in her opinion, Ironheart's wound had already bled him white.

The doctor had applied a token leech or two to Ironheart's arms and prescribed an infusion of black alder and agrimony to soothe the choler and help to balance the humours. He had drawn up a strict diet for the wounded man, consisting of ox-blood broth and dark bread soaked in milk until it made a kind of porridge upon which iron filings from a sword blade were to be sprinkled. It was small wonder that the invalid balked every time he saw her or her maid approaching him with a bowl and spoon.

'I have a bad feeling,' he complained as Linnet returned to his bedside. 'I need to go home to Arnsby.'

'A bad feeling about what?'

'I don't know. If I could put my finger on it, I'd not be so frustrated. All I know is that I have to go home.'

'Joscelin could go in your stead,' she suggested.

Ironheart shook his head impatiently and the two vertical frown lines between his brows deepened with anxiety and pain. 'It is not something Joscelin can do. I'm sick of lying here staring at that gaudy crucifix on the wall and swallowing that piss-faced chirurgeon's poisonous brews. One more day and, even if I have to crawl out of here on my hands and knees, I'm leaving.' He paused, out of breath, his skin shiny with the sweat of effort. Linnet wiped his brow, murmured soothing words until his lids drooped, and went in search of Joscelin.

She found him in a corner of the great hall sitting on an upturned half-barrel, patiently working the nicks out of his father's sword with a small, hand-held grindstone.

'Go and talk some sense into your father,' she said. 'He's threatening to leave his sickbed and ride home to Arnsby.'

Joscelin laid the sword carefully down and wiped his hands on a linen rag. 'I know. He spoke to me late last night. Does the sight of this bother you?'

She glanced briefly at the sword, its edges bright now and unstained. 'I can look at it without feeling sick any more if that is what you mean,' she said, 'but the sight will always bother me.'

'Once you have felt the killing force, it always does.'

A small shudder rippled down her spine. They looked at each other, the weapon lying between them, gleaming with dull, quiescent power. Joscelin rose from the barrel and, taking her by the hand, led her out of the hall into the courtyard.

'Where's Robert?'

'With Conan. He's taken him to see the hawks in the mews.' His expression was rueful. 'Much as I love the boy, I need some respite.'

'He kept asking for you when we were hiding in the cellars,' she said. 'And when you came, he thought you were a god to have answered his cry.'

They walked across the baileys to the small herb garden which was set in a quiet corner near one of the auxiliary kitchen buildings. 'But I'm not,' Joscelin said grimly. 'My feet are as much clay as any man's and if he believes otherwise he is going to be terribly let down one day. He clings to me so hard that sometimes it is like being eaten alive. I need to escape for a while.'

'And now I come to you to eat you alive with my burdens too,' she said as they entered the small garden and were assaulted by the scent of myriad varieties of herbs basking in the sunshine.

Joscelin squeezed her hand. 'Burden me with anything you want,' he said, and drew her down on to a turf seat situated under a rose vine. The flowers were just coming into bloom, the petals a rosy pale pink like babies' toes. Bees from the castle's hives hummed industriously among the blossoms.

She looked at him sidelong. In the cramped confines of the castle, beset by demands from every quarter, there had been no opportunity until now for her to talk in privacy to Joscelin nor he to her.

'Even with another mouth to feed?' she asked, smiling.

At first he did not understand, but she saw the moment

of comprehension brighten in his eyes and then slowly spread, lighting up his whole face. He kissed her, hard at first, then tender. 'You bring me not a burden, but a gift,' he said, hugging her against him. 'How long have you known?'

'A few days only. I had a suspicion when we were preparing to travel to Nottingham, and it has grown ever stronger. I do not believe my flux will come now.' She laughed and squeezed him back. 'The baby will be born in midwinter, I think, between Christmastide and Candlemas. I haven't told anyone else, but your father suspects. He has a very sharp eye for all he claims never to take notice of women.' She sighed with exasperation. 'I did wonder about using it as a lever to keep him in his bed – the opportunity to live to see his grandchild, but I think he would just bellow at me and rupture his stitches. He's a stubborn old mule.'

'The news might sweeten him a little,' Joscelin said thoughtfully, 'but then again, if he already suspects, he'll already have spent time mulling over the prospect and it won't keep him occupied for long.'

'What if we told him the child was to be given his name?'

'He would say that it was only his due, but would be secretly flattered. I doubt it would have any strong hold on him.' Joscelin shook his head. 'If he wants to go home to Arnsby, then so be it. I may just be able to persuade him to be borne on a litter for most of the journey. It will be more than his pride can stomach to enter Arnsby flat on his back, so we'll have to provide a quiet horse for the final mile.'

'He is mortally sick,' Linnet objected. 'He lost a great deal of blood and he hasn't the strength to fight off the fever if it sets in. A day's jolting in a litter will be extremely dangerous for him. He says that he wants to die at home in his own bed. That is surely what he will do, doubtless with his wife gloating over him.'

Joscelin sighed. 'It is his choice,' he said. 'I believe he is dying anyway, and if I can fulfil his wish to do so at home, then I will.'

'So you are not going to stop him?'

'I can talk to him, but I will not gainsay his final decision.'

Linnet rose to her feet and walked to a small sundial standing as a hub in the midst of a wheel of fragrant herbs. The sun was almost directly overhead and no shadow touched the smooth, silvery surface of the incised slate. She laid her palm on the warm stone. One life beginning, one drawing to a close, she thought, feeling the connection, and in between a lifetime's wheel of light and shadow.

Joscelin came up behind her and she turned into his arms, knowing that for her and Joscelin their time was now, and every moment too precious to be wasted.

CHAPTER 32

RAGNAR LEANED ON HIS elbow in the hay of the stable loft at Arnsby and watched Hulda, a kitchen maid, tidy her hair and brush ineffectually at the stalks of straw caught in her homespun gown. She slid him a look through her lashes. Her eyes were a bright, Scandinavian blue and, apart from her heavy, white breasts, her best feature. Her nose was big and lumpy, her lips thin and her hips fat. Still, she was athletic and accommodating, tight and moist where it mattered.

Hulda was frequently sought out by the castle soldiers because not only was she willing to lie with them for a pittance, she also had the added attraction of being barren. No man was going to plant his seed and then find a woman whining at his tunic hem demanding financial support for her growing belly. This being the case, the Lady Agnes turned a blind eye to Hulda's copulatory industriousness and only groused if it interfered with her work in the kitchens.

'I heard Cook say as your father's gone into Nottingham to fetch you a bride,' she fished as she secured her blond braid with a leather cord.

Ragnar said nothing and stretched. Tufts of red-gold hair sprouted in his armpits and poked above the level of his unlaced braies.

'Is it true?' Hulda pursued, undaunted. 'Are you really going to take a wife?'

Her eyes were avid and made him smile and bite the inside of his mouth. To lie with the lord's son was a source of power in itself, but to have snippets of information straight from his own lips was even more useful.

'When the time comes,' he said with a shrug and picked his tunic off the straw. 'Here's a penny for you to spend next time the new packman comes calling.'

She took the coin willingly enough, but he saw the sulky droop of her lower lip. His own mouth tightened. The slut need not think he was going to pay her with information.

'Go on, back to the kitchens, you've been away from them long enough!' He gave her rump a stinging slap.

She squealed and, rubbing her buttock, said reproachfully, ''Twas you who took me from my duties and kept me here so long.'

Ragnar laughed crudely. 'If you'd wanted a short ride, you should have let Ivo mount you!'

'P'rhaps I will,' she said and set her foot upon the top rung of the ladder. There was a loud commotion in the stable below. After briefly looking down, she tossed her head at Ragnar. 'I'll ask him now, shall I?'

In the stable, a hard-ridden horse was blowing loudly, its hooves circling and stamping as the groom unsaddled it. Hulda descended to the bottom step and stood aside, hands behind her back, her eyes coyly weighing up Ivo as he dismounted from the sweating courser.

'Where's Ragnar?' he snapped at her. She rolled her eyes towards the loft hatch. Ivo brushed her aside and set his own foot on the loft ladder.

'Ragnar, in Jesu's name, come down, there's news!'

Alerted by Ivo's flushed face and his breathing, which was louder than that of his hard-ridden courser, Ragnar came to the trap. 'Oh yes?'

His brother peered up at him, his chestnut hair sweat-dark on his brow. 'I met one of our messengers on the road. He'll be here soon, but his horse was tiring and mine was still fresh. It's Papa, Ragnar – he's been wounded in a fight, and they're bringing him home.'

Ragnar's own face flooded with colour, causing his brown eyes to seem light and gold. 'Who is "they"?' he demanded. 'Move out of the way, let me come down.'

'Joscelin and that wife of his.' Ivo was almost leaping up and down with excitement. 'They stopped off at Rushcliffe on their way to leave the brat and his nurse, so the messenger says. Joscelin's wife insisted on attending Papa all the way to Arnsby because he's in such a bad state. What's more, they're on their way here from the whore's chapel. Papa wanted to be taken there. He's dying, Ragnar.'

Ragnar strode from the stables towards the keep. He did not even give Hulda a second glance. She was nothing, a speck on the ground, dwarfed by the surge of elation sweeping through him. Ivo, shorter of the leg than his brother, had to run to keep up. 'Ferrers attacked Nottingham. Apparently Papa's house was sacked, but Papa escaped with the women into the cellars of the house next door.'

'How was he wounded then?'

'In a sword fight while trying to escape – a deep cut to the left shoulder.'

Ragnar grunted. If it was not all that he had hoped for, then it was still excellent news. Joscelin was bringing the old man home to die. They would ride straight into Arnsby's welcoming stone arms and never leave again. He glanced sharply at his scurrying brother, and was reminded of a rat. 'You didn't ride back along the road to greet Papa yourself then?'

'No, I came straight to tell you.'

Ragnar nodded and smiled thinly. As a younger son, Ivo's inheritance was slim and likely to stay so unless he married well. In Ragnar's opinion no father in their right mind would want such a spineless numbskull for a son-in-law. Ivo was dependent on the goodwill of the head of the household and it amused Ragnar to see which way Ivo had decided the wind was blowing.

'Go and give Mama the tidings, will you,' Ragnar said. 'She will need to prepare the main bedchamber if Papa is as bad as you say.' And strew it with wormwood, gall and deadly nightshade he thought. Maude was absent on one of her frequent visits to friends in convents and not expected home until the end of the week. His mother was always worse without Maude present to provide an absorbent ear.

Ivo glowered. 'What are you going to be doing?' he asked in a disgruntled voice.

Ragnar parted his lips, his teeth a narrow white flash. 'Preparing a welcoming committee, what else?'

'BLAST YOU, WOMAN, leave me alone, I'm all right, I tell you!' Ironheart snapped at his daughter-in-law.

'I haven't said a word!' Linnet protested indignantly.

'It's the way you keep looking at me. God's arse, I could ride before I was out of napkins. I've lived in the saddle all my life, and if I die in one I'll be a damned sight more happy than lying on a litter like an old woman!'

Linnet pressed her lips together and somehow held herself to silence. Ironheart looked dreadful. His eyes were sunken back in their sockets and their dangerous glitter was as much fever as rage. She had managed to get him to swallow a cup of feverfew potion when they were at Morwenna's chapel, but he had refused to the point of apoplexy to be borne in a litter and had forced his will beyond his broken, dying body in order to mount the grey stallion at the block by the chapel door. She had watched him wrestle with the horse, a great, aching lump in her throat, and angry words at his stupidity only just contained behind her bitten lips. Joscelin had said nothing at the time; he just held the horse steady while his father dragged his shaking body into the saddle.

Linnet glanced at Joscelin now. He was riding on his father's other side, affecting indifference, but close enough to grab him if he fell. She might have thought her husband cold had she not seen his anguish in the privacy of their own chamber. 'He hates sentiment and fuss,' he had said, staring bleakly out of the narrow lance of window into Rushcliffe's bailey. 'He's dying. Nothing can change that. I won't break his pride.'

301

And for the sake of that pride, William de Rocher now approached the stone Norman keep that his father had built to guard the lands that the de Rochers had seized at the time of the great conquest. Like the first William de Rocher he came astride a war-horse, a polished sword at his hip, his gaze glittering and hungry. But his ancestor had had thirty more years of life before him to build his first timber stronghold, marry an Anglo-Danish thegn's daughter and beget the next generation. Ironheart's own time was measured in hours.

The scaffolding still stood against Arnsby's walls, although on a different section to last year, and the same builders, masons and painters were busy about the task of maintenance. From the battlements flew the de Rocher banner. On a blue background the gold firedrake of the year of Hastings blazed a trail. The castle gates stood wide open, the road a sunlit white ribbon disappearing into the bailey.

The grey stallion, scenting familiarity, plunged and strained at the bit and Ironheart almost lost control of him, for only one arm had any strength left in it to pull back, and that was pared of flesh and fever-weakened.

Quickly Joscelin leaned over and grabbed the bridle. 'Whoa, steady,' he commanded the horse. Its ears flickered and the skin twitched upon its sweating hide, but its pace slackened.

Ironheart's face was grey apart from two scarlet flashes of fever upon each cheekbone. 'Leave go, I can manage,' he said in a hoarse, death-rattle voice.

'Papa . . .'

'Leave go, I tell you!'

Joscelin released the bridle and, setting his jaw, looked away. Linnet's heart ached for both men. She tried to catch Joscelin's eye. It was very difficult, but when he finally did respond to her stare, she saw the glimmer of unshed tears and the rapid movement of his throat. It was almost more than she could bear and she had to turn her own head.

In the bailey, the messenger's arrival had ensured that a

welcoming party awaited them. There were two serving men standing to attention beside a stretcher fashioned of latticed rope. Lady Agnes was present, attired in her best red wool gown and silk wimple. At her side, Martyn shifted from foot to foot, his hair damp and his face freshly scrubbed. Ivo, a frown on his face, had one hand on the child's shoulder, the other on his sword hilt as he watched the company approach.

It was Ragnar who stepped forward to take his father's bridle; Ragnar resplendent in a new tunic of grass-green velvet. Gold braid flashed on cuff, hem and throat, and tiny seed pearls were sewn in a spiral design over the braid. The body of the tunic was oversewn with small flowers in thread of gold. Ironheart's spare sword belt – the one he never wore because he said it looked as if it ought to belong to a court whore – was buckled around Ragnar's lean hips. Knee-high boots of gilded leather and bright yellow hose completed the magnificent ensemble.

Breath bubbling, Ironheart stared down at his heir. 'Why are you trapped out like a marchpane fancy?' he wheezed.

'To honour your homecoming, Papa,' Ragnar responded, his brown eyes wide, picking up golden lights from his costume. 'To accord you the respect that is your due.'

'You call this respect?' Spittle appeared on the old man's lips and his shoulders trembled with more than just the thud of his fever-driven heart. He stared round the silent group of his family and met his wife's bitter, triumphant eyes. 'When I am dead, then you can dance upon my grave,' he ground out, 'but by God, you'll not mock me while there's still breath in my body!' He wheeled the grey around and dug in his spurs. The horse neighed and gave a startled leap forwards before breaking into a gallop.

'Papa!' Joscelin tried to turn Whitesocks, but his way was blocked by other mounts and he could only watch helplessly as the grey bolted towards the gateway.

It was sealed. The massive oak doors had been closed

behind the party and even now the portcullis was squeaking down the slots cut in the great stone wall. The grey reared to a halt. Too weak to hold on any longer, Ironheart was thrown from the saddle and hit the ground loosely like a child's doll made of rags and straw.

Linnet reined her mare aside and Joscelin was finally able to turn Whitesocks and gallop down to the gateway. The grey milled round the bailey, head high, eyes rolling, avoiding the efforts of the groom to capture it. Joscelin flung himself down from Whitesocks and knelt at his father's side. Ironheart still breathed, his willpower holding him yet to life and consciousness.

'Tell the guards to open the gates,' he forced out, then stopped to cough. 'Tell them I command it.'

The two menservants approached with the litter, Ragnar pacing beside them.

Joscelin glanced at the four guards on gate duty. They returned his stare with a coldness that penetrated to his gut. He had never seen them before and, from the way their hands hovered over their weapons, he did not believe that they would respond to any command but Ragnar's.

'The fever has overset his wits,' Ragnar shook his head sadly and glanced over his shoulder. 'Mama, you had best take him to your chamber and care for him there. Obviously he has been neglected to the point of death.'

Ironheart made a choking sound. Joscelin jerked to his feet and faced Ragnar's gleaming smile. 'How long have you been planning this?'

'Planning what? I'm a dutiful son. Ever since I came home in the autumn I haven't set a foot wrong. The gates are closed for a good reason.'

Ironheart groaned as he was lifted on to the rope stretcher and Agnes de Rocher's lips curved with relish at the sound.

Joscelin stared at Ragnar. 'What reason?' he demanded stiffly.

Ragnar shrugged. 'My father is too weak and sick to go anywhere, and in such dangerous times it behoves me to keep those gates shut. The Scots are over the border again, did you know? And the Flemish will be sailing any day for the Norfolk coast.'

'The gates were wide open when we arrived,' Joscelin said through his teeth.

Ragnar gave him a pitying, superior smile. 'And how better to defend myself than by capturing my enemies? I have the proof of what you have done to my poor father. In the name of King Henry the Younger, I arrest you for treason and attempted patricide.'

Joscelin began to shake. 'You stinking, conniving, treacherous *nithing*!' he spat, and leaped, bearing Ragnar to the bailey floor. He succeeded in making of his brother's nose a scarlet squelch before the four gate guards managed to drag him off. Joscelin's soldiers were held from joining the affray by more of Ragnar's men. The ordinary castle guards, who had always owed their loyalty to Ironheart, looked on uncertainly, dithering. Ragnar might be overstepping his authority, and Joscelin might be Ironheart's favourite son, but Ironheart was dying and in the future they would look to Ragnar to pay their wages.

Ragnar regained his feet. Blood dribbled from his nose, masking his mouth and chin and dripping ruinously on to the bright green velvet. Joscelin struggled in the rough embrace of the gate guards. 'You have no authority!' he spat.

'I have all the authority I need,' Ragnar retorted, his voice thick and nasal. 'And to prove it, at noon tomorrow, I'm going to hang you from the battlements. Then I'm going to have you flayed and your hide nailed to Arnsby's gates.' A choking noise caused him to glance sideways and see Linnet retching into a kerchief.

'Take him away and put him in the oubliette,' he commanded the guards with a brief gesture. He dabbed at his bloody nose with his sleeve. 'Mama, I leave you to make arrangements for my father and Lady Linnet.'

Agnes stared at Ragnar as if he had descended from the heavens in a cloud of light. Slowly she folded him a deep curtsey. Open-mouthed, Ivo gaped at her, then at his brother. Beneath his frozen hand, Martyn's shoulder quivered.

'I won't let you hang Joscelin, I won't!' the child burst out. 'He hasn't done anything, you just want him out of the way because he's better than you!' He flung himself at Ragnar, screaming and pummelling.

'Hold your tongue, brat!' Ragnar sent Martyn reeling with a clout to the side of his head. 'It's not your place to speak of matters you know nothing about. Ivo, get him out of my sight!'

Ivo, a dazed look on his face, took Martyn by the scruff and dragged him away, still kicking and shrieking. The guards stripped Joscelin of sword, dagger and purse. Then they manhandled him towards the keep, jabbing him roughly with their spear butts to make him move.

Linnet screamed his name and rode her mare at the guards, but she was intercepted, the bridle was grasped and she was pulled down off the horse. Agnes de Rocher seized her arm in a vicious grip. 'You don't want to go where he's going,' she hissed, pinching Linnet's skin. 'The oubliette's no place for a gently-bred noblewoman such as yourself. You will come with me to the bower and learn from me how a sick man should truly be nursed.' Her gaze gloated hungrily upon Ironheart.

Linnet struggled to wrench herself free, sobbing with loathing, but Agnes held fast. Hung and then flayed. Nausea rose in Linnet's throat, burning and vile. Straining away from Agnes she was sick again. Agnes did not for one second relent of her fierce grip, but her brown eyes roved quickly over Linnet's slim figure and then narrowed.

'You're not really going to hang him tomorrow are you?' Ivo looked nervously at Ragnar, and ignored the steaming, skewered small birds on the trencher in front of him.

Shrugging, Ragnar took a loaf from the dish that the squire had just placed in front of him. He sat in his father's chair on the high dais, a white linen cloth covering the thick oak trestle. The best tableware had been set before him — silver-gilt goblets and expensive golden wine glowing through the incised rock crystal of a Byzantine flagon. He had exchanged his blood-stained tunic for one chequered in two shades of blue. Sky-coloured chausses and hose of midnight blue completed the outfit. The effect was not as opulent as the green, but it still flaunted his rank and displayed to advantage his strong bone structure and thick, red-blonde hair.

'What else should I do with him?' Ragnar broke the bread and took a voracious bite of the fragrant, soft interior.

'He's our brother too.'

Ragnar ceased chewing, his expression warily narrowing. 'Surely you're not squeamish?'

Ivo felt like a coney beneath the all-seeing eye of the hawk. 'I don't like Joscelin,' he said, forcing himself to take one of the loaves, 'but I don't hate him like you do. It doesn't matter who his mother was, he's still of our blood.'

Ragnar began to chew again. His throat rippled as he swallowed. 'I have never noticed yours being thicker than water before,' he said dangerously.

'You have never taken it this far before.' Ivo crumbled the bread between his fingers and then blinked at the mess on his wooden trencher. 'Papa heard everything you said in the bailey. I saw his face.'

Ragnar's expression darkened. He threw down his own piece of bread and lifted a knife from the table to drag one of the small birds off the spit. Amber fat dripped on to the cloth. 'I intended him to hear every word,' he said viciously. 'Let him have his first taste of hell even before he gets there.'

Ivo drank down his wine and wondered how long it would take to get drunk.

'Of course,' Ragnar added softly, his voice heavily nasal because of the dried blood clogging his nostrils, 'if you don't approve of my methods of government, you can always take to the tourney road or hold Joscelin's memory sacred by selling your own sword – although God knows who would want to buy it! I warn you, if you're not prepared to work in my interests, then get out now.'

Ivo bit his lip. 'And if I am prepared?'

'You have always coveted Papa's manor house near Melton. You can have that and the hunting lodge, and I'll find you a rich young wife to go with it. But only for your implicit obedience. I don't want you running here and there in your usual weasel fashion, carrying tales and blowing hot and cold.'

Taking his cup, Ivo left the table and went to stand before the deep firepit around which the eating trestles were grouped. Red heat simmered over him. The manor house had only been built six years ago and boasted a proper stone fireplace and a private room where the lord could withdraw to his pleasures, whatever they happened to be. The windows in the solar were fitted with real glass and the ceiling had a French design of gold knots upon a rich green background. Their father had not cared for luxury, but recognized that sometimes important guests had to be entertained and it was useful to have somewhere opulent to do so. A manor house was far less expensive to furbish than a castle.

His face fire-reddened, Ivo swung round to find Ragnar still watching him. 'All right,' he said. 'You have my obedience.' And at the back of his mind he saw the image of a man swinging from the castle battlements in the wind.

Ragnar smiled. A moist white sliver of chicken dangled between his forefinger and thumb. 'And you will do me homage for what I give you before witnesses. Tomorrow, in the bailey.' He bit the morsel in half with his strong white teeth and both portions vanished into his mouth.

Suddenly the image of the hanging man came sharply into focus and Ivo saw with foreboding that it was he himself who dangled on the end of Ragnar's rope, suffused and choking.

'Go and get Papa's scribe,' Ragnar said, wiping his fingers on a napkin. 'I've got messages to send.'

CHAPTER 34

I N MAUDE'S CHAMBER a single candle burned at the
dying man's bedside. The priest finished his ministrations and started to put away the vial of holy oil and
communion wafers in a small pyx of carved cedarwood.

Linnet watched the proceedings from a low stool in the
corner where she sat with Ella and Martyn. Agnes lurked
near the priest and Linnet had the fancy that she was a
demon, waiting her moment to dart in and snatch Ironheart's soul. This was her dark domain. The rooms belonging to Ironheart had been seized by Ragnar to underline
his authority and, besides, Agnes had insisted on nursing
him here.

Nursing him! Standing over him smiling like a gargoyle
Linnet thought, her soul shrinking within her. The nightmare, she knew, had only just begun and could not be
allowed to progress any further. And yet, trapped like this,
how was she to prevent it?

The priest turned to leave, murmuring that now was the
time for the grieving relatives to pay their last respects.
Linnet rose from the stool and quietly apprehended the
cleric as he approached the door.

'Father, I beg you to intercede with Lord Ragnar, make
him see that what he is about to do is Godless.'

He looked down at the hand she had laid upon his
sleeve, his distaste ill-concealed, and she quickly removed
it.

'Daughter, what will be will be and I cannot change it,'
he replied sanctimoniously. 'Lord Ragnar is not acting
without just cause.'

Linnet wiped her hand on her gown, wishing now that

she had not touched him. 'Just cause!' she choked. 'You call murdering his own brother a just cause!'

'Daughter, your loyalty commends you, but it is seriously misplaced. You must search your heart for the obedience to God's will.'

'To God's will I am ever obedient, Father,' she retorted, her face white, her eyes blazing. 'Perhaps you should search your heart too, if you can find it beneath the fear for your purse.'

The priest drew himself up but, full of disgust, she faced him, and refused to let his haughty stare beat her down, and finally he turned on his heel and stalked out.

Linnet released her breath, and her shoulders drooped. When she turned round, she discovered that Agnes de Rocher was watching her with malice. 'There is no way out,' she said softly, and a cold ripple ran up Linnet's spine as she realized that the woman was quite mad. Thank Jesu that she had owned the foresight not to bring Robert to Arnsby. But if Joscelin was hung, how long would her little boy be safe?

Ironheart groaned and Agnes's head rotated to the sound like a predator's. She scuttled to the side of the bed and leaned over her grey-faced husband. He was propped up on several goose-down bolsters and pillows. Everything about him was sunken, as if all his vital juices had been sucked out, leaving nought but a skeleton clothed in skin. Against all adversity a spark of life still glinted in the bruised eyes and it was directed not at his hovering, gloating wife, but at Linnet and his youngest offspring. With a tremendous effort, his hand wavered up, and he beckoned.

Linnet approached the bed and stood at the opposite side to the glowering Agnes. Her flesh crawled. Martyn hesitated, then came to stand beside her. He refused to look at his mother and Linnet felt his shoulders trembling as she put her arm around them.

Ironheart stretched out his hand to her and the boy. Linnet took it and felt through its thinness the raging heat of fever.

310

'You were right,' he whispered. 'I should have died in Nottingham.'

Linnet blinked and swallowed. Within her, a rage of bitterness demanded that she agree with him, but she held it down, knowing that it would serve no useful purpose. Nor would she show him anything but love and duty in front of his youngest son, and his gloating, mad wife. 'You were not to know what form your premonition would take,' she murmured, looking at the scarred, shiny hand within her own two smooth ones. 'For that matter, we should have kept you at Rushcliffe.'

Agnes snorted, and Linnet glared at her through a veil of tears.

Ironheart closed his eyes and Linnet saw him struggle, summoning what strength remained in his emaciated body for the effort of speech. 'The scribe . . .' he said. 'I have made my will known to him.' His eyes opened again and met hers, pushing a message at her. 'The scribe,' he repeated, as if rambling, but his gaze was lucid.

At first Linnet was bewildered, and then she remembered that Ironheart's scribe was none other than Fulbert, whom Joscelin had sent here rather than hang. Fulbert might owe Joscelin a life, but he was as spineless as a lump of new blancmange. It was a slim thread of a chance at the most, but nevertheless it was hope, and the spark of it filled her with new energy.

Agnes snorted again. 'Do not look so eager, girl,' she sneered. 'There's nothing in his will for you. The fool has made grants to the church and freed some serfs. Of course,' she added with a yellow smile, 'the bequest to the nunnery won't be necessary now, will it?'

Ironheart's lips curved cynically. 'Do not be so sure of that, wife. Ragnar won't keep you here unless it's under lock and key.'

'Ragnar and I have a perfect understanding,' Agnes said coldly.

'Yours or his?'

Agnes drew herself up, but he turned his head away

311

from her and faced Linnet. 'Have a care to yourself whatever happens,' he whispered. 'And my blessing upon you and Joscelin. Give it to him if you can. There is so much I wanted to tell him . . . so much.'

Linnet leaned over Ironheart and kissed him on his dry, hot lips. The presence of death was so close that it was almost a visible entity. Once she would have recoiled in horror from the very thought of doing this, but she was free of her fetters now. And she wanted him to know that he was not alone, that she at least would stand on the edge of the river and bid him farewell with sorrow.

Then it was Martyn's turn. He knelt at his father's bedside and Ironheart laid his hand on his youngest son's bright brown hair. Martyn flinched but once, then held his ground, his lips pressed together, his nostrils flaring, drinking in the putrid scent of death. Linnet could see that Ironheart was beyond speaking, and that the boy's composure was more than precarious as he struggled with his revulsion.

'If you die,' he suddenly burst out, 'Ragnar will kill Joscelin!'

Ironheart's lids tensed and squeezed. He drew in a wheezing breath and let it out, shuddering with dry anguish. Linnet quickly drew Martyn away from the bedside, gesturing the maids to come and take him, but he twisted in her arms and made the sign of the cross over himself. 'And then I swear by Jesus Christ that I will kill Ragnar!'

'Martyn!' Agnes marched around the foot of the bed and slapped her youngest son hard across the face.

'I will do it!' he cried. 'I swear I will!' His chin jutted defiantly. The handprint on his cheek slowly turned from white to red.

His mother quivered. From the bed there came a sound that might almost have been grim laughter, and Agnes whirled, her hands closing and unclosing, and her face scarlet with pent-up fury.

'You think it amusing, do you?' she hissed at Ironheart, leaning over him. 'Then let me make you laugh some

312

more. Let me tell you about your whore, your precious Morwenna, about how she died. You would like to know, wouldn't you?'

Icy-cold premonition rooted Linnet to the spot as Agnes bent over her husband, her lips tauntingly close to his in the parody of a lover's. She saw the man try to turn aside, but Agnes turned with him, her head moving like a snake.

'For all these years you thought she tripped on her gown and fell down the stairs. I saw her, you know, I was behind her at the time. She was so big with child that her balance was not good. One push was all it took, one small push in the centre of her spine and down she went, belly first, then head over heels.' Agnes spoke slowly, relishing each word, her eyes never leaving his face. 'She was still conscious when she reached the bottom of the stairs, so I dropped a loom weight on her head to make sure she was silenced. She never recovered her wits, and I saw you put in the hell you deserved.' Her voice sank to a whisper. 'Jesu, but it was worth it.' Her lips parted in a smile.

Ironheart's right hand whipped up and clamped around her throat.

'Poisonous bitch!' he whistled as, choking, she fought to free herself. 'I'll show you what hell truly is!'

Agnes clawed and struggled, but the man whose physical strength had once denied the bite of an iron sword–blade, only tightened his death grip, the tendons standing out bone-thick on his taut forearm.

Agnes collapsed to her knees at the bedside, her tongue protruding and her face the colour of ripe plums. Appalled, Linnet suddenly recovered the use of her limbs and ran to the bed to pull Ironheart and his wife apart. She wedged hip and shoulder against the strangling Agnes and grasped Ironheart's arm at the juncture of wrist and palm. Through her own hand she felt the violent shuddering of his fury. And then, as she strove to break his grip, crying at him to stop, his eyes suddenly widened. 'Morwenna,' he gasped, staring beyond the women at something only he could see. His fingers relaxed, and his arm fell limply to his side, and he did not draw another breath.

313

Wheezing, gulping for air, Agnes fell upon the floor. Linnet left her to the maids and, taking Martyn's arm, pulled him away.

He was trembling and pale. The eyes he raised to her were numb with misery and bewilderment. Linnet squeezed his thin shoulders – too thin to carry the burdens being placed upon them.

'We must save Joscelin,' she murmured, drawing him towards the door. 'Now is our one chance while your mother and the maids are distracted. Take me to the chapel and then go and bring Fulbert the scribe to me.'

He looked up at her uncertainly.

'Fulbert owes Joscelin his life. I am calling in the debt. It is the only way of sending a message outside. Does Ragnar read and write?'

'A little . . . only his name. He uses a scribe normally.' The words emerged stiffly, his lips barely moving.

'Good. Quickly now.' She urged him towards the door. A swift glance over her shoulder reassured her that for the moment Agnes was too taken up by her struggle to breathe to notice their exit, and the maids were all occupied in fussing round her.

Once out of the room with its death smell and dreadful images, Martyn rallied. A guard had been posted at the foot of the stairs, but he let them pass when the boy told him in an authoritative tone that his mother had bid him take Lady Linnet to the chapel to light a candle and say prayers. Linnet, the image of distressed modesty, kept her eyes lowered and shrank from the guard's scrutiny. Let him believe that she had no spirit.

A cold draught twisted round the newel post and fingered past her. She caught the familiar smell of dank stone, but there was an underlying elusive herbal scent. The guard must have noticed it too, for he turned and looked at the stairs behind him and even mounted them to peer around the newel post. Linnet shivered, thinking of Morwenna de Gael, and remembering Robert's tale of a lady in a green gown he had encountered here. 'If you can

314

hear me,' she entreated Morwenna's spirit, 'I call on you to help me to save your son and your unborn grandchild.'

She was answered only by the echo of her own whisper and the heavy fluttering of the torches in the sconces.

In the chapel, Linnet lit a candle and genuflected to the altar, then bowed her head to pray, seeking the strength to stay calm throughout the following hours. Martyn slipped away in search of Fulbert.

As Linnet eased her position on the hard stone flags, she heard a sound from one of the niches in the chapel wall. Her heart pounding, she looked round, half-expecting to see the luminous figure of Morwenna de Gael, but it was a man's form that rose from the shadows and began edging towards the rear of the chapel.

'Who's there?' she demanded, standing up. The man did not reply, but she knew that he had heard her speak, for he hesitated. Candlelight brushed across his hair, revealing it to be dull chestnut-red. A brief gleam of light caught the side of his face before he went out, and it was familiar to her. She wondered for whom or what Ivo de Rocher had been praying. Was his soul troubled at the prospect of fratricide? She wondered if she dared approach him for succour.

Hesitant footsteps pitter-pattered outside the chapel door, stopped, were silent for the space of several heartbeats, and then entered the dark sanctum.

'My lady?' The scribe's whisper was high-pitched with nervousness. 'It is not safe here. I just saw Lord Ivo, what if he says something?'

'He won't,' she said with more confidence than she felt and advanced to draw the scribe further into the church, before the altar so that the cross cast a long shadow between them.

Fulbert licked his lips and looked anxiously towards the door. 'I cannot stay long. I'm supposed to be visiting the garderobe.'

'I suppose I should be grateful that you have come at all,' Linnet said, allowing her disgust to show. 'Lord Joscelin spared your miserable neck once. Is it too much to expect that you should repay the favour?'

Fulbert ceased licking his lips and began to chew them instead. 'Of course I will help if I can, mistress, but I fail to see what I can do.'

'Because you would rather walk around in the darkness than risk the light!' she snapped, and watched Fulbert shuffle and look at his feet. 'It is obvious what you must do. Write to Sheriff FitzRanulf in Nottingham and the garrison at Rushcliffe telling them to come at once. You are responsible for giving sealed parchments to messengers, and Ragnar will have had much to send out today. It will not be hard to include another two.'

Fulbert swallowed audibly.

Linnet watched him wring his fat, pink hands and wondered how such bloated objects could create such wonderful, delicate script. Somewhere there had to be a hidden wellspring.

'Yea or nay?' she said fiercely, as the scribe continued to fumble and mumble and look at his feet.

'Mistress, I will do my best,' he flicked her a rapid look from beneath his brows and sidled towards the escape of the door.

A hole seemed to open within Linnet's breast and her heart plummeted through to her stomach. The man was a coward; she could read his intention clearly in his eyes. 'God grant you forgiveness, for I will not!' she hissed, her voice shaking, and then, hearing herself, she compressed her lips. Jesu, I sound like Agnes de Rocher, she thought. What if I become like her? And she knew that at noon tomorrow, if Joscelin died, she would not care what she became, or what became of her.

CHAPTER 35

TORCH IN HAND, Ragnar wound his way down into the bowels of the keep. The guards he encountered saluted him, their eyes nervous. The authority to command them was now his, but while his father still clung to life it was incomplete. And what he intended to do tomorrow did not meet with unanimous approval.

Ragnar responded to the sidelong looks with an air of supreme indifference, but behind his mask he was irritated by their uncertainty; indeed they made him feel nervous, for their attitude unsettled his own view of himself as being utterly in control. Once his father and Joscelin were out of the way, he told himself, everything would come right. The black bitterness would leave his soul and he would be healed.

He moved through the undercroft, the heat from the torch searing his face as he passed barrels, casks and bins of supplies, and came to the cells. Behind stoutly barred doors set with small iron grilles for observation of the prisoners, Joscelin's men were held captive together with those of his father's knights who had objected to his taking command of Arnsby. Seated at a trestle outside the cells, keeping watch, were two of the Flemish mercenaries he had borrowed from Robert Ferrers. They were unmannerly, rough types, but at least they seemed to know how to use their weapons, which half of their countrymen didn't, and they did as they were instructed without demur.

Finally, at the very end of the undercroft, where the shadows were deepest, Ragnar came to the bolted trap door covering the mouth of the oubliette. He stood upon the heavy oak planks with their wrought-iron banding, legs planted wide, and imagined Joscelin twenty feet below him, staring up into the pitch blackness and not even knowing where the trapdoor was. The oubliette was a deep, windowless pit. Originally it had been constructed with the dual purpose of storing roots and confining difficult prisoners with a view to demoralizing them into submission. Underground seepage, however, meant that there was always six inches of murky sludge lying in the bottom of the pit and the roots were far better stored in barrels of soil in the main undercroft. It was still, however, used occasionally for prisoners. A couple of days standing ankle-deep in cold water without food usually subdued even the most stubborn captives – if they did not die of the lung fever first.

Ragnar quivered. He could feel Joscelin's presence as if the two of them were bound together by an umbilical cord. The temptation to open the trap and peer inside was almost unbearable. What was Joscelin doing? What was he feeling, knowing that in the morning he was going to die?

Ragnar's mind wandered back to a hot, summer's day on the brink of adolescence. Joscelin had been fifteen then, big-boned and gawky with a voice like a cracked cup. Ragnar remembered baiting him, taunting and teasing, following him round, refusing to leave him alone. In the end, Joscelin's temper had snapped and he had turned upon his tormentor. Ragnar had been injured, but he had made far more of a fuss than his wounds warranted. Enough for their father actually to thrash his precious bastard son. Ragnar could still taste the triumph of that day. At the time, he had thought it worth every bruise.

Of course it had not lasted. Joscelin had run away, their father had blamed Ragnar for it, and the thrashing had come home to roost with a vengeance. Stupid old man. The torch sputtered and resin hissed at Ragnar's feet. He considered tomorrow's revenge and through the triumph felt a disturbing churning in his gut as he imagined Joscelin kicking at the end of a rope. A desperate need to see the thing accomplished warred with a feeling of utter revulsion.

A small voice in his soul was crying that he would never be free of Joscelin whatever he did.

The torch was growing heavy and making his arm tremble. 'Damn you!' he snarled into the darkness and, turning on his heel, strode rapidly away from the oubliette.

In the hall, he noticed that the scribe had returned from his visit to the garderobe and was busy with his quill once more. The atmosphere had a tense, waiting quality, like the edge of a thunderstorm, and Ragnar felt it raise the hairs upon his spine. Carefully he set his torch in an empty wall sconce and went over to the scribe.

'How soon will you be finished?' He braced his thin fingers on the trestle and leaned over the parchments.

'Soon Lord Ragnar, v . . . very soon.'

Ragnar eyed Fulbert's trembling hand and then the script. That at least appeared neat and flowing even if its creator was a gibbering wreck. Well, he needed the man for now, but he could soon and easily replace him. Scribes were ten a penny in Nottingham. 'Make haste,' he said. 'And have the messengers ride out immediately you have finished.'

'Yes, my lord.' Fulbert made bulbous swallowing motions like a frog. Then his darting gaze, which Ragnar had been unable to pin down and trap, settled beyond Ragnar's shoulder.

Ragnar turned round and saw Father Ralf standing to one side, his expression both grave and grim, his hands toying with a silver cross hanging on a cord from his belt.

'Sir William is dead,' announced the priest. 'I think that you should come to your mother's chamber, my lord. Apparently he had some sort of seizure in his last moments and assaulted the Lady Agnes. She is asking for you.'

Ragnar looked down and gently opened the fists he had clenched at Father Ralf's news. So now he was indeed 'my lord', with no one in the keep to gainsay his will. 'Tell her I will come as soon as I can,' he said, and was aware of a black desolation overshadowing his triumph.

★

His stomach rolling with fear, Fulbert finished working on the missives that Ragnar had commanded him to write, sealing them in hot wax with the ring the young man had pulled from his father's finger in the courtyard. His hands shook as he set all except two to one side. He paused to try to think, but was horribly aware of the grains of time slipping away with each moment that he procrastinated. Either he threw these two letters he had just written in the hearth and gave the others out to the messengers, or he did the reverse.

He imagined judgement day, his sins on one side of the scales and his good deeds on the other. He remembered Lady Linnet's accusing grey eyes. Then he thought of the fires of hell and came face to face with his own cowardice. He stopped the torture of thinking.

Rapidly, his hands went to the leaves of clean vellum at his left-hand side. He folded deftly, attached seals, scrawled salutations, but the pages were entirely blank. These he gave out to the messengers who were to ride to Robert Ferrers of Derby and the men of Leicester's and Norfolk's mesnie. The two letters most recently written he gave to the men with the best horses. Fortunately for his quaking knees, Fulbert was not questioned. It was only polite custom that the sheriff be informed of Ironheart's death, and if Lord Ragnar wanted letters delivering to Rushcliffe, then that was his own business.

When the last horseman had clattered out of the postern gate on to the road, Fulbert returned to his lectern and, screwing up the letters he had written on Ragnar's behalf summoning the rebels to Arnsby, tossed them in the great hearth. As soon as he was sure that they had been consumed by the flames, he went to rouse his wife and children and pack his belongings. The gates would open at dawn tomorrow to admit supplies and he intended, in the words of a popular folk song, to be over the hills and far away before Ragnar got wind of what had happened.

CHAPTER 36

I N HIS PRISON Joscelin stared upwards and listened to the footsteps recede. Not so much as a glimmer of light betrayed the whereabouts of the trapdoor, but he had felt Ragnar's presence above him. He had almost cried out, wanting to reason with his brother, but the thought of Ragnar's mocking smile had held him to silence. In his heart he knew that no amount of reasoning would alter his brother's decision. Ragnar had thought it out this time; he had taken rapid advantage of the situation and manipulated it to his own ends.

Joscelin had witnessed enough hangings to know what would happen. Hopefully, if the angle were right and the rope did not snag against the keep wall, death would be instantaneous as the force of the fall snapped his neck. If not, it would be a slow, strangling fight for air, flesh swelling and discolouring, bowels and bladder yielding their contents. Either way there was little dignity.

He wondered if Ragnar would force Linnet to watch. The thought tore through him like a spear and he wrenched himself around in the darkness and splashed through the cold mud until the wall brought him up short and he crashed into it with bruising force. Again and again he threw himself at its solid weight in frustration and rage.

At last, exhausted, he slumped against the wall. Every breath he took was invaded by the smell of mould and damp like the earth clinging to a corpse. Chest heaving, his body shaken by rigours of cold, he considered taking his own life so that when Ragnar came to drag him out to the gallows tomorrow he would be cheated of his final victory. He could dash himself against the wall until he knocked himself unconscious and drowned in the sludge at his feet. Or he could cut the veins in his wrists with the sharp notch on his belt. His breathing calmed while he considered the enormity of such a move. Ragnar would still have won, but not on the terms he desired.

Eternal darkness. Joscelin knew that he would be damned forever if he took his own life. So be it. He could spend eternity in pursuit of Ragnar. Slowly he put his hand upon his belt and unlatched it, rubbing his thumb over the notch of the wolf-head buckle.

Above him, at the trapdoor, he heard movement again, the gritty scuffling of footsteps, and the sound of something heavy being dropped on the trap. He ran the leather through his hands, to and fro, and stared aloft, licking his lips. The heavy bolts on top of the trap were being stealthily drawn back. Was it morning already? Surely not. Perhaps Ragnar was easing his conscience by offering him the comfort of a priest before they took him out to the gibbet.

The trap opened. Joscelin saw the dull glimmer of a small rushlight and the dark bulk of a lone human figure. It made no sound, save to grunt as it worked busily at something above. And then a thick hempen rope snaked down towards him and dangled to a halt at his collarbone.

For one horrible moment Joscelin thought that they had come to hang him here and now in the oubliette, swiftly in the dark without witnesses, but his common sense soon reasserted itself. If they were going to hang him now, they would have brought a ladder and more lights. And there would have been guards to restrain him while the noose was placed around his neck. Whoever had cast down the rope meant him well.

Breathing lightly, gazing upwards, he listened hard and thought he heard soft footfalls walking away. The trap remained open, and the rope ceased to quiver and hung straight down before his face. All was silent except for the drip-drip of water down the walls. In the faint light from above he could see the gleam of wet stone and the pale vapour of his breath. He latched the belt around his waist again and rubbed his palms upon his tunic, for they were suddenly slick with cold sweat. It was a long climb to the top of the oubliette, and if he fell from a height, his body would be broken, for there was not enough water in the base of the pit to absorb his fall.

Again he wiped his hands, paused to cross himself and murmur a plea to God; then he leaped, setting his hands upon the rope and winding his feet around it. The tough hemp fibres burned his hands as he struggled up the rope like a caterpillar on a stem. Hot pain lanced up his arms, and the earlier cold sweat of apprehension became salty-warm and slippery with effort, stinging his eyes and making his grip on the rope treacherous. Hand over hand, knees and thighs inching and gripping, he progressed towards the dull light of the trapdoor, knowing that at any moment he might be discovered and the rope cut.

By the time he hauled himself over the edge, his palms were blistered raw. Every muscle was screaming and there was nothing but red mist before his eyes. He was horribly aware that he was making too much noise in his efforts to breathe, that he was easy, conspicuous prey. He crawled to his knees, panting hard, trying to hold the sound to silence.

When his vision cleared, he saw that whoever had dropped the rope had left a candle burning on a pricket to give him light, and beside it a scramaseax – a common English man's weapon, mid-way between a sword and a knife. It was good and sharp, and made light work of severing the rope from the barrel of sand around which his rescuer had double-looped it to bear Joscelin's weight. He cast the rope back down into the oubliette and, after what seemed an eternity, heard it splash in the water below. He could still feel his heart thudding rapidly in his breast, but his breathing was easier now, and the fiery ache was leaving his muscles.

Tucking the scramaseax in his belt, he closed the trapdoor over the oubliette and refastened the iron double bolts so that to the casual observer all would seem normal. Who, he wondered, could have given him the grace of this chance to avoid death? He was sure that his first visitor had been Ragnar. He had felt him, blood and bone, and dark, bitter hatred. But the second time? There were several people in the keep who might have sprung the trap for him – he was Ironheart's favoured son and well known to the family retainers – but he doubted they would have been permitted past Ragnar's Flemish guards.

It was a mystery, and likely to remain so, for his rescuer appeared to desire anonimity – nor could he blame him. Joscelin picked up the candle and snuffed it out. Thus might his life have been quenched on the morrow. Thus might it still happen unless he succeeded in making his escape and freeing his men from the cells.

Joscelin moved tentatively through the undercroft, feeling his way past barrels and sheaves, laundry tubs and stitched-up sacks. Each footstep had to be carefully negotiated, for the darkness was almost complete and if he knocked anything over he knew that Ragnar's guards would come hurrying to investigate.

He found one of the stone columns that rose in an arch supporting the undercroft roof. Carefully he measured his paces between it and the next one. Ten. And another ten to the one after that. He knew that the dimensions of the undercroft roughly corresponded to those of the hall above, and that if he followed the pillars they would lead him eventually to the stairs.

Another ten paces, another column, and beneath his fingertips he felt lines cut in the sandstone. Investigation revealed that someone had carved out a nine-men's morris game. There was the outlining square, the two inner squares, and the peg holes at intervals. Every sense stood on edge as Joscelin realized he must be very close to the cells now. The carving would have been made by one of the guards at some time to stave off the boredom of a long stint of duty.

Joscelin moved to the next column, took another five steps and came up against some barrels. Wine for the hall,

324

he thought. That was always close to the entrance because of frequent use. Besides, he could see the dim outline of the casks. Beyond the next pillar two candle lanterns were hung from pegs in the wall and radiated a diffuse golden light. He caught the sound of voices, the rattle of dice in a cup, the clink of weapon mountings on mail.

He crept sideways along the row of casks until a short trestle table came into view between the pillars. Seated at either end was a guard. Mercenaries, he thought, examining their gear. There was more light now, for a half-burned candle stood in the centre of the trestle, adorned with strings of melted wax. A mutilated loaf stood on a wooden trencher and there was a stone ale pitcher beside it. They were not drinking at the moment, for one of the cups was being used as a shaker for two bone dice.

He could see that each man wore a sword and that their ash spears were propped against the cell walls. The cells themselves were barred from the outside with stout oak planks and had small iron grilles at the top. Guy de Montauban was looking out of one of them, watching the dice game.

'How long until dawn?' Montauban asked the guards.

'An hour, less perhaps,' answered one of them. He had dark, heavy stubble on his jaw and a strong Flemish accent. 'Eager to see the hanging and flaying are you?'

'It will be naught but cold-blooded murder. If you are a party to it, you will have signed your own death-warrant.'

The Fleming laughed, shook the dice, and rattled them across the trestle. 'At least you'll keep warm on all the hot air coming from your mouth,' he said, and rubbed his hands. 'Seven again, Joachim, that's your belt you owe me.'

The other guard groaned and, removing his scabbard, unlatched the handsome tooled belt from around his thick waist.

Joscelin rose silently from behind the barrels. Guy de Montauban saw him and his eyes widened in surprise. Then he began to shout and howl and scream as if possessed.

325

The guard who had been rolling the dice, leaped to his feet and went to the cell to see what was happening. Joscelin ran round the barrels and attacked the other Fleming. The man had no time to defend himself. Belt still in hand, mouth open in astonishment, he turned to face Joscelin. Joscelin aimed not at his mail clad torso, but at his legs which were only covered by woollen chausses and leggings. The scramaseax was razor-sharp and sliced like a cleaver through fabric, flesh and bone. Blood sprayed. Screaming, the Fleming fell. His fellow mercenary rasped his sword from his scabbard and turned from the cells to face Joscelin.

Casting aside the scramaseax, knowing that the Fleming's sword would far outreach it, Joscelin leaped over the bleeding soldier and snatched up one of the propped spears. Then he moved in again to the attack, jabbing and thrusting with the hard iron point. Behind him, the other guard screamed and thrashed on the floor.

The Fleming parried a couple of times, cast a rapid glance over his shoulder at the distance to the stairs, and cried,'Quarter! I yield! I yield!' And dropped his weapon.

Joscelin did not lower the spear. 'Unbar the cells,' he commanded brusquely, jerking the point.

The Fleming did as he was told, fumbling in his haste to lift the heavy wooden beams out of their slots.

'Now attend to your friend before he dies,' Joscelin said as the prisoners within pushed open their doors and burst out to freedom. 'Use that belt you so prized to strap off the bleeding.'

'Lord Joscelin!' Guy de Montauban's eyes were glowing with exultation and an excess of wild anger. 'How did you manage to escape?'

'Someone opened the oubliette trap and dropped down a rope. I don't know who; they did not wait to make themselves known. Did you see anyone go past?'

'Ragnar came before midnight, walking as if he owned the world, the whoreson,' Montauban spat, as if mention of the name had fouled his mouth.

'No one else?'

'I don't know. I think I must have slept some of the time. The rattle of their dice woke me up. What about you, Yves?' Montauban turned to a bow-legged sandy-haired man. 'Did you see anyone?'

'Someone did come.' Yves rubbed the side of his sharp, freckled nose. 'But I didn't see his face. He was wearing a cloak and a short hood – a blue one I remember. The guards knew him and weren't bothered.'

'Ivo!' Joscelin murmured with surprise. 'I always thought he was Ragnar's acolyte.' But then perhaps Ivo was no longer prepared to follow where Ragnar chose to lead. 'How many of us are there?' He took a swift head count. Six of his father's men, six of his own and himself. Thirteen, the unlucky number of the last supper, he thought with a grimace.

'We have two swords, two daggers, two spears, a scram, and a pair of mail shirts,' said Montauban, casting his eyes over the weaponry.

'There are spare lance-shafts stowed over there; they can be used as quarterstaffs.' Joscelin pointed to a stack of shaped ash staves leaning against a wall. 'We won't have to tackle every soldier in the keep, only the mercenaries loyal to Ragnar and, even then, their resistance is likely to be half-hearted.' He cast a look over his shoulder at the two Flemings. 'Ragnar is the target. Down him and the resistance dies.'

'You want him dead?' Montauban licked his lips.

Joscelin drew a harsh breath through his teeth. Every nerve and desire directed him to answer yes, but he held back, afraid of the blackness at his core, as deep and dark as the oubliette in which Ragnar had cast him. 'Hold back unless there is no other way,' he replied. 'Better if he is taken alive and dealt with by the Justiciar.' His expression became bleak. 'Otherwise I am no better than he.'

CHAPTER 37

LINNET WATCHED AGNES de Rocher raise a coffer lid, take from it a pile of garments, and bring them over to the bed where Ironheart lay. His hands were crossed upon his breast and his badger-grey hair was parted in the middle and combed and oiled as Linnet had never seen it in life. It had always been swept back from his forehead in leonine disorder, and very seldom had he used a comb to tame it.

Death had softened some of the harsh lines graven into his face but, without flesh or colour, he was already cadaverous, bearing little resemblance to the living man. And Agnes was revelling in her moment of glory. She was like an eager bride, her face radiant and her eyes sparkling as she went about her deathchamber duties.

Linnet had been escorted back from the chapel by two of Ragnar's Flemish guards and informed that if she wandered off again she would be tied up. Agnes had recovered from her near-choking, although her voice was nothing more than a harsh whisper and she had exchanged the light silk wimple of earlier for a fuller one of linen that swathed her throat and shoulders, concealing all marks.

Linnet had been forced to sit on a stool and watch Agnes prepare her husband to be taken down to the chapel to lie in state; forced to watch the woman wash his body as tenderly as a lover, dwelling upon the ravaged, calloused flesh with obscene, possessive joy. It had made Linnet sick. Twice she had had to run to the wastepit in the corner of the room, although there had been nothing to bring up but bile. And each time she returned it was to see Agnes crooning to her husband, smiling and stroking.

'You are mine now,' Agnes whispered, running the rosewater cloth over the body in long, smooth strokes. 'You cannot gainsay my will.'

Linnet shuddered at her tone. She harboured a fear that in her madness Agnes would cast off her clothes and leap into bed with the body.

'Of course, when it comes your turn to do this, your own husband will not be so presentable,' Agnes continued as she shook out the garments, hurling small, brittle pieces of bay leaf and sage from the folds. 'I saw a human hide once, nailed on the gates of a Jew's house in Newark. You couldn't really tell it was human — it was all yellow and shrivelled; they mustn't have tanned it properly.'

Linnet was overcome with nausea again, her reaction so swift and strong to Agnes's words that she had no time to reach the garderobe and had to use her wimple.

Agnes clucked her tongue. 'You are suffering, my dear, aren't you?' she said, a parody of concern in her husky, damaged voice. 'When is the babe due?'

'It is your behaviour that is making me sick,' Linnet swallowed out, removing her spoiled wimple. Jesu and his mother help me, she thought, knowing that she could not endure much more.

'Your heart is too tender, as indeed mine was once. Perhaps you see yourself in me?' Agnes cocked her head to one side, eyeing Linnet with a terrible shrewdness. 'But you *are* pregnant, aren't you? I have carried enough infants in my womb to know the signs.'

Rising, Linnet went to dispose of her stained wimple down the waste shaft. 'It is no concern of yours,' she said in what she hoped was a cold tone speaking of strength, not trembling terror.

'Oh, but it is,' Agnes murmured. 'In your belly grows the seed of Morwenna de Gael's grandchild. We shall have to do something about that unless you lose it of your own accord. It is no use looking at the door. There is a guard on the stairs and he has instructions not to let you pass unless in my company. Come,' she gestured, 'help me dress my

329

husband for the chapel. He cannot go before the altar in his shirt. It would not be seemly.'

Linnet backed away from Agnes's beckoning finger, sickened to the pit of her soul, backed away until her spine struck the wall and she could go no further. Agnes smiled and shrugged, and gestured instead to her maid.

Linnet slipped down the wall until a low, dust-covered oak coffer caught the back of her knees. She slumped upon it, fighting to stay conscious, terrified of the danger to herself and her unborn child. As if from a great distance, she heard Agnes directing her maid to lift and lower, pull and push as they dressed William Ironheart in his court robes, decking him out in the finery that his life-spark had shunned.

'Neither will it be seemly for you to accompany me to the chapel with your hair uncovered,' Agnes croaked over to Linnet. 'You will find a wimple in that coffer. Put it on and make yourself decent for the priest.'

Garish spots of light danced before Linnet's eyes and the room spun this way and that. She wanted to snarl defiance at Agnes, but knew that her only chance of escape lay in leaving this room, in persuading Ragnar that she would be better guarded elsewhere if he wanted to preserve her to use as a bargaining counter.

Gingerly, she turned round, knelt on the floor, and raised the lid of the coffer on which she had been sitting. The scent of faded herbs drifted to her nostrils as she looked upon folded chemises and summer linen under-gowns. Unable to find a wimple, she burrowed deeper, at last uncovering a rectangle of aqua-green silk and another larger one of pale blue linen. A small securing brooch in the shape of a small bronze horse was still pinned in its folds.

It was this second one that Linnet chose but, as she drew the wimple forth, the brooch pin caught on the garment folded beneath. She lifted both out in order to untangle them, and found herself looking at the gown lining the bottom of the coffer. It was made of green velvet, with a trim of tarnished silver thread. When she held it up, she saw that it was cut in the style fashionable when she had been a little girl, and that it had been adapted to fit a woman big with child.

'Dear God,' she whispered and looked over her shoulder at Agnes, but the older woman was busily adorning Iron-heart's body and showed no sign that she had intended for Linnet to discover the gown.

Linnet wondered if this coffer had been Morwenna's. Had she ever worn the blue wimple and horse brooch? Was the aqua silk wimple the one that belonged with the green gown?

Slowly, with fingers that shook, she covered her hair with the blue linen and brought an edge across to pin beneath her throat.

Agnes turned round. Her small eyes widened as she looked at the open coffer. 'Not that one,' she snapped irritably, 'the one next to it.' She pointed at another larger chest standing against the wall beside the one Linnet had used. Then she made a gesture of dismissal. 'It doesn't matter. Maude never uses it anyway.'

'It belongs to Maude?'

Agnes shrugged. 'I told you, it does not matter.'

Linnet drew the green gown from the coffer, shook it out and held it up. 'So this is hers?'

If Agnes had been capable of screaming, she would have done so. Her mouth open, she stared at the creased, green robe with its knotted hanging sleeves and rich silver bor-ders. Her colour faded to a sickly yellow and she dragged air into her lungs with painful effort. 'I gave orders that it should be burned!' she wheezed. 'The stupid, sentimental bitch, I should never have let her stay here to comfort William and the brat after the whore died. Give it to me!' Her hands extended to snatch, she stepped towards Linnet.

'You destroyed yourself when you killed Morwenna, didn't you?' Linnet side-stepped to avoid Agnes. Armoured with the green gown she was no longer afraid. 'You kept her fresh and young forever in your husband's mind.'

'Give me that gown, you harlot!' Agnes lunged. Linnet dodged. The tarnished silver braid glittered and the green velvet glowed with absorbed and reflected light as Linnet swept out of Agnes's reach. Agnes stumbled against the larger chest. Standing on it was a small, open basket containing her tablet-weaving materials. From amongst the hanks of wool, she withdrew her sewing shears and gripped them like a weapon. 'You whore!' Agnes whispered, her broken voice saturated with hatred. 'You'll not take him from me this time!'

Linnet jumped backwards, trying to avoid the wicked blades of the shears as Agnes lunged. Moving sideways, dodging, Linnet tried to reach the bed in order to keep its bulk between herself and Agnes, but Agnes was too quick for her and the direction of Linnet's movement only incensed the older woman further. 'Keep away from him!' Agnes hissed, striking at Linnet with the shears. The pointed blades ripped into the old green velvet, shredding the front from breast to hip.

Linnet narrowly missed being gouged. The force of Agnes's assault almost dragged the gown from her hands, but she held on to it. As the shears stabbed at her again, she raised the gown on high. 'Have it!' she cried, tossing it over Agnes's head, and ran to the door. She wrestled with the heavy latch, knowing that at any moment Agnes would win free of the gown and come at her again.

Sobbing with panic, she rammed the heel of her hand down on the latch, and felt it give. She wrenched the door open, intending to flee down the stairs to the guard, but her way was blocked.

'Going somewhere?' Ragnar said softly and, seizing her upper arm in a grip of steel, he turned her round and pulled her back into the room. He was not alone. Ivo, four knights and the priest followed him into the chamber.

'Your mother has just tried to kill me!' Linnet panted, struggling against his imprisoning fingers to no avail. 'She thinks I'm Morwenna de Gael!'

Agnes had fought free of the green gown and was

332

glaring wildly at Linnet, the shears still tilted at a wicked angle in her hand.

'She's a whore!' Agnes spat, her face flushed. 'And she's carrying a child. I'll have no spawn of a de Gael under my roof!'

Ragnar lifted his brows. 'Mama, she is useful to us for the moment. She holds the key to the Rushcliffe estates. There is no profit to be had in killing her.'

Agnes's complexion darkened. She compressed her lips mulishly, and her fingers tightened around her shears.

Ragnar gestured towards her work-basket. 'Put them down,' he said reasonably. 'We can discuss matters later, after the hanging. My father bought you a nun's pension before he died. Mayhap we can use it to endow a young widow instead?'

Agnes's lips remained tight, but she obeyed Ragnar and replaced the shears among the hanks of wool. 'I only have your good at heart,' she said.

'I know that, Mama,' Ragnar said gently, his tone imbued with a rare warmth. Releasing Linnet's arm, he crossed the room and looked down at the stiff composure of the corpse, at the wine-red court gown and the horny, battle-hardened hands clasped in an attitude of prayer.

'It doesn't look like him,' he murmured, and rubbed his hand over his lower face in a nervous gesture. Linnet could see that his composure was brittle. There were dark shadows beneath his eyes and downward tucks at his mouth corners. The act of murder was sitting like a gargoyle on his conscience, she thought.

'It isn't him,' Linnet said coldly. 'He might as well be a dressed carcass on a butcher's slab.'

Ragnar glared round at her. 'You will keep a civil tongue in your head, or I will lock you up alone in the undercroft,' he snapped.

'Is that what you are going to do to everyone who contradicts your will?' Linnet retorted. 'Lock them away, bully them silent . . . murder them?'

Ragnar's fists clenched. He swivelled and took two dangerous strides towards her.

'Ragnar, don't,' said Ivo in a wavering voice. 'Not in here, with Papa . . .' He gestured towards the corpse on the bed.

Ragnar stopped. A pulse thundered heavily in his throat and his eyes were narrow and wolf-golden. Linnet refused to be intimidated. She gave him back stare for stare, knowing that her own gaze was no less wild.

Ragnar abruptly turned his back on her. His fists remained clenched, and his voice was raw with his anger as he addressed Agnes. 'Is my father prepared for the chapel?'

'Yes, my heart,' Agnes said. 'See, I have dressed him fittingly in his court robes and set rings on his fingers.'

Ragnar smiled without humour. 'If you were to have dressed him fittingly, it would not have been like this, but in his oldest tunic and cloak,' he said.

Agnes stared at him, uncomprehending. Ragnar shook his head. 'No matter,' he said. 'You have done your best.' He kissed her cheek.

Agnes started to speak, but broke off abruptly as the sound of sword on sword and a choked-off scream twisted up the stairs from the guardpost at the foot of the tower.

Drawing his sword, Ragnar strode to the door and gestured to one of his knights to go down and investigate. The man hurried out and down. Almost immediately the occupants of the room heard the clash of blade meeting blade, and another cry. Ragnar's man backed up the stairs and staggered into the room, blood pouring from his shoulder.

'Bar the door!' he gasped through his teeth at Ragnar. 'Your brother and his men are loose and they're armed!' As he uttered the warning, he kicked the door shut, and leaned against it.

Ashen-faced, Ragnar stooped to pick up the draw bar leaning against the wall. Linnet saw the hope of freedom and ran to stop him from pushing the plank through the iron brackets. She blocked his way with her body, her arms outstretched. Ragnar thrust her violently away. She landed heavily on her side, bruising hip and shoulder, but rolled over on the straw, and grasped a handful of his tunic. Ragnar raised the plank and struck her on the side of the head with its corner.

Black stars burst in front of Linnet's eyes and she felt a spurting warm gush of blood. Her grip weakened and Ragnar tore free. Through swimming eyes, she saw him lift the draw bar to slot it into position just as the door was smashed wide by Joscelin and Guy de Montauban.

The wounded knight was thrown to the floor, and rolled back and forth, clutching his shoulder, his mouth thrown wide in agony. Ragnar dropped the wood and leaped backwards with the speed of a bounding deer. The sword he had sheathed while he manipulated the draw bar was snatched from his scabbard in a rapid flash of steel, and he turned in a battle crouch to face Joscelin.

The run upstairs had winded Joscelin and he was very close to the limit of his endurance. He saw Linnet near the door. She was struggling to sit up, her mouth working as if she wanted to cry out to him, but no sound emerged and she sagged back to the floor. Blood masked one side of her face and stained her wimple and gown. Joscelin's simmering rage boiled over and, with a howl, he flung himself at Ragnar. The blow was made of white-hot fury, mistimed and without control. Ragnar parried easily and made a smooth counter-strike, his own breathing calm and deep. The sword edge shrieked upon the ill-fitting mail shirt that Joscelin had purloined from one of the Flemings in the undercroft. He had the Fleming's sword too, the hilt worn and slippery in his grasp.

The room filled with the clash and glitter of weapons. The priest sidled quickly out of the door, delicately stepping over Linnet. Ivo allowed himself to be made Guy de Montauban's prisoner without even a token show of protest.

Ragnar's strength forced Joscelin backwards and he pressed his advantage, using his sword two-handed, swinging it almost as though it were a battle-axe. 'Side-by-side in the chapel,' Ragnar panted as he fought Joscelin into a corner. 'You and our sainted father, wouldn't that be fitting!'

Joscelin stumbled against a coffer and knew that it must be his last move on earth, but Ragnar lost his own footing upon a puddle of green velvet bunched on the floor, and his blow went awry, splicing the coffer instead of Joscelin's skull. The impetus brought Ragnar to his knees, his sword lodged in the wood. Before he could recover and free the blade, Joscelin leaped upon him, bearing him to the ground beneath his weight. The air burst out of Ragnar's lungs. His head struck the rushes, but he succeeded in landing a knee in Joscelin's groin and, as Joscelin recoiled, was able to twist free and grasp his sword once more. Both hands to the leather grip, he went all out to take Joscelin.

His sword rang out great hammer blows on Joscelin's blade as he beat at it, striving to win past the slender bar of steel and cut out Joscelin's heart. And Joscelin, on the edge of exhaustion, could barely hold him off; his body had taken too much punishment this past night and day to serve him through another bout. His vision started to blur and hot pain seared through his limbs as he parried and defended.

Sensing Joscelin's weakness, Ragnar gathered himself for a final, killing flurry and in that moment, poised on the brink of his triumph, Martyn burst into the room followed by Fulbert the scribe, who was wheezing like a set of bagpipes with the unaccustomed exertion.

'Soldiers!' Fulbert gasped out, clutching his side, his face purple. 'Demanding entry . . . the seneschal's just raising the bridge!'

Martyn shot between his two brothers. 'Stop, you have to stop!' he shrieked, his face white. 'You can't kill each other!'

'Get out of the way, whelp,' Ragnar snarled, his eyes never leaving Joscelin. 'You heard the scribe,' he spat. 'My allies have come. Either we finish this now, or you swing on a gibbet for their entertainment. Which is it to be?'

Joscelin stared dully at Ragnar. Every nerve and fibre of

his body was sodden with exhaustion; there was nothing he wanted to do more than let the weight of his sword hit the floor, but he knew that he would rather die by the grim mercy of a blade here and now than by throttling on a rope before a host of witnesses.

'It will never be finished,' he said hoarsely, and braced his trembling sword arm.

'Leave me alone!' Martyn yelled, wrenching himself free of his mother as she tried to drag him away from the two men.

Fulbert was twitching with terror, but he stepped resolutely forward. 'You do not understand,' he wheezed at Ragnar. 'It is the sheriff who is here, and Brien FitzRenard bearing the Justiciar's authority. They are in the bailey even now.'

Ragnar's face changed. He stared at the scribe in utter disbelief. Fulbert avoided his gaze and backed hastily away.

'What trickery is this?' Ragnar snarled.

Ivo brushed aside Montauban's sword and went to the window. Throwing the shutters wide, he stood on tiptoe to look out on the bailey. 'It's true,' he said. 'I can see de Luci's banner and the FitzRenard leopard.' He looked over his shoulder into the room, his expression half-afraid and half-relieved.

Uttering a roar of pure, incandescent rage, Ragnar swept Martyn aside as if he were no more than a feather and attacked Joscelin, his sword a hacking, slashing blur. Joscelin parried and ducked, was forced backwards, pushed and manipulated by Ragnar's superior stamina until the dark tower stairway was at his back, and he could retreat no further.

'I'll send you to hell, you whoreson!' Ragnar's lips were drawn back from his teeth in a white, feral snarl as he brought up the sword.

Joscelin feinted one way, dived the other and, as he hit the floor, yanked at the length of green velvet upon which Ragnar had been standing. He felt the impact of a heavy blow upon his chainmail, and a searing pain, and saw

337

Ragnar struggling to hold his balance on the very edge of the top step. Joscelin scrambled to his knees and clawed for Ragnar's tunic to try to pull him back into the chamber. The friction of flesh on fabric burned his knuckles; Ragnar's weight ripped back his fingernails. As Ragnar fell, Joscelin was brought down the first stone steps with him, only preventing himself from falling the rest of the way by jamming his feet against the newel post and his spine against the wall.

Time thickened and slowed. Sounds caught in it were distorted and hollow. The scrape of armour grinding on stone, the thud, thump of a body rolling over and over. The scent of flowers. Silence.

Joscelin moved very gingerly, his limbs feeling as if they were made of hot lead. There was pain across his shoulder and back. He could not feel the trickle of blood, but he knew that the sword must have split the hauberk from the very strength of the impact. He would have heavy bruising at the least and probably a couple of cracked bones. And Ragnar?

Like an old man, he inched down the stairs to his brother. The red-gold hair gleamed in the torchlight. When he turned him, so did the blood as it trickled from ears and nostrils. Ragnar's eyes were open, but there was only the thinnest ring of gold-flecked brown to be seen. The rest of the iris showed only the blackness of a lost soul.

'Christ Jesu,' Joscelin whispered and bowed his head. And behind him, he heard Agnes begin to scream hoarsely.

CHAPTER 38

LINNET FELT COLD moisture on her brow and heard Maude's comforting murmur. There was the softness of a bracken mattress beneath her, and feather bolsters supporting her head. Further into the room, she thought she could hear the low rumble of masculine conversation.

She dared to open her eyes. Pain throbbed hard at one temple, and the rest of her skull ached in dull sympathy. Through blurred eyes she stared around and wondered where she was. These were not her own chambers at Rushcliffe, but neither were they Agnes's rooms. The walls were austere, whitewashed stone that hurt her eyes. For a moment she wondered if she were in a monastery, but there was not even the adornment of a crucifix to relieve the bareness. Beneath her fingers was a thick blanket of the plaid weave common to the Scots borders, the kind that she and Joscelin had on their own bed.

'Where am I?' she whispered, and discovered that her mouth was sticky and dry.

Maude leaned over her. 'You're awake at last,' she said with relief. 'I was beginning to worry. A day and a night you've been asleep. You're at Arnsby, in my brother's rooms.'

Linnet tried to swallow, but started to cough. 'Thirsty,' she managed to croak out, the pain rippling through her head with a vengeance. Maude helped her to sit and held a cup of watered wine to her lips.

'Slowly, my dear, slowly,' she soothed.

Linnet sipped and then lay back against the bolsters. Her vision continued to clear and blur. She put her hand to the

339

pain at her temple and touched it gingerly. Her fingers encountered clipped hair and the thick hardness of dried blood.

'The leech said it was best to let it heal in the open air.' Maude gave her another sip from the cup.

Linnet frowned and, after she had swallowed, said, 'I remember now; Ragnar hit me with the hilt of his sword when I tried to stop him from closing the door.' Her eyes flew wide and she pulled herself to a full sitting position. 'And then he and Joscelin were fighting, and Joscelin was losing. I tried to move, but I couldn't. I don't remember anything except Ragnar and Joscelin and that open doorway . . .' She pressed her fingers to her lips, feeling sick.

'It's all right, loveday, don't you worry.' Maude enfolded Linnet in one of her famous, smothering embraces, but not before Linnet had seen the grief brimming in the woman's eyes. Struggling, she fought herself out of Maude's arms.

'What happened? Tell me!'

Maude blinked, and dashed one pudgy hand across her eyes. 'Joscelin is safe,' she said, her voice quivering with emotion. 'Never think that he isn't. Indeed, I will fetch him to tell you himself. I am upset for my brother, that is all . . . for the tragedy.' She sniffed loudly. 'William and Ragnar both. I know that he deserved it, but he was still my nephew . . . and Agnes has not spoken a word since, she just lies on her bed, her face all twisted to one side. She had a seizure, you know, the poor soul.'

'Ragnar is dead?' Linnet's head spun.

'He fell down the stairs while they were fighting and cracked open his skull. We arrived moments after it happened. William's seneschal opened the gates to us when he saw the Justiciar's writ – he had no choice. I almost feel sorry for the poor man. Conan and Brien FitzRenard were the first into the keep, and they found Ragnar dead and Joscelin in a state of collapse on the stairs to Agnes's rooms.'

Linnet bit her lip, trying to remember. Her mind was like an autumn scene with areas of drifting fog changing

340

the landscape from moment to moment. 'But how did you know to come?'

'I was on my way here and decided to stop at Rushcliffe for the night. That young red-haired Scotsman of yours, Malcolm, told me that William was dreadfully ill with a deep sword wound and that you and Joscelin had taken him to Arnsby. Then the messenger came with your cry for help, so we set off immediately. Apparently William's scribe used to be yours and took his life in his hands to send out the messages.'

Linnet smiled tremulously. 'I thought I had failed with him. I asked him to help me, but he would not meet my eyes when he said he would see what he could do. I will have to go to him, suitably humble now.'

'He is rather basking in his glory,' Maude admitted. She patted Linnet's hand and then looked round and rose to her feet as Joscelin approached the bedside.

Joscelin's eyes were all for his wife, and Maude tactfully made her excuses and left. The kiss she bestowed on her nephew's stubbled cheek before she departed was affectionate and understanding, her embrace for Linnet tender.

When she had gone, Linnet and Joscelin looked at each other, then in a sudden, simultaneous move were in each other's arms, kissing, holding tight. 'Jesu,' Linnet sobbed, 'I truly thought you were going to die!'

'So did I,' he muttered into the hair on her good side. 'If it had not been for Ivo, I would have done.'

'Ivo!'

He drew back and showed her the angry, blistered weals on his hands. 'Ivo threw a rope down into the oubliette, so that I could climb out. He says that it was the only rope on which he wanted to see me swing.'

'I thought he hated you.'

'Not as much as he loves the mortal state of his soul. Fraternal rivalry is one matter. Cold-blooded murder is another.'

Linnet shivered and pressed her cheek against his tunic, savouring a closeness she thought she had lost. 'And now Ivo is lord of Arnsby?'

'Not for long.'

She raised her head and looked quickly into his tired, unshaven face. 'You do not mean to dispute with him?'

'No. He says that he intends taking the Cross and that, providing he can have Papa's hunting lodge and manor house near Melton, he'll pass over his right in Martyn's favour.' He stroked her hair. 'It's not as strange as it sounds. Ivo's always trotted around in someone else's shadow. He does not know how to stand in the light.' He sighed heavily. 'I want to go home to Rushcliffe, I want to see Robert and sleep with you at my side for a week.' He paused, his hand clasped over hers, and added quietly, 'I want to forget ... Why do we always want the impossible?'

Without speaking, for her throat was tight, she took his calloused hand, and placed it against her womb, upon the hidden promise of new life.

EPILOGUE

Spring 1174

T HE WHITE AND GOLD chapel held two effigies, side by side, one a woman with a winsome smile and today a crown of saffron crocuses upon her alabaster brow. Her companion was a man wearing nail and surcoat, his sword carved at rest beside him and his hands clasped not in an attitude of prayer, but holding a shield bearing the comet blazon of his family line.

'It looks like Papa,' Martyn said judiciously, and ran his forefinger over the gleaming ripples and folds. 'He'll be happy here, I know he will.'

Robert copied him by setting his own smaller hand upon the effigy's chainmail shoe cover.

Joscelin lightly touched Martyn's shoulder and studied Ironheart's tomb. He had had to search hard among Nottingham's fraternity of alabaster craftsmen to find one who could carve the effigy as he wanted. No pious positioning of the hands or rigid garments confining the essence. He wanted Ironheart the restless, brusque warrior, not Ironheart the saint. By and large, the man had succeeded, although his father's hair had never succumbed to a comb the way it had succumbed in stone to the craftsman's

343

chisel. Ragnar had a tomb too, in the chapel at Arnsby, and that was rigidly conventional and blessedly resembled his brother not in the slightest. The same went for Agnes's memorial, although that was not yet finished, for she had only died the week before Candlemas of yet another seizure.

He would not dwell on the past. Linnet would rebuke him if she thought he was brooding, although she allowed him his moments of solitude and introspection. He heard her footfall now and turned to watch her walk up the nave towards him. She was wearing her thick winter cloak, for despite the sunshine there was still a sharpness in the air, and she had her burden to protect, but she walked gracefully, and he felt his heart and gut swoop together, producing a feeling of elation.

The others would be coming soon to fill the church and attend this mass that was to be said for the souls of William de Rocher and Morwenna de Gael, but Joscelin had allowed a space of time for the solitude of his own, immediate family, for the peace and breathing space to stand before the tombs of his mother and father and present to them their three-month-old granddaughter, dark of hair, green of eye – Morwenna.